Julie Caplin is the internat...... ....f the
Romantic Escapes series. H.................
charts in Italy, Germany, t'...................
and have sold over two ....
uplifting romantic comedie...................
across the globe, providing her reade....

Formerly a PR director, for many years Julie swanned around Europe taking top food and drink writers on press trips to sample the gastronomic delights of the continent. It was a tough job but someone had to do it. These trips have provided the inspiration and settings for her novels.

Julie also writes romantic and historical fiction as Jules Wake.

juleswake.co.uk

 x.com/JulieCaplin
facebook.com/JulieCaplinAuthor

Also by Julie Caplin

Romantic Escapes

CHRISTMAS ON FIFTH AVENUE

JULIE CAPLIN

One More Chapter
a division of HarperCollins*Publishers* Ltd
1 London Bridge Street
London SE1 9GF
www.harpercollins.co.uk
HarperCollins*Publishers*
Macken House, 39/40 Mayor Street Upper,
Dublin 1, D01 C9W8, Ireland

This paperback edition 2025
1
First published in Great Britain in ebook format
by HarperCollins*Publishers* 2025
Copyright © Julie Caplin 2025
Julie Caplin asserts the moral right to be identified
as the author of this work

A catalogue record of this book is available from the British Library
ISBN: 978-0-00-867083-2

For my dear friend Donna, one of the kindest and most generous people I know.

Chapter One

EVIE

'May I see your boarding pass and passport?' asked the woman at the desk at the entrance to the business-class lounge – yes, BUSINESS class.

'Absolutely,' I said, a tad overenthusiastically. I tried to be cool about it but even at the age of twenty-nine and a half … I couldn't. She gave me a polite smile, her bright red lipstick so immaculate, I did wonder if it might have been high-gloss red paint.

'And would you mind removing the sunglasses and hat?' she asked, peering down at my passport photo. So much for my attempt at a disguise. I'd hurriedly bought the hat and glasses after a couple of girls in the security queue had openly laughed at me and I turned as red as an overripe strawberry.

'Right this way, Miss Green.' I sighed with gratitude. Now this was travelling in style, the business-class lounge was huge with big leather armchairs, a free buffet, an open bar and stacks of newspapers and magazines – it was also very busy. After wandering around like a lost sheep for five minutes, I spotted a big wing-backed chair over in one corner. It was only when I staked my claim on said chair that I realised the opposite seat was taken, the high, wide design of the chair, hiding its occupant from view.

With his head bowed, he was intent on his phone. Like me, he wore dark sunglasses and a baseball cap. I'd hoped to sneak onto my chair without disturbing him, but I banged into the coffee table and sent an empty coffee cup rattling. He glanced up, clearly startled, his mouth slashing into an unfriendly flat line.

'Sorry,' I whispered and for some reason saluted the brim of my cap. I think it was to remind him we were incognito allies. For a minute, he stared at me … sometimes you can just tell even behind the dark glasses. Trying to play it cool, I gave him a nonchalant nod, as if I always travelled this way and I was part of the same gang.

He nodded back and ducked his head again, returning to his phone, his mouth crumpling in quick irritation as he read something.

The great thing about wearing sunglasses is that you can be subtle about checking someone out – okay, I admit it, ogling. He was very ogle-worthy. The Henley T-shirt he wore stretched across seriously broad shoulders. A weak spot of mine. What I could see of his hair, a dark chestnut colour, curled around the rim of his navy-blue cap, which had a stylised N and Y embroidered on the front. His face had a strong masculine jaw and aquiline nose. Male model? Actor? And the icing on the cake, he had the sexy, bad-boy stubble going on, which was an absolute killer.

Suddenly I realised that it was really obvious I was staring at him. I glanced away and studied my own phone but a few minutes later, I couldn't help myself.

There was something about the wary stillness of his posture that suggested he was ready for fight or flight at any moment. It drew my surreptitious gaze again and I studied him anew, watching as his mobile mouth mirrored emotions hidden behind his sunglasses. Frustration, anger, hurt … all quickly shaped his lips as he scrolled away, intently focused on his phone screen, holding himself stiffly in the centre of the seat so that it shielded him from view.

I knew exactly how horrible social media could be. I was on the verge of asking him if he was okay when I realised I was projecting. Projecting my recent online experiences. The vile comments, the trolls, the criticism, the complete lack of empathy or sympathy. I could relate to the slight, perplexed frown tugging at his mouth as he read.

'Excuse me,' I said, making a quick decision.

'Mmm,' he responded, not looking particularly friendly or encouraging. Maybe he didn't speak English.

'Er, would you mind,' I enunciated slowly and loudly, and in case he was deaf as well as foreign, I gestured at my belongings, 'keeping an eye on my bag.' For good measure, I actually pointed at my bag and did a walking-away motion with my fingers. There was a long pause, and I was about to rephrase the question when he responded with:

'Do I look like I offer babysitting services?'

I started at the blunt question, noting his American accent, but then I spotted the wry twist to his mouth. I gave him a careful up-and-down.

'Hmm,' I said with a considering nod. 'I think you probably do, but only low-level assignments.'

'Low-level?' Curiosity pitched in his voice as his mouth notched up another peg towards a reluctant smile.

'Yes, hand luggage and possibly a well-trained Chihuahua.'

He burst out laughing. 'A well-trained Chihuahua! Where did that come from?'

I took off my sunglasses and grinned at him. 'Truthfully…' I paused. 'I have no idea.'

He removed his own sunglasses to reveal dancing blue eyes and I felt a surge of triumph that I'd somehow managed to lighten his mood.

'If you don't mind,' I nodded towards my bag again. 'I'd like to get myself a drink.'

'Okay, I'll watch your bag,' he replied with a nod, suddenly serious before he smiled and added, 'providing it doesn't contain a small, well-trained dog.'

I shook my head and glanced around before whispering, 'I packed it myself, I'm pretty sure it doesn't.'

To my delight, he laughed for a second time.

'Thank you, that's really kind. I won't be long.'

I took a step away and then stopped, remembering the manners ingrained by my mum. 'Can I get you anything?'

His face sobered for a moment, as if he'd remembered something – it made me wonder if anyone had offered to do anything for him for a while.

'A drink or something?' I prompted.

I watched him swallow and push whatever haunted him away.

'I could use a beer and some chips, thank you.'

'Chips?' I asked.

'Crisps. You know.'

'Any particular flavour?' I asked.

'Cheese and onion,' he said with a quick grin. 'Is there any other flavour?'

'I'm rather partial to sweet chilli, but you only get those if they're posh crisps.'

'There are posh crisps?' His mouth quirked again. 'Who knew?'

'You know, the expensive ones,' I said.

'I'm not that much of a connoisseur.' He smiled, reassuring me that I wasn't making a complete idiot of myself.

'Back soon,' I said.

'I'll pay close attention to your bag,' he said, with another smile, producing a very cute dimple in the middle of his cheek, as if someone had poked a finger in there.

It was also as if someone had poked something at my heart and I got a funny fizzing sensation in my chest.

As I turned to go, I managed to knock into the coffee table again – adding a second bruise to my shin – and he jumped up and held out protective hands as if he were ready to catch me. The gesture pierced into my heart like an arrow into wood. No one had looked out for me in a long time.

'Thanks,' I said, managing to stay upright and catching the empty cup before it fell.

'Good save,' he said in smooth tones.

I walked away a little light-headed. Maybe it was just

the human connection but in that moment, it made me feel just a little bit less lost.

I did a quick circuit of the lounge; well, as quick as you can when everything is free. On the surface, in a purely material way, things were looking up. Life had been a bit shit in recent weeks.

I helped myself to a glass of champagne – the proper stuff, not prosecco – before perusing the selection of beer. I ummed and ahhed over what to pick up for my handsome neighbour. He'd been nice to me, when so many strangers of late had been unkind. I knew nothing about beer but as it was free, I grabbed four different bottles. I could always bring them back. When I explained my predicament to the handy bar man, he kindly lent me a bottle opener.

———————

'Here you go.'

Mr Handsome's eyes widened as he looked up at the beer bottles I held with one hand, the necks precariously sandwiched between my fingers. 'I didn't know what to get you.'

I put them down on the table one after another while hanging onto my flute of fizz.

His eyes crinkled at the corners. 'Thank you. I'd have been grateful for anything. That's … er … very thoughtful.'

'I thought so,' I said cheerily, sitting down and toasting him before taking my first sip of champagne, impressed that I'd managed to get it to the table without spilling a drop. I almost jumped at the instant effect of the effervescent fizz on my tongue and the sharp acidity of the bubbles.

'Oh, and I got you your chips,' I said proudly, pulling a packet from the pouch pocket of my sweatshirt.

'Thank you. You've spoiled me, except...' He leaned forward and chose one of the beers, looking at the bottle top and the table edge.

'Oh, sorry.' I delved into my back pocket. 'I borrowed this.' I handed the bottle-opener over. 'I need to take it back in a minute.'

'You've thought of everything,' he said with another one of those smiles that did strange things to my insides.

'This is the life,' I said with a happy sigh, taking another sip of the champagne. My mum would have loved this. My heart did one of those involuntary little pings when I thought of her. She'd been gone for five years but it was still there, that underlying sadness when I remembered all the things I'd never get to tell her. Like now. Going to New York. In December. Staying at *The* Plaza. It had been our dream. The thing we'd talked about while snuggled under a blanket together watching *Serendipity*, *Home Alone 2* and *Elf*, to name but a few of our favourites. The 'one day' that never came but which we talked about more and more as her life faded away, despite both of us knowing that one day was an elusive dream.

'Mmm,' said my new friend, taking a healthy slug of his beer straight from the bottle. 'Thank you again.'

'No problem, and thank you for looking after my bag.' I grinned at him. 'You did an excellent job despite being woefully underqualified.'

'So, do I get a certificate or something? For work experience?' He asked, putting his beer bottle down.

'Oh, yes. Absolutely. Well done.' I gave him a thumbs up. 'I could … er … er, WhatsApp it to…' My voice trailed off. Oh no, did that sound like I was asking for his number?

He gave me a gentle smile, relieving me of my embarrassment. 'Don't worry. I'll manage without.' He went back to his phone and I eased out a sigh of relief. I really hadn't been trying to pick him up.

I glanced around the room, still scarcely able to believe that I was really there, eyeing people carefully as if any one of them might snatch this amazing opportunity away from me as quickly as it had been magically bestowed upon me.

When The Plaza's marketing team contacted me, I'd ignored the email for a week before they emailed again. As a financial journalist for the online magazine *Money Weekly*, I know all about scams … or rather, I should have done.

To cut a very long story short, I'd fallen for a scam and lost a not inconsiderable sum of money.

So, obviously, when I was offered a second, albeit genuine this time, all-expenses-paid trip to stay at The Plaza Hotel, I was justifiably wary.

Thank goodness the lady in the PR department had been persistent.

And now here I was at Heathrow about to board a plane to New York to spend the next three weeks in the Big Apple staying at the five-star Plaza Hotel, right on Fifth Avenue and next to Central Park.

Sometimes good things happen to people. Even me.

Chapter Two

NOAH

As I returned to my phone, my face almost hurt from the unaccustomed smiling, as if my skin was protesting at the activity. The girl, whoever she was – I guessed, like me, she wanted to remain anonymous – had succeeded where no one else had for over a week, ever since the awful sound of bone cracking when I threw myself into an aggressive tackle.

From behind my sunglasses, I watched her smiling away to herself and envied her carefree attitude as she gazed around the room sipping with obvious delight at her champagne. Suddenly, with a furtive look around, she unloaded a bag of Minstrels from her sweatshirt pocket along with a KitKat, a packet of Mini Cheddars and a small tin of Pringles. She'd stashed them away in her bag like a squirrel planning for winter.

It made me smile again as I realised that being in the business-class lounge was a novelty for her. I'd gotten a bit too used to it, along with all the trappings of being a professional Premier League football player. Despite being able to get whatever I wanted, whenever I wanted, I was unaccountably touched that she'd brought me not one but four bottles of beer to make sure she got the right one for a complete stranger. Her confidence and slightly offbeat thinking were endearing. I thought about offering her my number for the 'certificate'; I would have done if it weren't for the fact that I was supposed to be keeping a low profile and leaving the country for at least three weeks to 'avert the gaze of the media' as my agent, Lara, so diplomatically phrased it. Basically, I was running away – on orders from her and my team manager. They'd decided that out of sight, out of mind would make the FA less inclined to push for a stronger punishment.

I stared down at the headline of one of the sports' news websites, feeling my gloom slip back into place and that familiar nausea burn in the pit of my stomach.

DIRTY TACKLE FROM SANDERSON ENDS
MENZIES' PREMIER LEAGUE CAREER

I inhaled a shallow breath, gnawing on my lip, shame overwhelming me. I wished I could turn the clock back. But no, even now in the busy airport lounge, I was back on the pitch, the Fulham vs Aston Villa game. We were two-one down. Second by second, I could remember the exact decision-making process. We needed a win. I needed a goal. I went for it. Going in hard. Sensing a chance to score…

If I hadn't been in public, in the busy airport lounge, I would have groaned and dropped my head into my hands.

I scrolled to another page.

TV PUNDIT CALLS FOR EIGHT-MONTH
BAN FOR SANDERSON

Currently, I had a six-match ban following the tackle on Rick Menzies which had broken one of his legs in two places, leaving him in hospital and unlikely to play in the Premiership ever again. I deserved everything I got, but I just couldn't afford to be out of the game for eight months.

For the sake of the team and my future place on it, I was doing as I was told. I owed too much to too many people to let them down, although ironically that fear had been what drove me to risk that tackle.

After two weeks off due to injury, and the team racking up four losses in the intervening period, I'd needed to make sure my comeback counted. To show the manager that I might be one of the older players on the squad but I was still integral to the team.

I sneaked another look at the girl opposite and she caught me, giving me another one of her smiles. It lit up her face. She clearly had no idea who I was, and that in itself was a relief. I'd got grief in the streets – even here standing in the check-in line.

A text buzzed through on my phone.

> Bon voyage. Have a safe flight. Behave and don't get into any trouble.

Lara. I winced. I knew as my agent she was on my side, but I had enough guilt of my own without needing a reminder to keep a low profile and be squeaky clean.

I pulled off my sunglasses to rub at my tired eyes, dislodging my cap. Sleep had been in short supply these last few days. Maybe going to see Rick Menzies hadn't been such a great idea. He hadn't wanted my sympathy, although he had accepted my offer to pay for surgery with a top orthopaedic consultant in Switzerland.

As I stretched and leaned back in the chair, I caught the glance of a man a few tables over. His eyes narrowed and I saw his muscles bunch like a bull about to charge. I casually looked away as if I was unaware of his sudden sharp interest, praying that he would leave it at that.

But no one was listening. With a menacing swagger, he barged through a group of tables, his Aston Villa shirt stretched over his beer belly, leaving three inches of hairy, bloated flesh on display.

The girl, perhaps alerted by the sudden shift of atmosphere, glanced back and spotted him coming. She shot a glance back to me and then back to him.

'Sanderson. You fucking arsehole,' he said, jabbing a stubby finger towards me.

Around us there was a sudden hush as he took a step closer.

'Oh, for fuck's sake,' said the girl, in a loud voice, rising to her feet, shaking her head and laughing. Her eyes sparkled as she tossed her coppery curls. 'If only I had a pound for every time someone mistook my husband ... I tell you, I'd be rolling in fifty-pound notes. I know he looks just the same, but I promise you this is Roy Ken … ton.' There was the briefest hitch in the word before she carried on. 'My husband – most definitely not famous and as ordinary as it gets. We're about to go on our honeymoon.' She paused and tucked her left hand – ringless – behind her back, then said with a world-weary sigh, 'So, if you want to thump someone, please could you pick someone else as I do *not* want pictures of him with a black eye.'

She dropped into my lap, throwing an arm around my neck and pulling me into her. A well of gratitude rose up inside me which made me want to clutch her close. Instead, I buried my nose in her neck, too surprised to say anything and distracted by the smell of her skin and her soft bottom landing on my lap.

'Thanks, darling,' I said, grateful to find the little angry guy's attention focused on her and not me. I pulled her in protectively.

'Shit, I'm so sorry, love.' He peered round her at me. 'Apologies, mate, you really look like him.'

I shrugged and said in what was my best attempt at an English accent, ''Appens a lot.' Definitely more Dick Van Dyke than charming Brit judging by the snigger the woman made.

'Right,' he said, already backing away. He crashed into a table and everyone around us who had been staring suddenly went back to their own business as he turned around and scuttled off.

We sat there for several seconds: me, shellshocked; her – I'm not sure. My hands were on her waist, and I didn't want to let go. She felt like something that had been missing from my life. Then the moment became awkward and she jumped up from my lap. 'Well, that was fun,' she said.

'Roy Ken … ton?'

She grinned and stroked her chin, nodding at my heavy stubble. 'Ted Lasso. But then I realised that sounded like a made-up name so I … elaborated.'

'I can't believe you just did that,' I said, amazed by her sheer cheek and quick thinking and, most of all, her willingness to jump in and save a complete stranger. It could have gone horribly wrong – and she would have been first in the line of fire. She'd put herself between me and a threat. If only she knew how little I deserved her generosity of spirit. Nausea rose up in my throat. Shame almost felled me. I needed to get away.

'That was really kind of you. Thank you, but I've got to go. They called my flight.' With that I gathered up my belongings and fled, trying to put as much distance between us as humanly possible. She was so kind, I prayed that she'd never find out her kindness was totally misplaced and that Sanderson was Noah Sanderson, the footballer who wrecked another man's career for the sake of proving himself. I'd hate her to realise that I wasn't worth saving.

Chapter Three

EVIE

'Business class have already boarded.' The man at the front desk pointed to the far side of the waiting area with a pained, patronising smile and I hurried over. Okay, so I'd got sidetracked in the duty-free shop, still coming down from the hot flush of whatever it was when I threw myself at that poor man. I was glad I had, even though he couldn't get away fast enough. I knew what it was like to have people who didn't even know you accost you and be unkind, although he probably thought I was a lunatic.

For the first time in my life, the cabin-crew member directed me to the left.

I flashed her a dazzling smile because trying to be cool was impossible. Oh, Mum, look at me now. Most people in business class were already seated as I skipped my way down the aisle. The seats in the fancy little cubicles that looked more like library carrels were bigger than I'd ever seen and the layout completely different to what I was used to. There were only four seats across in total. Single seats by the windows and then two in the central aisle.

My seat was in the central aisle.

The occupant in the seat next to mine might have had his head bowed but I recognised the familiar navy-blue ball cap and almost laughed out loud, although I was still reeling from his abrupt departure in the lounge. He was definitely going to think that I was stalking him or something.

'Hi,' I said, making my way to my seat. 'Is this seat taken?'

He lifted his head and his eyes narrowed, looking at me and then back down at the empty seat next to him. There was a brief flash of something in his eyes, a quick indefinable spark, before it was doused and his face went purposefully blank. Clearly, I'd disturbed his equilibrium, which was good because he'd disturbed mine.

'Actually, it is my seat,' I said, giving him what I hoped was a winning smile.

For a moment, several different emotions flitted across his face as if he couldn't decide how he was feeling.

'Right,' he said and settled on calm resignation, offering up a polite smile.

'Small world.' Then all my cool flew out of the window. 'Can I just say, I'm really not stalking you. I haven't changed my ticket or anything.'

He didn't laugh.

'I didn't think you were,' he said, and I knew whatever flirty vibes had been dancing between us earlier had been well and truly quashed. It was something to do with the name that angry little man had announced, but I couldn't fathom it. I'd been racking my brain. Sanderson? But it was like trying to pin down mist, the more I thought about it, the more the name eluded me. I was sure I must have heard of him.

He watched as I sidled into my seat. Well, not so much sidled, because there were bags of room. In fact, there was so much leg room you could swing a whole litter of kittens in there.

'Nice,' I murmured, patting the armrest, trying to look as if I flew business class all the time, while resisting the desire to riffle through the exciting-looking, complimentary White Company pouch of goodies.

Before I could even rearrange the blanket and the pillow to belt myself in, one of the cabin crew appeared with a tray of orange juice, water and champagne.

'Thank you,' I said with a grin, taking a champagne. Next to me, Mr Sanderson, whoever he was, helped himself to an orange juice and kept his head down. After the unpleasant encounter in the airport lounge, I could understand his reticence to be noticed.

I decided to ignore the Sanderson guy next to me and all pretence at being cool went out of the window as I tested all the buttons on the armrest. The bottom half of the seat slid out beneath my legs and the back tilted, so that I was reclining in comfort. I returned it to the upright position and delved into the little pouch of goodies to find an eye mask, a pair of socks, a little bamboo toothbrush and miniature toothpaste, some moisturising facial spray and a little bottle of perfume.

I pulled out the stiff card menu from the pocket in front of me and studied it. A brunch of scrambled eggs and smoked salmon with an English muffin, along with fresh fruit and organic Greek yoghurt would be served, as well as champagne. Later on, there would be afternoon tea with cucumber sandwiches, egg sandwiches, ham sandwiches, mini macarons, chocolate eclairs and mille-feuille finishing off with a fruit scone, clotted cream and strawberry jam. I replaced the menu with a happy smile and settled back into my seat. I could definitely get used to this.

Even though there was so much more space than I was used to on a plane, I was very aware of him sitting next to me and every movement he made. I could even smell him. He wore one of those lovely expensive rich cedary colognes.

As he'd made it plain that he wanted to pretend we'd never met before, I did my best to ignore him, watching the activity around me as the cabin crew delivered drinks to everyone, smiling and nodding every time I caught their eye.

The minute the aircraft doors were closed and everyone had finished filing through the cabin to their seats, Mr Handsome took off his cap and I removed my sunglasses and hat, giving him a conspiratorial smile.

'You think it's safe?' I asked in a teasing whisper, feeling that despite his recent reticence, our makeshift disguises and previous experience had created a common bond.

He shot me a wary look. 'You're a talker, aren't you?'

I eyed him warily. 'What does that mean?'

'On flights, you either sit next to someone who is happy to chat away for the whole time, or someone who would rather be left in peace.'

'Oh,' I said. 'And you'd rather be left in peace.'

His mouth tightened in what might have been a *that would be nice* look.

'Right,' I said, but I wasn't going to let him have the last word. 'Message received and understood.' I mimed zipping my mouth closed but gave him a cheerful grin to let him know I thought he was being a bit of an arse.

He turned back to his phone.

I listened avidly to the pre-flight safety talk and studied the instructions on the card in the pocket even though next to his indifferent nonchalance I felt unbelievably naïve. Once the plane took off, still aware of the silent man beside me, who was now plugged into a film, I decided to try out the entertainment system. It proved trickier than it looked because I couldn't even flip the controller out of its little slot. Trying to be subtle about it, so as not to advertise my complete incompetence, I kept going back to it every couple of minutes, like a cat playing with a cornered mouse but no matter which way I pressed or prodded I couldn't get the damn thing out.

There was a heavy sigh from my left and Captain Grumpy removed his headphones.

'Do you need a hand?' he asked.

'Oh, yes, thank you. Not used to this … model.'

'Here you go.'

Of course he popped it out straight away.

His fingers grazed my hand, and I almost dropped the stupid thing. He glanced at me quickly, his eyes narrowing before his gaze slipped down to my lips. The covert look was so quick, I could almost think I imagined it.

'Thank you. I don't know…' My voice trailed off because he'd already put his headphones back on. His movement, abrupt and sharp, and his body stiffening and leaning slightly away from me, as if he wanted to put as much distance between us as he could.

Hurt, yet at the same time amused, I ignored him – what was his problem? I began flicking through the entertainment system and to my amazement and delight I found that I could view a live football game. My team, too. Arsenal. It had always been my dad's team and after he died, Mum carried on supporting them but swapped allegiance to the women's team. Going to see a women's game at the big stadiums is much, much cheaper than the men's games, so Mum and I used to go to Arsenal to watch the ladies' side.

Donning my own headphones, I tuned into the pundits' preamble before the start of the first half.

Once the game began, I noticed that he shot several glances towards my screen, although that might have had something to do with the little twitches I gave whenever anyone took a shot in the box or came close to tapping a goal in. No doubt I was still annoying him – but he'd just have to suck it up. I've always been an active screen-watcher. I'm the sort of person that ducks when a plane flies towards the camera in a film.

When I groaned aloud at an easily missed penalty, I

caught him almost smile. That charming dimple haunted my peripheral vision.

Half-time arrived, with the offer of another drink from the cabin crew, and we both took off our headphones as we were served a beer and a glass of wine respectively along with packets of crunchy nibbly things.

'Cheers,' I said as I raised my glass – it was only polite – and took a sip of the very nice French wine.

'You like football?' he asked, his eyes scanning my screen.

'Only the women's game,' I explained.

'Right.' He looked delightfully confused and intrigued. 'And why's that?' He took a swig of his beer and leaned back in his chair, but the feigned indifference of his pose gave him away; I had the feeling that he was genuinely interested in my answer.

'One,' I ticked off a finger, warming to the subject, 'because the men are such drama queens on the pitch. Two,' I ticked off a second finger, 'the men are such drama queens on the pitch. Three, the women's game is a bit slower so you can appreciate the skill levels; they don't play dirty, they're not always falling over and they don't have enormous, oversized egos like the male players.' I shot him a satisfied smile. 'Also, tickets are way cheaper. I've been to Arsenal ladies quite a few times at the Emirates Stadium.'

'Right,' he said and smirked.

'Do you like football?' I asked and then checked myself. 'Sorry, that's probably a stupid question. You're American?'

He nodded.

'I should say soccer, then. But you probably don't know that much about it?'

Amusement danced in his eyes. 'We do play soccer in the States. I know about the offside rule.'

'You do know your stuff,' I teased. 'I'm impressed. I still have to explain it to my flatmate, Esther, and I've told her a dozen times.

My face faltered as I remembered that both my flatmates, Esther and Jamie, hadn't spoken to me for a couple of weeks. They were still furious with me, and I couldn't really blame them. I was never going to regain their trust.

'You okay?' he asked as my vision blurred for a second. His posture softened as if he was about to lean over towards me.

'Yes. Sure,' I replied, blinking, as a tear spilled out.

'So, where you headed?' he asked. I stared at him surprised by the unexpected conversational key change. Until then it was obvious he was keeping me at arm's length.

'New York,' I said and then forced a laugh. 'Obviously.' I spread my hands out, indicating the planeload of people all going to New York. 'I'm going there for Christmas.' I opted not to go into too much detail because I'd had chapter and verse from the online trolls about my stupidity. I didn't need to share it anew.

'Got family there?'

I shook my head and swallowed back the lump, wishing my mum could see me now. It had been our dream together.

'No, just having a holiday. How about you?'

'Flying home. Sort of.'

'So, is this flight business or pleasure?'

A brief flutter of alarm crossed his face.

'Sorry, I'm nosy. Hazard of my job.' I held up both hands. 'In the interests of full disclosure, I'm a journalist.' Even now, I got a buzz out of saying it. I'd worked hard to get there having done a ton of internships and a journalism degree.

'Shit.' Now he looked absolutely horrified.

'But I work for *Money Weekly*, so I'm not interested in celebrity gossip. Even if I did know who you are.' I wasn't about to confess that I was currently suspended. 'Unless you've cleared out your company's pension fund, are about to buy a bank or set up a new hedge-fund, then your secrets are safe with me.'

'You're a financial journalist?' he asked, immediately relaxing. Once again, I noticed that cute quirk to his mouth.

'Yes, I spend my days writing about interesting things like pensions and banking, as well as the really fascinating stuff like interest rates, stagflation and monetary policy.'

He raised an eyebrow, and I was pleased to see that he was giving me a second appraisal.

'I know. I don't look like one.' Something to do with the long, wild hair, dainty features and willowy build. No matter what I wore, and I'd tried, I never looked quite put together. I might wear a suit, but my shirt would never stay tucked in. Drape a scarf around my neck and it will be lopsided after five minutes. And don't get me started on the devil's work that tights are. They were born to be laddered and that's the ninety-million granny denier ones.

'I'm intrigued. What should a financial journalist look like?'

'Oh, you know. Foxy. Smart. Black or navy suit. Killer heels. Briefcase. Yeah, definitely briefcase. I had one once.' I pulled a face.

He laughed and we exchanged a grin. My pulse tripped. It made such a difference to his face, lighting up his eyes.

'What happened?'

'I could not get to grips with the stupid thing. Always bashing my legs with it. Honestly, I looked like I'd been in a football match with a bunch of donkeys. Covered in bruises.'

'I noticed you walked into the coffee table, a couple of times.' He glanced down at my legs. 'Maybe if you slowed down a bit.'

'You sound like my mum. She always said I was in too much of a hurry to do everything. I started walking when I was nine months.'

'Me, too. A fact that my mom is very proud of. I could kick a ball, too.'

'Impressive,' I teased, and his eyes sparkled back at me. 'And have you developed any more talents over the years?'

He raised his eyebrows, and I groaned.

'Oh God, I'm sorry. That was not a leading question.' I shook my head in mock despair before adding, 'Things just come out of my mouth all the—'

He sniggered and then it turned into a full-blown laugh.

I hid my face in the palm of my hand. 'I can't believe I just said that. What must you think of me?'

'Irritating but … you're kind of cute.' Even he looked surprised at his own words. 'I mean…' Now it was his turn to blush, and it was *so* unexpected and he did it so adorably that I had to rescue him.

'Hey, I'll take cute. To be honest, my ego could do with a little boost. It's been trampled on of late.'

'I know that feeling,' he said, his face softened with sympathy. 'Mine is shot to shit.'

'Sorry. Mine, too.'

We both lapsed into silence, each dwelling on our own issues.

'But,' I said brightly, 'we don't have to think about that now. We're thirty-thousand feet away from all that crap. We should just enjoy the flight. Looks like they're about to serve lunch.'

'Good. I'm starving. I had someone get me a measly bag of crisps hours ago. You know there's less than a single potato in one of those packs.'

'How inconsiderate of them. And they were free. You'd have thought they'd have brought you more. I have a spare KitKat in my bag if you want one.'

With another one of his smiley laughs, where his eyes crinkled at the corners, he shook his head. 'No. You keep it. You're really kind … I mean back there … that was above and beyond. Real kind of you. I could've been a bit more grateful. I was kind of surprised when you…' He looked down at his lap.

'Me too, to be honest,' I said. 'I just thought you

needed … some help.' I gave him a sympathetic smile. 'I've…' I wasn't sure I wanted to confess my recent history to him. Right now, he was impressed I'd rescued him. If he knew what a mess I'd made of everything, he might not feel quite the same. 'I've had a tough time recently. I get it.'

'Even so, it was quite something.'

'I know,' I said with a cheerful smile which made him laugh again.

Go me. I felt positively dizzy with triumph that I was getting this many laughs out of him.

Chapter Four

NOAH

'Are you going to eat that scone?' The girl next to me grinned, full of mischief, and before I could answer she scooped it up and took a bite.

'Hey!' I exclaimed.

She raised an eyebrow as if to say, 'And what are you going to do about it now?' She gave me a teasing smile and I couldn't help responding. Despite my earlier good intentions to stay aloof, it was impossible. There was something about her, like she understood me. Like she was doing her best to smooth away all the raw edges of my guilt and self-loathing – even though she didn't know me.

And then there was the physical attraction. I'd have to have been in a coma not to notice the buzz between us.

I raised my eyes to meet hers. We stared at each other for seconds longer than we should and when I dropped my gaze to her lush lips again, I was gratified to spot the movement of her throat as she swallowed. Her teeth caught her lip, but she held my gaze, and it felt like there was a current of electricity fizzing between us. There had been quite a few lingering looks, on my part as well as hers. From the minute she gave me that cheeky salute in the airport lounge, like we were comrades in disguise, something about her piqued my interest.

It's kind of inconvenient when I'm supposed to be leading a totally blameless life.

With the sassy comments and that wild hair which, for a fleeting second, I could imagine spread across my pillow, this girl was definitely the sort of trouble I should stay away from.

The trip to New York, which hopefully would be short and allow me to be back in London before Christmas, was supposed to be taking me away from the headlines and instead rebuilding my reputation. I wanted to do some hard thinking and focus on training and getting my mind set in the right place. Unfortunately, all my good intentions were already being eroded by the obvious connection between us. I was so aware of her sitting beside me; the subtle shift of her breasts as she breathed, the slenderness of her neck and the gorgeous, glossy corkscrew curls spilling down her back as well as the way she almost glowed as if fuelled by her own personal ray of sunshine.

I kept asking myself where the harm in a little light flirtation on the plane was. It wasn't like I was ever going to see her again – although something about her looked familiar. I was sure I'd seen her someplace before.

'So, what do you do when you're not financial journalist-ing?' I asked with a sardonic smile because it was such an obviously cheesy line and I kind of knew her answer would be entertaining. Now I'd started talking to her – despite my hopeless initial attempts to put her off – I couldn't stop.

'Oh, I do a bit of rally driving, mountain climbing and pole dancing,' she said with a wicked grin.

'Really?' I asked.

'No,' she shook her head, her curls bouncing. 'Just the usual run-of-the-mill stuff, going out with friends, clubbing and sleeping. I'm quite ordinary.'

'I don't think there's anything ordinary about you,' I found myself saying. There was something about her. She definitely was not ordinary. Her eyes met mine and there it was again, that spark of something.

When the pilot announced that we were due to start our descent, I'd started thinking about asking if she'd like to meet up for a drink.

'Are you staying in Manhattan?' I asked. Most tourists headed to Times Square or somewhere central to stay.

'I am,' she said, those beautiful brown eyes lighting up and sparkling with some secret delight.

I suddenly laughed as something occurred to me.

'You realise we've flown the whole way across the Atlantic and I still don't know your name.

She laughed back, although the sparkle in her eyes dimmed, and for a moment she seemed a little diffident, as if she weren't sure about something.

'Or we can stay incognito, like some romcom movie,' I suggested, so relaxed with her that I didn't even think how this might be construed or even thinking what her response might be to my name.

'I'm glad you said that and not me.' She grinned at me, and my pulse sped up. There was just something about her that made me smile, despite myself.

'I'm Evie, short for Genevieve, except no one ever calls me that.'

'Noah Sanderson.' I held out my hand. She went to take it and then at the very last minute, dropped her own hand away as if mine was a cobra about to strike.

'Noah Sanderson. I knew I knew you from somewhere,' she repeated, her shocked eyes staring at me with burning embers of accusation glowing in them, as if I should have come clean earlier.

'Yeah,' I said with a self-deprecating shrug.

I tended not to volunteer who I was; I don't get off on the fame and celebrity thing. Make no mistake, I loved playing football, but it was a job – my profession – and I took it seriously, although I hadn't always. Point is, it didn't define me, not like some of the team or my former friend and teammate Gabriel.

'I play for Fulham.' I wasn't mega famous but I was frequently stopped in the street and asked for a selfie with a fan or an autograph.

Not lately, of course.

That power of the tabloid press. Hero to zero in a matter of days. But aside from Villa fans, like the guy at the airport, most normal people were still civil to me.

I winced. All the empathy I'd imagined from her vanished in a second.

'Noah Sanderson,' she repeated, her lip curling. I closed my eyes because I knew what was coming. I could predict the disgust I was about to see in her eyes.

'It was an accident,' I said firmly, as instructed by my manager, my agent and my teammates but it didn't matter how many times I said it or how true it was – it didn't change the fact that my downright fucking dangerous tackle had finished Rick Menzies' football career. He was unlikely to play in the Premier League again and I will live that every day for the rest of my life.

'It was a genuine tackle,' I went on, gently, because I hated the thought that this girl would think that I'd done it on purpose.

She stared at me as if I were speaking another language.

'Do you usually go around putting the boot in?' she asked, a bitter twist to her mouth. Wow, she'd taken it personally – like a lot of Villa fans had.

I swallowed down my disappointment. She was right. I'd made a risky tackle. I couldn't contest my innocence; she had every right to judge me. It was just a damn shame because there was something about her. The kindness and impulsive willingness to help at the airport, combined with her sparky personality, was more than an attractive combination. Fun and thoughtful. We definitely had some sort of chemistry, or rather I did.

'You don't know who I am, do you?' she asked.

I shook my head, feeling like I'd stepped into shark-infested waters with a bloody steak strapped to my chest.

'I'm the woman you trashed online.'

'What?' I replied as something flickered at the back of my mind.

'Evie Green,' she snapped. 'Remember now?'

Oh, shit!

Her angry glare was a far cry from the flirtatious smiles we'd been exchanging.

'It must feel good, being so holier than thou,' she spat. 'Slagging off someone you don't even know when you don't even know the full story.'

'It sounded quite cut and dry. The fact is you stole from your flatmates.'

She was referring to an interview I'd done when the interviewer had asked what I thought about the TikTok video everyone was talking about. It was difficult to reconcile the woman in front of me with the swollen-eyed, ragged-looking girl who'd been trying to protest her innocence.

Evie Green had gone viral. Everyone knew about how she'd fallen for a scam – which seemed pretty obvious to me – where she'd won a competition, an all-expenses-paid trip to New York and a stay at The Plaza. The catch was that she had to pay upfront – I mean seriously? I'd heard it was over four grand. She was supposed to be a journalist. Didn't they fact-check and ask questions? It was still unbelievable to me how she could have fallen for it … and raided a savings account she shared with her flatmates. Understandably pissed off, one of them had filmed her pathetic, half-assed apology where she claimed she hadn't stolen the money, just borrowed it.

'I borrowed it,' she said with tight emphasis around every syllable. 'I had every intention of paying them back.'

'You took the money without their permission. How else do you define stealing?'

I winced. Stealing. It was a very sore point. On day one at the football academy when I first came to the UK at the age of seventeen, I met Gabriel. We got our first team breaks at the same time. We blew our first pay cheques together. We played hard and partied hard. We were the golden boys, foolish and arrogant thinking we were invincible. Then Gabriel stole from me and lost his first-team place – failed a drug test. It was a wake-up call – that and the chewing out I got from my mom. If it hadn't been for her, telling me I was embarrassing the family, I might have fallen as hard and fast as Gabriel.

I thought I was being a good Samaritan standing by him, staying loyal and turning a blind eye when money went missing. I had plenty and I didn't miss it – if I'd called him out and told it like it was – that it was stealing – it might have stopped his descent into addiction sooner.

Evie's angry voice broke into my thoughts.

'And thanks to your very public views, the matter was drawn to my boss's attention – my boss and lifelong Fulham supporter. As a result, I've been suspended and then outed as a financial journalist which then made all the tabloid headlines.'

'I can't be held responsible for a decision your boss makes,' I responded, getting angrier and more defensive by the second. I knew what it was like to be at the mercy of those headlines. I was on the plane to escape them. To escape the tackle. The knowledge of how much I'd fucked up. In the States they didn't care so much about soccer. I was a nobody there, which suited me just fine at the moment.

'Besides you've not done badly out of it. Here you are, in business class? And I heard you got yourself a sympathy stay at The Plaza.' Ouch, that was mean, but I was so mad at her. She did a stupid thing and received a reward for it. Gabriel did a stupid thing and nearly died; I did a stupid thing and ruined another man's life.

Screwing up her mouth, she fiddled with the ineffectual screen thing which was supposed to offer some sort of privacy between the seats.

Of course, the bloody thing was broken.

She cursed under her breath, glared at me again and threw herself back into her seat, yanking on her earphones and folding her arms.

I glared back at her. Yes, I was responsible for finishing Menzies' career, but I would have done anything to make up for that. At least I'd visited him to apologise and tried to make restitution by offering to pay for surgery.

She couldn't even admit she'd stolen. And how stupid do you have to be to fall for a scam like that? Yeah, it happens, but she worked in finance, for fuck's sake.

As she gave me the cold shoulder for the remainder of the flight, refusing to even look my way, I had a horrible thought. Oh, shit, I was booked into The Plaza for the next couple of weeks.

As soon as we landed, I'd be on the phone to my agent, Lara, to change the booking.

Chapter Five

EVIE

'Welcome to The Plaza.'

'Thank you.' I stepped out of the yellow cab and checked out his name badge before adding, 'Danny.' The doorman, resplendent in his grey wool coat and smart peaked hat, received no more than a quick glance before I gazed up at the impressive façade, the dark rows of windows stark against the white stone, stretching up and up, the image of which had been imprinted on my brain for more than a dozen years.

'And you are?'

'I'm Evie Green.' I looked back at the doorman, my mouth curved into a face-splitting beam that said it all. I was really here. He grinned back as if he understood just how momentous this was for me. Words couldn't express the gleeful pirouettes and jetés being performed by the butterflies in my stomach.

I wanted to capture the moment forever and keep it in a

little box so that I could relive these emotions whenever I wanted. Tears blurred my eyes.

'First time in the city?' he asked gently.

I nodded, and in a husky voice said, 'My mum always dreamed of visiting.'

With that innate sense of perception that must come with the job, he patted me on the arm as if he understood, before moving to the trunk (not boot) of the car and unloaded my battered suitcase with as much care as if it were Luis Vuitton luggage.

I paid the cabbie with the unfamiliar paper dollars and reserved a few notes to tip Danny, who had already loaded my suitcase onto a trolley and led the way into the hotel.

While he took the side door, I headed through the familiar revolving door, which I must have seen in umpteen films.

I stopped a few feet from the door to take it all in.

'Wow.'

The Christmas decorations were up already and dominated the foyer. Several Christmas trees, covered in white lights and red berries, were set in a group against the back wall, surrounded by arrangements of giant red and gold baubles and glitter-paper wrapped presents. Everything sparkled including the vast chandelier overhead that refracted the twinkling lights around the room.

It was magical. Yet again my eyes blurred as I turned 360 degrees, my head tilted upward. Danny waited for me, and I realised I was holding him up, so I hurried over to join him.

'I've always wanted to stay at The Plaza,' I told him.

He leaned down to me and whispered. 'I always wanted to work here.'

We exchanged a smile.

'This is Miss Green,' he said to the two ladies at the front desk, introducing me as if I was royalty.

'Oh, my,' said one of them. 'I'm Carol. Welcome to The Plaza. It's so good to have you here.'

'We're so glad you could make it for the holidays. I'm Sofia, if there's anything we can do while you're here to make your stay even better, just let us know,' said the other woman.

'Thank you,' I said, immediately charmed by the warmth of their welcome. I wondered if they'd been briefed to expect me but something about the smiles echoed in their sparkly eyes that made me believe their open enthusiasm was genuine. 'That's so kind.'

Both of them beamed at me. 'You're going to have such a wonderful time,' said Carol. 'We've got some great treats lined up for you. But first, let's get you checked in. You must be tired after the journey. Do you need something to eat?'

I shook my head. 'That's kind but I had afternoon tea on the plane. It was lovely. Although I'm a bit all over the place in regards to time. I think it's about nine in the evening in the UK.' I checked my watch and it was four o'clock New York time. Outside the light was starting to dim.

'Don't you worry. Can we book you a table for dinner?'

I hesitated.

'It's best to keep going as long as you can,' said Sofia. 'Say, six-thirty? That will give you time to freshen up.'

'That sounds perfect,' I said, a little overcome by how kind they both were.

'Fantastic,' Carol said. 'I'll book you in. And can I say, your English accent is just so darling. I know it's still early, but will you be dining with us on Christmas Day? The lunchtime buffet is something else and we only have a limited number of places for guests as we're all sold out to the general public.'

I had no other plans for Christmas Day, so I said yes.

I handed over my passport and had just started filling out the paperwork when I felt a prickle between my shoulder blades. I turned round and couldn't flipping believe it … Noah Sanderson.

My heart did one of those traitorous little flips.

'What are you doing here?' I blurted out.

He gave me a resigned, world-weary grimace.

'Small world, it would appear,' he said, making it quite clear he'd rather be anywhere but there.

Noah Sanderson could not dim my joy at being here in The Plaza and I decided at that moment that he was not going to get to me.

'You followed me.' I clutched my heart because I could either have fun or be upset. 'That's so sweet.' I turned to the ladies at the desk. 'We met on the plane. We had seats next to each other.'

They both beamed.

'Yeah, right!' he snapped, and then paused, taking in the fading smiles and disappointed looks of Sofia and Carol. This time his tone, although gruff, was a lot less antagonistic. 'It's a coincidence, I'm afraid.'

'Or *Serendipity*,' I piped up just to watch him squirm. 'Did you see the film? One of my favourites? I loved it. Did you?'

Carol nodded enthusiastically. 'John Cusack. Gorgeous man.'

'Ooh, has he stayed here?' I asked.

Her mouth was suddenly prim. 'We value our guests' privacy.'

'Right you are,' I said tapping my nose. 'You couldn't possibly say. I understand.'

Noah watched me. There was no sign of his charming dimple now. In fact, I could have hazarded a guess that he wasn't far from the steam-coming-out-of-his-ears stage.

Ignoring me, he stepped up next to me and put his hands on the desk.

'I have a reservation. My agent booked a room for me. Noah Sanderson.'

Permafrost tinged the air and both Carol and Sofia became blank-faced professionals.

'He's a football player,' I said conversationally. 'Soccer.'

'Welcome, Mr Sanderson,' said Sofia, looking at her computer. 'I have your reservation right here.'

I smiled at Carol and finished off my form with a signature. She waved over a bellboy to guide me and my suitcase up to my room.

'Have a nice stay, Mr Sanderson. See you,' I said sweetly and followed the bellboy across the busy lobby. It was full of people who'd clearly just returned from a day's shopping, weighed down by interesting-looking rope-handled fancy bags sporting brand names. Many of them were also waiting for the lift.

By the time a lift, or should I say, elevator, became available, Noah had checked in and once again had come to stand beside me.

Of course, the crowds had dissipated by this stage and when the lift arrived it was just the two of us, our respective bellboys and the unwieldy luggage trolleys.

'Floor five,' said one of them as the other pressed a button for our floor.

'Same,' said the other man – not really boys at all.

'Gosh, look at that,' I turned to Noah. 'We're on the same floor. What luck. You just can't get rid of me.' I shot him an overly bright smile. I really wanted to get under his skin, because ever since he'd made his pronouncement about me in that interview, he'd been like a thorn in mine.

'Wanna bet,' he growled under his breath.

I sneaked a look at his profile and the little angry pulse ticking in his temple. I grinned to myself and then realised he could see me in the mirror.

'Something funny?' he asked, turning to look directly at me.

'Maybe it *is* serendipity.'

'What?' he asked.

'Us. Running into each other all the time,' I said chattily.

'I have no idea what you're talking about.'

'Seriously, Noah, you need to get out more.'

I caught one of the bellboys stifling a smile as he looked down at his feet.

'It's a film. Romcom. Probably not your thing. You

probably spend all your time watching football training videos,' I said with faux sympathy.

'I do, although I'm wondering if catching up on a few serial-killer films might be more useful.'

I stared at him. Did he just crack a joke? It was as if battle lines had been drawn.

A ding announced we'd arrived at our floor. There were two directions to take on the corridor and I couldn't decide whether I was amused or appalled that the bellboys both turned left, with Noah and I trailing after them. A few doors down and we stopped.

Noah was in 502.

I was in 501.

'Howdy, neighbour,' I said brightly. 'What fun. I hope you're not too noisy.'

Noah's mouth curved into a cocky smirk. 'Not me.' He raised his eyebrows and then lowered his voice almost to a whisper. 'But I can't speak for my friends.'

I gulped, my imagination taking off at what he might be doing with his 'friends'. A wave of heat engulfed me, and I found myself staring at his damn mouth again. It did cross my mind to wonder how many friends he planned on entertaining in his room.

The bellboys both managed to keep their faces impassive as they opened our respective rooms and ushered us into them.

Just before I went into my room, I turned. 'Bye,' I called and blew Noah a kiss for the sheer hell of it.

All thoughts of Noah Sanderson – well, nearly all – vanished the minute I walked through the door.

Oh. My. God. I'd never stepped inside a suite, let alone stayed in one before. I nodded as the bellboy pointed things out, and hurriedly stuffed a tip into his hand, desperate to get rid of him. The minute the door closed I threw myself onto one of the sofas. Yes, one of the sofas – because there were three in my suite! The lounge was probably bigger than my entire flat in London. The sofa I sank into was soft and covered in cream velvet. Cream, for goodness' sake. Above me was another enormous chandelier, with twinkling crystals, which was reflected in the huge mirror above an ornately carved fireplace. A gilt table separated the three sofas, and beside each of them on smaller occasional tables were grand lamps. On the delicate console table on the back wall on the right was a gorgeous basket of fruit, a vase of flowers and a bottle of champagne in an ice bucket along with a couple of delicate flutes. If only I had someone to share them with.

My case had been wheeled into my bedroom, which was filled with a king-size bed and pristine, Egyptian cotton bedding and a pile of pillows just begging to be sunk into.

On the bed was a plush velvety robe in soft white, a pair of slippers and … my smile was a little blurry as I took in the little Lindor chocolate reindeer with the red bow around its neck. I glanced upwards. My mum had always bought me a Lindor reindeer at Christmas. I pressed my lips together to stop myself from starting to cry. She'd loved putting together my stocking, spending hours wrapping each gift no matter how tiny. The reindeer was always left so that it peeped out over the top of the woollen sock. I hadn't really bothered with Christmas much after she died. In the first couple of years, I'd gone to my aunt and uncle's and spent a couple of days with them and my cousins, but I'd always felt like the outsider. After that I'd worked at a restaurant run by a friend of my mum's. My dad died when I was six, so I never really knew him. My memories of him were like old photos, faint and blurry with a few standout technicolour ones. Mum and I had been our own little team. Until it was just me. But I was not going to feel sorry for myself. I was here.

Nothing was going to spoil my Plaza dream. I was going to enjoy every single minute here and do all the things Mum and I talked about, starting right now.

Chapter Six

EVIE

Danny waved as I coasted through the lobby out on my first foray onto Fifth Avenue, buzzing with excitement. As soon as I stepped outside, I was assaulted by the noise of horns blaring, a police siren in the distance and the cold crisp bite of the air, which had dropped several degrees since I'd arrived.

I wasn't planning on going far and was delighted to see Bergdorf Goodman, the iconic fashion department store, almost opposite the hotel. The big shop windows beckoned through the dark evening like a lighthouse in a storm. There were already several people videoing the extravagant glitzy displays. They were larger than life, brighter than bright and thoroughly beguiling with the flashy landmarks of New York theme. Each window had a predominant colour, purple in one with a central mannequin wearing a gorgeous feather-trimmed gown surrounded by giant-sized accessories, purple sunglasses, large, carboard dressmaker scissors and a pin cushion with brightly coloured, headed pins. Another window celebrated The New York Library, with a backdrop of red featuring a stylish typewriter and a huge fountain pen, all of which showcased a beautiful and very cute cream cape-style coat, which reminded me of Audrey Hepburn. I wondered what the price tag was. Each window was filled with lots of gorgeous details, and as I moved from each one, the smile on my face grew wider as I spotted the little secret nods to culture.

I decided to venture inside and walk into the expensive handbag department, buoyed up by the Coach bag on my arm. It was my very last Christmas present from my mum, and I couldn't tell you who got the most pleasure from it: my mum giving it to me or me receiving it from her because she knew how much it would mean to me. That bag has been with me through thick and thin, and it gives me a certain amount of confidence in any situation. The bags here were all way out of my league, but it was fun to look around. Some of the price tags were scary, over $2,000 on a handbag. I could hear Lady Bracknell from *The Importance of Being Earnest* in my head, saying in horrified tones, 'A handbag.' But they were beautiful, and I had to admire the craftsmanship in the expensive designs.

From there, I took the escalator up to the first floor to the shoe section. Oh, my God, I'd never seen so many gorgeous shoes – also some pretty ugly ones. I watched a woman who'd rolled her jeans up and was trying on a pair of elegant heels, walking this way and that and looking in the mirror trying to make up her mind.

'They're gorgeous,' I whispered as I sidled past.

She gave me a grateful smile. 'I know but…'

'Cost per wear,' I told her.

'What?' she asked in a New York accent.

I patted my Coach bag. 'If I worked on the basis of how many times I've used this bag, it's around a dollar every time I use it now.'

'I love your accent and I love, love, love your theory.' She flashed me a conspiratorial smile. 'If I buy these, they'll darned well be going in my coffin with me. Thanks for that.'

'No problem,' I said and sailed on, stopping at a display of truly hideous platform Goth boots in aggressively studded leather. They looked like small armadillos ready to go on the rampage. But it takes all sorts to make the world go around. They weren't my taste, but I patted the display and walked on.

I spent an hour wandering through the displays interspersed with Christmas trees and eye-catching decorations, but I was starting to flag and decided to head back to the hotel for dinner. If I eked dinner out over an hour and a half, surely going to bed at eight would be acceptable.

Tomorrow morning, I had a meeting at nine with the PR manager, Alicia de Vries, to discuss my itinerary. I was excited to find out what they had planned.

The dining room was serene and calm, with the familiar chandeliers hanging overhead. I wondered how I'd fit back into real life after three weeks here. Would I ever get over the little thrill each time I walked through the hotel doors and lobby, while people outside peered through the windows trying to get a glimpse of the famous interior?

'Good evening, Madam. Do you have a reservation?'

'Good evening. I do. The front desk arranged one for me.'

I gave him my room number and was led to a little round table in a discreet alcove. No sooner had I sat down and picked up the pristine white napkin, smoothing the dense fabric over my lap, than something, no more than a moth brushing past, made me look up.

Noah Sanderson was right in my eye line on the table opposite, and as fate would have it, because fate was a big fat bugger at the moment, he looked up at that very second. His eyes narrowed. And because he looked so irritated, I waved.

'Hello. Fancy seeing you here.'

To my surprise, rather than glare at me, he lifted his wine glass in an ironic toast. 'Evening, Miss Green.' His low drawl loosened a flurry of butterflies in my stomach.

Why him? I cursed my body.

Thankfully, a waiter came over and momentarily blocked my view, but the reprieve didn't last long as he stepped to the side and handed over a menu.

'Can I get you anything to drink?'

I considered the question and then unable to help myself I gave him a quick grin, putting my hand to one side of my mouth I said in a loud conspiratorial stage whisper, 'I'll have what he's having.'

Noah's mouth quirked ever so slightly before it flattened back into disapproval. Score one to me, I thought, relishing the tiny victory. I'd almost made him smile.

'The Californian Syrah. An excellent choice. Very good, Madam,' said the waiter and although his demeanour was all that was proper, he gave me a very quick wink before serenely walking away.

Pointedly ignoring Noah, I picked up the menu and began to read through the choices. They all sounded wonderful, though a little heavy for my body clock. Even though I had raised the menu like a barrier between us, I was aware of Noah watching me over the top of his wine glass, as if he were watching a tiger wondering what its next strike might be. It made me smile to myself. I liked the idea of keeping him on his toes.

'What do you think?' I asked, putting the menu aside. 'What are you having?' We were the only diners in this part of the restaurant; it seemed silly not to talk to him.

He huffed out a quick sigh of impatience at my continued impertinence. 'I'm having the soup.'

'Soup. Nothing else?'

'We were pretty well fed on the plane. Although someone ate my scone.'

'Scone,' I corrected his pronunciation. 'And I didn't want to see it go to waste.'

He had a point. I really wasn't that hungry. I returned to the selection of starters and the delightful realisation I could have anything I wanted. I was a guest of the hotel; I could drink champagne every day if I wanted. I didn't have to cook, or clean or do anything.

Not that I'd been much into cooking or cleaning, if I was

totally honest. I sat back in my chair revelling in this knowledge.

When I laid down the menu, the waiter appeared with a tall glass of red wine as if he'd read my mind. The service here really was something else.

'Please may I have the pork?' I asked.

'Certainly. And would you like some bread with that? The mustard sauce is excellent,' he lowered his voice, 'and deserves dunking.'

'Does it?' I asked smiling at him.

He nodded solemnly. 'My favourite.'

I flashed a grin at him and looked at his name badge. 'Thank you, Martin. I'll have some bread as well, please.'

'Very good.'

I took the first sip of wine.

'You've got good taste, Mr Sanderson. This is lovely.' This time, I raised my glass at him as if I knew anything about wine.

'Glad to be of service.' I could tell he was trying hard not to smile, and I had to purse my lips to stop myself laughing out loud.

'No, you're not,' I teased.

He put his wine down and rolled his eyes. 'Do you do this much?'

'Do what?'

'Stalk complete strangers.'

'I'm not stalking you. I was always coming. Why are you staying here?'

'Because my agent booked me in here.'

'Oh God, it really is serendipity,' I said.

'Or sheer bad luck,' he groused, but it was there again, that little lift to the side of his mouth. I reckoned he didn't find me as annoying as he liked to make out.

Martin the waiter arrived with his soup and while he fussed over Noah, I took another sip of the very delicious wine.

'Let me know if there's anything else I can get you?' he said and then turned to me.

'How's your wine?'

'Excellent, I was just saying to Mr Sanderson that he has good taste in wine.'

'Oh.' Martin looked from me to Noah and then back again and a little light of matchmaker winked in his eyes.

'Would you two like to sit together?'

'No!' we both snapped simultaneously.

He took a step back as if physically hit by the mutual wave of vehemence.

'Fine,' he said with a nod to both of us before scuttling off.

Noah picked up his phone with one hand and began diligently reading something on the screen as he tucked into his soup with the other.

I had a strong feeling that was it for the night. There would be no further interaction, or at least not deliberate, but there did seem to be quite a few occasions when I glanced over and he quickly looked away.

As soon as he'd finished his soup, he laid down the spoon, wiped his mouth with his napkin – why was I compelled to watch that?

He rose and said, 'Goodnight...' then paused, 'Evie.' The

way he said my name, even though it was obviously reluctant, sent a shiver rippling over my skin.'

'Goodnight, Mr Sanderson, I hope you sleep well.'

He gave me a grave nod and walked out of the restaurant. I watched him go, trying to ignore the way his lean, rangy walk made my breath catch just a little.

I was definitely going to look up how to build up some immunity against fearsome pheromones.

Chapter Seven

EVIE

'Wow,' I said the following morning reading through the itinerary that Alicia had put together, a little thrill running through me at the thought of ice-skating at the Rockefeller Center in front of the iconic gold statue of Prometheus. That, among other things, had been on my New York wish list. I'd been prepping for this visit for half of my life. All I had to do was have fun and post pictures on the Instagram account they'd set up, @EvieAtThePlaza.

'This looks amazing. I can't wait. I've always wanted to do some of these things.'

'I know,' Alicia gave me a kind smile. 'When I saw that reel and when you explained why you'd fallen for the scam and how you used to watch Christmas movies set in New York with your late mom, it really touched me and so many other people. My mom and I took a trip to Ireland this year, we'd been talking about it since I was a kid. We had such a blast and then straight after I saw that TikTok, I felt so bad for you. I mean, you did wrong, but it was really kind of nasty of those folk to post that reel.'

She held up her phone and I studied the infamous reel with fresh eyes. At the time, I had been outraged that my flatmates had posted an image of me at my most vulnerable, when I was shattered that I'd been scammed and that the dream of going to The Plaza and New York had been cruelly snatched from me. It brought back all my grief at the death of my mother and my tears were as much for her as they were for the shock and humiliation of being scammed.

Now, with a bit of distance and hindsight, I watched the reel as someone who didn't know the background. I was pitiful. A snotty, teary mess. First impression: pathetic, stupid and entitled. Trying to justify what I'd done, refusing to accept that what I'd done to them was wrong. So wrong. It hadn't helped that I was trying to explain about my mum and how much going to New York had meant to me while still in a state of high emotion. The reel showed me at my most vulnerable and incoherent, distraught and not capable of rational thought. 'I'll pay you back,' I wailed. 'I only borrowed it.'

I'd been pulled in by the classic, coercive urgency of the scammer. Time is of the essence… If you don't do this now… You must hurry… And like an idiot I'd fallen for it. If I didn't pay upfront for the flight, I'd lose it and for security reasons, it was quicker and easier to do it through them on my card as that would match my passport documentation. I didn't question it. Not for one moment because it was a golden opportunity to fulfil my mum's wishes. I basically handed them my bank account on a platter – or rather the house account where we were putting all our savings for our holiday.

Was it any wonder Jamie and Esther hadn't believed I was good for the money. How were they to know that my cavalier attitude about clothes, the future, relationships didn't extend to money? I might have worked in finance, but it wasn't exactly hot news over a pint and a glass of wine what that week's best interest rate was, or which stocks and shares ISA I'd recommend. Which had led my flatmates to assume I wasn't good for the money. Of course, I'd known I had the money, but I hadn't been able to convince them. My flatmates and the rest of the world had judged me – and now looking at the reel again, I didn't blame them one bit.

'So nasty,' said Alicia, again. 'I'm real sorry about your mom, you must miss her. I can't imagine not speaking to mine every day. It would make me a little crazy, too.'

I swallowed down the little lump and concentrated on being happy, like Mum would have wanted me to be.

'She'd be thrilled for me, and I have to be happy for her.' I hauled in a breath. 'But it's hard sometimes, especially now I'm here and she isn't.'

'Well, I promise you. We're going to give you a real good time and we'll look after you. The Plaza is renowned for looking after its guests. She gave me a friendly smile. 'So, I think that's everything.'

Alicia was everything I'd like to grow up to be one day. Not only was she kind but she had perfect white teeth, perfect red lipstick and wore an immaculate two-piece suit, the skirt of which stopped just below her knee to show off fabulous legs. From the smooth chignon of her blonde hair, right down to the tip of her gorgeous grey-suede shoes with their delicate heels – as unlike me as humanly possible – she was sleek and well groomed. Despite being up since five this morning – my body clock still had some adjusting to do – I had unmanageable bedhead hair and I'd taken the easy way out and scooped my errant curls into a messy bun. Clothes-wise, I'd just pulled on my favourite jeans and a jumper that had seen better days. I was panicking that I didn't have enough cold-weather clothes. New York was far chillier than I was expecting.

Alicia shot a quick glance at her assistant, an equally glossy, well-groomed girl who hadn't said a word yet.

'What size are you?'

'Size?' I asked, assuming she meant for the proposed shopping trip to Bloomingdale's, which was on my itinerary. 'I'm an English twelve, but I know your sizes are quite different here.'

She was already tapping on her phone. 'That makes you an eight.'

'That, I like,' I said. 'I don't think I've ever been an eight in my life.'

'Shoe size?'

'A UK Six.'

She tapped out something else then looked up again. 'Great. Have you got all that, Cora?'

Her assistant nodded.

'Okay, so we'll have all that sorted for you. We're gonna do a bit of a photo shoot this lunchtime. It'll be a lot of fun.'

'Great,' I said with a big grin, wondering if I'd get hair and makeup as well as the clothes. I couldn't wait. This trip was already exceeding my expectations.

'We're just waiting for Angel to arrive. She's your butler and will show you round the hotel and take you behind the scenes to get an idea of all the things that go on here.'

'Okay,' I said, excited to get started. 'That sounds brilliant.'

There was a knock at the door and a small dark head peeped around the corner.

'Hey, come on in, Angel, and meet your new charge. This is Evie Green.'

'Well, hello, Evie Green. Nice to meet you and welcome to The Plaza. I'm one of the butlers and I'll be looking after you.' Angel might have been small in stature, she was knocking five foot, but from the twinkle in her eyes, her low deep voice and wide grin, I could tell her personality outweighed her size.

'Hi, Angel, nice to meet you.' My own butler! How cool was that. I bet Noah snarky Sanderson didn't have his own butler. I hadn't seen him at breakfast this morning, although it had been an early one because I'd been awake for hours. I was the first and only person in the dining room for the first half an hour, and even then I'd had to wait until six-thirty for it to open.

Angel was dressed in a black suit, with comfy black shoes and wore heavy-black-framed glasses.

'Right, Evie,' said Alicia. 'We'll see you at twelve in the restaurant manager's office. Angel will show you the way.' She and Cora then hurried away as if they had important things to do, leaving me with Angel.

'And how are you finding The Plaza?' she asked, standing with her arms behind her back.

'Lovely so far. It's gorgeous.'

'And is everything to your liking?' she asked.

'Yes,' I said.

Apart from my neighbour in room 502.

'Good, that's a key part of what we're about at The Plaza. Nothing is too much for our guests, we want to make sure they have the best stay ever. Especially at Christmas.

Angel showed me every floor of the hotel except the fourth floor, which held The Royal Suite. 'It's occupied just now,' she explained. 'But next week I'll be able to give the full guided tour. It's quite something.'

'My room's quite something, too,' I said, thinking of the mosaic-tiled bathroom, the marble sinks – yes two of them – and the gold taps and fittings.

'So, is everything to your liking? Do you need anything? And when would you like a Christmas tree set up?'

'I don't know.'

'Or would you like to set it up yourself? We do that with some of the families that come for Christmas. They like that. It's a fun thing to do.'

'Mmm,' I said noncommittally. I hadn't actually had a Christmas tree since my mum had died. There just never seemed any point. Not so much of a fun thing to do when you are on your own. 'I'll think about it,' I said, knowing full well I'd avoid the issue unless it was brought up again. Why worry about something now when you could push it down the line until later and a decision absolutely had to be made.

We went and visited the maintenance team down in the basement. 'This is Bernard and his boys, they keep the place running and replace the crystals.'

'Howdy. How you doin'?' greeted Bernard.

'Good, thanks and you?'

'Just dandy.'

'What are crystals?'

He laughed. 'I'm not sure I should tell you. They're the little bits of glass on the chandeliers. Guests just love to take a crystal home as a souvenir.'

'Oh,' I said. The concept of souvenirs had kind of passed me by. I didn't like hoarding stuff. There never seemed much point.

He waved a screwdriver at me. 'Anything you need, just call – except for a crystal,' he said and continued rewiring the lamp on the table in front of him.

After that we skirted past the kitchens, where they were already preparing for lunch, and dropped in on housekeeping.

'Hey, Angel, how's it going?' called one of the women who was handing Sellotape to another woman wrapping a large parcel in luxury paper.

'Good, Joanie. Everyone, this is Evie Green. She's staying in room 501. Who's looking after that section.'

'Me! Hey, Evie,' called another woman. 'I'm

housekeeping for you *and* the hottie next door. Have you seen him? Phew.' She fanned herself. Another woman nudged her.

'Laetitia.'

I did not want to talk about Noah. 'What are you doing? It looks like Santa's grotto in here.' I touched one of the rolls of velvet ribbon in a bronze colour which coordinated perfectly with the cream paper dotted with bronze reindeer.

'Oh, that's for the Greenford family,' piped up Joanie. 'They come every year, with their children. Just the sweetest family, and those two little girls, they're adorable. Mr and Mrs Greenford order all the presents and have them delivered to us and we wrap them so that they're under the tree when the children arrive on Christmas Eve. It's a longstanding tradition. We've been doing it since the youngest was a baby. She'll be seven this year.' Laetitia held up a little fluffy rabbit and waved it at us.

'You wrap all their presents?' I repeated flabbergasted. My mum had loved wrapping presents, having a stranger wrap them for you seemed a little bit impersonal to me. But then when was the last time I'd sat down and wrapped presents? If I absolutely had to, for a secret Santa at work or the odd things for friends, I might, but quite frankly Christmas was something of a non-event, apart from binge-watching my favourite holiday movies.

'Come on, I'd better get you back to Raoul's office. You don't want to be late for whatever the next activity is.' Angel chivvied me along.

'How long have you worked here?' I asked as we trotted along. For a small woman she could sure walk fast.

'I've been here fifteen years. I started in housekeeping but then after my husband died, I applied to be a butler. I needed to earn more.'

'I'm sorry to hear that. You're very young to be a widow. That must be tough. What was he called?'

She stared at me and then her face softened. 'You know, no one ever asks that. They always shy away from the subject. And friends who did know him shy away from talking about him, I guess because they don't want to upset me. But it's like he didn't exist. I want to talk about him. His name was Tony. I met him when I was eighteen,' she smiled, remembering him. 'He was half-Italian, with this head of curly hair. Bit like yours. He worked for Amtrak and … there was an accident one day.'

I winced in sympathy as she continued. 'I still miss him, but I got a little girl and my mom to look after, so there's no time to mope. This job is demanding but it keeps me busy.'

'What sort of things do you have to do?' I asked, intrigued.

'I'll save that all for another day. Here you are, this is Raoul's office. He runs the restaurant during the day.'

A young dark-haired man, as neat as a penguin in black and white, appeared at the door.

'You must be Evie Green,' he said excitedly, with a touch of a Greek accent. 'I'm so happy to meet you and I'm thrilled you're taking over from me for today. Although don't get too attached, honey. You can't have the gig full-time because it's one of my favourites.'

'Hi,' I said, pleased by his warm, enthusiastic campy welcome. 'Raoul?'

'One and the same. Alicia sends her apologies, she got called into a meeting, but I can brief you.'

'Okay.'

'Now honey, the costume's right over there. If you want to get changed, I'll be back in five minutes to take you up to the restaurant.'

'Costume?' I looked at Angel.

She shrugged. 'I don't know nothing about that. I've got to collect some dry-cleaning and deliver it to some folks on the sixth floor.' With a cheery wave, she disappeared leaving me staring at the pile of clothes on the corner of the table.

'You want me to wear this?' I picked up a pair of red-and-white stripy leggings. Lying beside them was a little green felt tunic and a matching hat and next to them a couple of large wicker baskets filled with candy canes.

'Yes, you're going to be our Christmas elf!'

I stared, as much surprised by his words as by the children's-birthday-party levels of excitement in his voice.

'It's such a fun job.' He clapped his hands together. 'You get to decide who's been naughty or nice.' His eyelashes fluttered suggestively. 'And if they've been nice, they get a candy cane. Everyone just loves it.' He clapped again, his face lighting up with so much infectious enthusiasm I had to smile, even though that wasn't quite how I'd imagined the afternoon would go. So much for a fancy photo shoot. I picked up the hat with the little bell on the top and laughed out loud. Yes, this was much more my life than designer clothes. Who had I been trying to kid? I was the eternal hot mess, why did I really expect things to change?

'I'll leave you to get ready, Elfie,' he said, with a happy chuckle. 'You're really honoured, this is my favourite job of the year. You only get to do it today.' He winked. 'Be right back.'

Before I could say a word, he'd bustled away through the door and closed it behind him.

I looked totally ridiculous. My tangled curls, because I couldn't get my untidy bun under the hat, spilled out over my shoulders like a cartoon character who'd stuck their finger in an electric socket. The tights were a size too small, and the crotch was several inches short of where it should have been, and the tight lycra threatened to cut off my circulation mid-thigh.

The only positive thing I could say was that the little green curly slippers, again with bells, fitted perfectly. They tinkled announcing every step I took.

I sighed and looked in the mirror one last time.

'Oh, oh, oh,' cried Raoul, when I opened the door. 'Don't you look cute. Aw, the customers are going to love you. Make sure you say hi to Mrs Evans, she'll be in the corner with her little bichon frise, Monty. She's a widow. Has no family. Comes for the holidays every year. She's a doll. Mind you make a fuss of her. There's a dog treat in there for Monty. And there's a party of ladies in today who make an annual event of it and come for lunch on their shopping day. They tip real good, so smile and be real nice to them.'

Years of working Christmas Day in Paula's restaurant had been a good training ground for false cheer. I could do this. Tightening my elf belt, I trotted after Raoul, my bells ringing like Rudolf and Co's sleigh en route to the world's chimneys.

'Look who's here!' squealed Raoul at the entrance to the Palm Court Restaurant. All eyes turned my way and silence fell on the room. Absolute pin-dropping sort of quiet. For a moment I froze, and then I remembered this was supposed to be fun.

'Don't forget, Happy Holidays,' whispered Raoul in my ear as he strode into the room expecting me to follow. I hauled in a deep breath and stared down at the little brass bells on my toes. Finally I looked up, to find everyone still staring.

Gripping my basket, I shook one foot and stepped forward. 'Happy Holidays.'

Grateful for Raoul's heads-up, I darted to the elderly woman holding court in the corner, a little white dog perched on her lap. Elegantly dressed in an exquisite lavender cashmere sweater, she sat ramrod straight on her chair, surveying the room. Her soft white hair was beautifully styled and reminded me of the late Queen Elizabeth II.

'Hi, you must be Mrs Evans. Santa has asked me to make sure I stop by,' I yelled, a little too loudly. 'He said to say hello. And this must be Monty.'

'Why, you must be the Christmas Elf,' said Mrs Evans, thankfully playing along, otherwise I'd have looked a right idiot. Her powdered face lit up. 'What a treat, eh, Monty?' Her faded blue eyes wreathed in wrinkles shone with all the life of a twenty-year-old's, before she confided, 'He's been a very good dog this year.'

'Has he?' I blinked at her and then remembered the dog treat secreted in the basket.

'Then this is for you, Monty,' I said to the dog, handing over the paper-wrapped treat.

'Isn't that lovely. Say thank you to the nice Elf, Monty.'

The little dog lifted a paw. Enchanted, I took the paw and bowed, feeling a smile take over my face.

And how about you, Mrs E,' I said with a teasing wink because she was rather adorable. 'Have you been naughty or nice?'

'Darling,' she drawled the word. 'At my age, I can be as naughty as I like.' She gave a throaty, movie-diva chuckle, before adding. 'And I am.'

'In that case, you can definitely have a candy cane.' I handed it over. 'But don't eat it all at once.'

She patted my wrist with a blue-veined hand. 'I'll use it to stir my whisky, how's that?'

I burst out laughing. 'In that case, you'd better have two.'

She laughed delightedly back at me. Suddenly, this gig didn't seem quite so bad after all.

I bounded over to the large table of shopping ladies, making sure the bells on my toes tinkled.

'And, ladies. Which one of you has spent the most?'

They laughed and pointed to a woman on the other side of the table and chorused, 'Ava.' I tiptoed over to her. 'And have you been naughty or nice?' I asked her. She blushed pink at the attention. 'The present is for my husband,' she said quietly while the others teased her. 'So, I think I've been nice.' I handed her a candy cane.

'I think so, too.' I turned to the other ladies and eyed one of the louder ones at the end of the table. 'What about you? You look like a troublemaker.'

Her friends all laughed again.

'You got that right, sweetie. She's hell on wheels.'

'Yeah, Barb,' replied the woman, grinning. 'But I'm a lot of fun.'

They were all a lot of fun, and as I went round the table doling out the candy canes, I quickly got into the swing of being Christmas Elf.

My basket was nearly empty, and I'd worked most of the centre of the room with Raoul periodically giving me the thumbs up and passing me, whispering, 'You go, girl.' Hopefully he and his team weren't going to be missing out on their tips.

I'd just finished dispensing candy canes to two little girls, both dressed in matching frilly dresses and wearing the cutest patent Mary Janes on their feet when I had a feeling I was being watched. I mean I'd been at the centre of attention in the room for the last half hour, but this was different. When I turned and looked towards the table near the bar, I spotted him. Noah. I could have predicted it.

He lifted his coffee cup and gave me a cocky salute.

The gesture fired me up and I bounced over to him. 'Can I interest you in a candy cane?' I said, hamming it up because everyone was watching.

His stubbled jaw tightened, and a wary expression came over his face, as well it might. And as luck would have it, someone – I'd call it divine intervention – dropped a tray.

The crash reverberated around the dining room, silencing it momentarily once again.

I leaped straight in. 'And have you been naughty or nice?' I asked in a very loud voice and as suggestively as I could at that volume. Who knew it was so difficult to speak at full volume and be seductive at the same time? However, I must have managed it, because suddenly everyone's attention was on us.

'Have you been a good boy?' I tilted my head, one coquettish hand on my hip, waiting for an answer. A naughty spark lit in Noah's eyes and a slow smile spread across his face. It unnerved me, making me feel like I might just have poked a bear with a very sharp stick.

He looked me up and down, those blue eyes missing nothing, his mouth tilted in a wicked smile. I couldn't help the quick shiver that ran through my body at his slow diligent assessment, weighing me up inch by inch.

Well, I wasn't going to back down, was I?

I put my foot on the chair next to him, revealing my stripy leg in all its glory, like some mad elven dominatrix. 'Not got an answer for me?' I asked, poking the bear some more.

Our audience, because the assembled crowd were all tuned into the performance, giggled and murmured.

I was aware of Raoul taking photos on his iPhone, which to be fair he had been doing all the time, but now I felt like I'd stepped into no man's land, and I was in danger.

Noah's steady, unblinking gaze held mine.

'Well, what's it going to be. Naughty or nice?' I asked.

To my surprise, his eyes narrowed, and an unholy look

of glee lit up his eyes. Unknowingly, I'd just issued a challenge.

He ran a finger along my leg, from mid-thigh to knee and down my shin, suddenly shooting me a smouldering smile. 'Well, that depends on who's asking?' he murmured.

His hand circled my ankle with a firm, gentle but implacable hold. The bastard. I could have pulled away, but it would have spoiled the show, which he bloody knew. It was hard to resist the insistent tug deep in my belly telling me that I liked his touch and that hint of possession.

He was in total control. When his thumb caressed the inner part of my leg just above my ankle, I took in a sharp breath as a tiny tingle shot up my leg. As his thumb continued to brush over the same spot, my knees wobbled and heat pooled in a place it had no place going.

'Pardon?' I whispered, a little dazed.

'I think you heard me,' he said with a suggestive raise of one of his dark eyebrows. 'I can be naughty or nice. Which would you prefer?'

I gulped because, right at that moment, I wasn't sure which I'd prefer but either way I wanted it to be with me.

Aware of the interested gazes, my mind flitted backwards and forwards trying to work out the best way out of this. I'd started it, so I would see it through. I gently pulled my foot away with as much balletic grace as I could, which as it turned out wasn't much, and Noah, the bastard, rose to help me, that cocky smirk back on his face.

There was no way I was going to let him get away with having the metaphorical last word.

Curving my lips into a big smile, I stood on tiptoe and

chastely kissed his cheek and then, like a champion mime artist, I peered into my basket as if searching for just the right candy cane before I plucked one out. With a flourish and a bow, I presented it to him, blew another kiss and skipped out of the room to a cheer and a round of applause.

I wasn't sure which one of us was going to live it down.

Noah Sanderson: challenge accepted.

Chapter Eight

NOAH

After pounding the paths of Central Park for twenty minutes and five seconds, trying to rid myself of the can't-sit-still feelings racking my body, my watch signalled that I'd completed 5k. I slowed right down to a gentle jog before moving to the side of the path. I bent over, my sides heaving as I sucked in hoarse breaths.

A couple of teenagers gave me the eye as they walked past, and when I glared, just stopping short of growling at them, they giggled and walked on. I ignored them and strode to the edge of the lake, looking at the blue sky and skyscrapers reflected on the surface of the water. I wanted to throw stones and disturb the calm. The run was supposed to burn off my frustration at the world, but it clearly hadn't worked.

I did a couple of stretches and then sat down on the outcrop of rocks while I cooled down. I'd gone off fast to try and burn the antsy, pent-up feeling that I couldn't seem to shake. My thoughts kept circling back to Evie. Every time I resolved to ignore her, she made me smile with that implicit challenge to have the last word. I couldn't help myself trying to beat her at her own game. Everywhere I turned, she popped up, always in my peripheral vision. I checked over my shoulder and around at the quiet park, at the silent bare trees divested of their summer coverage, just in case I'd conjured her up and she was lurking behind one of the bushes.

Even getting a coffee in peace without her appearing was impossible, and today she'd surpassed herself. I laughed quietly to myself.

That girl did not know when to quit. I kind of admired her cheeky style, even though she was everything I wanted to avoid right now. She was impulsive and jumped before she thought. She was too reminiscent of Gabe. Evie was amusing, and I bet I could have a lot of fun with her, but I needed to get back on the team and not get distracted by anything or anyone.

Although, being totally honest, she'd livened up what was otherwise turning into a very dull day.

If I was going to be stuck in the city until my ban was overturned, I needed to make some new plans. My original idea had been that if I was still here, I'd spend Christmas with my sister. Unfortunately, those plans had been sunk when my sister told me that her mother-in-law was sick so she and her kids were travelling to Montana straight away and would spend the holidays there.

There were only so many hours a day I could spend in the gym, and I was already sick of the place.

Maybe I'd take in a ball game while I was here. I hadn't been to one in years. I'd hoped to meet up with my college buddy, Todd, but he was out of town.

My phone buzzed and I seized it gratefully. Someone to talk to.

It was my agent.

'Hey, how's it going?' asked Lara. 'What are you up to?

'I've just been for a run.'

'Good boy. You can't afford to let your fitness go.'

'I'm bored,' I said. 'I can only train so many hours a day.'

'Bored! Noah, you're in one of the world's greatest cities. Go play tourist.'

'Is this the sort of advice I'm paying you for?'

'Yeah, and it doesn't come cheap, so pay attention.'

'I could come home. Any news on the appeal for my suspension?'

'No, you need to be patient.'

'Easier said than done.'

'Noah, you, the manager, the team and I know that was a risky challenge. We can change perceptions about that, but what we can't change is the fact the guy broke his leg in two places.' I felt sick when she said it. I felt sick every time I heard it.

'Unfortunately, we've got some work to do to rehabilitate your rep. You need to be squeaky clean. Don't suppose you could find a nice girl to fall in love with? The tabloids love a romance.'

'Very funny,' I told her. 'I don't have time for that sort of stuff.' I needed to prove I deserved my place on the team and that I would do what it took to keep it.

'You just told me you were bored. Go out and have some fun. You can afford a few late nights. Not too many, though, and don't go out and get stupid drunk and be pictured leaving a nightclub with anyone. If you have to be seen – be seen coming out of a museum or having some good clean fun.'

'I'll do my best,' I said wryly.

'Seriously, Noah, take this time to do stuff. Go to the Guggenheim, the High Line – and that café, the Central Perk.'

I groaned. 'You do know that was in *Friends* – it's not real.'

'It isn't – are you sure?'

'Real sure,' I replied firmly responding to the disbelief in her voice.

'Well, even so. I'd love to do those things but some of us are too busy. Go out, do stuff. For my sake if not your own.'

'Okay, Lara. I'll go out and do stuff.'

I finished the call and looked up at the skyline around me. She was right, I was in one of the world's greatest cities, I should make the most of it but that was easier said than done. It would be more fun with someone. I knew one person in particular who seemed to find fun in everything. I pushed the thought away.

Maybe I'd do as Lara suggested and check out a museum.

Mind made up, I picked myself up, loosened the

sweatshirt from around my waist and slipped it over my head.

'Excuse me,' a voice from behind me intruded on my thoughts. 'Would you mind taking a…' I turned around.

It was almost as if I'd manifested her presence by just thinking about her. Evie Green stood in front of me, wrapped in a long black shapeless coat and a scarlet scarf, wrapped several times around her neck so that only her face above her nose was visible.

'You,' she said taking a step backwards. 'What are you doing here?'

'Running. What are you doing here?'

'Following you, of course,' she replied.

'Are you?' I asked, raising an eyebrow.

She tutted loudly even as she blushed, and I got a definite kick out of the way a streak of pink stained her cheekbones.

'Mr Ego. Of course I'm not. We are within spitting distance of the hotel that we're both staying in. It's not that much of a stretch to imagine we might bump into each other here.'

'I guess,' I responded. 'Well, nice seeing you but some of us have things to do.'

She fell into step beside me, and my body hummed in silent satisfaction.

'Like what? What do you recommend doing? As a native?'

'Not so much a native. I grew up in Bridgeport in Connecticut.'

'I meant American, and I'm not even going to pretend I know where that is.'

Unable to help myself, I laughed, as there was something so refreshingly honest about her. 'It's about sixty miles northeast of here along the coast.'

'Close enough to be local in my book. You must have visited the city.'

I thought of my mom. 'We came to see Broadway shows a lot, my mom's thing.'

'A Broadway show. Good idea. I'll have to check what's on.'

Her hair danced in the stiff morning breeze, and I had to keep my hands at my sides to resist the temptation to brush it away from her face. I found myself volunteering more information than I needed to.

'My mom always used to go see the Radio City Rockettes Christmas Spectacular.'

'And that's a bit of a mouthful,' quipped Evie.

I laughed again because she was right. 'I went with her a couple of times when I was younger – my sister and I got dragged along. I couldn't get out of it. Not that I'd wanted to, although I wouldn't have admitted it at the time. It was a lot of fun.'

'So, what happens?' Evie's genuine interest was obvious, her big eyes were focused on me and there was a thoughtful look on her face. She might be a lot of things I didn't approve of, but she was very open and had a warmth about her that was kind of endearing. And I liked the way she was so ridiculously outspoken. When she walked beside me, she was in step, keeping up easily, and I was fascinated by that mass of hair. I was itching to find out if it was as soft and silky as it looked. And then there was the infectious smile, which, when she turned it on me, felt as if the sun had come out.

'It's like a real, old-school Hollywood musical Christmas deal. Big cast. Lots of singing. Dancing. They have a couple of traditional numbers, the 'Dance of the Wooden Soldiers' and the 'Living Nativity'. You should go, if you can get tickets.'

'I know a woman who probably can,' said Evie with a grin, and I was immediately reminded of what brought her to New York and why I was here, too. I wasn't here for fun. There was a man lying in hospital because of me. I needed to train hard and focus on being the best I could, so that when I got back on the team, everyone would know I deserved my place.

I shot her a tight smile, thinking of her scamming free tickets. I get offered a lot of freebies, but there's no such thing as a free lunch. I don't take anything for granted... And shit, don't I sound like old misery guts. Of course, I take tickets and stuff for friends, but I try not to blag too much (and that's how English I've become in the last ten years. Blagging is such an English word).

It seems wrong that Evie's benefitting when she messed up.

'Are you going to milk this?' I asked.

'Sounds like you don't approve. There's a surprise. Are you always this much of a killjoy?'

'No. I prefer to think of myself as a responsible citizen who pays my way.' I sounded prissy even to myself, and then when her face turned pale and her eyes dulled, I felt a bit of a shit, but I couldn't take the words back.

'I'd forgotten what a high opinion you have of me, Mr Sanderson.' I didn't miss the sudden crumpling of her mouth and wondered for a moment if maybe I'd judged her too harshly.

Chapter Nine

NOAH

'Who's the girl in the elf costume?' Lara's accusatory words rattled out of my phone like a spray of machine-gun bullets. Bleary-eyed, I focused on the phone screen. 2:22am 'What?' I spluttered.

'I told you to behave. Not get yourself all over social media. I've had a tip off – a very reliable one – that a certain TikTok reel featuring you and a fetching elf has gone viral and the *Sun* is asking who she is.'

'You're shitting me,' I said and fell back against my pillows. I scrolled through my apps to Instagram and searched for Evie Green. Just one look at the results told me all I needed to know.

'Fuck.'

'Indeed,' said Lara. 'I told you to keep a low profile. Instead, you're pictured, feeling up a festive fucking elf.'

I winced and looked back at the image of me with a filthy smirk on my face as if I'd got evil designs on the very sexy elf. It reminded me of what I was thinking at that very moment. Let's just say those thoughts weren't the least bit pure.

'Sorry, Lara. It's not how it looks.'

She sighed heavily. 'Nothing to be done about it now. They'll print the usual, "Sanderson was unavailable for comment".'

'Do you want me to issue a statement?'

'No, I just wanted to give you a heads-up. I'll try and come up with some damage-limitation strategy. We don't want to draw any adverse attention to you at the moment, not while management are appealing the length of your suspension. If you're going to appear on social media, we want Mr Nice Guy, not the villain of the dirty tackle, and definitely not Mr Playboy. It's the sort of thing the press will lap up and won't do your cause any good. Public opinion could sway the FA.'

She wasn't telling me anything I didn't already know.

'Who is this girl and why is everyone so interested?'

'She's Evie Green, the sobbing girl.'

'That's her. How funny? She's … pretty, and she looks a hell of a lot better than she did in that video. So, what's she doing at The Plaza? I thought she was crying because she couldn't go.'

'They felt sorry for her,' I drawled, making my disapproval apparent, 'and they've given her a complementary stay. She's documenting her visit – a promotional campaign run by the hotel.' I learned this from the restaurant manager after Evie had danced off on her tinkling toes. It's called @EvieAtThePlaza. Like *Eloise at The Plaza*.'

'Who's Eloise?'

Sometimes things come up that are a stark reminder of the cultural differences between the UK and the US. It's not just the difference between sidewalk and pavement, sweater and jumper. There's a whole popular-culture divide.

'It's a famous series of kids' books.'

'Right,' said Lara but even from across the miles, I could tell her mind was elsewhere. 'Leave it with me, Noah. I might have something.'

'Like what?' I asked, immediately suspicious. Some of Lara's ideas could be a little off the wall. For the last two years she'd been trying to get me to do *Strictly*. I fancied the *Dancing on Ice* gig – but the higher likelihood of injury put the kybosh on that one.

'Like I said, leave it with me. I need to make a few calls!' And with that, she disconnected the call.

I laid back on my pillows in the dark, deeply regretting my foolish impulse to tease Evie in the Palm Court Restaurant. There was just something about her that got under my skin and made me act out of character. I needed to stay away from her, because I never knew what she was going to say or do next. Like Lara said, my appeal was going to be heard in a matter of days. I was hoping my six-match ban would be overturned and I could get back to the UK to play the Boxing Day fixture. Surely in a hotel this size, I could stay out of her way.

I woke up several hours later to a dozen text messages, including a very pissed-off missive from my manager. He was not impressed by the low-profile approach. With the transfer window coming up, the last thing I wanted to do was upset Marco, the Fulham manager. I rather liked my Chelsea apartment, and after living in Central London for the last three years, I'd got to know my way around. Even though I was a long way away from my family, London was starting to feel like home. Mom and Dad had come to visit several times and got a kick out of visiting the city and playing tourists.

I phoned for room service and ordered breakfast. At least that was one way of avoiding the curly-haired menace. Man, her hair was wild, and again, I wondered what it would feel like under my fingers, fanned across her naked back. And whoa! Where had that thought come from?

Despite her annoying, perky attitude and ability to turn up everywhere I went, there was a definite pull between us. Even though it wasn't my style, or maybe because it wasn't, I liked her unpredictability and the way she pushed me off balance. And those quick comebacks… It was more, though, there was the way she'd instantly plunged into rescuing me at the airport, not even pausing for thought. Clearly there had been a touch of empathy there because she'd suffered at the hands of anonymous keyboard warriors, but she'd done it because she wanted to help. Help a complete stranger. Not many people stepped up like that.

At this time in the morning the traffic was quiet, headlights flickered through the trees on the edge of the park and a refuse truck chugged along one of the inner paths collecting the trash. I liked the sensation of peace before the city woke, and felt slightly pleased with myself that I got to enjoy it before everyone else flooded in. I passed a few other runners, all of whom acknowledged me in that running-community way with a quick nod. The brief interaction reminded me of the camaraderie and power of sport, the joy of your body working in sync along with the miracle of the power of muscles, tendons and bones all coming together.

Nearing the brightly lit rink, I slowed, my breath steaming out in foggy puffs. Now I'd warmed up a little, I kept up an easy jog. There were a couple of skaters out on the ice. Two men happily chatting away, arms loose and casual as they circled the rink at a leisurely pace looking as if they were out for a gentle stroll, completely at home on the ice. One skater caught my eye, a girl in the middle of the rink. She wore a red cap over a long plait that hung down her back, a short red skirt and black tights, top and gloves. I smiled. The red skirt which fanned out as she moved was trimmed with a border of white fur. Very Christmassy. She looked like Santa's granddaughter as she moved across the ice with fluid, easy grace. I stopped to watch her as she suddenly flipped and started skating backwards, weaving across the glassy surface in a smooth figure of eight. Then she skated to the far end and gathering speed raced across the centre of the rink executing a series of jumps and spins in the air. I watched mesmerised, appreciating the discipline she must have exercised to perfect those moves. It reminded me of all the hours of practice I'd put in. Playing soccer was all I'd ever wanted to do. I might not be the best player on the field, but I worked the hardest and I was the hungriest. I thought of both Gabriel and Rick Menzies. Not everyone made it, and even if they did, it could be taken away again with one bad tackle or a series of bad decisions. Gabriel had never made it back to football, his well-publicised addiction problems making him an outcast.

I almost tripped over a tree root as I carried on watching the girl gliding across the ice, her arms outstretched and clearly enjoying every moment. As a kid, I'd loved watching ice hockey, I still caught a game now and then, and envied the way the players were so at home on the ice. Skating for me had been out of the question because my mom had broken her arm very badly on the ice once and was fearful I might do myself an injury and ruin my chances at playing soccer.

The girl's limbs were long and lean, her arms graceful and there was sheer joy in the way she moved, embracing the speed and space around her. It reminded me of those magical days on the pitch when everything all came together and that moment when I'd draw back my leg knowing I'd score. There was nothing quite like it.

Talent like that took dedication. When I was partying hard, I'd eased up on the practice and it had showed. I nearly lost my first-team place – and would have, if my mom, in a rare temper, hadn't reminded me that life was about moderation and balance and that she hadn't continued a career in teaching to put me through soccer academy so I could throw it all away having an excess of good times.

It had been a timely intervention. It would have been nice to have a connection with someone who understood the relationship between hard work and making it. A lot of the women I met were more interested in me being a professional soccer player, assuming that my life was fast cars, bougie nightclubs and big bucks. And yes, sometimes it was, but most of the time I was putting in the hard yards to maintain my fitness and keep my skills at optimum level. Not everyone understood the sacrifices that had been made along the way or the time I put in, week after week.

I upped my speed, keeping an eye on her in the distance as she sat down to unlace her skates. By the time I reached that side of the rink, there was no sign of her.

I grinned to myself, there was no harm in coming back this way again tomorrow at the same time. Who knew, she might be interested in a post-skating coffee? I could do with a distraction from Evie Green, who was popping into my thoughts a little too often.

Chapter Ten

EVIE

Bloomingdale's. I stood and looked up at the signage at the front of the store, another one of those little fizzy thrills going through me. I'd been in New York for a couple of days now, and I still got a thrill every time I set foot out of the hotel. My grin must have been visible from the moon. Honestly, my system was on permanent high-excitement alert. I checked my watch. Ten minutes to find the floor where I was meeting my personal stylist. *Personal stylist.* Me. I was running a little late after having breakfast with Mrs Evans and Monty this morning. It had become a regular event, as she seemed to like the company and I certainly enjoyed hers. Her devotion to her little dog was an obvious sign that she was a good human.

I hurried through the perfume department like the white rabbit, accepting a quick spritz from one of the glossy girls on duty before rushing on to the lift. I did not want to be late for my very important date. Alicia had fixed everything up.

'Hey there, you must be Evie Green. I recognise you from your picture. I'm so happy to meet you.'

'Hi, you must be Debbie.'

'One and the same.' The blonde woman with perfect teeth gave me a friendly smile, and the tension in my shoulders receded just a little. I'd been worried that she might be a bit snooty and snobbish. I think I may have watched *Pretty Woman* one too many times.

Debbie wore smart black trousers and a fuchsia-pink silk shirt and exuded enviable effortless chic at the same time as looking kind and motherly. She was probably in her early forties and looked as if she should be chairing an important meeting at one of the investment banks I occasionally visited in my job. At work, no one cared what I wore, and I'd never really made much effort. I didn't see the point and had stopped making any effort a long time ago.

'Well, we are going to have some fun.' She shot me an encouraging smile. 'But first, let me get you a drink and we can sit down and have a chat about the look you're trying to create.'

I stared at her. 'Sorry?'

'What style are you looking for?'

I shrugged my shoulders in bemusement. 'I … I don't know.'

'Don't worry, honey.' She patted me on the arm and steered me over to a small seating area. 'Coffee, tea or a hot chocolate?'

As she got the drinks, I sat down in one of the little leather tub chairs. I'd never even thought about having a style. Was it something you 'created'? That was news to me. I just pulled on clothes every morning without an awful lot of thought. I bought things on impulse, although nine times out of ten they never fitted that well or looked that good, but I never got round to taking them back so I ended up wearing them and having a wardrobe full of crap. My mum had liked to dress up whenever she could. And she'd loved a dress. The smarter the better. Even when she was feeling poorly she would insist on wearing one of her favourite dresses – although they hung from her thin frame – because it made her feel better. I'd buried her in her favourite Roland Mouret knock-off, with its signature neckline. Suddenly I felt guilty that I'd not made any effort with my appearance. I could see why now – it was my way of kicking back, internalising my anger. Because it hadn't done Mum any good, had it? Looking well-dressed and smart hadn't made any difference to her in the end.

'What do you do for a living?'

'I'm a financial journalist on a weekly magazine.' I stood up a little straighter. I'm good at my job, really good. I've even won an award. A lot of people think money and economics are boring but it fascinates me. Although I've had to work twice as hard to get where I am, because I'm female and whatever the HR positive stats attempt to say, finance is still very much a man's world. I can cite a ton of examples where I've been underrated, overlooked or ignored. Like the time I was left sitting outside an office for over an hour because my interviewee, when he saw me, assumed I was a temp awaiting a brief and went back to his office. Or the time a banking executive only talked to a colleague (male of course) and avoided every one of my questions.

'So, a lot of desk time,' observed Debbie, with a warm smile. 'Do you meet many people? Do you work in an office or at home?'

'Sometimes I go and interview investment bankers, fund managers – that sort of thing. I work one day a week at home. The rest of the time, I'm in the office. It's better … otherwise I end up spending all my time in my bedroom.'

She nodded. 'And how would you dress for those meetings and for the office?'

I glance down at my navy chinos and sloppy sweatshirt and shrug. 'A bit like this, really. Maybe I might put on a shirt.'

She frowns. 'But aren't they all in suits and ties?'

'Yeah, but they're finance people. I'm a journalist.'

'Okay,' she says, nodding, 'And what about out of work. What do you like to do?'

'Socialise with friends. Go to the pub. Go out to eat. Go for walks. That sort of thing.'

'Do you have a partner?'

I shook my head.

'So, what about dating?' Her eyes crinkled with a quick smile. 'Do you want some dating outfits? Knock their socks off?'

I laughed. 'Chance would be a fine thing. It's really hard meeting people these days.' Even harder after I'd had so many dodgy, trolling messages after my video went viral, along with more dick pics than I could shake a stick at and a lot of people telling me how ugly and stupid I was. My shoulders sagged. That video had really exposed me, and although I put on a brave face and had embraced a fight-back through @EvieAtThePlaza, my confidence had taken a serious knocking and I was nervous about the response. I hadn't read any of the comments on the posts yet.

'Do you want to meet someone?' she asked, which surprised me.

'I guess. I mean I'm not desperate.' I shrugged again. 'I'm not really into long-term commitment but I'm happy to have some fun.' Life was too short to tie yourself down to one person or make too much of an investment in them. People could go boom or bust at any moment. There were no guarantees, so it was best to steer clear of too much long-term planning. You could lose someone so easily. Like I did my mum. The best way of investing in yourself and your own personal equity was to protect yourself from known risks. Love was far too high-risk.

'Okay,' said Debbie again and I realised that it was her non-judgemental way of disagreeing with me.

'Are you married?' I asked.

'Yes, but we're not talking about me. I want to find out about you, so that I can find out what you want to wear.'

'Sounds a bit like therapy,' I said, thinking of the grief-counselling sessions I'd gone to before I'd given up. After three, I couldn't see how they could possibly help. Maybe I should give them another try.

Her smile was kind this time. 'I like to think that I can help people.'

Help people? I didn't need help. I just wanted to… What?

I really had no idea. I'd kind of deliberately not thought about clothes because that was something my mum had done. I'd hear her voice in my head. We disagreed about clothes being important. I thought people should take me as I am, she thought it was important and it hadn't been, not in the end. It had made no difference to her treatment, to her health. She'd died anyway.

Debbie gave my current choice of clothes a passing glance and her mouth tightened. 'Can I be honest with you?'

'If you must,' I said with a smile. 'You sound like my mum.'

She smiled. 'We sometimes know what we're talking about.'

I nodded, wishing that I could listen to my mum again. Wishing that she could dole out her wisdom. Even if I disagreed, I'd still love to have heard her one more time.

'Of course, you don't have to listen to me but the fact that you're here makes me think that maybe you want to listen.'

'You do know this was set up by the PR lady at The Plaza.'

'Yes. I know Alicia. She's a smart cookie. I also know that you wouldn't be here if you weren't a little curious or interested. You're a journalist. Isn't it your job to be curious about things? To dig beneath the surface to find out more?'

I stared at Debbie, ashamed to realise that I'd underestimated her.

'Yes, it is,' I said, lifting my chin. I took pride in my job, and it was clear that it was also the case with her.

'Well, honey. I'm a great believer in clothes make the person. Your clothes tell me that either you don't care what people think of you or that you're too arrogant to worry about making a good impression. I don't think the latter is the case. What worries me is why don't you care? Don't you value yourself?'

I shrugged again. Embarrassed.

She walked in a circle around me, weighing me up.

'Your shoes are scuffed and need polishing – and the heels need repairing – and your trousers are so loose and baggy they don't flatter you at all. And that jumper should go in the bin.'

I stared at her. Where had cosy, comfortable Debbie gone?

She smiled and softened. 'I know comfort is important, but so is making a positive impression. I bet you already know as a journalist that people make an impression of you based on the first seven seconds of meeting you. And that they come to eleven conclusions about you, including your education level, economic level, success level and trustworthiness. Additional research suggests that a first impression is made within a tenth of a second.'

I nodded. I did know all this stuff although it was never front of mind. I'd forgotten more of it than I paid attention to.

'I think you're a bit lost,' said Debbie, her eyes locking on mine, with a sympathetic gaze.

My stomach lurched as if I'd fallen out of a plane and tears pricked my eyes. I was horrified to realise that she might just be right.

Chapter Eleven

EVIE

Weeping all over your personal stylist was possibly not the done thing but Debbie took it all in her stride. I suspected I was not the first client to do this. She sat me down with a cappuccino and took the seat opposite.

After a moment, I told her about my mum and the silly reason I've been so resistant to thinking about clothes.

'It sounds so stupid,' I said, snuffling into a tissue she'd handed over from a small travel pack, in exactly the same way my mum used to. 'I was so mad that she died and that she'd put so much effort into looking well turned-out all the time, and it hadn't made any difference to life. She still died. And isn't that the stupidest thing you ever heard?'

'Not at all, I understand that,' said Debbie, standing up and crossing to a rail of clothes. 'Here,' she said and held out a pair of wide-legged trousers in a dark navy. 'Try these on.' She ushered me to the curtained-off changing room.

As soon as I was inside, she passed through a white top and the cutest little boxy cashmere jumper, that was so soft I immediately stroked it across my cheek. A minute later, she handed me a pair of chunky loafers in studded black leather.

I assumed our conversation was done, but as I was buttoning the trousers in the cubicle, she started talking again.

'You were trying to take control of a part of your life that you felt you could control. It's a very normal response. Clearly, clothes and her appearance were important to your mom, and a big part of who she was – if your reaction is anything to go by. I think perhaps you're avoiding thinking about your clothes, and the way you present yourself, so that you're not constantly reminded of her. It sounds as if you are deliberately hurting yourself. If you don't care, then you don't have to care.'

I swallowed a lump in my throat, so hard that it was painful. *If you don't care, then you don't have to care.*

The thought settled in my brain, and when I pulled the sweater over my head and slipped on the shoes, it was as if the movement of my body coordinated with my mind and when I stepped through the curtain, it all made sense. I stared at her, struck by her point. She was right. I'd deliberately stopped caring – not just about clothes, but lots of things – because … what was the point. Nothing lasted. Good things got taken away from you. Lives, homes, security.

'Do you have a degree in psychology or something?' I asked her, catching a glimpse of myself in the mirror and suddenly standing a little taller. It made a change from feeling like the world around me was just a little too big and

I was just a little bit too small. For once, the image of me in the mirror looked like she had a place in the world and was worth noticing.

Debbie's smile was soft, her eyes gentle. 'Or something. There's more to this job than colour wheels.'

I nodded, my eyes fixed on the mirror.

The colour of the jumper suited me, and the long, wide-leg trousers accentuated the length of my legs. Even though it was the simplest of outfits, I felt I could face anyone in this.

'Lovely,' said Debbie. 'Now you dress this up or down.' She held up a big, chunky gold necklace that mirrored the neckline of the jumper, folded the sleeves back a couple of turns, added a row of boho bracelets and then threaded a contrasting belt through the trouser loops and tucked one corner of the jumper into the belt.

'Wow,' I said.

'Now, how do you feel?' There was a directness in her bird-bright gaze that told me nothing less than honesty would do.

I huffed out an exasperated sigh. 'Amazing.' I turned and looked at myself over my shoulder. I sighed with pleasure. The shape of the soft wool outlined my broad shoulders and flattered my less-than-stellar boobs, giving me a bit of shape and femininity. It also felt so soft on my skin. I loved it.

She smiled, but it was a warm 'I've got you' smile rather than holding any sense of triumph or smug satisfaction. I got the impression she wanted me to be happy.

'I'm thinking that you don't like fuss or to look as if

you've made too much effort. I think you want to keep your look clean and simple. And this look really suits you.'

I nodded, because she was right on all counts.

'So, I'd suggest carrying this style through by adding another couple of sweaters in a different colour.' She held up two very similar boxy-style jumpers, one in a deep russet colour with a twisted cable running down the middle and the other in a bright kingfisher blue. Both were gorgeous.

'This gives you three basic outfits for everyday wear, that you don't need to think about too much and if you need to be a bit fancier you accessorise with jewellery. I've got a selection here we can go through.'

For the next hour, she showed me how different colours and shapes looked, as well as making me try on costume jewellery that I'd never have picked in a million years.

I did a final twirl in the mirror, thrilled with what I saw.

'You're really good at this, and also the psychology stuff,' I said.

She beamed at me. 'I'll let you into a secret. I'd been doing the job for six months when I decided to become a qualified counsellor. That was six years ago.'

It made perfect sense. She'd made me so at ease.

'Now, you'll need some smart clothes for evening wear, and you need a showstopper.'

'I don't think so.'

'You should always have at least one of those in your wardrobe,' she said with a mischievous sparkle in her eye. 'And you need a dress for Christmas day. Lunch at The

Plaza is quite a chi-chi occasion. You'll want to look the part.'

While I tried on some black, wide-leg crepe trousers and the cutest little black, sleeveless waistcoat in the same fabric, Debbie disappeared, telling me she'd be right back.

As soon as I looked in the mirror, I loved the outfit, but looking at myself in it saddened me. Had I really let my grief control me so much?

When Debbie came back with an armful of more clothes, I found myself blurting out:

'I went to a grief counsellor, a few times.'

I let it hang in the air for a minute. Debbie clearly picked up on the *few times*, I saw the quick quirk of her eyebrow but in that clever counsellor-y way she left me to fill the gap.

'I couldn't go back. I felt my grief was wrong, like I was wallowing in it, and I knew my mum would have hated that.'

Debbie stood behind me and gave the beaded top a little tug, making it sit better as she said, 'There's no such thing as the wrong sort of grief.' Her eyes met mine in the mirror. 'I'm sure your mom would have understood that. We all process things in different ways. There are also different styles of counselling. It takes a while to work with a counsellor for you to build trust.'

'I didn't want to forget my mum and I thought that's what the counsellor wanted me to do. To carry on functioning when inside part of me felt dead and that it would never grow again.'

'And how do you feel now?' She hung a pendant around my neck.

'There's that same barren patch.' I felt ashamed that I'd not been able to move on or at least reseed it. I missed my mum all the time. I clutched the pendant as if it was a talisman.

'It might always be there but that doesn't mean you can't enjoy the other things around it,' said Debbie.

'I've always wanted to come to New York. It was our dream.'

She did that eyebrow-lift thing again.

'I wanted to come,' I said, just a little defensively. 'But maybe…' I nodded in acknowledgement of the truth, 'I felt I had to.'

I rubbed at the necklace. 'I thought about making the trip loads of times but never quite got around to booking anything. When I won the competition, I thought it was a sign, reminding me that my trip was long overdue. I should have come before. I'd been delaying. So, I wasn't thinking straight. When the competition organisers – scammers, I realise now – said I had to pay upfront for the flights and hotel, I didn't even think about it. I just booked them before I could chicken out and let my mum down. It never occurred to me that they wouldn't reimburse me.' I swallowed back the shame of my stupidity, but Debbie gave me an understanding look.

'You thought by not coming before that you were letting her down?'

I nodded miserably. 'Taking the money from my flatmates was honestly a moment of madness. I told myself

I was just borrowing it. I'd get it straight back. But then, of course, it was a scam. And worse still, I should have realised because I'm a financial journalist for fuck's sake. I paid them back as soon as I could but it was too late. Even though they took the TikTok reel down, by then the story had gone viral and everyone made their judgements about me. I got suspended from my job. It's not really a great look when you go to see the CEO of an investment bank and you've been very publicly exposed for borrowing money without asking.'

Debbie winced in sympathy. 'You have had a tough time. So, what are you going to do about it?'

'Sorry?'

'Are you going to lift your chin, learn a lesson and come back fighting – or are you going to take it *on* the chin and try to stay under the radar?'

'Come back fighting,' I said without a second thought.

'I thought you'd say that.' Debbie's nod was approving. 'And that's where I come in. I'm going to give you some armour and a bit of advice.' Her expression became stern. 'You talked about not being respected by the people you interview and work with. But I'd ask if you don't care about your appearance and dress the way you do now, what sort of impression would that give. It's probably one of the few places of work where people of both sexes are still expected to be smart: suit, shirt and tie, dresses or pant suits. You walk down Wall Street, you'll see it.'

'But the way I dress doesn't affect my job,' I protested. She gave me the eyebrow treatment again.

'It affects how people perceive how well you can do

your job. If I was wearing overalls, spattered with food, would you consider me as qualified to be your personal stylist or if the guy serving in the canteen was dressed like that, how would you feel about the canteen's hygiene standards?

'Clothes can also shift a perception. One moment, forgive me for being blunt, you're the ugly-sobbing girl in sweats, with a mascara-streaked face and wild hair.' She steered me back to look in the mirror. 'But you don't look anything like her now.'

My heart sank. 'You've seen the video?'

Debbie nodded. 'I can tell you straight, now I've met you, you are not that girl. You're so much more and you need to start showing people. You're smart, intelligent, funny, sweet and kind and thoughtful.'

'Wow, you got all that already?'

'Seven seconds.' She winked. 'Body language tells a lot, too. And,' she looked at her watch, 'we've been doing plenty of talking. I had something in mind originally but,' she shook her head, 'I had to make a quick adjustment because that's not who you are or who you want to be.'

Intrigued, I asked, 'What did you have in mind, originally?'

'I thought you'd be an influencer, keen to show off that you're on top of the latest trends and want to be showy, but that's not you at all. So, I put back the winter high fashion and went for something more subtle. At work, you want them to take you seriously and you need a new job ... so you need something else entirely. You're tall, with long legs and those broad shoulders. You can really pull off a pant suit and I have just the designer for you. One suit, a couple of really severe white shirts and a handbag that pops with colour. Come on. We've only just got started.'

Debbie also insisted on taking me to the hair salon where they braided my hair into a cool fishtail, which looked great with my new wide-leg trousers, chunky cream sweater and a fabulous pair of thick-soled black ankle boots.

By mid-afternoon, a manicure and a pedicure later – my nails scarlet, with the cutest little holly leaves on the tips of my index finger – Debbie declared her work was done. I had a pile of new clothes and a special dress for Christmas Day. As she packed everything up, my stomach had taken to vociferously complaining with loud, very unladylike rumbles, which made her giggle – though that could have been because she was happy with her work. Not long after, I swanned into the hotel lobby like I was Julia Roberts, a fistful of expensive shopping bags in hand.

'Somebody's been shopping,' said Danny opening the door for me. 'Can I give you a hand with anything?'

'I'm good, thank you,' I said with a broad grin, giving him a little twirl and showing off my fabulous new Burberry trench coat.

I was just opening my room door when Noah's opened. I hadn't seen him for a couple of days, and it was gratifying when he did a double take.

'Where's Evie Green and what have you done with her?' he asked.

'Have you considered stand-up if the football doesn't work out?' I asked sweetly.

'No.'

'Just as well,' I replied with a faux smile. 'You'd starve.' I swanned through the doorway without looking back and closed the door behind me, grinning at scoring yet another point.

Chapter Twelve

EVIE

Over the last few days, urged by Mrs Evans, I'd been to visit the Guggenheim, MoMA and the Botanical Gardens to see the Holiday Train Show, which was quite the most adorable thing ever. A model railway set among the landmarks of New York, running through the conservatory with friendly conductors dotted around, live music and food and drink. It was definitely Christmas holiday heaven. With the pictures I posted of my magical tour of New York, I acquired loads of new followers every day and Alicia was delighted with the way the campaign was going.

Before each of my outings, I'd made a morning pilgrimage to the ice rink, the times varying each day depending on what had been arranged.

This morning, my feet whispered across the plush thick carpet and my down coat shushed quietly like a disapproving theatre goer at rustling sweet eaters, the sounds cocooned by the corridor as if it were in on my secret. These quiet dark early morning hours had quickly become my favourite part of the day.

Despite this, there was an air of anticipation to the day. The hotel was just waking up, and behind the scenes, I could sense the practised hum of preparation and activity. The calm, quiet lull before a full day's storm of activity. I could hear the subdued chink of china and clatter of cutlery from the restaurant as the place was readied for breakfast, and saw Martin, the waiter, carrying a stack of plates into the room. From somewhere beyond me, there was the distant back and forth hum of a vacuum cleaner and the up-and-down squeak of cloth on glass as someone cleaned a window on the other side of the lobby.

Bernard the maintenance man was up a ladder, underneath the huge, central chandelier, which hung above the group of six Christmas trees, their tips just brushing the dangling crystals. I watched as he twisted one of the little pieces of glass back into place, bathed in the glow from the trees below. 'Morning,' he said with a cheerful wink.

'Morning,' I said, grinning up at him. They had to be the prettiest trees I'd ever seen.

With their frosted branches and the plethora of tiny sparkling white lights, they looked as if they were encrusted with diamonds, and the tiny boughs of cranberries glistened like rubies. It reminded me of Narnia through the wardrobe.

'Morning, Evie,' said Carol from her usual lookout post on the front desk, which was swathed in garlands of dark green yew interspersed with fat white velvet bows. Along the counter were groupings of elegant silver stags, so well sculpted that they looked as if they might startle and flee at any moment.

Nothing got past Carol without her knowing it. With eagle-eyed awareness and a near photographic memory, she knew all the comings and goings in the hotel. 'Going to be a beautiful day. What have you got planned today?'

Before I could answer, her face lit up with an enthusiastic smile. 'Can I just say. I loved those clothes you got at Bloomingdales. That lady really has an eye.' She shook her head. 'I've decided I hate the outfit I got for Carla's wedding. I'm gonna book myself in with the lady you saw. See if she has better ideas. No one wants to feel like a dowdy on their little girl's big day.'

I eyed her smart uniform and her pinned-up hair which was wrestled into a tidy updo with a dozen clips and grips, clearly for extra insurance. 'I'm sure you won't, but,' I leaned forward, both in empathy with her insecurity and because I'd learned a surprising amount from Debbie, 'you want to feel good about yourself on Carla's big day. So, if you're not happy with the outfit, why not? What have you got to lose? You haven't got long. What is it? Two weeks now until the wedding?'

'Yes.' Carol's face lit up. 'What was the stylist's name, again?'

'Debbie, and I can highly recommend her. She's lovely and really knows her stuff. You must be getting excited and a bit nervous.' A couple of my friends had got married in the last few years and there seemed a ridiculous amount of planning to do for one day. Personally, I thought people were crazy spending so much money and effort on one day when it could all be snatched away so easily. Life is short, they should just get on with it.

I'd heard all about the childhood sweethearts. That Carla was a teacher and her husband-to-be was a fireman. A fireman! I would never say anything to Carol, but how did she feel about her daughter marrying someone with such a dangerous job?

A firefighter's life expectancy is ten years lower than the average persons. I'd looked it up. Did she not realise that he might not come home from work one day?

Before Carol could reply, she was interrupted by the phone on the reception desk. 'Good morning, The Plaza. How may I help you?'

I gave her a quick wave, mouthed goodbye and hurried on through the revolving door.

'Morning, early bird,' said Danny with his customary bright smile.

'Morning. How are you?' I asked, wondering if he ever had an off day.

'Doing just fine, ma'am,' he said, touching the brim of his hat. 'You going for your usual constitutional?'

'I am.' I said and hitched the heavy tote bag higher on my shoulders. On my first morning out, I'd said I was going for a walk, and now it was easier to let him think that I was doing nothing more than taking a leisurely stroll around the park. Skating was my private thing and always had been. Out on the ice I had to concentrate so hard that I was able to let go of everything else in my head. I was completely free, mind and body.

'Want me to bring you a coffee back?'

He grinned. 'I would love it, but not on duty.'

I visited Starbucks each morning and couldn't decide which was my favourite Christmas drink: Peppermint Mocha (Yum), Caramel Brulée Latte (double yum) or Chestnut Praline Latte (absolutely divine).

With another goodbye I swung sharp left and crossed over the road sucking in a big breath of the crisp winter air. Today the clear dark sky highlighted the moon glowing beyond the skyscrapers, but there was a softer glow heralding sunrise. Anticipation fluttered through me, with gentle butterfly wings brushing my stomach.

It was a brisk walk to the Wollman Rink, just inside Central Park, and when I arrived I did as I'd done for the last few mornings – I stood for a moment, marvelling that I was finally here. Just like in the movies. The bench, when I sat on it, was cold and hard, dusted with a light frost. But I didn't mind. It was worth it. With great care, I removed my skates from my bag and gave the soft red leather a covetous stroke. I loved, loved, loved them and all they represented – a special reward after years of practice in borrowed smelly rink-rental skates. The stainless-steel blades were sharp and shiny, perfectly balanced and all mine. I'd only allowed myself to buy them once I'd perfected a double axel – which, for the uninitiated, is a forward jump in the air with a double rotation before landing on one foot without falling over – it took me a very long time to master.

My determination to learn to skate bedded in after Mum and I watched *Serendipity* and from that moment, I'd decided that when we did get to New York, I would be able to glide effortlessly across the ice and surprise her. Of course, that was never meant to be, but at the time I didn't realise that Mum would die, I thought we'd beat the cancer together.

After Mum died, I moved near Alexandra Palace and signed up for lessons. I had no desire to be an Olympic champion or anything, I just wanted to be good enough to look as if I were in one of those iconic New York winter movies we'd always watched together. And now it was my time.

When I'd come for my inaugural visit on my second day here, the rink had lived up to all my expectations, one of those pinch-me moments – although minus a handsome stranger, but there was still time for him to show up. Adrenaline and nerves fired through me as I stepped out onto the fresh surface only marred by a couple of tracks.

With a swoosh, I pushed my blade forward, the ice unforgiving beneath my blade but I immediately felt the freedom as I pushed my feet across the surface. Picking up my speed, I sailed along, the breeze whipping through my hair as I did a swift circuit. Joy filled my heart like air trying to burst a balloon. I whizzed along, revelling in the pace. I felt so free, swooping like a bird, gliding with ease. Graceful, elegant and together. Here, I knew what I was doing, I'd practised and trained for no one but myself. None of my friends knew I could skate like this. It was a secret part of me. After Mum died, I wanted something that was just for myself, that no one else could judge or comment on. Here, I was confident that when I took off on an outside edge I could land with accuracy. If anything went wrong, it was down to me. I was in control and that couldn't be taken away – as long as I focused and concentrated on my feet, my muscles and the positioning as I took off. I liked the precision of skating, the absolute science of knowing when I made the right effort and concentrated, by the laws of physics, I would get the right results. Of course, it didn't always work out like that – I'd ended up on my bum plenty of times – but the principle of it comforted me.

I whirled and twirled with the abandon of a snowflake in a snowstorm, feeling the endorphins flooding through my system, exhilaration bouncing through my veins. The sunrise splintered through the trees, golden beams piercing the shadows to reveal a perfect pure-blue sky and the promise of clear, bright day.

After half an hour, I was on a high, if a little tired from the exertion. When I felt my legs start to wobble with effort I knew it was time to head back. Besides, I had a meeting with Alicia. She'd texted me late the night before to tell me she had some exciting news.

I walked slowly back through the park, watching two girls walking along, arm in arm, giggling together and taking selfies and then comparing shots. They were oblivious to me, and their self-absorption highlighted my loneliness. At that moment I would have killed to have a friend to share this with me. But look at what I'd done to my friends.

And because I wasn't looking where I was going, I bumped into the one person I'd rather not have.

'Oof,' I said as they cannoned into me.

Strong arms steadied me, and I looked up into Noah's face.

'You,' I said, annoyed by how sexy he managed to look. Despite the temperature, he was wearing a tight-fitting running top and shorts, which left very little to the imagination.

'Morning, Evie,' he said. 'You're up early.'

'So are you,' I pointed out.

'I'm training,' he drawled, as if I wouldn't know the meaning of the word, but he was gazing over my shoulder as if he were looking for something.

'Lost something?' I asked.

He squinted into the distance towards the ice rink. 'No,' he said but it was the sort of quick denial that said the opposite.

'Well, don't let me stop you,' I said, intrigued, and also cross with myself, because at the sight of him my pulse had started jumping about like the Easter Bunny. I hadn't seen him for a few days, and I had to summon up my blasé I'm-totally-used-to-this-level-of-hotness-in-a-man face because I'd forgotten the effect he had on me.

I gave him a snarky smile. 'I wouldn't want you to get cold.'

'Don't you worry, Green.' He winked at me. 'I run hot.' With that he jogged away leaving me feeling more than a little hot and bothered.

Chapter Thirteen

EVIE

Slipping on one of my new Helmut Lang sweaters from Bloomingdale's, and my Vivienne Westwood trousers, I finished off the outfit with a big chunky necklace and gave a little twirl. I was starting to feel like I had my New York legs, and thanks to the ice skating, was ready to face anything. I opened the door, prepared to seize the day by the scruff of the neck and then jumped slightly as the door to room 502 opened at exactly the same moment.

Noah had showered, and his earlier stubbled jawline was now smooth. My mouth dried at the sight of him and I had an inexplicable urge to run my hand across his face.

'You've shaved!' I blurted out, and probably looked as shocked as he did.

'Am I supposed to be flattered you noticed?' His blue eyes locked on mine.

'No,' I did my best to sound blasé and not give away the fact that I noticed every darned thing about him. 'I just thought you looked like a footpad when I saw you earlier.'

'A what?'

'Footpad – an old English term for a … Regency for mugger.' Note to self, stop watching so much *Bridgerton*.

He narrowed his eyes and shook his head as if he didn't know what to make of me. I could hardly blame him.

We both took a pace forward, almost falling into step together. He made an ushering gesture to allow me to go first. There was no getting away from the fact that we were both headed in the same direction to the lifts, so it was only polite to initiate conversation.

'Got a busy day?' I asked, still all pleasant smiles.

His mouth twitched. 'Not especially.'

For some reason his answer quelled me. Was I feeling sorry for him?

We stood in silence as the lift took its painstaking time to reach our floor.

'This is the part where you could ask if I've got a busy day,' I suggested.

'I'm sure you have, judging by your recent posts.'

My eyes shot to his, just as a dull flush flared above the collar of his casual shirt as he realised what he'd said.

'Aw, that's sweet. You've been following me.' I looked him up and down.

'You look like you're going to a banking convention.'

'What can I say? I'm going to a meeting.'

The lift door pinged, announcing its arrival. Noah waited a beat before letting me step in first.

'Ground floor, I assume,' I said cheerily.

'First floor,' he said, only a tad patronisingly, reminding me that I was using British terminology.

'You say *tomayto*, I say tomato,' I quipped.

He stared at me, as if I was a bug he just couldn't identify, before looking away, but not before I caught the slight smile on his lips. Surreptitiously, I studied him until he turned around and tilted his head enquiringly.

'Yes?'

'Nothing,' I said, realising that I'd been given away by the mirrors in the lift.

I stared down at the floor for the remainder of the descent and we travelled down in silence. When we reached the *ground* floor, I said, 'Have a nice day,' and walked away, following the now familiar route, aware that Noah was following me.

I gave Carol at the front desk a nod, noticing that Noah diverted to speak to her. I cast one last glance his way, taking in the tall, slim frame and handsome profile. With a small sigh – regret, confusion, I wasn't sure which – I walked away down the corridor, through a side door, and down the narrow flight of stairs that guests never see. There was a sharp contrast between the polished wood floor, luxurious rugs, cream-painted gilded walls above stairs and the practical lino tiles and plain white matt-paint finish down here. After nearly a week here, my feet knew their way down to the little suite of offices and the conference room, where I was due to meet Alicia.

She was in the conference room, along with her assistant and the open laptop screen showed an image of a woman I didn't know who'd clearly phoned in to join the meeting.

'Morning, Alicia,' I said.

'Hey, Evie. How's it going? Thanks for joining us this

morning. Can I introduce you to Lara Jennings?' She waved a hand toward the screen.

'Hi, Lara,' I said and lifted a hand in greeting.

'Morning, Evie. Nice to meet you.' I was slightly disconcerted by the way she used my name, which suggested she was way more prepared for this meeting than I was.

'Oh, you're English,' I replied, wondering who she was and why she was here – as it were.

'I certainly am.' She gives me a business-like smile, with the eyes and teeth of a shark.

'Grab a coffee, Evie,' Alicia said, indicating the thermos flasks on the sideboard. I was just pouring my coffee into a cup when she added, 'We're just waiting for—'

Right on cue, there was a knock at the door. I turned round … and carried on pouring coffee into my cup, my saucer and onto the floor.

Noah.

'Er,' Alicia's assistant interrupted, and I looked down at the coffee overflowing onto the floor.

'Sorry.' I hastily put down the jug and stood there like an idiot with coffee dripping over my hand.

What the hell was Noah doing here? I grabbed a handful of napkins, dumped the coffee cup and started cleaning my hands, while Alicia's assistant dabbed at the brown puddle on the carpet tiles.

I didn't dare look at Noah, instead I bobbed down and helped mop up coffee.

'Morning, you must be Noah Sanderson. I'm Alicia de Vries, The Plaza's social-media manager. Come on in.'

'Are you all right down there, Evie?' Again, he was wearing that superior smile which drew attention to his damn mouth.

Why oh why does he always catch me behaving like some street urchin?

I nodded, standing up with a handful of coffee-soaked napkins in my hand.

'Hey, Noah,' called the woman on the screen. He sent an uncertain wary glance my way before he turned and addressed her. 'Lara.'

'Glad you could make it.' The smile she gave Noah was sickly sweet. 'Play nice.'

What was going on? And why was he here?

Alicia, clearly aware of the undercurrent of tension, clapped her hands together as if she were rounding children up at kindergarten.

'Right, we're all here. Why don't you take a seat here, Noah? And you here, Evie.' Thankfully, Alicia's assistant relieved me of my soggy burden, handed me a clean napkin and sorted me out with a fresh cup of coffee.

Noah and I faced each other across the table, with the laptop to my right and his left and Alicia opposite.

My teeth were firmly gritted, a frisson of anxiety nagging at me.

'Lara,' Noah narrowed his eyes at the woman and got straight to the point. 'What is going on?' I could see a tic in his jawline, the tiny pulse giving away his tension. I couldn't decide whether it was reassuring that he had no idea what was going on, or alarming. I had absolutely no idea why he was here, either.

There was that sharky smile again. It might have been mid-afternoon in London when most people's makeup had worn off, but Lara still wore killer glossy lipstick.

'I told you I'd sort your mess out for you,' she said, folding her arms, and even though I didn't know her, I could tell she was preparing for an offensive. Suiting up like Joan of Arc going into battle.

'Hear us out. I've found a solution to all your problems. I've been talking to Alicia, and we've come up with a brilliant plan.'

'Sorry,' I interrupted, still trying to get my head around what was going on. 'How do you and Lara know each other?'

'She's my agent,' said Noah with a terse frown.

'And?' I looked at Alicia.

'Evie, sorry, I know you two met in the dining room – the TikTok went through the roof, but I guess you didn't stop to introduce yourselves. Evie, this is Noah Sanderson, he's an international soccer star and plays for one of your English soccer—'

I held up one hand. 'I know who he is.' I shot Noah a surly look.

'Ah, well, that's great. And that video – the two of you ... the chemistry. Honestly, the engagement. People online loved it. So, it makes perfect sense.'

'What makes perfect sense?' I asked.

'For you two to combine forces.'

There was one of those dumbstruck pauses in which you could practically hear our brains scrambling for a response.

'Combine forces?' Both Noah and I said it at the same

time, and it would have been comical if it weren't so horrifying.

'Yes,' said Alicia, bright and enthusiastic, bringing in a counteroffensive on the other side of the table. 'We'd like the two of you to do a series of posts together, exploring the magic of the city, showing everyone how gorgeous The Plaza is, and all the lovely things people can do here. We want the two of you with trees, ice-skating, shopping and exploring. It's a perfect development for the @EvieAtThePlaza story and I think it would give the whole campaign a real boost. When Lara contacted me and suggested it, it was like Christmas came all at once, especially as engagement has been dropping off just a teeny little bit over the last couple of posts. This will give the posts a real uplift and we just know it's going to completely re-energise the campaign.'

I pursed my lips, as did Noah.

Lara took over again. 'As we discussed, Noah, your rep needs a bit of rehabilitation and what better than a little romance.'

I started. Romance? Where had that come from?

Noah lifted an eyebrow in outright James Bond scepticism. The way his back stiffened like an angry cat almost made me giggle, except this was no giggling matter. They had to be kidding. This sort of thing did not happen. In a million romance tropes, yes, but not in real life.

'Sorry?' he asked, in a way that was not sorry at all, anything but.

'Fake dating,' Lara's face was encouraging, her voice authoritative. 'Works a treat and everyone laps it up.'

Alicia interjected. 'We thought it would be really cute if you joined Evie on some of her holiday adventures. As dates.' She clasped her hands together. 'What do you think, Evie?' She winked at me.

What did I think? With the buzzing in my ears, I thought I was having an out-of-body experience.

I opened my mouth but nothing came out. There was a temporary stranglehold on my vocal cords.

'Great, then,' said Lara. 'I'll leave you to work out the details of the first date with Alicia.'

I pursed my lips. I couldn't decide whether I might burst out laughing at Noah's look of outrage or wail and gnash my teeth with frustration.

Silence descended on the room. I didn't dare look at Noah. This was … I didn't know what it was. A disaster? A nightmare? Downright weird? I wanted him to say something.

'She's a force of nature,' said Alicia approvingly. 'I hear she's one of the top sports' agents in the UK.'

'I'm guessing she told you that,' said Noah.

'Er … well.' Alicia blushed and his face softened.

'She's good at what she does.'

Alicia chewed her lip and then turned her attention to me. 'What do you think, Evie? I wanted you to come out here to enjoy yourself, but we also need a really dreamy social-media campaign, full of Christmas sparkle."

I knew she'd worked hard to persuade her boss this campaign was a good idea, and I didn't want to let her down.

'Our best engagement came from the video of you and

Noah in the dining room. When Lara suggested this, it seemed perfect. What do you say, Evie?' She looked pleadingly at me.

I really didn't want to go home, nor did I want to let Alicia down. Surely putting up with Noah was a small sacrifice. I was spending Christmas at the freaking Plaza!

'I don't mind,' I said risking a look at Noah.

He eyed me with resentment.

'But of course, if Noah doesn't want to do it, I'm not going to force him,' I said as magnanimously as I could. 'I can't imagine he's much of an actor. All his talent is in his feet.'

Alicia turned towards him and behind her back, I mouthed, 'Chicken.' Childish, I know, but I did enjoy getting under his skin.

'I'm not happy about it,' said Noah, folding his arms across his chest. 'Lara, can I have a private word?'

Lara looked pissed off, but she nodded.

We all vacated the room to stand outside. Noah waited until the door was closed.

'You have to be fucking kidding me.' His words came through the partition wall loud and clear. 'I thought you wanted me to keep my nose clean and stay out of the limelight.'

'That was the plan originally, but that reel of you two, it got so much positive engagement. People forgot that you're a pariah.'

'Hmmph,' grunted Noah.

'Noah, the two of you looked great on camera together and she looks cute and relatable.'

'Yeah, and annoying with it. She always has to have the last word.'

'It will do you good,' said Lara. 'Seriously, Noah, right now you need all the help you can get. The FA are still holding out on the ban. This will look good. Besides it's just a bit of fun. You can pretend to like her for a photo or two, surely.'

'I'm not so sure about that. I'm supposed to be focusing on my training.'

'You also need some positive publicity to show the FA you're human.'

A minute later, Noah opened the door, and we filed back in.

'So that's a yes, is it?' I asked. 'You've agreed with your agent you can pretend to like me?'

His face flushed as he realised we'd heard every word, before his mouth firmed into a flat line. 'It's a professional commitment. I can smile for the cameras. That's all I need to do, I presume.' His expression was implacable. And unaccountably sexy. He looked mean and moody and all bad-boy. Quite irresistible.

Chapter Fourteen

NOAH

Evie was already in the lobby when I stepped out of the elevator. I stood and watched her for a moment, taking in her carefree smile as she chatted to one of the doormen as if they were old friends. She had a warmth and ease about her that drew people to her.

'Hey, Noah,' she called across the open space when she spotted me, completely oblivious to the hushed silence in the lobby.

I acknowledged her with a nod, ignoring the sudden uptick of my pulse at the sight of her face and the crazy curls.

'Green,' I said repressively as she bounded over like a goddamn golden retriever puppy let out for the first time.

'Don't be a boring old fart,' she said, and to my surprise, she tucked a hand through my arm and led me out onto the steps of the hotel. 'If we're going to be stuck together, let's try and enjoy it. Just remember, this is temporary. Lucky you. You're not stuck with me permanently.'

Outside, there was a line of people hoping to come and take a peek at the hotel's Christmas decorations. I'd stood in this very line when I was a kid with my mom and dad, long before I could afford to stay here. I could still remember Mom's excitement as she handed out candy bars to me and my sister as bribes to keep us from getting too fidgety while we waited.

'Where are we going?' I asked, looking round for a cab.

'We're walking,' she said.

'Walking? In New York?'

'Yes.' She tutted and nodded down at my legs. 'I thought you played football. It's only a couple of miles.'

'Only tourists walk.'

'We *are* tourists. Or I am,' she pointed out with a consoling smile. For once Evie seemed happy with the silence as we walked across the road onto Fifth Avenue. Her head bobbed this way and that taking in the shop displays and the enormous crystal decoration suspended above the cross walk, which faded from vivid green to azure blue and to rose pink. Swirling snow was projected onto the Apple Centre and everywhere we looked, shop windows were ablaze with tiny fairy lights and filled with fantastically detailed decorations, from holly and ivy wreaths to scenes containing cute Santas and elves, through to glittering displays of stars and crystals. Doorways were framed with boughs of greenery threaded with gold lights or snow-laden branches interspersed with glittering baubles.

The whole of the Luis Vuitton building in its signature livery was wrapped in the most enormous red bow while the jewellery store opposite featured in one window a tableau of stately black-and-white penguins, each with an elaborate diamond choker around its neck. In the second window was a set of shy fawns complete with sparkling tiaras as they grazed beneath a giant snow-dappled Christmas tree in front of a Swiss cottage, its carved wooden exterior frosted with more diamonds. In the final window was a full-sized stag, complete with a glowing red nose and hanging from its antlers were several pairs of long dangling earrings of twinkling gemstones.

Evie was absolutely enchanted and almost had her nose pressed against the window.

'Isn't this just the cutest thing you've ever seen?' she asked, grinning, her cheeks a little flushed. 'And have you seen the size of those diamonds?' Her enthusiasm was infectious and I found myself agreeing while wondering what she might look like with a diamond tiara in that glorious shock of hair of hers.

'Oh look, Tiffany's. I must get some pictures of their windows. My mum was mad about the film *Breakfast at Tiffany's*. Actually, you can take some pictures.'

Before I could respond she was hurrying to cross the road.

The Tiffany windows had already drawn quite a crowd, with lots of people taking pictures and videos. The gathered group murmured its appreciation of the tiny animated crystal birds hovering in the small square window display, carrying expensive rings with dazzling gemstones in their beaks. My mom would love it and I took my phone from my pocket and snapped a few pictures to send her. She loved this place and I've been window shopping with her and my sister quite a few times on our annual Radio City trip, although in those days we didn't have the bucks and always came away empty-handed.

A thought struck me. 'Do you want to go inside?' I asked Evie. 'Do some Christmas shopping?'

She stared at me, eyes almost on stalks, and I felt an odd little skip inside at her surprise. Who knew? I'd surprised Evie Green.

'Would I? Can pigs fly?' She barrelled past me to the doors.

Once again, I couldn't help laughing. 'I'm pretty sure they can't.'

But she was already inside the store, saying hi to the doormen and wishing them happy holidays.

Her face lit up with enthusiasm. Who wouldn't get a kick out of her infectious wide-eyed delight? She stared round at the luxurious cabinets positioned throughout the huge room like an actual kid in a candy store. I could see why. The contents sparkled and twinkled as brightly as all the Christmas lights in Manhattan.

'Wow,' she said and stood there. This was something else. The huge open space with enormous windows had the hushed awed feel of a cathedral but with the additional elegant details of an art gallery where every last feature had been curated for style and taste.

'This is so exciting,' Evie whispered, and I got it, because it was the sort of place you felt you had to whisper. 'Who are we buying for?' She moved forward a couple of paces towards one of the glowing display units and then stopped dead in front of me and whirled round. 'Oh! Do you have a girlfriend? Of course you do. Footballers always have WAGs.'

'Not this one.' I laughed at her sudden concern, as if that possibility had only just dawned on her. 'Something for my mom.'

She looked up at me. 'I forgot.' She was still talking in a low murmur. 'You must be rich.' She studied me with narrowed eyes. 'You don't act rich, though. Well, not that I know many rich people. But you … well, you seem quite normal.'

'That might be the nicest thing you've said to me since we met.'

'I'm sure it isn't,' she said blithely. 'So, what are we looking for? What are you going to buy your mum? Diamonds? Earrings? A necklace? This is going to be so much fun. I love spending other people's money.' She rubbed her hands together with bright-eyed joy. 'Although I'm much better at saving it for them.'

I glanced at her; I'd forgotten she had a proper job. Understandable, given that she seemed so easy come, easy go.

'I haven't given it that much thought,' I confessed with a quick shrug, now wondering if coming in here was a good idea, after all. It suddenly seemed a bit personal to be involving her in shopping for my mom. 'I only just decided.' Before I could talk myself out of it, I added, 'But my mom will be so thrilled to receive a blue Tiffany box, with a white ribbon that she won't really care what's inside.'

'Pshhaw,' Evie scoffed. 'I bet she will. Is she a diamonds-

and-mink sort of gal?' Evie put on an American drawl, or at least what she thought was one.

'No.' I laughed, thinking of my mom. Jeannie Sanderson. Elementary school teacher. Practical, efficient and into her crafts. And not afraid of telling anyone how it is. 'Absolutely not. She might be thrilled but the first thing she'll do is tell me off for wasting my money.' I pictured her face. 'Then she'll cry, and my dad will pat her on the shoulder and tell her it's okay and wink at me because he'll know she loves it.'

Evie stared at me and her face softened. 'That's so cute. Sounds like you miss them.'

I shrugged again. 'I guess.' I didn't normally talk about things like this. It was personal and private. I was used to being on my guard, especially in interviews when people were trying to pry information out of me. I didn't want to drag my family into the limelight any more than they wanted to be there.

Since hitting the big time, the only thing my parents had let me do for them was pay off the mortgage on their house and buy Mom a new car when hers died. They made so many sacrifices for me when I was a kid. Remortgaged the house. Drove for hours to get me to games all over the country. Paid a fortune for coaching, boots, camps, gas and overnight stays. Despite all that, they refused to take any more of my money. My sister was the same, although she at least accepted a college fund for my nephews.

I owed my entire career to my parents and I didn't ever want to let them down. The time my mom chewed me out during my partying days had stayed with me. She didn't guilt me into changing, she just reminded me how hard I'd worked to get where I was and how much she and Dad believed in me.

We wandered around the displays. Evie browsed each case we passed, occasionally stopping to give a piece a closer inspection. It was only when we passed a case with a display of necklaces that I realised I'd left her behind. I returned to her side and found her focused on a set of gold chains each bearing delicate golden keys, some intricately designed and dotted with twinkling diamonds, others plainer with simple filigree embellishments. I was surprised, because after her interest in the previous jewellery store, I'd expected her to make a beeline for the expensive, diamond-encrusted rings, the ones that flashed and sparkled like fireworks in a dark sky.

'These are pretty,' she said, pointing.

We moved on to the next cabinet full of diamond-encrusted bracelets.

'Madam, would you like to try something on?' Neither of us had noticed the sales associate approach.

I was about to say no when Evie's face lit up, literally – brighter than the diamonds on display – but then, she said, 'That would be so cool but,' she shrugged, a gesture I was getting used to from her, 'I'd better not. We're not shopping for me.'

She gave me an overbright smile that made my heart ache a little. In that moment, I realised that she did a lot for others. She always had a friendly word for the hotel staff and even before we'd met properly, she'd been kind to me. Before I could think better of it, and taking a leaf out of her book, I said, 'I don't know, Evie, who knows what Santa might bring. I think you should try something on.'

For a moment, at least a whole ten seconds, she didn't say a word.

I nodded at the sales associate.

'What about one of the key necklaces?' I pointed back to the cabinet we'd just come from. 'You were looking at those.'

She still hadn't said anything. I crossed to the cabinet and chose the one she'd spent the most time poring over.

'That one, I think,' I said, looking back at Evie who had regained her composure.

'Really?' She grinned at me, every inch the mischievous elf again. 'Darling, you spoil me.'

I simply raised my eyebrows and smiled back at her.

'Ah, the Tiffany gold knot with one-point-four carat of diamonds. An excellent choice, sir.'

With a touch of ceremony, the sales associate donned a pair of white gloves and removed a gold chain with a gold key encrusted with small diamonds, placing it on a black velvet pad before putting it reverently on top of the glass counter.

The thing sparkled and twinkled as if it had a life of its own and Evie stepped forward gingerly touching it with one finger, as if it might bite.

'It's beautiful.'

'May I?' I picked up the necklace.

Evie lifted her mass of hair to reveal the pale skin of her neck. Such a simple gesture of complete trust, that I faltered for a moment.

It took a second for me to straighten up. With the same focus as if I was about to take a goal kick, I stepped behind her and looped my arms around her neck. My hands shook slightly as I draped the chain in the hollow of her collar bones. As I fastened the tiny catch and my fingers brushed the soft skin of her neck, I held my breath. I itched to stroke the delicate nape, tangling one finger in one of the downy curls that crept from her hairline.

Beneath my fingers, Evie shivered and then she turned to look at me over her shoulder, her lips slightly parted and her eyes wide. I was a whisper away from kissing her when I remembered where we were. I held myself back, flexing my hand behind my back, to hide the sudden sharp need.

'Let's see,' I said, my voice huskier than I'd intended.

She turned and lifted her chin. I touched the necklace, my hand shaking slightly because I really wanted to touch her mouth, move my thumb over her soft pink lips.

'It suits you,' I said, looking at the gold glowing next to her skin.

She turned back and looked in the mirror. 'It's lovely,' she said, and I saw her swallow, the movement lifting the necklace. She touched the key pendant, a wistful smile on her face. She looked at me in the mirror and gave me a brief nod as if to say thank you, and then turned to the sales associate. 'But not today.'

She handed the necklace back. 'Thank you, but we really are here to buy his mum a present. We shouldn't get sidetracked, should we?' She shot me one of her wicked grins which brought me out of my head and back to the present.

'Yes, you're right. Mom.' I swallowed down the thoughts about pushing back her pullover and kissing my way down her spine.

'Let's go up to the silver floor. They do some beautiful silver designs.'

'And you know this how?'

'Tiffany website,' she said with a *duh* roll of her eyes. I couldn't decide if I was relieved or not that normality had returned and the Evie I knew was back.

We headed up the fancy staircase which spiralled up around a huge bronze statue.

The silver floor was more my mom. I circled round the cabinets of bright highly polished silver and studied heavy link chain bracelets, diamond-studded hoops, delicate filigree pendants and sculpted rings.

Evie, it seemed, knew her Tiffany silver and beckoned me over to a cabinet of Elsa Peretti designs – full disclosure, I'd never heard of the woman, but Evie pointed to a pretty, stylised silver starfish on a silver chain.

'How about that one? Or you could buy the classic Tiffany heart pendant, but I think your mum might like this more. It's less obvious.'

I smiled at her with gratitude. 'Thanks, Evie. It's perfect. My mom will love it.'

When we left the store, she was positively skipping along beside me. 'That was amazing. I've always wanted to go in there, to buy something, even by proxy, and to have the little blue bag. My mum would have got such a kick out of this.'

'Why was your mom such a fan?'

Evie's face turned solemn, and she shrugged. 'She just was.'

Her voice was suddenly quiet, with that sort of deadness to it that made it clear she didn't want to talk about the subject. She wouldn't thank me for feeling sorry for her, so I said, 'Okay, so now I've set the bar really high with my mom, what am I going to buy for my sister?'

Evie's usual, cheerful expression returned. 'Oh, you're in good hands. I'm brilliant at shopping.' She rubbed her hands together gleefully and I almost saw her tucking her grief back in its box.

Chapter Fifteen

EVIE

The Edge was exactly as the name suggested: all sharp, angular lines with acres of clear glass, and the statement-making Observation Deck that sliced dramatically into thin air, thousands of feet above the city. The whole place epitomised sleek and modern, along with being an absolute engineering triumph. Not that I knew anything about the latter, but you didn't need to, to marvel at the construction.

A little awestruck – Noah too, I guessed, as neither of us said a word – we climbed down a flight of steps, lined on either side by huge plate-glass panels, to the triangular deck below. Thanks to clever construction and an uninterrupted wall of glass, there was a complete 360 view of the city. During my initial steps, I tried hard to shelve the thoughts about what would happen if this sleek shark's fin of glass and concrete failed, but then the magic of the panoramic view mesmerised me. The whole city spread out before us, like an architect's model. The bird's-eye view took in the wide expanse of the Hudson River, the cluster of buildings in the financial district not too far away and the Empire State Building, which was dwarfed by this building. Distant windows twinkled in the sunlight, the river sparkled and the cool crisp air felt as if it were filled with ice chips.

While the view was exceptional, I could almost hear my mum's voice in my ear. 'But it's not the Empire State Building, is it?' I had to go there for her, that was why I was here. For Mum. This was just a detour on the way.

'This is cool,' said Noah, standing next to me, and I watched as the big broad grin spread across his face, his eyes sparkling, reminding me of a small excited boy.

'Yeah, although I'm not sure what everything is.'

'That's the Empire State Building.'

I nudged him with my elbow. 'Wow! You really know your New York.'

'Very funny. The Chrysler Building, Lower Manhattan.' He leaned into me, his warm breath on my cheek, and his hand touched the small of my back as he steered me to a different angle and pointed. 'Over there, that's New Jersey – and there, you can see the Statue of Liberty.'

My gaze followed the direction he indicated. I could just make out the iconic landmark.

'And back that way, you can see Central Park.' He turned his face in profile and I took a quick glance at his strong jawline, lightly stubbled with tiny, glistening bristles. It was tempting to brush my fingers over them, to feel the texture of him, as if it might help me to get to know him.

'I still want to go to the Empire State Building.'

'Absolutely.' Noah's face softened and he smiled. 'You

should.' He leaned down and whispered, his eyes brimming with amusement. 'And don't tell our host but it's my favourite place. I promise you, there's something special about it. The romance, the history – it's magical.'

My heart almost missed a beat at the unexpected confidence. It felt as if Noah was actually opening up a little to me and wasn't quite the arrogant, pain in the arse I'd first thought.

'Good to know,' I whispered back. 'It's actually top of my list.'

'Now, it's selfie time.' I held up my phone as Noah groaned. 'Smile,' I urged, my finger hovering over the button. 'I've got a mouthful of your freaking hair,' he said and lifted his hand to push it back over my shoulder as I took the selfie. I swallowed as I looked at the first picture, with his thumb brushing my cheekbone and the intense focus in his eyes as he did so.

A few minutes later, we headed inside to meet up with our guide for the next part of the tour. 'Hi, Chad,' I said.

'Hey, guys, welcome to City Climb – the highest open-air ascent in the world,' he added a verbal flourish to the final words.

'Sorry?' I sounded very English. 'Open-air ascent. Like Everest?' Now that sounded interesting, if terrifying.

He grinned at me. 'Without the snow and ice. Don't worry. It's awesome. We just need to get you all suited up.'

'Cool,' I said, as a little tremor of excitement rippled in the pit of my stomach. Who didn't love an adventure?

'City Climb?' said Noah, clearly refusing to be bowled over by Chad's encouraging smirk and pleased-with-himself attitude. 'What does that mean?' Noah's jaw was locked and he folded his arms in a classic defensive, no-way-on-Earth pose. 'Climbing? Up there?' He asked and peered up the narrow corridor to the glass wall beyond.

'You scared of heights?' I asked.

'*Scared*, no, it's healthy self-preservation,' said Noah.

'It's all perfectly safe.' Chad cocked his head. 'We're gonna take a walk on the wild side. You're going to scale the outside of the skyscraper. Twelve-hundred feet up. It's the highest platform in New York. And perfectly safe, you're all harnessed and tethered the whole time. I've never lost anyone yet.' He winked at me. 'Seriously, you're safer up here than down on the street where you're more likely to get hit by a cab.'

'That's good to hear,' I said grinning back at him as little bubbles of excitement started to dance under the surface of my skin. 'So, we just walk up the side of a skyscraper?' That sounded pretty amazing.

Happy as the proverbial lamb, I followed Chad into the changing room, where he handed us matching blue overalls. 'Pop these on, grab a helmet and I'll see you outside for the safety briefing.'

Noah in overalls was pretty hot. They outlined his broad shoulders and height and could have been custom-made for him, especially around the bum.

'This is going to be fun,' I said, zipping up and wedging the helmet on my head.

'Fun?' Noah laughed. 'I'm not so sure about that. Dangling off the side of a skyscraper, thousands of feet above the city, is not most people's idea of fun. I think you might be unique there. Adventure, I'd say, and not for the faint-hearted.' He smiled at me. 'Do you ever stop to think things through, or do you always jump into shark-infested waters with both feet?'

'Don't be such a baby.' I grinned back at him. 'Life's too short.'

'I'm not being a baby. And exactly, although this might shorten it further. Sometimes, it's worth slowing down and taking the time to weigh up the risks.' For a moment his face looked sombre. He swallowed and spoke quietly, and I knew he was remembering the accident with the other player. 'Sometimes we ought to take a step back before we commit to something … dangerous.'

I stared at him with sympathy. 'True, but we might never get to do this again. We could die tomorrow.'

'We could die today and then you'd miss out on the Empire State Building, and I'd hate you to miss that.' He smiled at me, his eyes meeting mine and holding my gaze for a moment. 'I know it's important to you.'

The words made an unexpected warmth bloom in my chest. I was sure it didn't mean anything but it was sweet that he understood.

To cover my sudden emotion, I said quickly, 'Yeah, yeah, yeah. Come on. Like he said. We're in more danger on the street.'

Once we were cleared to start, Chad led us out onto a small platform, several scary floors above the Observation Deck, which now we were out there, looked a disconcertingly long way down. I gulped, suddenly not quite so confident. Being out in the elements made everything very real. The brilliant blue sky and the protection of the glass barriers down on the deck had lulled me into a false sense of security. My adrenaline spiked. Although the view was breathtaking; so, too, was the sharp icy wind that stole my voice. Fierce gusts swirled around us, tugging and pulling at our overalls with vicious fingers.

I grabbed the handrail feeling a little wobbly.

'You okay, Green?' asked Noah, immediately noticing.

'Yeah,' I said. 'Just a bit windier than I was expecting.'

'We'll get used to it, but I'm right here, if you want to stop or hold onto something.'

I nodded, wondering how he'd feel if I clung to him like a monkey.

Now that we were a very, very, *very* long way up, with no protection from the strong air streams whipping around us, I felt out of my depth, barraged by the unfamiliar sensations of noise and chaos. My hair streamed around my face, flapping against my helmet like Medusa's corona of snakes around my helmet. But I couldn't back down now, could I?

Noah covered my hand gripping the rail and gave my white knuckles a gentle pat.

'Ready?'

With the wind buffeting our bodies, it was quite a struggle to round the corner to the first metal-latticed step. I glanced up at the intimidating steep flight of steps hugging the angle of the building. The gusts hitting my face were so strong that my cheeks vibrated, and my eyes streamed as the cold temperature kissed my skin with icy needles.

It really did feel like this might be like the final assault on Everest and I regretted my earlier gung-ho attitude. Maybe Noah had a point about jumping in with both feet. I'd honestly thought that this would be a breeze, and now I wasn't so sure.

We battled our way up into the headwind, taking one step up at a time. My legs had turned to jelly, and I was struggling to keep up.

Noah looked back, and much to my disgust, his eyes were alight and his mouth curved into a big smile. He was bloody enjoying himself. 'You okay?' he yelled.

My eyes locked on his and I think he could see the uncertainty in them. Taking a step backwards – he couldn't turn around because of the safety measures – he slowly backed down the stairs until he stood in front of me.

'Why don't you come right up behind me and I can shelter you from some of the wind. Hold on to my waist,' he said. 'Take it slowly. We're not in any hurry to get to the top.' He grinned at me then, his eyes shining and his face full of mischief. 'I'm sure you said this was going to be fun.'

'Very funny,' I muttered before adding, 'the quicker we get to the top, the quicker we can get back down,' I ground out under my breath, more to myself than him. I don't think he heard over the wind, which whistled through and around the metal staircase.

'Remember what you said. We might never get to do this again. Just stop and take in the view for a moment. It's awesome.'

I lifted my gaze, which had been fixed on my feet, and cautiously looked around. We were far above all the other nearby buildings. I tried to respond to Noah's enthusiasm and gave him a faux smile and a thumbs-up.

The climb seemed interminable and my legs were starting to wobble, but as we neared the top, Noah held out a hand and said, 'You can do this.'

'Mmm…' I nodded and took his hand, grateful for his strong grasp and his reassuring confidence in my ability.

'Now, the fun bit,' said Chad. 'We're going to hang out over the city.'

'Okay,' said Noah. I glanced at him and saw that his eyes were bright and his cheeks ruddy. All of a sudden, he was fizzing with excitement. Clearly on the way up, he'd acquired his skyscraper legs while I appeared to have acquired those of a newborn foal.

Chad attached a couple of extra safety ropes to our harnesses and told us what to do.

Lean out.

Lean out! He had to be kidding. Butterflies were dancing the salsa in my stomach.

I stood on the edge of the platform, my back to the view, gripping the nylon rope attached to my harness with both hands. The rope gave just a little, and for a brief stomach-swirling moment I felt as if I were falling. My pulse roared in my ears and I felt a little sick. What the hell was I doing? One by careful one, I moved my hands from the rope to my harness, holding onto the shoulder straps for dear life. I realised I had my eyes shut tight. When I finally summoned up the courage to open them, I discovered my feet, which were on the platform, were now a foot or so in front of me. I was leaning backwards over the sheer drop. My stomach did a couple of somersaults, backflips and belly flops and I sucked in a quick gasp of air.

'You okay, Evie?' asked Noah from beside me, his voice low and firm. It felt like an additional lifeline.

Slowly I turned my head, keeping the rest of my body very still. 'I think so,' I looked at him and he gave me an encouraging smile and then stretched out both arms. His fingers brushed mine and he took one of my hands, giving it a gentle squeeze.

'I'm right here.'

I looked over at him and to my chagrin, he was the one embracing the experience, standing there with his other arm thrown out wide, looking happy. 'It's amazing. Take a look.' He squeezed my hand again and then interweaved his fingers through mine, locking his hold on me. 'I've got you.'

I nodded and, feeling a little braver, although that was relative, I peeped down.

'Oh, wow,' I said with a nervous giggle.

'Awesome, isn't it?' said Noah. 'Just awesome. We could be flying.'

'Mmm,' I said noncommittally, squinting to focus on the criss-cross of streets far below, just a little bit galled at our role reversal.

'Give us a big smile,' said Chad, who was filming everything because we weren't allowed to have our phones up here.

Noah raised our arms as he grinned at the camera, as if we had just bloody topped the summit of Mount Everest. I squeezed his fingers, holding on tight while grimacing at the camera and hoping it looked as if I were smiling a little.

Noah squeezed my hand back and looked over at me.

'You okay?' he asked again.

I nodded even though my stomach was doing umpteen loop-the-loops in complaint.

We hung there for far too long although it was probably less than a minute, Noah marvelling at the view with far too much flaming enthusiasm – what happened to the killjoy I was used to – before we were winched back in, thank God.

Being vertical again felt so much better.

'Right, time to turn around,' said Chad, all too cheerily to my mind.

'Sorry?'

'This time you get to lean out forwards. Cool, huh?'

I glanced back over the edge. He had to be flipping kidding. But no, he was already adjusting the harnesses.

'Are you sure this is safe?' I muttered.

Noah slipped a hand in mine and I fully expected him to say, 'What could possibly go wrong?' or something to remind me of his earlier now completely understandable reservations, but instead of revelling in my terrified face, he said, 'You don't have to do anything you don't want to, Evie. We can go back down now.'

'But you want to,' I said, aware of the glow of excitement and the shift in his body language.

'Not if you don't,' he reassured me. 'We can go back right now.'

I hauled in a deep breath realising that despite being scared, I was actually getting a kick out of seeing this side of Noah and him letting go a bit. He really was enjoying the experience.

'No,' I said. 'Let's do this.'

'Sure?' he asked.

'Yeah. Like I always say, life is short, and what could possibly go wrong?'

He smiled at me and laced his fingers between mine. 'We'll go together.'

When Chad was happy that we were secure, we stepped onto the edge.

'Look at me,' said Noah. When I did, he pulled a funny face and it was so unexpected I laughed.

'Now, lean forward,' called Chad.

Just the very thought of it made my heart thud so hard, I thought it might burst out of my chest.

'On the count of three,' suggested Noah, giving my hand another one of those reassuring squeezes. In that moment I knew I could rely on Noah. It wasn't an attribute I'd ever really valued in anyone before, but the knowledge came to me in a rush and made me feel unexpectedly warm. He had an innate ability to make me feel safe. No one had ever made me feel like that.

'One, two, three.' He leaned forward and I followed a second behind him.

And oh, oh, *oh*. Amazing. The rush to my head that came with the brief sensation of falling. I looked down. Oh, my God. We were hanging off a building, hundreds and hundreds of feet up.

Noah's hand moved in mine.

'Amazing, isn't it?' he said, his arms spread wide again like an angel embracing the view.

I gingerly spread my arms out to copy him.

The weight of my body tugged at the harness, and I tried not to think that all that was holding me was the metal carabiner. As I got used to the unfamiliar sensations and the wind gently buffeting me, I relaxed and took a few long slow breaths. A sense of peace and euphoria began to fill me. We were the only people up here and we might as well have been the only people in the city.

'It's like flying!' I laughed with pure joy.

'Isn't it incredible?' Noah grinned at me, his sparkling eyes lit up with enthusiasm.

'It is incredible,' I agreed and couldn't resist adding, 'bet you're glad I talked you into it now.'

Noah laughed at me. 'Evie Green. What are you like? I'm taking the fifth.'

'You know I'm right,' I teased.

Our eyes locked and something clicked inside me, sealing the magical moment.

'I'm never going to forget this,' I said.

'Me neither,' said Noah, more sombrely. 'And yes, you were right.' He pulled my hand to his mouth, opened my fingers and placed a soft kiss on my palm, his gaze holding mine the whole time. 'It is fun.'

The intimate gaze and quick brush of his lips sent fifty gazillion volts through my body, frying every last one of my hormones. It was the sexiest thing ever and all I could do was stare at his mouth, even though we were hanging above the city.

I gave him a tremulous smile.

'Incredible view,' he said, his eyes warm and his mouth curving as he held my gaze for several of those heart-flopping seconds before he looked back down at the distant street below.

My heart expanded in my chest as I gazed at his profile. I'd never seen it coming. His unreserved reassurance had reinforced the initial attraction I'd felt for him, which throughout the day had been gently twining its way around me like ivy. Slow, steady and sure.

Suddenly I wanted him to like me. Not to be the annoying, pesky companion he was stuck with. I wanted a lot more. Way more. I wanted to know what those lips would feel like on mine. Did he feel the same way or was this just an adrenaline high, born of the exhilaration of the moment?

Chapter Sixteen

NOAH

'Woohoo, I feel amazing after that,' Evie said as she raised her glass of champagne at the bar afterwards. 'Wasn't that just amazing? I can't wait to see the pictures and the video. That was just awesome.'

But I'd crashed back down to earth.

Hanging off the side of a skyscraper wasn't a good look while Rick Menzies was looking at the end of his career. I wasn't supposed to be enjoying myself and getting a headrush of adrenaline. I was supposed to be showing remorse. Showing that I was someone that had learned his lesson from playing too hard and aggressively.

The crunch of bones replayed in my head. I shouldn't be doing stuff like this.

I certainly didn't deserve to be having a good time when someone would never play football again, thanks to me. And Rick was a pertinent reminder that, to use a soccer analogy, I couldn't afford to take my eye off the ball. I needed to focus on getting back to playing. The whole point of being with Evie was for the Hallmark moments to show I was a nice guy really and getting the rest of my match ban overturned. Every game I didn't play was potentially career damaging. It only took another player to shine in my absence and take my place. It only took a few disastrous decisions, and I could lose it all. I wasn't going to let that happen, I'd worked too hard and let my family make too many sacrifices.

'Here you go. Congratulations.' Evie lifted her glass and toasted us both. 'To the next adventure.'

'I'm not sure there should be another adventure,' I said, rubbing at my temple.

'What do you mean?' Although she'd asked the question, her eyes were sympathetic.

'There's a guy lying in a hospital room because of me, and I'm hanging off skyscrapers.' I sighed.

She leaned over and put a hand over mine. 'Noah, you do know you're still allowed to have a life?'

'Yeah, but the point of this…' I indicated Evie then me with my hand, 'is supposed to be something else. Making me look good. Like a responsible, nice guy. Not rubbing the guy's nose in it.'

'Did you have fun?'

I gave her a reluctant smile. 'Yeah, more than you, I think, but I'm supposed to be a role model. Kids look up to me and I should be showing them that I'm trying to be better.'

'You're allowed to be human,' said Evie. 'You're allowed to live a life.'

'Given your history, I think you're the last person to give advice,' I said and immediately regretted it.

Evie's face fell and then she jutted her chin out trying to style it out, but I knew I'd hurt her.

'Sorry, I shouldn't have said that.'

She shrugged. 'No, you shouldn't have but you did, because that's what you really think of me, isn't it? That I'm a thief and don't think about the consequences of things.'

'Look, I'm sorry. I'm taking my guilt out on you.'

She glared at me for a full thirty seconds before tilting her head to one side. 'At least you're honest about it. So I'll forgive you...' She paused. 'But it's a one-time deal, you arse.'

'Fair enough,' I said. 'I'm real sorry.'

'You've said it. We move on now,' said Evie matter-of-factly.

I studied her expression, but she seemed sincere which made me feel even more shitty for being such a dick.

'Still want my help shopping for gifts?' she asked.

If I hadn't spent a fair bit of time with her, I would have missed that tiny plaintive note of hope in her voice. Evie was desperate for approval. I suspected that in her own way she was as guilt-ridden as I was.

'Yes,' I said decisively, earning a quick look of surprise from her. 'My mom is going to be thrilled. You can help me choose something for my sister and my nephews. And I need to grab a Christmas decoration from the shop here before we leave.'

Her face brightened and she picked up her phone.

'What are you doing?' I asked, impressed by her quick

change of mood. It was refreshing to find someone who didn't bear a grudge. I thought of Rick in his hospital bed – who had every right to bear one.

She grinned at me. 'Figuring out just how rich you are.'

'I earn well.' I'd already made an anonymous donation to Rick via the Players Association, because his income was going to take a catastrophic hit.

'Woo! It says here Premier League footballers earn around sixty thousand a week.'

Again, I winced thinking of how Rick's loss of career would impact on his lifestyle.

'Hello, earth to Noah.' Evie waved a hand in my face. 'Do you really earn that sort of cash?'

I shrugged.

'You do!' She beamed. 'Hell, yeah, we're going shopping. I'll help you find a present for your sister and her family.'

After interrogating me about my sister for half an hour, insisting on seeing her Facebook and Instagram pages, Evie declared herself ready, having ordered a second round of champagne. I think she'd have ordered a third if she wasn't the type to sit still for too long.

Before we retraced our steps back to Fifth Avenue, I picked up a couple of decorations from the Edge shop as souvenirs for me, my sister and my mom.

'Are you one of those guys whose body is a temple?' she

asked suddenly, startling me with another one of her random questions.

'I watch my nutrition but I'm not evangelical about it,' I said, wondering where this was leading.

'And how do you feel about eating in the street?'

'I don't have a problem.'

'And how do you feel about buying me my very first New York hot dog?'

I groaned. 'Seriously? That is the most roundabout way of asking someone to buy you lunch I've ever heard.'

'I know.' She shot me a winsome grin. 'Cute, eh? It's only so that I can say on Insta that Noah bought me my first New York hot dog.'

'It wouldn't do to be factually inaccurate, I guess,' I said, pulling out my wallet.

'Also, you're the one with the bucks. If it was an expensive meal, I'd insist on going halves.'

Her logic and blunt honesty amused me. It was also a novelty. Most of my dates never even questioned who should pay.

We swung by a hot-dog cart on the corner of Fifth and Thirty-Seventh.

'Mustard or ketchup?' I asked.

'Mustard,' she said. 'The bright yellow stuff. And onions, please.'

I paid for the dogs and handed her one. The smell made my stomach rumble, but before we were allowed to take a single bite, she had to get her Insta shot. Then we wandered along, chomping happily in companionable silence – I've always thought that an overrated expression but it really did feel companionable. I didn't feel the need to talk and Evie, her head turning this way and that, was clearly enjoying the festive atmosphere that spilled out from every single shop we passed.

Eventually we arrived at Saks, discarding our sticky napkins in one of the trash cans on the sidewalk.

'Right,' she said, and pushed up imaginary shirt sleeves. 'You ready for this?'

'As ready as I'll ever be.' I huffed out a resigned sigh, more to make her laugh than anything else. 'Be gentle with me.'

The storefront was decked out with hundreds of fairy lights hanging from every surface, sparkling in the fading light.

'Right, I think your sister would appreciate a really smart handbag, for the days she gets to be a grown-up.'

'You mean a purse,' I interrupted.

'Purse, handbag.' She wrinkled her nose. 'But big enough to carry around all the mum stuff she might need if her kids are around. I'm guessing she likes a bit of luxury now and then.'

I nodded, once again her logic was impeccable and I liked her no-nonsense assessment.

'I think a frivolous colour.'

I raised my eyebrows. 'What's wrong with black?'

'Nooo!' she said, clearly horrified. 'A gift should always be something you love but would never buy for yourself because it's too much of an extravagance or impractical – a busy mum is always focused on the practical. So, the gift should be something delightfully frivolous but still functional. So not navy or black or tan.'

'Okay,' I repeated, folding my arms.

She tugged at them. 'Stop doing that.'

'Doing what?'

'Standing like you're a bodyguard or something. You look forbidding.'

'Good,' I said with a smirk.

'How do you expect me to do frivolity if you're being forbidding.'

I dropped my arms by my side. 'Frivolous but functional,' I repeated. 'Not navy, black or tan. Got you.'

'So, the frivolity is in the colour, I'm thinking,' said Evie sagely, her face contorted as she considered various options. 'And as you're paying. It definitely has to be designer.'

By the end of her second circuit of the bag department, she'd disrupted six displays and stood almost equidistant from them all in the middle of the shop floor.

'So, there's the orange Ralph Lauren – quite a bold choice. The teal-blue Kate Spade, which is classy. The burgundy Coach, which is a bit staid but a safe choice. The dark-purple-almost-blue Marc Jacobs, which is a lot of fun. And the red Ferragamo, which is the most gorgeous statement and very Christmassy.'

She looked at me expectantly.

And I looked back at her.

'Now it's your turn.'

'What do you mean?'

'It's your gift to her, so you have to make the final

choice. I've narrowed it down for you but you have to pick one.'

I glanced at the purses with a touch of panic. Seriously? They were purses. She was the expert.

'Breathe. Don't overthink it. Go with your gut. If I held a gun to your head and said pick one now or I'll chop your left leg off, which one would you choose.'

'You can't chop a leg off with a gun.'

'Stop stalling, Sanderson. Pick now.'

'The teal blue.'

'Why?'

'Because she'll love that colour and I know diddly about *handbags*.' I put on a faux English accent to highlight our cultural differences.

'Don't worry about the handbag. That's my department. Excellent choice, by the way.' Once the purchase was made, Evie insisted on carrying the smart shopping bag, swinging it with great gusto when we left the store.

'Now, who else do we need to buy for?'

I glanced down at her animated face, amused by the *we*. 'My nephews, Barney and Oscar, and a couple of others.'

'This is going to be so much fun.' She skipped beside me. Actually skipped.

I rolled my eyes, but I couldn't help thinking that spending time with Evie was a lot of fun.

Chapter Seventeen

EVIE

I rapped on Noah's door. And then I rapped a second time. After my third knock, he wrenched the door open wearing nothing but faded blue jeans, his hair standing up in damp spikes. The moisture in my mouth evaporated at the sight of his tanned skin and the droplets of water dotting his collarbone. I wanted to lick them off, there and then.

'Where's the fire?' he asked, scowling at me.

I stared at him for a moment – Noah had one hell of a body. A tasteful dusting of dark hair across each pec and muscles in all the right places. I did my best not to ogle his lean hips, firm abs and the arrow of hair snaking down beneath his waistband.

'Downstairs,' I said, grabbing his arm, my fingers landing on warm skin.

'What?'

'Not a fire. But I need you. Angel is giving me a tour of The Royal Suite. Come on.'

'Er, Evie. I'm not dressed.'

'I know.' I beamed at him. 'It's perfect. Come on, she's holding the lift. She's got the all-clear from Alicia to send up some champagne.'

'I'm busy.'

'Noah, you are not busy.'

He stuck his chin out in stubborn denial. I patted his stubbled chin and gave him another gentle tug forward. As he stepped over the threshold, the door clicked shut behind him.

'And now I'm locked out,' he growled, the bass in his voice sending a little frisson through me.

'It's fine,' I said, my fingers tingling at the touch of his bare skin. 'Angel will … will have a master or something.'

'Hmmph,' said Noah, glancing up and down the corridor.

'Don't worry, it's not like anyone's going to take offence at the sight of you.' I patted his arm again, because I could. 'You might even make someone's day. An early Christmas present. Those pecs should come gift wrapped. Do you wax your chest?'

A resigned snort exploded out of his mouth. 'Evie, you ask the most random things.'

'I know,' I said. 'Can't seem to help it when you're around.' It was the truth, he had the strangest effect on me. My filter around him was shot, maybe because I knew he already totally disapproved of me.

His mouth flattened but I could tell he was trying really hard not to smile. 'Was there a compliment hidden in there?'

'Yeah, I think so,' I said, trying to brush it off. 'Don't let it go to your head. I didn't mean it. Come on.'

'I don't have much choice,' he grumbled and fell into step beside me down the corridor to the lift. We had to go down to the ground floor in order to access the private lift to the suite.

As Noah crossed the lobby with his naked chest and bare feet, both Carol and Sofia did a discreet double-take, as did the other occupants of the lobby. Not that I blamed them.

'Hello, Noah,' said Angel, greeting us in the lobby of The Royal Suite. Being a complete professional, she didn't bat so much as an eyelash at the sight of his naked chest. Although behind his back once he'd stepped out of the lift, she looked at me and mouthed, 'Wow'.

I mouthed back. 'I know.'

'What do you think?' I asked, ushering Noah into the living room.

It was so big it contained a grand piano, along with several sofas and a dozen chairs. I glanced up at the ceiling with its elaborate plaster mouldings and the grand chandeliers, their crystals shimmering in the light. The room epitomised understated elegance with the sort of cream upholstery that only someone who didn't worry about the cost of dry-cleaning bills would ever pick. In the corner of the room by the window overlooking the lights and decorations of Fifth Avenue was an enormous Christmas tree trimmed in hues of gold and red and decked out with warm white lights that twinkled. In the room opposite was a black dining table, which could easily seat eight – twelve at a pinch – which was laid with gold cutlery, red damask napkins, gold candles and an enormous glass vase containing an elaborate bouquet of red roses, eucalyptus, pinecones and fir branches.

'Very nice,' said Noah, looking around.

'There's a gym, a study, a library and a kitchen,' I said. The entire suite was probably five times the size of my shared flat.

'Everything your average billionaire needs,' said Noah with a smile.

'Don't tell me, you probably live in one of those small mansion houses out in the home counties, an hour's drive from London, with extensive garaging for your Ferrari, Range Rover and, oh wait, you're American, I bet you have one of those great, big trucks.'

Noah laughed. 'I've lived in London and Europe for nearly ten years now. I don't need a truck. I don't need a mansion. I do have an apartment, and as you clearly want to know, it's in Chelsea overlooking the river. Wonderful views.'

I wrinkled my nose. 'Seriously? That's a bit boring. I prefer to fantasise about you being a rich, self-indulgent bastard. That is much more rewarding.'

'Sorry to disappoint,' said Noah, with a twinkle in his eyes. 'If it's any consolation, I drive an Aston Martin and I also have a place in Vale do Lobo, in Portugal.'

'Ooh. I'm almost impressed. Are you going to take me out in the Aston Martin?'

'Don't be, and no, I'm not.'

I grinned at him.

'But you want to,' I said with an encouraging smile. 'I've never been in an Aston Martin.'

'I don't want to,' he said. 'Now, why have you dragged me up here?'

I pouted and he grinned at me, completely unperturbed. There's just something about a man who never gives an inch especially when he's owning it standing barefoot and bare-chested.

'It's the master bedroom en-suite, I really want you to see,' I said, and led him into the luxurious bathroom with its gorgeous hip bath.

'Fancy,' said Noah, turning a complete circle. 'I've seen it. Can I go now?'

I folded my arms. 'And do what? Alicia says engagement has gone through the roof since...' I wasn't going to mention the kiss on the palm. I still got tingles thinking about it, as, it appeared, did my followers. 'What do you suggest we do to keep followers interested?'

'I don't know,' he said. 'Don't really care.'

'Noah. Noah. Noah. Am I going to have to tell on you to your agent? How about we take some pictures in the suite?' I grinned at him encouragingly as I built up the plan. 'I've cleared it with Alicia and she's on board. She's sending a bottle of champagne up. In here would be great.'

'What?' he said slowly. 'In here?'

'Yes. In the bath.' I indicated the large, roll-top enamel bath with its gold-plated taps and the gold-leaf decorated tiles on the wall before looking at him and then back at the bath. I grinned adding, 'Toasting each other with champagne.'

Noah shook his head in disbelief. 'No, just no.'

'It's very romantic, and it'll show your softer side.'

'I don't have a softer side.'

'Everyone loves a will-they-won't-they build up.'

'Will-they-won't-they what?'

I sighed. 'Kiss … it's all about perception. Remember. It's not for real. It's just for the campaign.'

Noah looked at Angel, who nodded. 'I think she's right,' she said. 'People love a romance. Let me rustle up a couple of glasses of champagne. I think we can make this work.'

I did not want my New York adventure to end prematurely, and Alicia had told me that yesterday's video had got far more engagement. We needed to keep building on that. 'If Angel takes the picture from the right angle, we could get in the tub and neither of us would even have to take our clothes off.' Beneath my sweatshirt, I was wearing a sleeveless tank top, and it would take me two seconds to pile my hair on top of my head in a messy bathtime-style bun.

Noah frowned. 'Are you sure?'

'Positive,' I said with my usual utterly misplaced confidence. I had no idea.

'Why don't you hop in the tub and we'll see,' said Angel with a mischievous smile.

I clambered in at the taller end of the hip bath, raising my arm pretending to hold up a champagne glass. Noah stood at the edge of the bath looking down at me, his mouth flattened into its usual noncommittal flat line.

'Sorry, Evie. I can see your tank. Why don't you take it off and put a towel around you?' suggested Angel.

She tossed me one of the uber-fluffy towels from the pile on the side.

'Turn round, Noah,' I told him.

I stripped off my top and bra and wrapped the towel bandeau-style around my boobs and climbed back in the bath.

'How's this?' I asked.

'Perfect,' said Angel. 'You look naked.'

'Great,' I replied. 'Your turn,' I told Noah.

'Are you sure this is necessary?' he asked.

'No, it's not necessary.' I paused and gave him a taunting smile. 'Or are you too chicken?'

He raised an eyebrow and stepped into the bath.

I really hadn't thought this through. The bath was big, but not that big. I hugged my knees to my chest to give him some room, but kept sneaking glances at his chest. It was quite distracting. He stretched out his long legs and a wave of heat rushed over me.

I stretched my denim-clad legs out and shifted to one side. My hand touched one of Noah's muscled calves, which I could feel through the fabric of his jeans.

'Sorry,' I said moving my hand quickly. I wondered what they'd feel like on top of mine. Another burst of heat barrelled its way across my chest and I felt the flush charging up my neck. Please don't let Noah notice.

Angel held up my phone and screwed up her face, shaking her head.

'No good, Evie. I can see yours and Noah's jeans. In fact, it's really obvious there's no water in there.'

'Okay,' I said.

'Hey, guys.' Alicia popped her head around the door, waving a bottle of Piper Heidsieck and two flutes. 'Aw, that is so cute.'

'Yeah, but it's not quite working,' I said, standing up and looking down at Noah who was reclining half-naked with his arms propped on either side of the bath. With his tanned skin, dark against the crisp white enamel, he looked ten types of hot – thank goodness we had an audience.

'Alicia,' said Angel, 'I've got to go. Can you take over here?'

''Course I can. See you later.' Angel hurried away.

'You need to put some water in there,' said Alicia, 'and let the bubbles do their thing. That would totally work.'

'But…' I said.

'But we need to keep followers engaged and it's going to look sooo romantic.' Alicia beamed. 'I should have got some rose petals. Make sure you put lots of bubbles in.'

'Okay,' I said, getting into the spirit. 'We can make it work.' Then I started thinking about the practicalities. 'Lots of bubbles and we keep our underwear on.'

'Are you sure?' asked Noah stepping out of the tub.

'Yes,' I said as if it was no biggie. I could be blasé about these things.

Noah raised an eyebrow, looked down at the bathtub and stood up to shuck off his jeans. I'd expected him to put up a bit more of a fight and narrowed my eyes in surprise. He gave me an amused smirk. 'This was your idea.'

Alicia had already stepped forward, turned on the taps and dumped half a bottle of gardenia scented bath essence into the water.

'Okay,' I said overbrightly as Noah stepped out of his jeans. Suddenly taking my clothes off didn't seem such a good idea. He was all muscle, I was all saggy bits around the middle, which normally didn't bother me. But normally I wasn't standing next to a footballing Adonis.

Was it very warm in here?

'Don't worry, Evie,' said Alicia. 'No one will see anything.'

'No, I know,' I said, still reluctant to take my jeans off.

'If you're feeling uncomfortable, we don't have to do this,' said Noah, with a gentle expression on his face. We stared at each other, and his eyes were soft, for once not mocking or scowling. The sudden hiccup in my chest and the swirly feelings in my stomach were the things making me feel uncomfortable. Noah looked perfectly at ease. Of course he did.

'Are you feeling uncomfortable?' I asked, trying to regain my confidence and be my usual cocky self.

'No,' he said, and gave me a slow, ever-so-slightly smirky smile. 'But then I don't have a problem with nudity. I'm a professional athlete. I often have photos taken of me in not much. My body is my tool.'

'You keep your tools to yourself,' I teased, trying to keep things light but suddenly feeling a bit insecure. He was used to being photographed, often with women in the same sort of league as him, not an unfit, average-looking female whose weekly exercise consisted of weight-lifting a packet of digestives and a daily climb up the stairs to my first-floor flat. 'You might be used to parading about the locker room and sharing showers with the team with no clothes on, but not me.'

'Evie.' Noah's tone was chiding and teasing at once. 'You're happy to make me dangle off a thousand-foot skyscraper when we might actually die.'

'This is completely different,' I said, wrinkling my nose.

'And not dangerous. But you really don't have to do it if you don't want to. If it's any consolation, I'll probably be in more danger from your toenails than anything else.'

'Nobody's in danger from toenails, that's completely spurious.' I pursed my lips, trying not to laugh.

'Evie. I promise I'll keep my eyes closed and you can arrange the bubbles so I can't see anything.'

'But I'll know,' I said.

'Know what.'

'That you might see my boobs.'

'Are you chicken?' he asked with that quirk of his eyebrow.

'No,' I replied, jutting my chin out realising that one had come back to bite me.

'Are they exemplary boobs?' he asked.

I glanced down at my chest. 'They're all my own.'

'I've seen boobs before.'

'They probably don't measure up to your standards. I bet you've seen plenty of exemplary, model boobs.'

'It's okay,' his face softened and there was kindness in his eyes, as if he understood my stupid insecurities, 'I'm not a boob man.'

I realised this was a ridiculous conversation.

'Promise you'll keep your eyes closed.'

'Yes.'

'No, you have to promise.'

'I promise.'

'On your legs.'

'What?'

'It's something important to you – like swearing on your mother's life.'

He sighed. 'I promise on my legs and my mother's life that I won't look.'

Chapter Eighteen

EVIE

Me and my big mouth. As soon as I stepped into the lovely hot water, the scent of the bubbles enveloping me, I realised I'd outmanoeuvred myself. Thank God I'd shaved my legs recently and put on good underwear, although my knickers were going to be translucent. I arranged myself at one end, making sure the bubbles covered me, and tucked my knees up to make room for Noah.

'Ready,' I said, although as Noah stepped into the bath bringing his body that much closer, I realised I wasn't ready at all. There was nowhere else to look. All I could see was how well his snug jersey boxers clung to his muscled thighs, the dark happy trail that arrowed down his taut stomach and the bulge beneath. Awareness of him fizzed across my skin and I felt a little kick in my stomach. An involuntary half-squeak came from nowhere and my eyes darted to meet Noah's.

'You okay?' he asked.

I nodded, swallowing, not daring to speak because my vocal cords were crippled by panic. I had a horrible feeling my voice would come out in a pitch several times higher than normal. More for something to hold onto while I was having this weird out-of-body experience, I clutched my knees to my chest as he sank into the water. I pulled the foam towards me so that my boobs were covered and gingerly lowered my legs, so that they draped over Noah's. He was much closer to me than I'd planned. I could reach forward and touch him.

'Comfy?' asked Noah.

I nodded, still unable to speak. This had been a crazy idea. I wasn't sure if the water was really hot and steamy or if my temperature had rocketed up to close-to-fainting level.

'Excellent,' said Alicia, 'that looks great.' I'd almost forgotten she was there. She handed us each a glass of champagne and I risked putting out a bubble-covered arm to snatch it from her as I made sure the foam was covering me. The bubbles were pfft-pffting around us, melting away already.

'Smile, Evie,' said Alicia.

I did my best to dredge up a smile, but I had severe stage fright. It had been a while since I'd been this close to a man, and certainly not in daylight, half naked. My recent sexual encounters were of the fleeting, mainly pissed, in the dark and of the one-night stand variety – where I had absolutely no intention of seeing them again. This was all a bit too up close and personal for comfort.

'Relax,' said Alicia. 'This is supposed to be cheeky and

fun. You look as if there's a shark in there with you, Evie.' Which, of course, made me freeze up even more.

Noah started humming the *Jaws* theme tune and tracking a finger down my calf, suddenly grabbing my ankle. I squeaked with surprise, throwing my champagne all over him.

He grinned and then said in the most ridiculous faux-sexy voice. 'I hope you're going to lick that off.'

I burst out laughing because it was so unlike Noah.

'Which porn movie did you pick that up from?' I asked in a low voice, still giggling.

Noah's eyes twinkled and he pouted, which was actually very cute, before he said in a whisper, 'You just had to go and ruin my favourite fantasy.'

I raised my eyebrows and leaned forward, murmuring, 'That's it? That's all you got?'

Then he grinned at me, lifted his champagne glass and suddenly the temperature went up dramatically as his eyes met mine. As if through a layer of cotton wool, I heard Alicia say, 'Perfect. Oh, that's brilliant. Great pics.'

The rest of the world receded as I stared at Noah and he stared back at me. My gaze dropped to his chest where the drips of champagne ran down over his chest.

Alicia's phone rang at that moment. 'Oh, I need to take this. Can I leave you to it? Angel will sort everything out later. Just leave when you're done. There are plenty of towels, use the robes when you come out. And help yourself to anything. The suite isn't booked now for a couple of weeks. Enjoy.'

Neither of us even looked her way as she scuttled off, her heels tapping on the tiled floor.

In the sudden silence, there was a zing of awareness. Noah's eyes were trained on my lips and everything else faded into the background.

I swallowed and looked at his chest again, mesmerised by the smooth golden skin.

'How would you feel if I licked that champagne…' I nodded towards his body, itching to slide my hands over it, to feel the firm taut flesh.

'You wouldn't,' he said, but his words were husky.

'Are you daring me?'

'I'm guessing you'd never back down from a dare.' I saw the dip of his Adam's apple as he swallowed.

'Never,' I said.

'I'd be okay with it, if you were.' His words sounded constricted, and I saw the cords in his neck were stiff with tension.

My breath caught, and for a moment I wondered how I came to be here, in this sumptuous bathroom, in an amazing suite with a truly gorgeous man with the air filled with the rich fragrance of The Plaza's signature gardenia scent? Against my skin, the bubbles felt silky and decadent, enveloping me in luxury. Even in my wildest fantasies I couldn't have dreamed this, but I was going to make the most of every moment and all the indulgence on offer, which included the opportunity to touch Noah's naked skin.

I slowly scooted forward, my eyes holding his as I moved closer, reaching out to touch his chest, my thumb dipping into the champagne. I took it back and slowly licked it. 'Wouldn't want to waste it,' I said.

'No,' he said, his eyes widening. I heard the rasp of his breath.

Before I'd even thought it through, I'd lowered my head and brought my lips to his warm skin, my tongue lapping at what was left of the champagne. The taste was a combination of the acidic wine and his slightly salty skin. Intoxicated by that initial touch, I couldn't stop now. I wanted more and I let my lips kiss their way to his throat, the pulse that beat at the juncture of his neck, feeling the furious thud beneath my lower lip. When his hands gently moved to my hips, his thumbs stroking my skin in mesmerising circles urging me on, I looked at him. His eyes darkened, fixed on me. I swallowed. Serious Noah. The focused intensity of his gaze tripped a switch inside my chest. Serious Noah was seriously sexy. An instant flood of desire bathed me with sharp heat as I stared back at him.

For a few seconds we just looked at each other, anticipation building and burning between us like a physical flame. When he finally pulled me towards him, I sighed as his mouth met mine and his fingers tightened on my hips. Scorching. White heat. The kiss was incendiary and went fast and furious in seconds. His lips were hard against mine, then soft as they explored and devoured. Noah was thorough and meticulous as his mouth seared over mine. I moaned trying to capture his kisses, hold on to each one, but his lips seemed determined to discover and claim me. I collapsed against him, chest to chest, my nipples hard and aware of each gentle graze of his skin. My hands locked around his neck as I tried to anchor myself, trying to find some sense in the whirl of feelings. I'd never felt such hot, sharp desire before. Beneath my thigh I could feel the hard length of him straining against me. His mouth moved down my neck, trailing fiery kisses, and I pushed against the enamel surface of the bath trying to raise myself to give him greater access, my skin burning for his touch. My hand slipped and I fell back on him sending water sloshing up the sides of the bath like a mini tsunami, hitting the tiled floor with a splash. It stopped us dead and for some reason we both dissolved into giggles.

Noah eased me off him and I immediately missed the long lean length of his body. He stepped out of the bath and snagged one of the towels before tossing it over his shoulder. In one fluid move, he turned and lifted me out of the bath, before placing me in front of him and then gently wrapping the towel around me. My heart literally melted, and as I was looking up at him all gooey-eyed, with my heart a little puddle inside, he grinned down at me and kissed me on the nose before grabbing his own towel. He gave himself a brisk rub down over his chest and shoulders before casually tucking the fluffy white towel around his hips.

While I was still gaping at him, because he looked even hotter, he dabbed at my shoulders and then gently looped my towel around my chest and tucked it in bandeau style at the front.

It was rare for me to be speechless. No one had ever taken this much care of me.

'Thank you,' I murmured, lifting on my tip toes to kiss his neck.

'My pleasure,' murmured Noah, his head dipping to find my mouth again.

We sank into another long, deep kiss, my fingers trailing into his damp hair, while his hands roved up my thighs beneath the plush towel. I could feel the ridge of his erection pressing into my stomach and that delicious sensation of being desired filled me. I wanted him, too. As I pressed against him, trying to get closer, my towel loosened and he took full advantage, lowering his head to kiss the swell of my breasts. His stubble slightly abrasive against my skin. I moaned as his lips captured one nipple, his tongue swirling expertly over the pert bud. I tilted my head back and took in a gasping breath as he took his sweet time. Tight desire coiled, the pressure building. Then with unhurried ease he moved to my other breast, his hand cupping the first one, his thumb moving over the sensitive nipple, while his mouth and tongue assaulted my other nipple. With twin points of sensitivity being tortured over and over by his hot, wet mouth I could feel my knees weaken and I held onto him, sighing half-finished words, incoherent with mindless pleasure.

His hand moved higher up my thigh and I parted my legs because I needed his touch, right there.

'Ahh,' I moaned as he teased me, circling with the tip of his finger.

'You're so wet,' he murmured, lifting his head and staring down at me, his eyes dark with satisfaction.

'It would appear so,' I managed to respond between

breathless pants, desperate for him to push his finger inside me.

Suddenly the intercom phone in the bathroom began to ring, bringing reality back like a bucket of cold water.

We both stiffened and jumped apart.

Holding my towel between my breasts, I picked up the phone.

'Hello.'

'Hey, it's Alicia. Just realised you need a key card to get out of the suite to use the lift. I'm sending someone up to leave one for you. Stay as long as you like. And I've found the most gorgeous thing for you to do tomorrow. You're going to love it. I'll keep you posted. Gotta go.'

With that she hung up and I wondered if she had any idea of what she'd just interrupted and whether Noah would be willing to pick up where we left off.

Chapter Nineteen

EVIE

'And now this isn't awkward at all,' I said, walking through to the lounge area, where Noah sat in a robe, tied loosely so that I could still see all that golden skin.

'Not really,' said Noah, who uncharacteristically seemed completely at ease with the situation. He leaned back against the sofa, one arm stretched along the back. It was me that usually jumped into situations without thinking things through or worrying about the consequences, but now all my alarm bells were beginning to ring.

'I've been wanting to kiss you for a while. Well, since the first day I saw you.'

That stopped me, my heart fluttered at his words which made the alarm bells even shriller, although I just had to ask, 'Have you? I thought I irritated the hell out of you.' What was wrong with me? Being all needy for his approval, when I should be slamming the brakes on here and running for safety.

'You do that as well,' he said with a smile. 'I'm never quite sure what you're going to say next.'

'Oh,' I said. That wasn't so bad, although not exactly a compliment.

'Like now.' He grinned at me triumphantly. 'It's really cute seeing you lost for words for a change. Flustered.'

'I'm not flustered,' I protested.

Oh yes, I was. Very. Because he was making me feel things I'd avoided for a long time.

He stood up and handed me one of The Plaza branded, soft velvet robes, wrapping it around me and doing up the belt. It would have been so easy to tilt my head and kiss him, instead I looked down at my feet.

'I guess we'd better be sensible given Alicia or Angel could turn up at any moment,' said Noah but there was a question in his voice, which made me want to forget my fears and give into the desire to kiss him again.

'I guess,' I said with a little pout, which was ridiculous because I needed to be sensible. Noah's gentle care was stirring emotions that had no place in my life.

'And don't pout.' He touched my lips. 'It's too cute. I might forget myself. I'd rather take my time and not worry about an audience.'

'Oh,' I said. That was bad. I felt another flutter in my chest.

He grinned. 'It really is cute when you're lost for words.'

'Don't get used to it,' I muttered almost wanting to cry because I had to stop this, but his words flickered warmth into places that had been cold for so long. I'd managed to live life on my terms for the last five years, secure and confident that I was mistress of my own feelings. Life was simpler and easier without emotion messing things up.

'You do realise we're both going to have to go commando to get back to our rooms.'

Noah frowned at the sudden step change. I gave him a cheeky grin, determined to alter the mood, and helped myself to a glass of champagne, walking around the coffee table to one of the sofas opposite, where I sat, making sure the robe covered my legs. I was relieved when Noah took my lead and sat opposite. I could see that while he was a little puzzled about my withdrawal, he was also respectful, and that made my heart give a little pang of regret. He was definitely one of the good guys.

Trying to appear nonchalant, I relaxed back into the sofa and took a sip of champagne, looking at the Christmas tree in the corner, inhaling the subtle pine fragrance perfuming the room and ignoring the low, persistent clamour of my body muttering, 'Why have you stopped?'

'This is quite nice,' I said, sounding horribly like I was making small talk at a party. 'Christmassy. Do you have a tree in your apartment?'

Noah shot me a quick frown but to my relief he followed my lead.

'Usually. I didn't get round to it this year.' He sighed. 'First time I haven't. It's always been a big deal in our family. Me and my dad would go out and cut one down.'

'Cut one down. Get out of here,' I said with faux brightness, but I was genuinely amused. 'What with an axe and everything?'

'With an axe and everything.' He smiled and suddenly it wasn't awkward anymore. 'And then we'd drag it home on a sled—'

'Hallmark Christmas alert,' I interrupted.

'Or a golf trolley, if it hadn't snowed yet.'

'I like it.'

'And we'd take it home for my mom and my sister to inspect. Dad's job then, would be to put the lights on, and then me and my sis would bicker about which ornaments to put on.'

'I've never had a real tree,' I said wistfully, thinking of the battered white tinsel tree that had had its final outing in Mum's bedroom when she was no longer able to get downstairs. 'We always said we would, one day when Mum was better.' I gave in to the grief. 'Except she never did get better.'

'I'm sorry, Evie. Sounds like Christmas was difficult.'

'No,' I said, determined not to be a Debbie Downer. 'We loved Christmas. That's why we watched all the films. It was something we could do together. Maybe one day I will get a real tree. This one smells just like Christmas.'

'There's nothing quite like it,' Noah said with a sigh as we both stared at the beautiful tree shimmering opposite in a halo of gold. 'Although ours never looked as well coordinated as this one. We have a motley collection of ornaments, none of which match. We still have things me and my sister made at kindergarten.'

I smiled thinking of the tatty tree and the homely decorations which had made a reappearance every year without fail while Mum was alive. 'My mum refused to throw anything I'd made away. No matter how crappy. She kept the paper one I made with a handprint for Rudolf's antlers, which was Sellotaped together, and the string of snow – white wool threaded with cotton-wool balls, all of fifteen centimetres long. It looked ridiculous but it had to go on the tree every year.' I swallowed. 'When she died, I got rid of them all.'

'Why?' asked Noah, his voice gentle.

'Because it didn't feel right celebrating Christmas without her.'

We lapsed into silence, lost in our memories. I sipped at my champagne and listened to the traffic outside several floors below. It felt as if we were in our own private cocoon up here, shielded from all the difficult parts of life.

'How old were you when she died?' asked Noah after a little while.

'Twenty-four,' I said. 'But she was ill for a long time.'

'That's tough.'

'Yes, but also we knew she was dying, so we got to spend a lot of time together. We said everything we needed to.' As usual I tried to put a positive spin on it. Those years looking after Mum were tough, even though she did everything she could to make sure I didn't end up caring for her, it was impossible in the end when the money ran out.

'What about your Dad?'

'Oh, he died when I was young.'

'So, you dealt with your mum's illness, on your own.'

I shrugged my shoulders, really not wanting to have this

conversation. It brought back too many memories. Too much terror. Too many sleepless nights. Too much angst about how I was going to keep the lights and the heating on.

'Thank goodness for the NHS. And also, Mum had some savings.' I gave a brittle laugh. 'They weren't much, and they were badly invested. So badly invested.' I shook my head. 'That's when I taught myself about the stock market and investments so that I could make her savings go further.' I paused, remembering how hard it had been to juggle everything but the interest that Mum had taken. She loved helping me.

'And this is a depressing conversation to be having when we're sipping champagne in The Royal Suite of The Plaza. Come on, I'm never going to get to do anything this fancy again. I'm going to make the most of it. I'm hungry. Alicia said to help ourselves. There must be a minibar and snacks.'

Noah picked up the bottle of champagne and topped up my glass.

He tilted his head and studied me.

'What?' I asked a touch irritably. I didn't like the way it felt as if he could really see me.

He frowned but didn't say anything.

'So, what do you think your nephews would like for Christmas?' I asked, desperate for a change of subject. I didn't want Noah looking too hard at me. He might just see beneath my carefully erected shell that beneath the hot-mess confidence and sass, I was an even bigger hot mess who had pretty much given up any long-term planning for my future.

I gave him a little smile, to emphasise that we were back in the 'fun Evie' zone.

'And, more importantly, I'm officially starving, you can take me down to dinner.'

Chapter Twenty

EVIE

'Wrap up warm,' had been Alicia's only instructions for this evening's excursion, the day after our session in the suite. Neither Noah nor I had any idea where we were headed, even when we crossed the famous Brooklyn Bridge. When the car finally pulled up in a distinctly residential area nearly an hour later, we stepped out of the car into the chilly, crisp night.

'Hey,' called a gruff voice from across the street. 'Evie Green.'

I turned and saw an elderly man waving at us from the front of what looked like a horse-drawn sleigh, except it had wheels. Dressed as Santa, he sported a flowing white beard and a broad beam as he waved again.

'You've got to be kidding me,' said Noah, examining the sleigh, in front of which were four horses, each wearing light-up reindeer horns.

'It's adorable,' I said, nudging him in the ribs.

'We've come all the way out to Brooklyn to have a horse-drawn ride. We could have got that in Central Park.'

'Don't be such a buzzkill,' I said as Santa bellowed, 'Happy Holidays,' as we approached. 'And welcome to Dyker Heights.'

'Ah,' said Noah, 'now I get it. This should be fun.'

'What is it?' I whispered to Noah.

'You'll find out.' He laughed. 'You're going to love this.'

'Okay, then.' I took Santa's hand and climbed up into the seat in the back of the sleigh, followed by Noah. As soon as we'd both sat down in the very snug seat – clearly the sleigh was built for elves not humans – Santa tucked a thick soft faux-fur blanket around our legs.

'There's a flask of mulled wine in the trunk there, help yourself and there are cookies, be sure to save one for me. Ho! Ho! Ho! I'll give you a minute to get yourselves settled and then we'll begin the tour.'

I squirmed a little but there was no getting away from the touch of Noah's leg wedged up against mine. Thankfully, he seemed totally oblivious as he opened the little trunk to reveal a small star-shaped plate of iced Christmas-tree-shaped cookies and a big thermos jug. When he opened the jug up, fragrant steam wafted into the air with the enticing scent of cinnamon, cloves, oranges and red wine.

'Mmm,' Noah said inhaling. 'That smells so good. My mom always makes this for us on Christmas Eve when we go watch the church choir in the mall. Like some?'

I nodded and held out the glass mug for him to fill.

'Your Christmas is starting to sound like something out

of *The Gilmore Girls*.' In fact, his whole family sounded rather adorable.

'My mom would love that, she adores that show.'

With a laugh, he cupped my hand with his while he poured the wine for me, and an alarming little frisson ran up my arm. I kept my face impassive and did my best to ignore it, because it didn't mean anything. Except the memory of those hot, steamy kisses yesterday seemed to be playing on repeat in my head.

Just a natural response, I told myself, taking a slurp of the rich, full-bodied wine, feeling the spices warming me inside. You haven't had sex in a while, it's just good, healthy lust. But I knew if that was all it was, I wouldn't be fighting against it so hard. I took another slug of mulled wine and cast a sidelong look at Noah. He was sitting back in his seat, looking relaxed, as if my proximity didn't affect him at all, whereas I was very conscious of his firm thigh wedged against mine.

I gave an involuntary shiver.

'You okay?' asked Noah.

'Yes, fine,' I said with what was surely a giveaway squeak.

With a sudden jerk, the sleigh began to move and the horses moved more quickly than I expected. Unfortunately, wedged in as we were, the motion made any attempt to put even so much as a centimetre's distance between us impossible.

I was grateful when within a few minutes, we rounded a corner and I discovered why we were there.

The huge house in front of us blazed with lights, strings

of white fairy lights ran around every window and door and along each of the wrought-iron balconies on the upper floor. A life-sized and rather realistic Santa climbed a ladder up to one of the balconies, brightly coloured presents tumbling from the sack on his back, all up-lit from below. A crowd of elves posed, hauling up one of their number over a balcony railing. A pair of moving reindeer sat on the front lawn, their heads lifting every now and then, with the one on the right sporting a glowing red lightbulb nose.

This, as I quickly realised, was one of the more subdued and restrained displays. On the next street, the entire garden of one house was full of every style and shape of nutcracker, each carefully lit, while the house had big red bows surrounded by lights at every window, flashing wreaths across the walls and a huge neon sleigh on the roof. It was loud, exuberant and definitely festive. Small children ran around the garden taking photos with their parents, some of whom stopped to wave at our sleigh as we passed.

The next house, an enormous mansion, had the entire cast of characters from the song 'The Twelve Days of Christmas', including seven swans swimming serenely across a pond in the garden. On the balustrade around the roof, were eleven pipers piping, complete with the sound of bagpipes drifting towards us. The *piece de resistance*, looking like a gateway to another realm, was a huge gold ring around the porch.

'Wow, these people really go to town,' I murmured.

'Do you wanna stop and get some pictures?' asked our driver when we pulled up outside the next house, which was lit with red and green flashing lights outlining every last feature of the house and the garden. I nodded.

Noah stood first and lowered himself to the ground and I got up to follow. Before I could stop him, he put his hands around my waist and lifted me down. I glanced up into his face and our eyes met and locked. He held my gaze as he lowered me to the ground, his hands still on my waist.

'Thank you,' I murmured, unable to wrench my gaze away. It was one of those ridiculously cheesy romantic moments that almost never happen in real life.

'My pleasure,' he replied, with a smile that almost undid all my good intentions. Why did I want to kiss him so much? Why did he make me want something I knew was bad for me. Getting involved with people was a sure path to heartache and I'd had enough of that to last me a lifetime.

I slipped out of his hold and deliberately held up my phone to take a selfie of the two of us with the house behind. I knew exactly why Alicia had sent us here. I owed her for all these fabulous experiences. If it weren't for her, I'd probably be eating canned soup on a cold damp night in London instead of enjoying mulled wine and the biggest and best Christmas light show I was ever likely to see.

Chapter Twenty-One

EVIE

Alicia bounced over to me the next morning as I was having breakfast with Mrs Evans and Monty.

'Morning, Alicia,' said the older woman as she pulled out the chair opposite me.

'Morning, Mrs E, how are you doing?'

'I'm having a wonderful time. It's always fascinating to see what Evie will get up to next. The Dyker Heights lights were extraordinary. Quite hideous in most cases. I'm a great believer in less is more.'

I turned, surprised that she had seen them.

'What? You think I'm too old for Instagram. Darling, Monty has his own account with thousands of followers.'

'Of course he does,' I said, looking at the dog. 'He's a cutie.'

'Don't let him hear you say that,' she slapped my hand. 'It will go to his head and there's nothing worse than an insufferable dog.'

Alicia sniggered while I tried not to laugh.

'So, Alicia, what news. You look as if you're about to burst,' said Mrs Evans. 'You young people ought to practise restraint sometimes, it doesn't do any harm to cultivate an air of mystery, you know.'

Alicia laughed. 'Sorry, but holy shit, Evie.' Her eyes shone. 'You'll never believe it. Everyone loved the bath pictures and the latest reels from last night. FAO Schwarz, the toy store, have invited you guys on an official visit. It will be so sweet. Excellent work, Evie.'

Mrs Evans rose to her feet. 'Please excuse me, ladies, but Monty has a date this morning and I need to get him to the dog groomers.' With that she sailed off with the little dog in tow.

Alicia and I waited till she was out of sight and then burst out laughing.

'She's quite a character,' said Alicia.

'Yeah, but she's adorable and always very kind to me. It's nice to have breakfast with her.'

'You never quite know what she's going to say next.'

'That's part of her charm.'

'Well, I'll head off. Looking forward to today's pictures. You've got a full-on schedule and I'd better let you get on.'

I met Noah in the lobby at eleven o'clock. A black beanie hat framed his chiselled face, reminding me once again just how handsome he was and he wore a dark grey wool pea coat along with black jeans and tan lace-up boots. He exuded man-about-town, laid-back elegance.

I was glad that I'd put on the Burberry trench coat that Debbie had rightly insisted would take me anywhere.

'Ready to go?' he asked.

'Where are we going?' I asked.

'I thought we'd do a detour – we've got all day. There's a place I'd like to take you to and then we can go via Times Square because, as a tourist, you have to see it. Then we can cut across to Bryant Park. There's a place there that does the best Christmas cocktails.'

'Okay,' I said. 'So, what's with the bossiness today?'

'I'm not being bossy. I'm being assertive.'

I nodded, rather liking assertive Noah.

Even though we were off the main drag, it was still busy, but it didn't take us long to reach our first destination, a small shop on Seventh Avenue.

'Christmas Cottage.' I read the shop sign.

'Yeah, they do Christmas all year.'

'Fun,' I said with a sigh, not meaning it at all.

Noah gave me a quick sidelong glance. 'Whenever we came into the city, we would always come here to get a new decoration for the tree. A family tradition. I want to get a couple for my mom and sister.'

I followed him into the store, which, as its name suggested, was crammed with every Christmas decoration and ornament you could possibly imagine. It was difficult to know where to look first but being a magpie, who couldn't resist any sort of trinket, I was drawn to a display full of New York-themed ornaments.

'Oh, look at this,' I said picking up a little yellow cab driven by Santa with an elf in the back. 'This is cute.' There were tree ornaments of every possible design from pizza slices, hot dogs, Christmas-themed Big Apples and festive crystal Statues of Liberty sporting halos through to skyscraper cityscapes and Santas on skates. My eyes kept darting this way and that trying to take it all in. Maybe some bits of Christmas *were* fun.

On another display were more fairy lights than I'd ever seen before, old-fashioned candles, little LEDs, fancy gingerbread men, tiny angels. I was rather taken with some pretty, warm gold lights, which were so tiny they looked like fireflies winking in and out and would be nice all year round.

I drifted through the store, unexpectedly entranced by the sheer choice available. At some point, I lost Noah. He'd probably got bored, but I couldn't get enough of the place.

There were the sweetest felt stockings, pretty snow globes and wooden nutcrackers with startled soldier faces in every size, from a few inches tall through to five feet. At the sight of the familiar traditional wreaths bursting with holly berries and fir boughs in every size and the ornate garlands festooned with everything from velvet bows to dried orange slices through to plastic snowballs, I could hear my mum's voice cooing and sighing in childlike pleasure.

'Evie, look at this one.' 'How cute is that?' 'What about that one?' 'Isn't this the sweetest?'

I almost laughed out loud. She'd had terrible taste. The tackier the better when it came to … well just about everything. She would have loved it in here, and I held it together until I came to stand in front of one of Santa and

Mrs Claus kissing with the words, '*I love you to the South Pole and back*', when my eyes blurred. To the moon and back and back again, Mum had always said to me. I blinked hard, trying to remind myself that she'd be happy for me. That I should be enjoying myself for her. I turned away. Mum wouldn't have left this place without at least a dozen ornaments, but I couldn't bring myself to choose one. There was no point. I wasn't suddenly going to start getting a tree each year.

'How are we doing?' asked Noah. 'I'm getting hungry. Do you fancy a coffee? There's a great coffee bar down the street and they do amazing donuts.' His eyes shone with sudden enthusiasm.

'Have I just found your kryptonite?' I asked.

His boyish shrug was endearing. 'What can I say? I love donuts, and this place does really great snowman donuts.'

'You've been shopping,' I said noticing his bulging carrier bag.

'Just picked up a few gifts,' he said. 'Come on, I'm starving.'

When we stepped out of the store, the sky was filled with swirling snowflakes.

'It's snowing!' I squealed and, laughing, held out my hand to catch a flake, tipping my face up to feel the cold kisses of snow. I stood for a minute, closing my eyes to feel it flutter against my eyelashes like the gentle touch of an angel. At least that's what my mum believed it felt like.

When I opened my eyes, Noah, with snow settling on his eyebrows, was watching me, a tender smile curving his lips. His expression hit me straight between the ribs and I caught my breath. Running scared, I brushed the flakes from my cheeks, even though I wanted to smooth them away from his brow and touch his face. 'Come on, you promised to feed me.'

The donut shop was everything he promised and more. Donut heaven. And the snowman ones were to die for, each covered in thick white frosting with a little carrot nose, chocolate-button eyes and a red M&M as a mouth. And of course, they oozed with jam.

'Do you know what? I'm going to take one of these for Danny, the doorman. He can have it with his coffee when he's warming up on his break.'

'That's a real nice idea.'

'In fact, they're doing boxes of four. I can get one for Carol and the other lady on the desk, and for Angel – and one for Alicia – although she might not thank me, she's so slim. Oh, and then there's Cora, her assistant.'

In the end I bought two boxes.

'You're going to have to carry them around all day,' said Noah being very sensible, eyeing the paper bag I was handed.

'Oh, well,' I said, having not considered that. Hopefully they wouldn't get too battered.

From there we walked to Times Square, the snow swirling around us but not really settling. Like us, lots of people were looking up and children were excitedly trying to catch flakes with their wool mittens. People milled around us, taking pictures and stopping to gawp at the sights. Brightly coloured billboards promoting all the popular shows, like *Wicked*, *The Lion King*, *Frozen*, *Stranger*

Things and *Chicago* festooned every building, while digital screens flickered with adverts for internationally familiar brands like Coca-Cola, Nike and Sony. It was both familiar and alien at the same time. Many of the images were commonplace but seeing them altogether was an assault on the senses, heightening my feeling of being out of place.

Noah was an excellent guide, explaining that although long gone, *The New York Times* offices had been based here in the early 1900s, and that was when it became a tradition to gather there on New Year's Eve. Now, of course, it was famous for the huge predominance of theatres in the area.

Bryant Park was the most charming Christmas Market. It was impossible not to be swept up by the festive atmosphere, especially now that it was snowing. Stallholders handed over paper bags of goodies to happy shoppers, the food stalls shared little tasting bits and the smell of chocolate, gingerbread, coffee and cookies tantalised the senses. My mouth watered as I stood in front a cookie stall – so many to choose from – iced, plain, chocolate-chip, double-chocolate-chip, cranberry and pistachio – and in all sorts of shapes, fir trees, snowmen and reindeer. Then there were the gingerbread stalls with elaborately constructed houses, little cottages with jellybean flowers and chocolate-button roof shingles, along with grand mansions with candy-cane curlicued balconies and stained-glass windows made of boiled sweets. Another stall displayed gingerbread postmen, builders, dancers and clowns, the features delicately iced in a variety of colours, with ribbons threaded through them to hang on the tree. Noah picked up a pack of those and added it to his by now bulging bags. Every time I turned around, he'd disappeared and then reappeared with another purchase.

'What have you just bought?' I asked giving into my curiosity.

'Oh, just something for my cleaner. Have you seen these?' He pointed to a stall brimming with pretty glass ornaments in myriad colours. There were dragons, elves, teddy bears, all wearing traditional Santa hats, along with a selection of old-fashioned angel Christmas Tree toppers with blue eyes and golden hair fanning out around their shoulders.

'Oh, the dragons are adorable,' I said, completely falling in love with one of the little creatures in bright scarlet. I couldn't help touching the sinuous shape with a covetous hand, but I withdrew it quickly because I didn't need it. What would I do with it? My eyes lit upon a particularly pretty angel topper, her dress a delicate shade of mauve, her wings a gauzy metal. 'She's lovely, too,' I said.

'Yeah, I think my sister might like it. Why don't you go on and I'll catch you up.'

I sauntered past a couple of stalls and along to one that was selling cashmere hats and gloves in rich jewel-bright colours, a deep sapphire-blue, ruby-red and sunshine-yellow. I touched the soft wool and was almost tempted to buy one of the hats but then Noah came up behind me.

'How are you doing? Ready for a cocktail?' asked Noah.

'I'm always ready for a cocktail,' I said.

'I know just the place.' He led the way through the stalls to a quieter area, which was fenced off. He spoke to the man at the gate, and we were ushered through to an area containing four little wooden Swiss chalets, complete with snow dusting the roofs and tiny reindeer around the doors. Snowflakes still danced in the air, landing with gentle poufs on our clothes before melting away.

'Oh, this is adorable,' I exclaimed. It was the cutest thing I'd ever seen.

'This is us,' said Noah and gestured to the end cottage. He pushed open the door for me and I stepped inside to find a roaring fire in front of a two-seater sofa piled with blankets and cushions.

I smiled broadly, taking in the fairy lights that lined roof trusses, the picture of Santa and Mrs Claus on the wall, along with a row of nine stockings, each emblazoned with the name of one of his reindeer. Along the mantelpiece were berry-laden holly boughs interspersed with fat white candles, their golden flames flickering and dancing. Above the sofa, a huge branch of mistletoe was hanging so low that I could see the white berries glistening. Immediately I thought of Noah's lips on mine two days before, and a tiny shiver rippled down my spine.

I let out a little laugh, belying my sudden nerves. I so wanted Noah to kiss me again.

'This is just the best. I love it.' I did a little twirl in the centre of the room, trying to avoid sitting down just yet. The plump-cushioned sofa suddenly felt like the elephant in the room. I didn't mention that I thought it was impossibly romantic.

To my surprise, Noah blushed with pleasure. 'I heard about it from my buddy, Todd, who writes a restaurant column for a New York magazine. He says they do a mean cranberry mojito.' He spoke quickly, as if to fill the gap between either of us knowing what to do.

He picked up the menu on the table and handed it to me. 'What would you like?'

'There's quite a choice,' I said, noticing the little handbell on the table with a sign next to it, reading, 'Ring me to order'.

The list included a Christmas Cosmopolitan, Poinsettia, Elves Eggnog, Festive French 75 as well as a Holiday Harvey Wallbanger and a Merry Manhattan.

I chose the Poinsettia, a mix of triple sec, cranberry juice and prosecco, and Noah followed suit and then rang the bell to place our order. We were still standing, when a young woman in an elf costume, not dissimilar to the one I'd worn, bounded into the room.

'Happy holidays and welcome to Blitzen Cottage. What can I get you? And can I put another log on the fire for you?'

She took our orders and then banked up the fire.

'Come y'all, take a seat. Make yourselves comfortable. Take the weight off.'

The invitation was just what we needed and I shed my coat, brushing off the damp. Because it was so cosy, I removed my jumper and took a seat on the sofa, watching the fire as it popped and crackled in the grate.

Noah sat down next to me, and awareness fizzed in the air.

'I bet if you cut down your own Christmas tree, you have an open fire,' I blurted out.

Noah smiled. I wondered if he knew I'd got the jitters

and was nervous of being alone with him. It was starting to get harder and harder to resist the pull to kiss him.

'My parents do. It's my dad's thing.'

'Do you roast marshmallows and whole hogs?' I asked.

'You really buy into the whole Hallmark thing, don't you?' he teased.

'Hell yeah, it always looks so much more cosy than real life. Although I have to say you've surpassed yourself with this place.'

'I aim to please.'

We lapsed into silence, both of us watching the flames dance and sway.

The cocktails, when they arrived, lived up to expectation and the sharp tang of cranberry was softened by prosecco, the gentle bubbles bursting on my tongue. Along with the drinks was a selection of beautifully prepared canapés on holly-leaf-shaped platters, which our friendly elf placed on the coffee table in front of us. My stomach rumbled in anticipation at the sight and smell of the tiny parcels filled with smoked salmon pate and topped with bright, ruby-red roe, pigs in blankets, sausages wrapped in pastry, which although not the same as at home, were delicious, rolls of roast beef on rye bread with hot, yellow mustard and miniature pecan pies that glistened in the candlelight.

'This is Christmas heaven,' I said a little while later patting my stomach. 'Absolutely perfect. Your friend has great taste.'

'Never tell him that, he's cocky enough as it is,' said Noah with a laugh. 'You should meet him. You'd probably like him. He's a journalist, too. He loves it.' Noah turned to look at me. He was so close I could see the colour of his irises, darker blue flecks among the deep blue and they softened in what I guessed was sympathy when he asked, 'What about your job? Do you enjoy it?'

I caught my lip between my teeth, reliving the gut punch when my boss had told me I was suspended. 'I was good at it,' I said, my voice suddenly plaintive. I hated that I sounded pathetic, but I couldn't help it. 'I don't think they're going to reinstate me.' Fighting for control, I turned on him, a touch belligerent. 'I bet you wouldn't blame them, would you? Hardly the greatest advert for their magazine. A financial journalist who can't even spot a financial scam.'

'Don't be so hard on yourself,' said Noah and he put a hand on mine. 'I'm sorry I said what I did, before. I didn't know the background. Now I understand why you were so keen to believe that the prize of a trip to New York was real.'

He squeezed my hand. 'Those bastards touched a sore spot.' He looked at me and his eyes flashed. 'If they'd known … well, they deserve to die a long and ugly death. Although I'm guessing they just got lucky with the scam and you. It doesn't seem fair that you might lose your job as well.'

I felt as if a huge weight had been removed. I took in a breath to see if I could breathe easier. It seemed as if I could. Someone understood. Someone on my side. Someone looking out for me. I hadn't had that for a long time.

I shrugged, doing my best to hide that his words had touched a part of me and it was getting harder and harder to keep hidden under the layers.

Noah continued and I listened because it was a relief to hear. 'These scammers are good at what they do. Lots of people get caught out. At least you didn't lose too much. I've heard of people who have lost hundreds of thousands. Old people losing their life savings. Students being taken for every penny they have.'

'I know,' I said, realising he really was trying to make me feel better and remind me I wasn't the only idiot on the planet. 'It's happening all the time. In fact, it's not talked about enough. Most people, me included, are too embarrassed to admit what's happened. I wouldn't have told anyone if it wasn't for that flipping TikTok going viral.'

'But people need to know,' said Noah, gently. 'You could write about it. As someone who's been through it, I'd have thought other people would be prepared to open up to you and share their stories to help prevent other people being scammed.'

I shrugged again, not really wanting to talk about this aspect. Why draw further attention to my stupidity and risk more people knowing how incompetent I was? That wouldn't help me get another job. Instead, I replied, 'You might be right, but my editor didn't quite see it that way. He said I'd undermined the magazine's credibility and that as a journalist I should have been more savvy.'

'I disagree. I think the message is that even the most savvy of us have to be on our guard.'

'Sadly, he doesn't think like you.' I sighed. Would they fire me in the end? I was good at my job, I hoped that might count for something. But right now, I didn't want to talk about it anymore.

'I love the picture of Santa and Mrs Claus, who do you think the models are?'

I was pleased to see that Noah coped admirably with my tendency to veer off on conversational tangents, something that my work colleagues and flatmates frequently commented upon. I sometimes wondered if maybe there was something wrong with me, but then I decided that there was no point holding back if I had something to say. Life was short. Life was messy. Why did people pretend otherwise? It was better to get things out there when you could.

We spent another hour in the cosy cottage before we reluctantly left the warm cocoon to go over to the ice rink to watch the skaters. I was saving my powder for the Rockefeller Center because that had always been the dream. I'd always wanted to skate on the rink in front of the iconic gold statue of Prometheus that had appeared in *Elf* and *Home Alone* and countless other Christmas movies. That would be the culmination of my dream and the ultimate promise to my mum. She'd said that one day we'd skate together at the rink.

Still dreaming of my moment of triumph, I walked next to Noah out onto the street and around the corner to the imposing New York City library. With its two regal lions, Patience and Fortitude, flanking the arched entrance – I'd read up in advance – the landmark from so many movies, once again felt almost familiar. Although today, each lion guarding the building wore an enormous wreath, which didn't detract from their imposing majesty.

'We have to see the tree here,' said Noah. 'It's a famous one.'

'Of course it is,' I said.

'No, this one is special,' he said. 'It's quite unique.'

I followed him, fully expecting another gaudy, glitzy extravaganza but when we got inside, I was charmed by the unexpected whimsy of the tree. It was decorated as if it was a tree in the forest. Towering over us at well over twenty feet tall, the tree's snow-covered branches bristled with life, tiny robins with beady eyes, snowy white owls in mid-flight, a squirrel peeping out from beneath a fir cone, red cardinals nestled between the boughs, along with bright goldfinches collecting twigs. Enchanted, I stopped in front of the tree, spotting more and more tiny natural vignettes.

'This is…' I turned to Noah. 'Absolutely lovely and totally unexpected.' My eyes shone, I couldn't help it.

Noah's eyes met my mine, and they softened as he looked at me. 'I'm glad you like it.' His voice lowered and I had to strain to hear his words. 'It's my favourite tree in the whole world.'

For some reason, my heart lit up inside my chest and I said very quietly back to him, 'Thank you for sharing it with me.' To my surprise he took my hand and gave it a quick squeeze.

'My pleasure. I thought you'd like to see it because it's original, bursting with life…' He paused. 'It reminds me of you.' Touched, I interlinked my fingers with his and together we stood and gazed up at the tree in complete accord. It was a Noah and Evie moment. Not a film moment. Or a Mum moment. But our moment.

'Hey, would you guys like a picture?' asked the man behind us, thankfully breaking the moment.

'We'd love one,' I said and handed my phone to him.

Noah slung an arm around my shoulder and pulled me in tight. I was happy to tuck into him and just inhale the scent of him.

'You smell nice,' I murmured, because I had to share just a little bit. It was like my weakness was leaking out bit by bit.

'Aim to please.' He hugged me a little tighter for a second as the man took several different shots, even going down on his knees to capture the whole tree behind us.

'Thank you,' I said, feeling a little bereft when Noah dropped his arm. As I looked at the pictures, my smile was bittersweet. You could almost imagine we were a couple. I wasn't sure I wanted to share this one on Instagram. 'What next?' I asked.

'The Empire State Building, of course.'

'Really?' I squealed because, hello, it was second on my list.

'Yeah.' He shook his head at my excitement, but he smiled, too.

'We need a selfie,' I said looking out over the view towards Central Park. The sun was setting and the light fading fast. The sky glowed, a pink sheen tinged with lavender dappling the horizon. Much as I'd loved the view from the Edge, Noah had been right, this was something else. The history, the spirit, the story of this building resonated. The pictures of its construction back in the 1930s were striking, especially the terrifying ones of the workers thousands of feet up sitting on a beam eating their lunch with the city below them. And then of course there were the films, *Sleepless in Seattle, An Affair to Remember … King Kong*. Not quite so romantic, that one.

'A kiss might be good here,' I suggested coyly, although inside I was dying to taste him again. Would it be so bad to give into the undercurrent of want? It wasn't as if it would be anything I needed to worry about. We were both headed in separate directions very soon. Maybe I could play with fire just for a little bit…

'Would it?' teased Noah deadpan.

'Yes, it's one of the most romantic, iconic spots in the city. Did you see *Sleepless in Seattle*?'

'Is that the Meg Ryan one? I seem to recall the ending was a bit cheesy.'

I rolled my eyes. 'It's one of the all-time greats.'

'If you say so.'

'You have no soul.' I gave him an exasperated glare. 'This would be a really good opportunity to give social-media followers the kiss.'

'Hmm,' said Noah enigmatically, not giving anything away, he seemed totally indifferent to the idea. 'Shouldn't we string them along a bit longer. I thought you said the will-they-won't-they build up was what kept people interested.'

I couldn't help feeling a little disappointed. In a matter of days, Noah and I might never see each other again. I was safe from any emotional entanglement, and this would be the icing on the Christmas cake of my once-in-a-lifetime trip. Plus, we owed it to Alicia to give our followers a good show, I told myself.

'You only had to ask.' Noah had caught my expression.

I looked up at him and then the world went still as he looked down at my lips. There was just him silhouetted against the sky and the pink tendrils of clouds behind him, backlit with gold, spread across the horizon.

All the feelings in my heart collided. I was on top of the world with a man who made my heart, body and soul sing. I'd been trying to protect myself from the feelings, but they were breaching every dam I'd attempted to put in place. Now, at the top of the Empire State Building, of all places, I wondered why I was fighting so hard to keep him at bay. What did I have to lose? While these thoughts raced around my head, he'd walked around the corner to the view out over Central Park which spread in a long finger towards the horizon, the snow-covered greens of the trees and parkland bounded by the sharp building blocks of high rises and skyscrapers. I followed him and stopped to admire what was my favourite view from up here.

'It doesn't look real,' I murmured. 'More like toytown or Legoland.'

'I forget how incredible it is,' agreed Noah.

He was so close I wanted to lean against him as we stood there taking in the view. When had the need for contact suddenly become so vital to me? I'd worked hard not to need human contact or support, to be self-sufficient. This was messing everything up.

'My mum would have loved this,' I said with a sigh.

Noah waited a few beats before he said. 'But what about you?'

The words punched into me, weightier than they should have been.

'Me?' I asked, lifting a careless shoulder in one of my usual shrugs.

'Yes,' said Noah, the word suddenly sibilant and heavy with meaning. 'You.'

'What do you mean?' Defensive, I knew, but I wasn't sure where this was going and I wasn't sure I liked it. Another layer being peeled back before I was ready.

'What do you want?' asked Noah, his eyes keen now, his gaze sharp. There was no escaping the sudden spotlight. 'Why are you here?'

'I'm here because … we always talked about coming.' My answer sounded lame and passive.

'You and your mum.'

'Yes.'

Noah scrutinised my face and a sense of foreboding scurried down my spine.

'But when…' he paused, 'when, Evie, do you do things for yourself?' I felt pinned to the spot. 'When do you do things for yourself, instead of this pilgrimage for your mum? Instead of hiding behind the daydreams and what the two of you might have done together.'

'I don't know,' I admitted in a small voice. I didn't dare look up at him, in case he saw all the things that were rising to the surface.

'We need to take some pictures. Sunset at the top of the

world,' I said hurriedly and pulled my phone from my pocket. 'That's what we're here for.' I suspected that on this occasion my bright smile wasn't fooling him, but he was making me look too hard at myself all of a sudden, and I really didn't like it. I wanted to go back to being the fun, irreverent, never-look-ahead Evie who jumped into things without thought. Noah was getting too close, and it scared the pants off me. I was stupid to think I could play with fire, give in to temptation... If I wasn't careful I'd get seriously burned.

Chapter Twenty-Two

NOAH

'No, we're not walking,' I said, ushering Evie into the yellow cab outside of the front of the hotel. As she began to protest, I added, 'It's too cold and too far – and pretty as the snow is, this will be warmer.' The weather hadn't been able to make up its mind today and had veered between sudden unloading of snow to bright blue skies and sunshine. Part of me wished it would snow properly. It wasn't Christmas without snow.

'Okay, boss,' she said, shaking her head. 'It's only a little bit of snow.'

'Are you sulking because I won't tell you where we're going?' I teased. It was fun to mess with her. I was taking her out to lunch somewhere really Christmassy, because after the last couple of days, I'd begun to realise she'd been denying herself pleasure at this time of the year, and I wanted to give her some happy memories.

'I don't sulk.' She stuck her bottom lip out. 'I pout prettily.'

Once again, she made me laugh. 'You do. And it's a surprise. If I tell you where we're going, you'll google it.'

'True,' she said, her face wreathed in a smile. 'I don't like surprises.'

'Now that does surprise me.'

'Why?'

'Because you're spontaneous, ready for anything, always up for a laugh or a challenge. I thought surprises would be "right up your street", as they say in England.'

She wrinkled her nose. 'I don't like having the rug pulled out from underneath my feet. There's a long way to fall.'

Although her expression suggested her comment was light-hearted, I got the impression she meant it. I thought of her earlier talk of her mum and leaned over and squeezed her hand. Sometimes her sadness sneaked through her defences. She'd coped with so much on her own; no wonder she preferred firmer footings, although I wondered if she ever admitted that to herself. She kept up a shield, but I was learning that there was a whole lot more to Evie than I'd first realised.

I linked my fingers through hers and clasped her hand with my other hand with quick understanding. 'I promise this will be a good surprise.'

As we drove along the busy street in the cab, she gave me a soft smile.

'Thanks, Noah.'

After we'd been to the Empire State Building, yesterday, something had shifted between us and even though she gave me a wary, grateful smile, I suspected she was starting to accept someone looking after her.

The stores were lit up in all their Christmas finery, a rainbow of coloured lights and festive scenes as we passed. 'It's just like all the movies,' said Evie a touch wistfully.

From what she'd revealed earlier in the day, I realised that she'd actually missed out on a lot of Christmas traditions and the sense of community and family that so many people enjoyed and took for granted. It seemed that she and her mother had lived vicariously through films because it was an escape from the reality they were both facing. Now it made complete sense as to why she'd been so desperate to come to New York, why she'd fallen for the scam so easily and why she'd stolen her flatmates' money. She wasn't a bad person at all. Just a bit bruised and battered, and most of all, lost. Something inside me ached for her. Wanted to show her that life could be kinder to her. That there was more to Christmas than all the outside glitz. The displays, the materialism. If my parents were back, I would have taken her home and spent the rest of the holiday there. But they weren't, so I was going to bring Christmas to Evie. Give her a Christmas to remember, one that she could enjoy and participate in, rather than look on as if she were still watching a movie. And suddenly I had a dozen ideas of what we could do over the next couple of days.

We pulled up outside Rolf's German restaurant. I'd never been before but I'd heard all about it, and by the slimmest chance had bagged a booking today.

I let Evie lead the way in, with my camera at the ready. It

was the perfect shot when she turned round to face me, her mouth wide open, her eyes shining and behind her the spectacularly glitzy, over-the-top Christmas decorations. The place was like a grotto with stalactites and growths of baubles covering every last inch of the ceiling. It reminded me of a man-made Christmas coral. The undulating outcrops of baubles were interspersed with crystal icicles, while white fairy lights wound their way between them. Every surface was covered, the lampshades, the pillars and the windowsills were also covered bringing a cosy atmosphere to the place.

'Wow. This is Christmas on steroids,' she said. 'I think I love it.'

'I know. Crazy,' I agreed looking round. 'It's more than I could have imagined.'

I gave my name to the waiter, who led us to one of the tables and I ducked my head as we went, worried I might hit it on one of the overhead decorations. The table was laid with a simple white tablecloth, which contrasted with the explosion of colour, sparkle and shine around us.

Evie was already snapping pictures of the decorations. Then she took a selfie of us both.

'I've never really had German food before,' she said.

'I played over there for a little while. In Bundesliga.' I picked up the menu and my stomach growled. I was going to be hard-pressed to choose something. All my favourites were listed.

'You played in Germany? Why didn't I know that? What do you recommend?'

'Everything,' I said. 'And yes, I played there but only for a season on loan.'

'I can't have everything.' She rolled her eyes. 'Seriously. What's good?'

I studied the menu, almost groaning out loud.

'To start with, potato pancakes with apple sauce or potato salad. Both are delicious. Then for the main course. Oh, I don't know where to start. Any kind of schnitzel is good. But then the pork loin with red cabbage is delicious. And wurst is always good.'

'You're no help at all,' she muttered.

'You were happy to follow my lead in the restaurant at The Plaza on the first night.'

'I had jetlag and couldn't have made a choice to save my life that night. Food was just a means to stay awake for longer.' She lifted her head and shot me a mischievous grin. 'And an opportunity to wind you up.'

'Mission accomplished. I thought you were the most irritating woman on the planet.'

'And now?' she asked with a coy smile.

'Same,' I said.

She giggled and nudged my leg under the table with her foot. 'Good. I like to keep you on your toes.'

The waiter arrived to take our orders and I selected a paprika schnitzel, while Evie opted for chicken schnitzel with mashed potatoes and green beans. We both chose the potato pancakes to start with.

'Thanks for bringing me here. Come on, admit it, I've stopped irritating you.'

I realised she'd retreated to teasing/flirting, which made her feel safer because she was keeping things light.

'You've grown on me,' I said casually, even though inside I felt far from casual about her. I felt completely mixed up, but I was horribly aware that I should be focusing on getting back into the team. Evie was too much of a distraction, she made me forget that, as a result of my actions, I'd finished a man's career. I needed to remember how easy it would be to lose everything.

But despite knowing all of that, I was finding it harder and harder to resist Evie.

She made everything light up when she was around. It was like the sun came out inside, and I found myself wanting to spend more time with her. Not that I was the melancholy type. Life of late had been muddied and full of guilt and shame, but when Evie was around it was as if everything was brought into sharper focus. There was no doubt I was attracted to her. It saddened me that for her Christmas was all about the show. It didn't seem as if she'd held onto or developed any special traditions. I couldn't imagine what it would be like without my family at Christmas. It was my favourite time to spend with them.

So I wanted to show her what Christmas could be like if she let it, and I knew just what to do. I consoled my mixed-up brain with the thought that if nothing else, it would be a great photo opportunity.

Chapter Twenty-Three

EVIE

The loud rap at the door startled me.

I opened the door and was surprised when a member of The Plaza staff wearing a Santa hat stood there with an ice bucket and a bottle of champagne.

'Happy holiday delivery for you, Miss Green.'

'Thank you.'

Behind her was another member of staff, this one in a reindeer costume with a pile of boxes in his hand.

I held the door open as they trooped in, followed by two more staff members, one at the head and the other at the bottom of a large Christmas tree. After them came another couple of staff with more boxes and then finally, Noah.

I burst out laughing at the sight of him in fairy wings and a string of tinsel wrapped around his forehead.

'And who might you be?' I asked.

'I'm your Christmas Fairy Godmother.'

'What's going on?'

'I thought we could decorate a tree together,' he said, as the trail of people began exiting the room.

I turned and looked back into the lounge area, where the tree had been placed in the window. My eyes blurred a little.

'A tree.'

'Yes. I thought you might like one.'

I couldn't get the words past the big lump lodged in my throat.

Noah closed my door, and I walked up to the tree and was immediately wreathed in the smell of pine. I reached forward and touched the coarse needles on the nearest bough.

'A real tree,' I said for want of anything else to say, because I really was a little choked and overcome.

'Yup, although not chopped down by me, I did go out and choose it.' He rattled off the words, as if he was trying to make out it was no big deal.

I gave him a startled glance.

'When?'

'As soon as we got back.'

'You went back out in the snow?'

He nodded. 'Yeah, I've obviously spent too much time in the UK.'

My heart swelled in my chest and for a moment it felt as if the floor beneath my feet swayed. I was completely out of my depth. While I'd been reclining in a hot bath thawing out and breathing life back into my frozen and aching feet, having insisted we walk off our lunch, he'd gone out again.

I stared at him, unable to remember the last time anyone

had done anything for me. I blinked, not wanting him to see the rush of emotion on my face. I'd been on my own for so long. Although I had to wonder now if I'd deliberately pushed people away.

I turned away from him and summoned up inner reserves. I wasn't going to melt all over him, even though I wanted to. I was so used to being self-sufficient, it was hard to lower my barriers.

'And what about all this?' I asked, my voice brusque, pointing to all the boxes and bags.

'You'll have to wait and see. You can open them in a minute, but first we have to put the lights on and open the champagne to toast the tree. That's part of the Christmas tradition.'

'What Christmas tradition?' I asked, still admiring the tree which was slightly taller than I was.

'Yours, now,' he said. 'Christmas can be anything you want, but this feels like a fresh start for you. I think you've been hiding from Christmas since your mum died. Maybe now it's time to start embracing it and making your own traditions.'

I shot him a quick look, surprised by his acute perception. 'I don't know what you mean.'

'Yes, you do, Evie,' he said, so gently that it brought tears to my eyes, because he knew me.

I sniffed them back and he smiled at me before simply picking up one of the many bags, although I noticed the logo on the outside, Christmas Cottage. From it he withdrew a large plastic box and handed it to me.

Inside was a tightly coiled string of fairy lights. My

mouth dropped open. They were the pretty warm gold lights I'd admired in the shop.

'Lights always go on first,' said Noah.

'Is that a Christmas rule?' I asked.

'No, it's just common sense,' he said, and I laughed.

'Here, plug them in, make sure they work first.'

I plugged them in and then spent a couple of minutes playing with the numerous different settings.

'Disco or calm?' I asked, trying to sound calm myself, except my pulse was leaping about all over the place, totally overcome by Noah's kindness.

'You're the one who has to live with it. You decide.'

He had a point. While I loved the exuberant flashing, it would get old quite quickly.

We switched the lights off as we wound them round the tree, or rather Noah did. He quickly took over because there was a technique, apparently. So I stood back lending a hand and every now and then he weaved the strand of lights in and out of the tree branches so that the green wire was hidden.

'You're a bit of a pro at this,' I teased. I'd have just laid the lights on top of each layer of branches and wouldn't have been half as painstaking as he was, but the careful concentration on his face was cute. When he'd finished and we switched the lights back on, I could appreciate his care. The sparkling lights peeped from in between the branches, just like the fireflies I'd imagined before.

'It looks so pretty.' I grinned at him, feeling light-hearted.

'Now the toast.' He opened the champagne and poured two flutes.

'Do you know I've never drunk this much champagne in my life? I could get used to it,' I said. Although I knew it would be back to the prosecco when I got home – if I could afford that. There was still no word from my editor following my suspension. I was hoping to be reinstated soon. But I wasn't going to think about that now. It was out of my control.

'To the Christmas tree,' I said raising my glass.

'To Christmas, whatever it may bring,' said Noah, chinking my glass before taking a sip.

'You take this Christmas thing seriously,' I observed.

'Yes, it's always been a special family time. Especially in the last few years when it's the only time we all get together. It's weird, this year, my family being away. I kind of understand how difficult it must be you being on your own.'

'Not really,' I said glibly. 'I usually avoid it. On Christmas Day I work in my godmother's restaurant. It's always fully booked, so it's a busy day. By the time it gets to the evening, I'm so knackered, I just collapse in front of the telly with a pile of leftovers from the restaurant and a bottle of wine.'

'Sounds lonely,' said Noah.

'Well, it isn't,' I said with a sarcastic smile.

Noah stepped in front of me and kissed me on the lips. 'You can admit to being lonely, you know.'

'I can, but I'm not going to,' I said, my bravado

shrinking by the second, my heart completely won over by that quick, careful kiss. 'Now, what else have we got?'

Noah put down his glass and sat down on the floor next to the table and dug into one of the bags, handing me a tissue-paper-wrapped bundle.

'Here you go. This is for you.'

I unwrapped the tissue paper and this time my eyes really did fill up. It was the little yellow New York cab ornament from Christmas Cottage.

'That's … thank you. Sneaky. I didn't know you'd got this.'

I held it in the palm of my hand, watching the light reflect off the silvery surfaces, my heart swelling with … I wasn't sure I could put a name on it.

I glanced at Noah who was watching me with a gentle smile on his face, but he didn't say anything, just let me absorb my feelings. I really liked him for that, not trying to step in and ask if I liked it, looking for approbation and making it about him.

I turned away to the tree and sized it up carefully, wondering about where it should go. High up. Where I could always see it. I fastened it to one of the upper branches and smiled at the sight of it.

It was the thing that broke me. I had enough of fighting against my feelings, trying to protect myself from emotions.

I went over to Noah, held his face in hands and kissed him on the mouth.

'Thank you, I love it.'

'My pleasure,' he said and the warmth in his eyes brought a rush of heat over me. I didn't know how to react around him. My normal MO was to dive in and see where things went without a second thought. But Noah had already demonstrated that wasn't his style.

'Next,' he said holding up a box of medium-sized gold ornaments.

'Aren't you going to help?' I asked and gave him a couple.

Together we hung them at random, but my gaze kept straying back to the little taxi and I couldn't help smiling.

'There,' I said stepping back and exchanging a grin with him.

'Looking good. Here's another one.' From the plastic bag he handed me another tissue-wrapped parcel.

Inside this one was one of the Big Apple decorations, the red fruit topped with skyscrapers.

'Do I get another kiss?' he asked as I held it up to the light.

'When it's hung to my satisfaction,' I said haughtily.

I put it near the top again.

This time the kiss was of the lingering variety and my fingers weaved into his hair at the back of his neck. 'Thank you, Noah.'

'I should have bought the whole store,' he said and tugged me to him, giving me another kiss. 'However, there's more.' He pulled away and handed me a box of large red glass baubles and a couple of strings of tinsel in silver and gold.

It took a while before I was happy with the placement of the tinsel, and he rearranged a couple of the baubles because I'd bunched them all together and there were too many at the top, apparently.

'You need to save space for the special ornaments. These are the fillers.'

'Oh,' I said.

'So, here's a special one.' This parcel contained an Edge snow globe ornament.

'When did you get that?' I asked, my voice pitching in surprise.

He shrugged. I put my hands on his shoulders and kissed him again before turning to place the ornament on the tree.

As soon as I turned round again, he handed me a hot-dog ornament, which made laugh, reminding me of the hot-dog cart we'd visited.

Then he handed me another box.

'You really have been very sneaky,' I said. He had, he'd sneaked into my heart and for tonight I was done fighting it. 'I had no idea you were buying any of this stuff.'

'Good.' He grinned.

This time I almost burst into tears. 'Oh, Noah.'

I lifted the pretty crystal angel from Bryant Park and held it up by the thread between two fingers, the light sparkled through the pale mauve glass. 'It's beautiful. You shouldn't have.'

'There's more.'

I delved into the tissue paper and this time withdrew the tiny scarlet glass dragon I'd admired so much. 'You bought me this?'

'You liked it,' said Noah simply.

'I do. I love it.' A tear spilled down my face and I caught my bottom lip in my teeth.

He lifted my chin, kissing me on the forehead. For some reason the gesture almost floored me. I wrapped my arms around him and hugged him. He held me, my head tucking into the crook of his neck and the world slowed. I felt the seismic shift inside. I could love this man. For a moment I clung to him, savouring the feeling of coming home. I felt him kiss the top of my head. I couldn't let go, even though I knew I'd have to, eventually.

'There's more,' he said sheepishly and produced a couple more packages. 'I've probably gone a bit over the top but…' I unwrapped each one to find an owl just like the one on the tree in the library, a little ice skater in a red dress and red boots which reminded me of watching the skaters at the Rockefeller Center, and finally one of The Plaza, topped with a wreath.

'Noah, this is brilliant.' I hung each one and then stood back to admire the tree. I could see that there was a souvenir of everywhere we'd been together in the last few days.

He came to stand behind me and wrapped his arms around my waist, resting his chin on my shoulder. 'I wanted you to have a Christmas of your own to remember.'

Noah had officially unearthed my heart. I turned around within the circle of his arms. When his mouth lowered to mine, I leaned into his lips pouring all my hope and longing into the kiss.

It was Noah who pulled back, with a rueful smile. 'I think we should switch the lights on and finish the champagne before it gets too late. I've got an early start in the morning.'

'Early start?'

'I've got a training session in the morning. My agent fixed up for me to go out to Orangeburg to do some drills training with New York City Football Club.'

'Wow, that's great.'

'Mmm,' he said, tracing my lips with his thumb in a way that made my knees weak.

I patted his cheek and tried to hide my disappointment, even though I should have been feeling relieved that he was the one slowing things down. 'Oh, the trials of being a professional athlete,' I said flippantly, trying to hide that I was in danger of turning into an uncharacteristic puddle of mush.

'It's a tough life, but someone's got to do it.' His smile was quick, and we both knew that this was merely a raincheck, and the anticipation of what was to come was a rather lovely thing to hold onto.

Chapter Twenty-Four

NOAH

Rolling out of bed on a dark morning before sunrise was never my favourite thing to do – especially when it had been so tempting to take things further with Evie – but I couldn't afford to miss a training opportunity, let alone a prestigious one.

I made myself a coffee and picked up my phone to catch up on what had been going on back in the UK. There was a text from the football club in Orangeburg.

'Training cancelled. Issue with the pitch. Reschedule tomorrow.'

I huffed out a disappointed sigh. I was up now. I might as well head out for a run. There was always the chance that I might see Ice Skating Girl. I'd been on the lookout for her, every day. Two days ago, I caught another brief glimpse of her but again when I reached the rink, she'd gone. Although I'd kind of forgotten why she'd intrigued me so much. My head was now full of Evie Green.

'Morning, Mr Sanderson.'

'Morning, Danny. Cold enough for you?' I asked as I stepped into the brisk morning chill.

He smiled and tucked his hands in the pocket of his heavy overcoat and then produced a pair of handwarmers. 'Swear by these. Warm hands, warm feet – that's all you need.'

I nodded at him and headed towards the park, jogging slowly to warm my muscles up.

As always, the park was quiet, the way I liked it. I don't bother with music when I'm training, I like to focus on my own internal rhythms and listen to my own body. I could hear the thud of my feet on the paths, the bird song and the quite background hum of the city, the traffic, sirens and horns.

I was sweating by the time I reached Gapstow Bridge and I stopped for a breather hunched over my knees before standing up to take in the view of The Plaza. I smiled. What would Evie be doing right now? Would she still be sleeping? An image of those cascading curls spread across a pillow leaped into my head.

Shaking my head to push the thought out of my head, I forced myself into a fast sprint, pushing as hard and fast as I could. I stopped once I was back on the bridge, chest heaving. At least it had done the trick.

I turned to face south at the ice rink, still hauling in oxygen.

And there she was. The ice skater. Today her hair in a high ponytail, bouncing along behind her as she streaked across the ice, weaving in and out of a series of fluorescent orange cones. I straightened, intrigued again because there was something about her that looked … familiar. No, I was imagining it. It couldn't be. I had Evie on the brain.

I set off to the rink side, still trying to work out if I'd conjured up some sort of mirage and determined to find out if my brain was playing tricks on me.

She was still skating on the far side of the rink when I arrived and took up my position by the exit. I unhooked the sweatshirt from around my waist and pulled it on while I waited for her to come closer.

And now suddenly she was skating at twelve o'clock, dead ahead and coming straight towards me, her hair flying behind her. The curls dancing in the … I stared, unable to believe that I'd missed it before.

'Noah?' Evie said, coming to a graceful halt. 'What are you doing here?' She glanced over my shoulder and then around with a definite look of guilt. I looked behind me.

'What are *you* doing here?' I asked.

It was cute the way she suddenly put her hands behind her back, as if she had something to hide and her face turned all cheerful and bright-eyed.

'Skating,' she said. 'Did you see me?' Her eyes were wary, and I wanted to reassure her, tell her how amazing and glorious she was.

'Yes, I saw you. You're incredible … just…' I waved my hand, a little overcome by how brilliant she was. 'You look so happy, so full of life, so free.' I paused, but I had to say it, 'So incredibly lovely.'

'Oh,' she said, so wide-eyed, I leaned forward and kissed her. She blushed. 'It was going to be a surprise. I was going to bang it out at the Rockefeller Center. A sort of, "why, Miss Jones, you can skate" moment.'

I laughed because she looked so crestfallen.

'Would you like me to forget what I've seen?' I asked with a quick grin because she was so ridiculously funny and sweet.

She wrinkled her nose. 'Just don't tell anyone.' She walked as elegantly as anyone could in skates over to one of the benches, where she sat down to remove them from her feet.

'Who am I going to tell? You're really good. How long have you been skating for?'

'Six years. I started about six months before my mum died. I wanted to surprise her. We each had the things we wanted to do if we ever got to New York. Her thing, like I told you. was to visit the top of the Empire State Building. Mine was to skate at the Rockefeller Center.'

'Did you take lessons?'

'Hell yes. A ton of them. When Mum died, I spent all my time at the rink. I started taking lessons then. It was an escape. No one there knew me or anything about me.'

'You must have put a lot of hours in,' I said, still not quite able to believe that this was Evie. It was like I'd picked something up expecting it to be feather-light and it had turned into a twenty-kilogram kettlebell. It overturned so much of the way I thought about her. She had staying power, determination and ambition. It put her in a whole new light.

'Some,' she said.

I raised an eyebrow.

A smile tugged at her mouth. 'I've been going to the rink three times a week for the last two years. Before that, it was every day after work, I'd go and work at the rink in the evenings to pay for my ice time and lessons.'

It took me a minute to absorb this. 'It's so obvious how much you love it.'

'No one can take it away from me,' she said in response with a shrug. 'I don't tell people about it because it's something I do just for me.' She smiled. 'Even Danny at the hotel thinks I just come out for a walk most mornings.'

'Most mornings? I've been … I haven't seen you.' Damn, I'd given myself away.

Evie gave me a sharp look.

I held my hands up, keen to show I'm not a crazy stalker. 'One morning, I saw you from the other side of the field over there, and there was something about you. I wanted to see you again. I had no idea who you were.'

Her eyes lit up and she smirked. 'Do you know what that is?'

'No,' I shook my head.

'Serendipity,' she said with a quick grin.

Chapter Twenty-Five

NOAH

As we walked back into the lobby of the hotel, Alicia appeared.

'Just the people,' she said with a satisfied smile. 'Evie, I've sorted the Swanson lounge for you. You've got it,' she flicked a glance at the watch on her wrist, 'for the next two hours.'

'Brilliant,' said Evie and tugged at my arm pulling me in the opposite direction of the lift.

'Where are we going?' I asked.

'I have a plan,' she said with a triumphant grin.

'Am I going to like this plan?' I asked, smiling back at her because she was so full of fun.

'You're going to love it,' she replied, linking her arm through mine and leading me to a small lounge. In the centre of the room, surrounded by a dozen Christmas trees covered in gold lights, was a glossy black grand piano.

'*Fabulous Baker Boys*? *Pretty Woman*?' I asked, several

famous movie scenes involving pianos flitted through my head. All of them from memory pretty hot. I grinned at her.

'No,' she sighed. 'I wish I'd thought of them. We … are going to recreate the piano scene in the movie *Big* for when we go to the toy store.'

I stared at her, amazed by her ambition. 'We are?'

'Yes. You could do the easy bit on the right-hand keys and I'll do the fancy bits with a C chord, although I'll have to improvise because I've only got two feet but it'll still sound okay.'

I was completely confounded by her evil genius. 'You're either mad or brilliant.'

'I know,' she said, 'but you'll nail it. I've seen your fancy footwork.'

'You have?' It was a throwaway remark, but I was surprised to see that she turned red.

With a shrug she said, 'Might have checked you out on YouTube. Cracking assist for that goal against Crystal Palace earlier in the season.'

'Why thank you,' I took a bow, feeling more pleased than I should that she'd checked me out.

Half an hour later, surrounded by flip-chart paper with the notes emblazoned on them, Evie having run back and forth between the piano, playing the notes and then writing them down, we were well into practice.

'Count of three,' she said cueing the music, which she'd recorded on her phone. This was our fourth attempt, and it went well until we got to the post-C octave, when of course Evie couldn't remember what she was supposed to be doing. But Evie, being Evie, didn't stop, she just improvised, skipping along the paper singing, 'Dee dum da da da,' and then tripping over her own feet as she stumbled and, mid-jump, cannoned into me and I slipped on the smooth surface of the paper and went down taking her with me. As if we'd been playing Twister, we landed in a tangle of arms and legs, with Evie's curls tickling my nose as she giggled helplessly.

'S-s-sorry,' she spluttered, trying to get herself upright and putting her hand right on my crotch. Her head shot up and her eyes widened as she looked at me. 'Sorry.' She moved so quickly her shoulder hit my chin. 'Sorry,' she said again, and then tried to pat my chin but dug her elbow in my ribs at the same time.

I clamped my hands on her waist, touching bare skin where her jumper had ridden up. 'Stop moving,' I growled, wincing in anticipation at her next potential jab.

'Sorry,' she said again and went limp, making me aware of the soft curves of her body pressed against mine.

Her skin was so soft and I couldn't help myself, my fingers grazed the surface of her back.

Her eyes, bright and full of laughter, met mine. So, Evie. There was just something about her. She was always so alive. Right now, there was a hint of challenge in her eyes, as if to say, go on, I dare you.

Why was I fighting this? It had almost been inevitable since the moment she'd given me that cheeky salute in the airport lounge. I tried to remember all the reasons we shouldn't be doing this as the world around us receded and it was just the two of us. I wondered if she could hear the thud of my heart, or feel it banging against her ribs as she nestled against my chest. With a calculated and deliberate move, I dipped my gaze to her mouth, but I still held off. I wanted this kiss. I wanted it to count. I was going to be in control. If I was going to give in, this wouldn't be one of Evie's spontaneous, go-for-it, fun-girl moments. She moistened her top lip with her tongue and her eyes widened. I heard her tiny inward gasp of breath. Anticipation danced lightly over my skin.

The silence was loud in my ears, a rushing noise as I slid my hand into her hair and pulled her head down to mine. Her body softened against mine as our lips touched in a slow, silken glide. The touch sparked a flicker of heat lower in my belly. I wanted to go slow but now that her mouth was on mine, I wanted more. My fingers massaged her scalp in tiny circles as I fought the urge to open my mouth and ravish hers. I slanted my mouth with a teasing kiss, a gentle exploration but my control was slipping. Beneath me, Evie groaned and that sent me over the edge, I opened my mouth and gave her a deep searching kiss, trying to capture some elusive something. I'd never felt this pulsing need before. Evie matched me, move for move, pushing me on.

My blood was thudding in my veins. Even as I kissed the pale skin of her neck, my lips trailing down the smooth column, one hand skimming up her ribcage, the other anchoring her against me, I wanted to touch her, hold her, with a need more desperate than I'd ever felt before. As my hips rocked against her, she responded, pressing against me. 'Noah,' she murmured, her fingers tangling in my hair.

Her head was tilted back, and I could hear her harsh breaths as I palmed her breast. I took my time, gently massaging her through the fabric of her bra, my fingers stroking the skin just beneath the lacy edge. She squirmed beneath me, pushing as if driving for more, but I captured her mouth again, slowing the kisses, slowing the pace. I wasn't going to be hurried about this. I wanted to take my time, tease, taste and savour. I wanted to be in the driving seat for once and give Evie time and attention.

I felt it, the moment she gave in, when she finally conceded, gave up the battle for control. Her body calmed beneath mine and I heard her sigh in pleasure as I worked my fingers into her bra and began to tease her nipples, all the while kissing her, my hips keeping up a gentle nudging pressure.

She wriggled out from me, rose to her knees, wrenched off her top and threw it on the floor.

With dishevelled hair, eyes bright and almost feverish, she glared at me. 'For fuck's sake, Noah.'

Her impatience fired my blood, but I was determined to lead. Evie needed someone who would stand up to her, not roll over at her command all the time.

I kneeled in front of her, holding her gaze before dropping it to look down at the creamy swell of her chest.

'Take your bra off,' I demanded. I could play my own game. I saw the flash of surprise in her eyes. She lifted her chin and put her arms behind her back to unclasp it and let it drop.

She had perfect breasts, round and firm, with tight pink nipples. I leaned forward and touched them one at a time, watching her face the whole time.

'I'd say these are exemplary breasts,' I growled,

watching her face. 'And I lied when I said I wasn't a boob man.' When I grazed my thumb over one tight bud, she caught her lip between her teeth, and I heard her gasp.

'Like that?' I asked, coolly.

She nodded, uncertain now. It made a change. I liked seeing her that way.

'Want my mouth on you?' I asked, my thumbs skimming around each nipple, watching her squirm.

She nodded.

'And what about here? Are you wet for me?'

I let my hand drift down to the juncture of her thighs. Her sharp inhalation was almost a squeak and I felt myself harden even more. Talking dirty had its downsides. I was running out of patience myself.

I took her tight nipple into my mouth, licking and sucking, quickly falling into a rhythm as she began to moan, alternately panting my name and saying please. With my other hand I rubbed at the seam of her jeans, feeling her trying to grind into my palm. Each time she did, I removed the friction until she learned that she wasn't going to be taking control. Not this time.

Her hands went to my waist, and I could feel her tugging at the top button of my jeans. I put a hand over hers, sucking her nipple harder. This time her moan was louder, and she arched her back, pressing her breast against my mouth. I grinned to myself, eased off and licked the taut skin.

'Oh, Noah, please,' she said.

I moved back to her mouth and murmured against her

lips, my hand still pressed against the seam of her jeans. 'What Evie? What?'

'Oh God, I don't know. You … you.'

I kissed her, feeling like I'd won for a change. My hand moved to the front of my jeans…

Suddenly there was a distant bang. And then the sound of heels on the tiled floor.

'Shit,' said Evie, lurching away and grabbing her top. I stuffed her bra down the back of my jeans as she pulled on her T-shirt.

I picked up a sheet of paper and held it up as if I were studying it.

'Hey. you two.' Alicia, her voice bright and bubbly, appeared in the room.

'Hi, Alicia,' said Evie with a fake smile and a very strained voice.

'Hi,' said Alicia. It was like a Mexican stand-off.

'Thanks for all the stuff. It was perfect,' said Evie, referring to the flip chart, paper and marker pens that Alicia had arranged.

'No problem.' Alicia's eyes were darting around the room trying to work out what we'd been up to. Evie hadn't told her the plan. Alicia stepped over to the taped-together sheet of paper, which Evie had turned over to hide the letters that she'd scribbled on there.

She glanced over at Evie who suddenly grinned at her. 'Still not telling you.'

Alicia huffed out an irritated sigh. 'I'm not good with surprises.'

'It's not a surprise, surprise, is it, Noah?

'No,' I said. 'More like making sure we get it right.'

'What's that supposed to mean?' asked Alicia.

'All in good time,' said Evie winking at me.

'I'm starting to regret pairing you two up, now,' she said sulkily.

'No, you're not,' said Evie, still clutching a piece of paper in front of her braless chest and giving the other woman an awkward hug.

'No, I'm not. Although do you think you might manage an on-camera kiss? You know, give them want they want?'

'We're working on that, too,' said Evie with another cheeky wink at me. 'Aren't we, Noah?'

I rolled my eyes, but inside I wasn't so sure I wanted whatever this was between me and Evie being documented so publicly. These bright, sparkly, exciting feelings were too special to put under the social-media microscope. I wanted to nurture them and see where things between us might go. Whatever we had was special, I was sure of it. I just needed to convince Evie because I knew emotion and commitment scared her.

Chapter Twenty-Six

NOAH

'So, who are these people we're going to meet?' Evie asked as we neared Grand Central Station late the following afternoon. It was a brief port of call on our way out to dinner with a friend I wanted Evie to meet. I thought they'd have something in common, both being journalists, and that he might help her because it was obvious she was worrying about not knowing whether she had a job or not.

'Todd. I told you about him, remember? We were at college together. Both played on the soccer team. He was one of those naturally gifted players who didn't care that much about ... well, anything.' I pulled a quick face, remembering the front he'd always put on.

'Right,' Evie said, sounding a little disappointed.

'Sorry, that doesn't paint him in a good light. He's rich, hot and had a shitty upbringing.'

'Still not selling him,' she said, wrinkling her nose. 'How come you're friends with him? He doesn't sound very you at all. Aren't you close with your family?'

'We are but I don't make a big thing of it.'

'No, you hide it well – not part of your bad-boy image.'

'What bad-boy image?' After my partying days and Gabe losing his way, I'd done my best to avoid a bad-boy image, which is why the recent adverse publicity had been so galling.

'Todd is the one with the bad-boy image, although he loves my family. Probably more than he likes me. He's very loyal to his friends. He always has my back. Always used to come home with me on spring break when we were at college and he keeps in touch with my mom.'

'Okay. He's inching back up the scale,' said Evie, screwing up her face with a begrudging twist of her mouth.

'My mom loves him. He's got a girlfriend now, and … well … according to my mom, it's been the making of him.'

'Don't tell me, and now she's nagging you to find a nice girl,' she teased.

'No, my mom's cool with my current status,' I lied. Mom was super-keen for me to settle down.

'You know you have a tell when you lie,' crowed Evie. She folded her arms as if this statement was set in stone.

'I do not.'

'Yup, you do. Your eye crinkles up in the corner. Right there.' She pointed and touched the outside corner of my left eye. 'I bet she worries that girls are only after you for your money. Or because you're a Premier League footballer.'

I sighed, because as usual Evie was bang on the money. 'She's just concerned about how I'll find the *right* girl. That's all.'

'Must be difficult,' she said, laughing at me. 'Being so irresistible and rich.'

'You're so not funny.'

'Your eye is doing that thing again,' she teased, even though I was sure it wasn't.

'You're nothing but trouble, Evie Green.'

'I know, but you wouldn't have it any other way. At least I'm fun.' Her eyes sparkled. She was far too much fun, and I was enjoying spending time with her more than I should.

'Todd works for *CityZen* magazine.' I laughed suddenly thinking of the regular column he wrote. 'He writes the *Man about Town* column, he knows all the best places to be seen and is invited to all the best places. He told me this bar has a three-month wait list.'

'Now he sounds interesting,' said Evie.

'Here we go. The station.' I'd never been before but the building's reputation was legendary.

Evie hooked her woollen gloved hand through mine and picked up her pace. We walked in through one of the side entrances under an arched roof and quickly came into the large main hall, which at this time of the evening, just after seven, was quietening down. Several purposeful commuters strode across the marble floor in response to the tinny-voiced announcements calling people to platforms but there was also an air of calm as if a higher order was presiding over events. Both of us immediately craned our necks to look up at the vast vaulted ceiling, painted in a striking shade of green with gilded illustrations of the zodiac and constellations.

'It's stunning. Imagine coming through here every day

on your way to work. Do you think people ever stop noticing?' asked Evie, walking in a circle as she looked up.

'I hope not,' I said.

'Probably do,' said Evie mournfully.

I smiled, watching her as she frowned in thought. I couldn't help myself, I stepped forward, to rub away the little scrunched up v above her nose. 'I don't think you ever would.'

Evie would always notice the things around her. It was part of her charm and what made her special.

She brightened and grinned at me. 'I think you're right. Did you ever see that film—?'

'*The Fisher King*,' I finished for her.

'Yes,' she clapped her hands in delight.

'Sorry to disappoint you, but no, I've never seen it. For a while they held New Year's Eve waltzes here to celebrate the film, but they've stopped now.'

'Shame. It's a gorgeous scene. The whole of Grand Central Station starts waltzing, all the commuters pairing up. It is quite magical.' She sighed, looking wistful. 'I guess most people don't even know how to waltz these days.' I heard her humming to herself and recognised the familiar one-two-three, one-two-three refrain. I stepped back from her and searched up a waltz on my phone.

I wasn't sure what had got into me, but as the music started, it was worth the whimsicality to see Evie's head lift and the smile of pure enchantment that touched the corners of her mouth. I bowed because it seemed appropriate, and I knew she would love it. 'Dance with me?'

'Oh.' She stood motionless for a moment, and I could tell that I'd surprised her.

I took her in my arms then held out one hand and she placed hers into it. I stepped forward, with my left foot nudging her opposite foot backwards. The steps came back easily and for the first time in my life I was grateful to old Mrs Robbins who'd insisted our class learn to dance.

Evie followed my lead, shuffling at first until her confidence grew, and then we were gliding around the small patch of floor that we'd commandeered, not bothering anyone or getting in their way. Eventually, the music faded and we stopped.

Evie gave me the most angelic smile, standing in a beam of light and I felt my heart go boom inside my chest, as if it had ballooned so hard and fast it had filled my entire chest cavity. For a moment, all I could do was stare back at her.

'That was lovely, Noah. Thank you,' she said simply. 'I'll remember this forever.' She took my hand and linked her fingers through mine with a quick squeeze.

A couple walking past gave us a discreet burst of applause, reminding us that we were not alone.

'Let's go up,' said Evie, tugging my hand and leading me over to the split staircase up to the next level.

We leaned on the stone balustrade looking out over the station. Even a level up, the roof was still a long way above us.

'This really is gorgeous,' said Evie, her eyes soft and luminous with appreciation. 'I'm not sure I'll ever forget this.' She turned and smiled at me. I felt a little tug, like a silk ribbon wrapping around me and easing me towards her.

We spent another fifteen minutes gazing up at the roof. It seemed neither of us were in a hurry to leave and we kept turning to each other and smiling. It struck me how often we were in accord, as much in the quiet introspective times as during the busy, active periods when it was easy to chat and laugh.

As I stared at Evie, at her pretty face and the curls spilling down her back, I realised it would be hard to say goodbye to her. Maybe … I could invite her on a date in London, once I was back on the team and things had settled down.

———

The bar had a speakeasy vibe, and Todd had warned me I'd need a password to get in. I thought he was jerking me around, but when we arrived at the unobtrusive doorway and opened the door, we were greeted with a sharp stare from a balding man sitting on a high stool reading a copy of *The Great Gatsby*.

'Help you?' he asked, sounding disinterested and vaguely irritated that we'd disturbed his reading.

Evie and I exchanged a quick look, and I had that quick frisson of uncertainty. Had I got the correct address?

'We're meeting someone here?'

'Who?' he asked with a long-suffering sigh.

'Todd McLennan,' I said, expecting to be told that we

had the wrong place and to leave forthwith and never darken his door again.

'Downstairs,' said the man and went back to his book.

Evie's face creased up, the silent amusement written all over her face. Like chastened school children, we crept down the concrete steps, hemmed in on either side by walls painted in oxblood red. It wasn't the most inviting entrance and I was beginning to wonder if Todd was playing some elaborate joke, especially when we arrived on the floor below, it was just an empty space, except for a large armoire-style wardrobe.

A petite woman in an overcoat with a brown trilby stepped out from behind a curtained alcove and tilted her head, staring at us expectantly.

'F Scott Fitzgerald,' I suddenly blurted out.

She gave me a nod, opened the wardrobe door and ushered us through.

'Curiouser and curiouser,' murmured Evie, following me.

On the other side of the wardrobe and, yes, we had to push through a few coats, we stepped out into a bar in full swing. The sudden contrast was like a punch to the face. Dark panelled wood covered the lower parts of the wall, the upper part in plush, rich-red wallpaper. Waiters, with a strong barber-shop vibe dressed in waistcoats and striped drainpipe trousers sporting waxed moustaches darted about carrying cocktails, decorative glasses filled with brightly coloured liquids and the occasional tall half pint of golden beer. Judging from the level of noise rocking the place, the loud chatter punctuated with bursts of laughter and shouts of approval, people were having a really good time.

Evie's eyes darted this way and that drinking it all in.

'I think I like your friend already. This place is so cool.'

It took a minute for my eyes to adjust to the light and then I spotted Todd and a woman in one of the small alcoves.

'There they are.' I led the way over.

'Hey, man.' Todd jumped up and gave me an enthusiastic hug. 'Long time.'

We studied each other for the minute demanded when you haven't seen someone for a couple of years.

'Hey, good to see you.' He looked exactly the same as he always had; the asshole had been blessed with the cream of the crop when it came to genes. He was your original all-American boy, except now I noticed something different about him. There was a soft glow about his smile, stripping away the cynicism that had frequently marred his face. Before I could say anything else, he was pulling the woman at his side to her feet.

'And this is Sophie.' Even the way he said her name made it obvious that Sophie was something special. 'Sophie, this is Noah, he plays English football and lives over there. So, you might have something in common with the jerk.' His grin softened the insult. 'We were at college together, so don't believe a word he says about me.' He beamed at her, and I almost fell over in surprise at the way he proudly put his arm around her shoulder and puffed out his chest.

'Hi, nice to meet you,' she said.

'You're English,' I blurted out.

'No shit, Sherlock,' said Todd, rolling his eyes with his usual good humour. He leaned past me and held out his hand to Evie. 'I'm Todd, this is Sophie.'

'Hi, I'm Evie.'

'And you're English, too.' He winked at her. 'What brings you to our shores and how the devil do you know Noah?'

'Long story.'

'Ooh, I like a good story.' Todd rubbed his hands together.

'Play nice, McLennan,' said Sophie. 'Ignore him. Would you like a drink? We were just about to order.'

'Thank you.' Evie took the menu Sophie handed over.

'This place is all about the cocktails. They're really good, and Todd's paying.'

'Nice to see she has a civilising influence on you,' I said to Todd, who simply beamed.

'She brings out all my best bits.'

Sophie blew him a kiss. 'I just pander to his ego, it's easier.'

Evie shot me a quick look. 'Looks like you have interesting friends, Noah.' She turned back to Todd and Sophie. 'Nice to meet you. You can spill all the dirt on Noah. I'm hoping that he really misbehaved in college.'

Todd shook his head. 'Nah, he was always wedded to his soccer.'

I was grateful he decided to be circumspect. I'd been no angel at college.

'Hmm,' said Sophie. 'Next to you that isn't saying much.'

He kissed her firmly on the mouth. 'You know you love me.'

She rolled her eyes but they exchanged one of those secret smiles and I felt a quick nip of … I thought it was envy at first, and then to my shock, I realised it was recognition. It was exactly the sort of smile Evie and I had exchanged in the station.

We ordered drinks and the conversation flowed easily. Todd, Sophie and Evie all had plenty in common, given that they were all journalists. While Todd and I caught up, I kept half an ear on Evie's conversation with Sophie.

'Do you miss going home at Christmas?' Evie asked.

'Not really. Todd and I have been together for three years now and he's not that close to his parents. We'll be spending Christmas with his cousin, Bella, and her husband, Wes. The thing I really miss is mince pies!' said Sophie vehemently. 'This year, I've made my own mincemeat. A ton of it.' She laughed. 'I'll be giving it away.'

'I love a mince pie. Me and my mum used to make them together.' Although Evie's smile was bright, I could hear the echo of grief in her words.

Our drinks arrived, craft beers for me and Todd and fancy cocktails for Evie and Sophie.

'So, how did you and Noah hook up,' Todd asked Evie a little while later, after she had relayed the story of how she came to be in New York.

'Good question,' she said, and looked at me as if checking for my permission to tell the true story.

'It's all right, I trust Todd,' I said. 'We're doing this social-media thing to rehabilitate my lousy reputation after I snapped Rick Menzies' leg in two,' the familiar sickness rolled in my stomach as I said it, 'and to increase awareness of Evie's TikTok account.'

'I heard Menzies has issues,' said Todd.

'Where did you hear that?' I asked, scoffing slightly. It was the first I'd heard of it, and I heard all the locker room gossip.

'I have contacts.'

I raised an incredulous eyebrow. 'In the UK?'

'*Sports World Illustrated* is across the floor. I told Conrad, one of the guys there, that I was meeting you. He mentioned it straight away. In fact, would you be interested in doing an interview with him?'

'No,' I said. 'I'm not talking to anyone at the moment.'

'What if he promised not to mention the tackle?' asked Todd.

I shook my head.

'So, what happens next?' Sophie asked Evie diplomatically, picking up a slender long-stemmed glass of white wine.

Evie lifted her shoulders in one of her trademark *I don't really care* shrugs. 'Hopefully, they'll reinstate me in the New Year, otherwise I'll have to look for a new job.' She pulled a face.

'It's hard,' sympathised Sophie. 'Magazine jobs are being cut all the time. It's all right if you've got minor-celebrity status and a following like McLennan here, but it's important to have another string to your bow. I've set up an online recipe and cooking channel. I use TikTok a lot and I've got some followers—'

Todd dug her in the ribs. 'She's got a ton of followers and her last tip about making herbal ice cubes went viral. She's being modest.'

'I've got a good base and I'm starting to earn from it,' said Sophie with quiet modesty. 'Which the magazine likes because it attracts new readers, so I'm protecting myself.'

'That's a great idea, except "financial journalist" isn't that sexy,' said Evie a little despondently.

'You need to make it sexy,' said Todd with a quick grin.

'Says the man who writes the male equivalent of *Sex and the City*,' mocked Sophie. We all laughed.

'I'm glad to see you're not letting his ego get too big,' I told her.

Todd took her hand. 'She loves me just the way I am.' Although he said the words with a cheeky grin, there was no doubting the veracity of his words. It was a revelation. Sophie was completely different from any of the women I'd ever seen Todd with before. She was pretty, very pretty, but in an understated way. Before, Todd had always swum in a glamorous pool filled with well-dressed and well-heeled women. Sophie, in a simple sweatshirt and jeans, looked positively wholesome in comparison. She balanced him, I realised. Opposites did attract.

I glanced over at Evie and she smiled at me. It was another one of those little moments, when I realised we were both really enjoying the company and we were completely at ease in the situation. Did we balance each other out? Was Evie having a good influence on me? I felt so much lighter when she was around, but then we were both on holiday. This wasn't real life. Was it?

'They were very nice,' said Evie, wrapping her voluminous pink scarf several times around her neck as we walked back down Fifth Avenue to The Plaza. I huddled down into my coat, the tips of my ears already cold. The temperature had dropped and snow was forecast.

'Yeah, to be honest I'm amazed. Todd, well, he won't mind me saying it, but he was always a bit of a womaniser. And now. Well, I can't believe how happy and settled he looks.'

'The love of a good woman,' said Evie, arching her eyebrow.

'More than that.' I thought about it for a moment, remembering the Todd I'd known through college. 'His demons have been settled.' That was it. There'd always been an undercurrent about him, an almost invisible resentment in his cynicism and superficial charm as if he always mistrusted happiness. 'He's happy, and it shows. He'd always been pretending before.'

'Whereas you've always been settled,' said Evie thoughtfully as we came to a crossing and waited for the green light. 'I can tell from the way you talk about your mom and your family. I think I'm like Todd was. Unsettled. Rootless. Aimless, with no idea where I'm going or what I'm doing.' She sounded more despondent than I'd ever heard her and I sneaked a glance at her profile, not knowing what to say.

'Apologies, I sound sorry for myself. Don't mean to be. But Todd and Sophie are proper grown-ups, aren't they?

They seem like they've got it all sussed, whereas I feel as if I'm wandering around in someone else's shoes, that not only don't fit me but aren't my style either.'

Her mouth drooped and when she looked up at me, I was moved by the sadness in her eyes.

'I'm lost,' she said. 'No purpose. No focus. When I go back to the UK, I'll just be going back to going through the motions.'

I reached for her hand as we bumped shoulders, avoiding a boisterous crowd of young people in Santa hats singing 'Jingle Bells' rather tunelessly.

'Evie, don't be so down on yourself.'

Initially I wanted to give her some reassurance, but as I thought about it, I realised that not only was she doing herself a disservice, I had been, too. Yes, she was bright, bubbly and fun, but Evie also brought so much more to the table. I'd actually had more fun with her in the last few days than I'd had in weeks or even maybe the last year. Even when Gabriel and I were ripping up the party scene, it hadn't been fun like this. Half the time it had been anxiety-inducing, wondering if I could keep up. Evie brought a vital new perspective to my life.

'You're an inspiration,' I told her earnestly, stopping in the middle of the sidewalk outside one of the Bergdorf & Goodman windows just across the road from The Plaza. 'You squeeze more enjoyment out of life than anyone I've ever met. You think about other people, you're kind to them and light up their days. I'm the one that's going through the motions. I do my job ... but what happened to the passion I had for football once upon a time? I work hard all the time because I'm scared of losing it all. When did I stop looking forward to things instead of worrying all the time about what I might lose? When did I stop doing new things?'

'What, like hanging off skyscrapers?' she teased, looking upwards.

'What if I told you I enjoyed it?' I'd loved it. The rush, the thrill of doing something out of my comfort zone and the satisfaction of enjoying it as well as achieving a new challenge.

'I know you did. Whereas I'm supposed to be the fun one and I was bloody petrified.'

'You overcame your fear,' I said encouragingly.

'So where does that leave us?' She turned to me with one of her sudden about zigzags of thought. 'I really fancy you, but would jumping into bed with you, because I can, be a stupid idea?'

I stared at her, poleaxed by the characteristic abrupt direction change and by the subject matter. How had we gone from talking about skyscrapers to sex?

'Sorry,' she spoke again before I could say anything. 'There I go again. Jumping in with both feet without thinking.'

'Actually, I was going to say, it doesn't sound entirely stupid. I'm quite keen on the idea, in fact.'

'You are?'

Should I be insulted that she sounded surprised?

'Yes, Evie, but I want to sleep with you because we both want to and we've been building toward it. Not because it feels like a good idea right now or why the hell not? I want to go to bed with you, take my time and savour you.'

'Oh.' Her eyes went as wide as dinner plates. 'Oh.'

I loved it when that was all she could say.

'Maybe have a little fun,' I added. 'Come to bed with me, Evie Green.'

Her mouth opened and shut a couple of times as she stared at me. Adorable confusion clouded her eyes as she chewed at her bottom lip.

She clutched my arm. 'Now I feel … sort of shy and a bit nervous … because I've always just jumped in.' She caught her lip between her teeth again. I lifted a finger to her mouth to release her lip, soothing the skin.

She paused, and then added, 'So how do we go about it?'

I laughed and hooked my arm through hers as we crossed the road towards the hotel, our pace, by mutual agreement, picking up.

'Seriously, you need to ask?'

Chapter Twenty-Seven

EVIE

I'm not sure who was moving faster, me or Noah, as we hurried across the road towards The Plaza.

'Evening, Evie,' said Danny the doorman. 'Cold enough for you?'

I nodded.

'You had a nice night?' Danny pointed upwards to indicate the first few flakes of snow tumbling out of the sky. 'Ah, look,' he said, and beamed. 'They said it would snow tonight. I reckon we'll get a good few inches. I love it when it snows. The city goes quiet for a few hours. You wait 'til morning. It's magical in Central Park.'

A couple of flakes landed on Noah's gorgeous face dusting his long lashes. I wanted to kiss him, capture those flakes with my lips. I sighed with longing, the anticipation almost bubbling beneath the surface of my skin.

'Well, we'd better go,' I said lamely. 'I hope you don't have to stay out here too long.'

'Enjoy the rest of your night,' said Danny.

'Will do,' said Noah, tugging at my hand.

We ran up the steps into the hotel and both began to giggle as we crossed the lobby to the elevator.

'I thought we were going to be there forever,' I said. 'And now I feel bad for not talking to him.'

'I'm sure he'll forgive you, whereas if we'd had to wait out there for much longer, I might not have done.'

As soon as the elevator doors closed, Noah yanked off his shearling gloves, shoved them into his pockets and caught my cold face between his warm hands lowering his head to capture my mouth with icy cold lips.

I wrapped my arms around him and drew him closer, sinking into the kiss.

When the elevator doors opened, we stumbled out, mouths fused as we tried to simultaneously walk and kiss down the corridor.

'Your room or mine?' asked Noah, lifting his head for a brief breath.

'Mine,' I said on a gasp and, still kissing him, fumbled for my key card in my messenger bag.

We almost fell through the door when it opened and Noah pinned me against the wall, his mouth roving over mine while his hand tugged at the zip on the front of my coat and his other hand pushed at one coat sleeve trying to divest me of the down layers. We were like a pair of octopi, all arms and legs as I tried to unbutton his heavy wool coat.

There was a thud followed by a rustle as both coats dropped one by one to the floor.

'You've got too many clothes on,' he said as he unwound my scarf.

I was already hauling up his sweater and the long-sleeved tee beneath it.

He yelped and cursed, tossing my scarf aside. 'Your hands are freezing.'

'Sorry,' I said, relinquishing his mouth to pull his clothes over his head.

I kissed his smooth, taut chest. God he was gorgeous. Nicely muscled with defined pecs leading to a flat stomach and a smattering of hairs that led below his waistband. My mouth watered and I wanted to kiss my way down his stomach. I dropped to my knees and kissed his belly, my lips grazing the smooth skin before nuzzling the soft hair. My fingers were already grappling with his belt buckle.

'Evie,' he murmured. But it wasn't a 'stop, Evie', I was pretty sure it was a 'yes, please, Evie'. I pulled open his jeans and pushed them down to his hips to reveal black jersey boxers and a tented bulge.

'Someone's pleased to see me,' I murmured, cradling him through the fabric.

He grasped my elbows and hauled me up. 'Not yet. I told you. I want to savour you.'

I lifted an eyebrow. 'Savour me?'

'Oh, yes,' he said. 'Every last bite of you.' He gave me what I could only describe as a wolfish grin and my heart fluttered in my chest. I pressed my hands against his chest and stared into his eyes and his gaze softened. 'We're not in a hurry, are we?'

I shook my head, unable to speak, overwhelmed by the rush of feeling.

'I'm going to take my time with you, Evie Green.' His

fingers sneaked under my jumper and circled the sensitive skin just above the waistband of my jeans. He leaned in and kissed me again. A long slow open-mouthed kiss which had my heart singing and made me dizzy with lust.

He pulled off my sweatshirt and then kissed me again, before his fingers drifted to my shirt. He undid the first button and skimmed my collarbone sending light shivers across my skin. When he released the next button, the fabric fell away and he kissed my sternum down to the next button. He worked his way down to my stomach, pulling my shirt from my waistband. His mouth roved over my belly, and I sucked in much-needed air. Then he pushed my shirt back and my sleeves halfway down my arms so that I was caught fast in the material. I stood before him, mute, in my bra.

'Pretty,' he whispered and kissed the swell of my breasts. I wriggled, trying to get free but he'd bunched the material behind my back with one hand and I was held tight. He paused and stroked my face, his fingers tender on my skin as he pushed stray curls off my cheeks. I met his heated gaze, drinking me in as if he were a man dying of thirst.

'I want you, Evie.' His hand glided down my throat to my chest without touching my breasts, his gaze intent. 'Do you want me?'

I nodded, almost but not quite shy. This soft tenderness was new to me and now I knew what he meant by 'savouring'. I wanted to hold onto these feelings, this quiet intimacy, the lull before the storm. For once, I'd made this choice. I'd not just given in to impulse.

With his other hand, he undid my jeans and pushed them down, showing remarkable dexterity as they dropped to the floor around my ankles.

'Mmm,' he purred, looking down my body, and my insides turned themselves inside out. No one had ever taken this much time to seduce me, and although the heated ache between my legs was starting to burn with insistent desire, I wanted to see where it would lead.

He pulled my bra down and his hot wet mouth closed over my breast, sucking in my nipple with one quick pull. My knees almost buckled as I let out a long low moan. The intensity of feeling almost too much to bear. It felt as if we'd been building this bonfire for days, and any moment I might spontaneously combust into flames of pure lust.

His mouth teased and tormented and then he lowered to his knees, his tongue sliding down my belly. His hand palmed my mound. I was so focused on the hot bundle of nerves at my apex that it was only then that I realised he'd let go of my arms. I wriggled out of my shirt and thrust my hands into his hair as he opened his mouth over my damp underwear, nuzzling at my seam. I bit my lip, aware that I was coming apart and any second was going to call his name over and over. I was losing all sense of control.

Noah stood again, his hands undoing my bra and then both his thumbs circled my nipples again.

I almost fell against him, light-headed with desire. 'I don't do this,' I whispered against his throat. Shocked and awed and more than a little scared by the rising tide of emotion washing through my body. I wasn't sure if he heard me or not, because his hot wet mouth closed over my nipple again and I lost the ability to think straight.

I pushed my hands into his briefs and pushed them down, watching as his erection sprang free. I immediately grasped the hard silken length of him, a burst of heat thrilling through me at his low groan.

He captured my mouth again in a long, open-mouthed, drugging kiss, pushed my hand away, shuffling us back to the bed, falling backwards and taking me with him. We landed on the soft mattress, side by side. He shucked off his jeans, taking something out of the pocket and made quick work of my panties. And then we were lying skin to skin. That first full-body-length contact sent a static burst of excitement spiralling through me. I arched into him wanting to feel as much of him as I could.

I heard the rustle of protection.

'This okay,' he asked as he slid the condom down the length of him.

I nodded, mesmerised.

'Come here,' he said and pulled me on top of him his hands caressing my butt cheeks and moving down to separate my legs. The yearning between them was now almost unbearable. Then he rolled us both, until his weight pressed into me. I welcomed the security of his body cradling and cocooning me.

His eyes searched my face for one second before he circled his fingers around my opening.

'Please, Noah,' I begged and lifted my hips.

The desperate invitation was all he needed, and he nudged at me, his thick head easing inside. I gasped at the sensation as inch by delicious inch, he filled me. When he was fully seated, he looked down into my eyes and I felt a quick thread of fear. This was too much but … not enough. I clasped his back and pulled him closer, hiding my eyes from him. I bit him lightly on the shoulder, tasting his salty skin.

'I want more,' I whispered, wanting to lose myself in passion, so I didn't have to think or worry about these feelings of need and hope.

Noah kissed me and then pulled back before pushing home in one smooth achingly perfect thrust that set my nerve endings sparkling with pleasure. He set the pace, and I lifted my hips, sighing his name with each slide and pump, matching his rhythm, until I was breathless and incoherent with desire and desperation.

I felt my core tightening and the little rush of heat before I went over the edge, the orgasm bursting over me drenching me in ecstasy. A second later, he moaned and I felt him pulsing inside me as he came with a loud heartfelt groan, 'Evie, oh God, Evie.'

I clutched him to me and hung on, realising that I might have just made a terrible mistake.

How was I ever going to let him go?

Chapter Twenty-Eight

EVIE

I woke tucked up next to Noah's furnace-hot body, and for a moment, still drowsy, I luxuriated in his warmth. Then gradually the doubts started to creep in. What had I done? What happened next? How did I—?

Then I told myself to stop being so stupid, I was getting ahead of myself. We'd had sex. Very good sex. That was all it was. I could walk away at any time. Noah might not even want a relationship. Maybe what happened in The Plaza, stayed in The Plaza.

Comforted by this thought, I reached out for my phone to check the time. Six o'clock in the morning. We'd slept all night, although it was hardly any wonder. I smiled to myself, when Noah set his mind to something he was assiduous in his detail.

I scanned the screen and a red dot on my email icon caught my attention. Even though I knew I should ignore it, I couldn't stop myself opening up the email. What I saw on the screen made my heart sink.

Noah's hand snaked over my waist, his arm warm and heavy, pulling me back to him.

With my nose pressed to his chest, my hand still clutching my phone, I whispered, 'I've just had an email.'

'Mmph,' he murmured and kissed my forehead.

'From my editor.'

His fingers slid up my back, soothing my skin with quiet reassurance.

I closed my eyes as if that might seal me off from possible bad news. Maybe if I didn't read it, it wouldn't be real. I felt Noah pull back and rearrange himself, sitting up, dragging his pillows up to support him. Then somehow, he scooped me up, putting an arm around me and pulling me into his side, his hand squeezing the top of my shoulder. For the first time in a long time, I was grateful that I had someone to lean on, even if I knew I shouldn't get used to it.

I sighed a tiny sigh of… I wasn't sure what it was, but my heart flip-flopped in my chest, sending sweet warmth radiating through my body and thawing out the deepest frozen parts of me, parts that until then I hadn't realised were still in ice.

Strengthened by Noah's support, I opened up the email and scanned the words. I really liked that Noah didn't try to read them, he let me get on with it, without judgement or putting his spin on things. He just held me as my eyes tracked the message, key components of the sentences registering like blows.

Contract terminated forthwith. Bringing the magazine into disrepute.

I sucked in a breath as comprehension and the consequent fallout spread fast through my brain.

Out of work. Dispensed with. No longer required. The rejection was as sharp as the realisation that my job was the one thing that I'd been good at. The one thing that had given me a source of pride. The thing that gave me some credibility. The thing that I'd carved out for myself after I'd lost my mum.

My throat worked as I struggled not to cry.

For the first time since Mum had died, it felt as if I'd finally reached the bottom. For so long I'd survived, tumbling from one ledge to the next, each time clinging on until the next fall. This was the fabled rock bottom, and now I understood what it meant – I had no place left to fall.

'They've fired me,' I said brokenly.

'Evie...' He breathed my name into my hair and kissed me on the temple. 'I'm so sorry.'

I nodded, not daring to speak because I knew I would cry. I burrowed into him, telling myself I was buying time to pull myself together, and not giving into the comforting warmth of another human body and the simple reassurance that it brought. What the hell was I going to do? Would anyone else employ me?

After a while, Noah spoke, asking, 'Can you get another job? You said you were good at your work.'

'Like Sophie said, magazine jobs are like gold dust.'

'Could you do a YouTube channel like she does?'

I shrugged. 'Like Todd says, finance isn't sexy.'

'If anyone could sex it up, you could.'

I laughed in spite of myself. 'Thanks, Noah, but I think sexing up finance is beyond even my capabilities.'

'Do you know what I think you should do?' said Noah, and I liked the way he phrased it, making it clear he wasn't telling me what I should do, just offering a suggestion.

'No, I'm not a mind reader,' I said, trying for humour because I didn't do feeling sorry for myself.

'I think you should enjoy every last minute of this trip, and have as much fun as you can. Don't let this ruin your dream.'

I leaned into Noah and kissed the side of his throat, my lips brushing the stubble emerging through his skin. 'That sounds like a very good idea. Do you have anything in mind, at this very moment?'

'Funny you should say that. I normally go out for a run first thing, but in the interests of having fun, I can think of another form of exercise.'

'And what might that be?' I asked as his mouth sought mine.

'Sure you haven't got that mind-reading thing down yet?'

'Funny you should say that,' I murmured as I felt my body stirring in response.

———

Half an hour later, I opened the curtains. It was amazing how being with someone else and sharing your problems made things feel a little less insurmountable.

'It's snowed!' I squealed to Noah. 'Proper snow. We have to go out. We need to build a snowman.'

'We do?' He came to stand behind me, looking out of the window over my shoulder, his lips nuzzling my neck.

I turned in his arms, gave him a hard kiss on the mouth. 'Snow time,' I said firmly and pushed against his chest.

'What about breakfast? Coffee?' he asked plaintively.

I rolled my eyes. 'Snow fun first.'

'Okay. I'll go back to my room, shower and dress.'

I beamed approvingly at him, glad that he'd got on board with the programme so quickly. 'That was easy,' I said with a teasing grin.

'I'm getting to know which battles are worth fighting with you,' said Noah with one of his easy smiles. The words touched me. Not only getting to know them, but respecting them too. Noah was very good at letting me be me.

'I'll see you downstairs in twenty minutes.'

'Twenty minutes?' I grumbled.

'I've got a couple of things to do,' he said, tapping my nose. 'Miss Impatient.'

'Always,' I said.

He smiled. Kissed me and pulled on my robe.

'I'll bring this back later,' he said over his shoulder. I sighed at the sight of him in the white robe, pure sex on legs. He opened the hotel door and went back to his room next door.

The water in the shower pulsed over my body, the warm touch reminding me of all the places Noah had touched last night. I felt well used and relaxed, with an overdose of smug satisfaction. He certainly knew what he was doing, and he wasn't a man to be hurried, even though he'd worn my patience to its absolute limit, racking up the tension and torturing me until I could bear it no more.

His skill with his tongue and fingers more than equalled his fancy footwork.

Once out of the shower, vanity dictated that I take a bit of time to put on a little makeup. Just for any photo opportunities, I told myself, as I applied a careful layer of mascara and slick of lip gloss. With a few minutes to spare I hurried to the lift to meet Noah in the lobby.

There was no sign of him, and I hadn't heard him leave his room. I'd even knocked because it seemed the logical thing to do but there'd been no answer.

'Morning, Evie,' called Carol from the front desk with her usual friendly smile.

'Morning! Have you seen the snow?' I called, bouncing over to her. As always, she was immaculately turned out, but this morning, in a nod to the approaching holiday, she was sporting bright-green enamel holly-leaf earrings with berries dangling from her earlobes.

'Hello, some of us had to get through it to get here this morning,' she said, a reproving roll of her eyes.

'Sorry. It's just we don't get snow very often in England. Not like this. I love your festive jewellery. Very classy.'

'Thank you.' She flicked them with one finger and then

her gaze slipped beyond me. She sighed. 'Now that's one gorgeous man looking very fine this morning. And bearing caffeine.'

I turned and there was Noah, his dark hair flecked with snow, holding two takeout cups in his hands. My heart, still tender from our night together, stuttered at the sight of him.

'Cappuccino,' he said and pushed one of them into my hand. 'Keep us warm.'

'You went out and got coffee?' I asked.

'Despite your enthusiasm for snow, I thought you might need one,' he said. 'I might have a cookie in my pocket, too.'

'I bet you say that to all the girls,' I joked, but I inside I was touched by the gesture, warmed all the way through by his care.

Carol was obviously equally impressed because she piped up, 'You're a keeper, Noah. Want to marry me?'

'I think your husband might have something to say,' said Noah with a boyish smile.

'There is that,' agreed Carol dolefully, and as she turned to answer the phone beside her, she handed him a small plastic bag, which he tucked into his pocket. My eyes narrowed at the exchange but before I could ask about it, Noah took my spare hand.

'Ready?' he asked and led me out through the hotel lobby into the snow-softened morning. White flakes whirled their way down from the thick cloud cover, caught like feathers on eddies of wind that funnelled through the skyscrapers around us. I tipped my face skyward and they landed on my skin like crisp ice kisses.

Around us the snow blanketed every surface, softening

the hard edges of the city and muffling the usual, harsh metropolitan orchestra of sound.

Clutching our steaming coffees we headed towards Central Park. Ahead of us, I could hear a group of children calling and shouting, and through the trees I saw them bundled in brightly coloured snowsuits, wearing Wellington boots and scooping up snow with their mittened hands. I smiled at the sight of them and their unfettered delight at the first snowfall of the year, as they kicked their way through the fluffy carpet.

Our feet crunched in the snow beneath our feet with a waxy squeak as we strode along Central Drive.

We came to a large playground. Today it was deserted, and the large area where people normally played football was empty, unmarred by a single footstep.

'This looks like the perfect spot,' I said gleefully.

I began rolling a snowball, which very rapidly grew, and Noah took pictures until it was so big I needed his help to push it. Once I deemed it big enough, I started on a second ball, grateful that I had Noah to lift it onto the first.

'He needs a name,' I said, studying his blank face.

'Frosty,' suggested Noah, straight-faced.

I shook my head and sighed disparagingly. 'You can't call him that. It has to be something better. Something that suits him. You can't name him until he has a face and some other bits…' I looked around for inspiration and then scouted round for twigs for the snowman's arms.

'Of course we can't,' said Noah, smiling at me.

With a flourish, he pulled the bag from his pocket and produced a carrot, six black buttons, a marker pen and two brown cardboard coasters as well as a length of red fabric, which on closer inspection turned out to be a table runner embossed with tiny Christmas bells and holly.

'Allow me,' he said.

'Where did you get those?' I asked delightedly.

'I asked Carol on my way out if she could procure me a carrot and anything that I could use for eyes. She outdid herself.'

'She certainly did,' I said, taking the red makeshift scarf from him and tying it around the snowman's neck. Next, I stuck the carrot in and arranged the buttons in a curved smile underneath it.

I coloured in semi-circles in the coasters to give the snowman a quizzical expression, which I was rather pleased with. It gave him a distinct personality and now I was ready to christen him, but first I had to give credit where it was due.'

'Thanks, Noah. You thought of everything.'

'Carol's the star. The staff really do go the extra mile.'

'They do. They're amazing. You probably think this is a crazy idea, but I was wondering if I should throw them a Christmas party. Very low-key. Invite them up to my room for drinks. Do you think they'd come?'

'I'd come.'

'I'm not offering to have sex with them,' I said, and he let out a shout of laughter.

'Evie Green!' he leaned in and kissed me. 'Of course they'll come. Because they like you. They love you because you take the time and trouble to notice them and talk to them. You're nice to them when not everyone is.'

I shrugged, uncomfortable with the praise. I was just being me with them, not trying to impress anyone.

'I can't decide between Sid or Norman,' I announced to change the subject.

Noah shot me a perplexed frown.

'For his name.' I thought some more. 'I know, Snorman the Snowman.' It was a good compromise between the two and these things were important.

'Snorman's not a real name,' Noah said with a laugh, shaking his head.

'He's a snowman, he can be anything I want,' I declared, grinning up at him.

'I'm fascinated by the way your brain works,' said Noah, smiling.

'Admit it. I'm a lot of fun.'

'I've already admitted that,' he said, grinning. 'And I'm sorry I misjudged you.' He shook his head. 'I didn't know you and I judged you. Unfairly. I didn't understand the context. And I didn't look beneath the surface. It's funny, the first time I saw you skating I made a completely different judgement about you, even though I thought you were a stranger. You're a good person. A really good person.'

'I try. So, will you help me put together a party? I'm going to need to do some shopping and planning.'

'Of course I will.' He glanced at his watch. 'Don't forget. We've got a hot date at the toy store this morning. We could get anything you need after that.'

'I haven't forgotten twinkle toes,' I said. 'We'd better head back.'

'Ahem?' said Noah waving his phone.

I shook my head. 'No. No photos today. This is for us. Real fun. Just us. Don't you agree?'

Noah put his arm around me and kissed my cheek. 'I do.'

Chapter Twenty-Nine

NOAH

F AO Schwartz was decked out for the holiday season and was full of families bouncing with excitement, shiny-faced with anticipation. The store's famous toy-soldier staff, one of the star attractions, were busy showcasing and demonstrating many of the toys on display.

'It's very different to when I was a kid,' I murmured to Evie, trying to take in the hubbub around us. There were Build-A-Bear booths, Lego-building workshops, a Brio train experience, elves blowing bubbles and a Barbie and Ken styling station. Children swarmed around us, darting about like silverfish, high voices exclaiming at each new discovery.

'This is a bit scary,' said Evie, staring around her, as wide-eyed as the children. 'There are so many small people in here.'

'Tell me about it,' said Alicia, who'd come along to film us, because there was no way, talented as she was, that Evie could film us and play the piano with her feet at the same time. Alicia stepped back in alarm as three pre-schoolers weaved around her.

'They're just children,' I said, laughing at the pair of them, remembering Christmas Day with my nephews last year and their innocent joy upon finding that Santa had visited and delivered their presents down the chimney. 'Don't you remember Christmas as a child? The magic of waking up on Christmas morning. Finding presents under the tree.'

Evie looked at me and suddenly her smile was brilliant. 'Do you know what. I'd forgotten.'

I could almost see the memories filtering back.

'Before my mum was ill,' she paused for a moment before allowing the moment to pass. I realised it defined so much of her life and I wondered when it had stopped her being properly present in it. 'When my dad was still with us. Christmas morning was always special.' Her eyes looked a little haunted. 'I always had a stocking from my Dad.' Although she tried to laugh, it emerged as a sad huff. 'It was always full of random stuff that he'd collected throughout the year.' She looked over at the display of toys opposite, and her mouth curved in amusement. 'Honestly, so random. Plasters with Disney characters. A compass from the previous year's cracker. Liquorice allsorts, because he knew I loved them. Socks with puffins, which we'd seen in a gift shop one Easter. A pencil sharpener from a museum visit. A harmonica. Fridge magnets from holidays. A pack of patterned tissues. Sugar lumps.' She smiled at me. 'He was inventive, I'll give him that. My stocking was always an adventure.'

'Reminds me of someone,' I said.

'Yeah, maybe you're right.' She stared at me. 'I don't think about him that often. After he died, Mum didn't like talking about him.'

'Did he have any family?'

'Only very distant relatives. When Mum was dying it seemed insensitive to ask her.' I felt Evie's loss, there was no one cheerleading for her. I realised just how damn lucky I was with my family and how much I owed my success to them and their unflagging support.

'Are you two coming?' asked Alicia, bustling over.

'Sorry,' said Evie, and like chastened children we followed her through the throng to the second floor where the famous piano had been reinstated after the original store had been relocated to the site at the Rockefeller Center.

There were already plenty of children running up and down the keys, creating an ear-splitting cacophony of clashing notes. I wondered how the staff bore it, all day, every day.

Evie handed her phone over to Alicia, who'd brought along a professional-looking tripod, which helped us to encourage the children to let us have a turn on the piano.

'Ready?' asked Evie as the pair of us lined up.

'As ready as I'll ever be,' I said, glancing down at my hand, where all the notes were written. That sharpie Carol had lent me had come into its own today.

'On three,' Evie said, and Alicia nodded.

'Okay. One, two, three.'

On Alicia's cue we both jumped onto the white plastic keys. Evie clicked her fingers to keep the rhythm going and keep us to time while Alicia filmed us.

Nerves and unfamiliarity got the better of me and I muffed the second lot of notes.

'Sorry,' I said to Evie.

'No problem.' She pulled a face. 'It feels very different to bits of paper on the floor.'

'True.'

'Start again,' said Alicia. It had seemed so much simpler in the privacy of the ballroom, without an avid audience. It hadn't taken long for a crowd to gather around us.

On our second take, a couple of kids decided to join in – only they weren't playing any of the right notes, let alone in the right order. Evie chased them off with a fierce glare, telling them if they let us finish, they could have their turn.

'Third time lucky,' said Alicia cueing us up once more.

This time, it all went to plan, and I only had to look at my hand a couple of times. It was a relief to jump on the final notes and I let out a long breath. Our performance was perfect.

'We did it,' said Evie giving me a high-five then running up and down the keys in a discordant victory dance before throwing herself at me. I caught her and without thinking kissed her.

'We did it,' she crowed, linking her arms around my neck, her eyes dancing with delight. She kissed me and hugged me as the crowd began to clap.

Suddenly we both froze, realising that Alicia was still

recording. We glanced over at her and she gave us a big thumbs-up and mouthed 'Perfect.'

Evie gave me an uncertain look.

As soon as we stepped off the piano, the children rushed forward clearly inspired by our virtuoso performance as they tried to copy our moves.

'Brilliant,' said Alicia. 'And I loved the kiss at the end. It looked so natural. Perfect timing. People have been rooting for some action. That was spot on.'

Oblivious to our discomfort, she began packing away the tripod.

Neither of us said a word, just shifted on the spot. We hadn't really discussed this. Then Evie gave one of her laconic shrugs. 'We aim to please.'

Alicia hurried off with all the footage, which she was planning to upload later that afternoon.

'That was fun,' said Evie, picking up her coffee and taking a long slurp. 'I needed that.'

After our piano duet, we'd wandered around the shop before taking refuge in a tiny coffee bar just off the main drag.

'I can't believe the toys kids have now,' she said, marvelling at the bags I had at my feet. 'That Lego is so amazing.'

'And yet they still prefer to play with the wrapping paper and the packaging,' I said, remembering one year when my nephew, Barney, had spent most of Christmas Day climbing in and out of a big cardboard box. To be fair he was only five then. Now at twelve he had more sophisticated tastes.

Evie nodded but she had that faraway look in her eyes again.

'So, when exactly did you last celebrate Christmas?' I asked.

'The year my mum died.' She shrugged and I wanted to grab her shoulders and tell her to stop it. It was her way of pretending things didn't bother her.

'That's your tell,' I said.

'What?' she narrowed her eyes.

'When you shrug,' I said.

She did it again. 'I don't know what you mean.'

'You do it a lot.'

She froze, and I knew she'd been about to repeat the gesture, instead she lifted her chin, deliberately defiant. 'So, what does my tell, tell you?'

'That you're pretending not to care about Christmas. That you pretend not care about a lot of things, but you do really.'

Her mouth firmed in a line and she stared at a point over my shoulder. Then she slumped.

'I told you I keep busy, I work over lunchtime on Christmas Day.'

'What about the evening? Doesn't your godmother invite you to stay.'

'She does, but I always tell her that I'm going to friends.'

'Why?' I asked.

'Because … what's the point? Christmas is about families, and I don't have one. It seems pointless. And it's never like the movies, is it?'

'Family doesn't have to be blood you know. You can find your own family.' I thought of Todd and Sophie and their plans for Christmas. They'd invited me to join them, but I hadn't given them an answer yet. 'And Christmas can be anything you want it to be. 'My neighbour and her children last year had Chinese duck and pancakes because her partner had to go and spend Christmas lunch with his elderly mother in a nursing home.'

'That's one way of putting a positive spin on the day, I guess,' said Evie. 'If it were me, we'd have a whole plate of pigs in blankets and forget the turkey. And I'd have stuffing. And roast potatoes. And no Brussels sprouts – I can't bear them.'

'Would you eat prime rib? That's what my mom always cooks.'

'Ooh, nice, but only if I could have Yorkshire puddings as well.'

'I'm not sure I could persuade my mom to make Yorkshire puddings.'

'So, what do you have for lunch?' she asked.

'We tend to have Christmas dinner rather than lunch,' I told her, thinking of my mom's traditional feast. 'Usually the beef, sometimes a glazed ham, and Mom makes the most amazing mashed potato and we have green beans and carrots. For dessert, my grandma always brings her famous pecan pie, which is the best.'

'Never had it,' said Evie, pulling a yuck face, 'but it's got to be better than Christmas pudding. That's disgusting. My gran would always serve it when I was little and insist I try a piece, even though she doused it in brandy trying to set fire to it. Although she did make brilliant mince pies. I love a mince pie. That's about the only thing I'm going to miss this year.'

'Why not find something different to replace them with?' I suggested. 'Like a cranberry muffin or pumpkin pie.'

'Ooh, listen to you, being all positive and inventive. You sound like me.'

I laughed. 'Christmas should be what you want it to be. You make your own traditions. You can celebrate in whatever way you want but you don't have to avoid it.'

Evie sobered. 'I don't know what my Christmas would look like. I've deliberately avoided putting any roots down anywhere.'

'So, you've got a clean slate. You can do whatever you want.'

She shrugged and then caught herself. 'Maybe I will one day. Now, are you going to be long with that coffee? I need to go shopping and think of some gifts I can give everyone without breaking the bank – now that I don't have a job.'

'Want me to come with you?' I asked.

Looking up she shook her head. 'No, you'll only hold me up. Besides, you've got your tell, too. The last thing you want to do is more shopping.'

'I need to go and do some training. I want to be match-fit, in case my suspension is quashed in time for the Boxing

Day game.' I was still clinging onto the possibility that I might get a reprieve, although I was beginning to wonder what Christmas would look like at The Plaza. It would be very tempting to stay.

Chapter Thirty

EVIE

Noah's text popped up on my screen just after I'd got back from my ice-skating session. There was something completely exhilarating about skating in the snow, although I'd forgone my little red skirt in favour of something a bit warmer. I had something special saved for our trip to the Rockefeller ice rink scheduled for tomorrow.

> Meet me for breakfast at 9am. I have plans for us.

I raised my eyebrows in surprise. He hadn't mentioned this to me yesterday.

I hurried to change as there wasn't much time, and dashed down the corridor to the lift. An air of quiet calm ruled the dining room in the mornings, as if preparing and fortifying the guests for a busy day ahead.

'Morning, Elfie,' said Raoul. 'Usual table?'

'Yes, please,' I said and headed for the table in the alcove.

'Morning, Evie,' said Mrs Evans, lifting Monty's paw and waving at me.

Morning, Mrs Evans. Morning, Monty,' I said and sat down opposite her.

'Your young man joining us?' she asked.

'Yes,' I said, glancing at my watch. 'I thought he'd be here.' It was ten past nine. Not like Noah to be late. Then I looked up and saw him weaving through the tables towards us, carrying a box with as much care and delight as if it were the World Cup trophy in the box.

'Good morning, ladies,' he said and placed the box on the table.

'Morning, Noah, dear. Have you been training this morning? You look…' Mrs Evans's eyelashes fluttered, 'hot.'

He smiled at her. 'And you're looking very elegant this morning. How's Monty? Did he have a good night?'

'He did. I didn't,' she said indignantly, patting her perfect white helmet. 'He had the most terrible gas.' Her voice boomed out through the dining room. 'Honestly, I might as well have a husband. Although at least he doesn't snore … well, not too loudly. I bet you don't snore, do you, Noah?' Her coy expression made me smile and I watched poor Noah to see how he would handle her.

'A gentleman never tells, Mrs Evans. How was your poached egg this morning?'

Mrs Evans's eyes twinkled. 'I'm tempted to say unfertilised, alas, but that wouldn't be proper, and I wouldn't like to embarrass you two young things.'

I almost spat my tea out at that one. The woman had

mischief in spades, it was probably written all the way through her like a stick of rock.

'Are you going to tell us what's in the box, Noah?' she asked. 'You're looking very pleased with yourself. Is it a selection of sex toys?'

Martin, who was more than used to Mrs Evans and her wickedly direct tongue, wasn't on duty this morning, and the poor boy standing in for him turned bright red, his eyes bulging as if he weren't sure whether to laugh or run away.

Noah, on the other hand, was more than man enough for Mrs Evans. 'Funnily enough, it isn't. Although it is something for Evie.' He gave Mrs Evans a wink.

'I knew I liked you,' she said approvingly, taking out her hip flask and putting a quick dash into her coffee cup.

I craned my head towards the shoe box. 'A present for me?'

'Not exactly,' he said. 'You'll have to wait to find out. But you'll both like the outcome.'

'That's cryptic,' I complained, and my hand strayed towards the box, which Monty was sniffing enthusiastically.

Noah moved it out of reach. 'Not until after breakfast. We have a date with Maxim, one of the chefs.'

'In the kitchen?'

'I believe that's where chefs are generally found,' he said, a smile dancing around his eyes.

'Oh, don't be tedious, Noah. I hate surprises and I'm sure Evie does, too.'

'Not always,' I said, remembering Noah turning up with the Christmas tree. That had been a nice surprise. I usually preferred to be the one doing the surprising, though. I liked to know what was going on, which gave me the choice of opting out of something I didn't want to do.

'Right, let's go find Maxim,' said Noah twenty minutes later, having eaten breakfast. He picked up the box.

'Have a good day,' chirruped Raoul as we left.

'Another one to add to my guest list,' I said. 'And Martin.'

'How long is the list?' asked Noah.

'Long enough – but I'm not going to be able to buy gifts for everyone.' That was worrying me, because obviously there were people like Danny, Carol and Angel that I wanted to buy for, but I didn't want anyone else to feel left out.

'Don't worry, I have an idea,' said Noah.

We met Alicia in the lobby. Guests weren't normally allowed anywhere near the kitchens, but she had worked her magic.

The kitchen was vast – or rather, it was a series of kitchens, each responsible for different things. There was a strict hierarchical control at each post, with teams of white-clad staff moving quickly but with purpose. It was obvious that everyone had a place and it all worked with mechanical precision.

Alicia introduced us to Maxim, a tall rangy man with a very full, reddish moustache and a broad chest.

'Good morning and welcome to The Plaza kitchens. Let me take you to the patisserie section.' With an amazing turn of speed, he led us to another area weaving through the throng, despite his size, with a dancer's grace. In fact, the whole scene reminded me of a ballet, with people swirling in and around a giant stage with carefully choreographed moves.

He led us to a large stainless-steel table and Noah put down his box. Now I was really intrigued. As Maxim produced a couple of aprons, Noah opened the box.

'Sophie sent these over for you,' he said and pulled out two large glass jars which had been nestled in bright red tissue paper. There was also a typed recipe sheet.

'Oh, my goodness! Mincemeat,' I exclaimed with a hot rush of happiness. 'What a sweetheart.'

'I thought maybe you could make them as gifts to give out at your party, but the deal is we have to let Sophie have some.'

'Was this your idea?' I asked him quietly.

He shrugged, and I immediately thought of what he'd said about me shrugging. 'That's my tell!' I laughed.

'I've got nothing to hide. I like mince pies, too.' There was a tinge of pink along his cheekbones. I circled the stainless-steel table and kissed him on the cheek.

'Thanks, Noah.'

'It's nothing. Besides, it'll make a great photo shoot. The wholesome couple cooking together.' He winked at me. 'It'll do my rep the power of good. The hard man in touch with his baking side.'

I laughed. 'What hard-man rep?'

He wrinkled his nose. 'Yeah, I'm no Roy Kent.'

Maxim interrupted.

'I'll leave you to it.' He waved at the table, which was set up with everything we'd need. It reminded me a bit of the domestic science class at school. 'Please send someone for me when you're ready to put the mince pies in the oven. Patrice here will be around if you need anything.' He indicated a small dark woman working at the next table who was piping meringue swans onto greaseproof paper with great precision.

'Gosh, that looks very clever,' I said, impressed by her nimble fingers and each perfect swish of the icing bag.

'By the time you've done a hundred, you get quite proficient,' she said, with a smile. 'They're for the Christmas Day buffet. So they have to be perfect. We've been planning for it for weeks. It's a really big deal in New York. Tickets are over two hundred and fifty dollars a head and sold-out weeks ago. It's a real tight operation. Are you planning to come for lunch?'

'Yes,' I said, remembering that it had been one of the first things Carol on the front desk suggested when I checked in.

Patrice turned back to her work, while I eyed the unfamiliar brand of flour and the pats of butter.

'Okay, boss, where do we start?' asked Noah. 'I haven't got a clue.'

I picked up the recipe that Sophie had kindly included and smiled at the words she'd typed beneath it. *Good luck and have fun.*

'First we have to make the pastry,' I said.

'Why does that sound like a threat?' asked Noah. 'Doesn't it come in packets in the supermarket?'

'Not at Christmas!' I told him with mock horror. 'My mum always made the pastry.' A vision of her in the kitchen, running her wrists under cold water to make sure her hands were cold popped into my head. 'She always said, "The secret to good pastry is cold hands and a warm heart."'

'Why the warm heart?' asked Noah.

I sighed, remembering asking a similar question as a child. 'Because if you care when you cook it always tastes better ... according to my mum. Funny, I'd forgotten that. I haven't made mince pies in years.'

'And cold hands?'

'Ah, that's easy,' I said with a dismissive wave, 'if your hands are warm, it releases the fat from the butter and makes the pastry less flaky.' I was still thinking about Mum and the other things she'd said that had remained deeply buried. She'd said the same about wrapping presents, making sure all the corners were tucked in neatly, even though we used newspaper or brown paper and last year's ribbons. She put a lot of thought into presents, and because we were broke, most of them were homemade or charity-shop finds. Despite that, she was meticulous about wrapping each one as beautifully as she could. Then they'd be finished off with a gift tag made from the previous year's Christmas cards, which we'd cut up with an old pair of pinking shears that had belonged to my gran.

I gripped the table, suddenly stricken with guilt, hollow with regret that I'd abandoned Mum's traditions and let them die with her.

'Evie, are you okay?'

Trust Noah to notice.

'Not really,' I said, so quietly I wasn't sure he'd heard over the noise of the busy kitchen.

He came round the table and put his arm across my shoulders. 'Hey. Want to tell me about it?'

I lifted my face, my eyes brimming with tears. 'Not really.' And I didn't. I didn't want to own up to my cowardice to Noah. Not admit out loud that I'd been running away from Christmas all these years, deliberately avoiding the pain and memories. Mum had loved Christmas, every last minute of it. She made it bright, fun and happy, even when she was desperately ill. I felt ashamed that I'd not adopted her spirit but let my grief hang over me like a pall, deliberately eschewing any enjoyment and happiness. It was not what she would have wanted for me. I'd been going through the motions, focusing on the material elements of Christmas instead of the meaning.

I straightened up. Now was as good a time as any to start making some changes. Mum had loved making mince pies – and she'd insisted they were done properly with tiny holly leaves and berries decorating the top of each one. We had work to do.

At my direction Noah weighed the flour and the butter while I put the mixing bowls in one of the freezers to make sure they were ice-cold, which is exactly what my mum had done. His earnest expression made me smile and made me feel mischievous.

I stepped behind him, deliberately bringing my body flush with his and put my hands around him. He smelled so good, I couldn't resist kissing the side of his neck.

'Like this,' I said, touching his hands and guiding them to the bowl.

'Now what?' he asked huskily.

'Like this,' I whispered against his neck, standing on tiptoes, taking his hands and dipping them into the flour.

'Feels soft,' he murmured, 'like your skin.' A flush streaked up my body. He wasn't supposed to turn the tables.

'You rub the butter between the flour and your fingers but gently.'

'I know how to be gentle,' he said, pressing back against me.

I giggled. It turned out, trying to show someone how to rub butter into flour from behind isn't that easy. I sidestepped and moved in front of him.

'Like this,' I showed him, and it was my turn to pay the price as he caged my body against the counter, tugging my ponytail to one side to scatter kisses down my neck.

'Behave,' I muttered, looking around, but the kitchen staff were all focused on their work, not even glancing our way.

'Why?' asked Noah.

'Because making pastry needs to be done with care.'

'I thought that's what I was doing,' said Noah with a suggestive raise of his eyebrows.

'Focus on the job,' I told him.

He pouted and it was the sweetest thing I'd ever seen. 'I seem to recall you started this.'

'And now I'm stopping it.' I laughed. 'Otherwise we'll never get this pastry made, and I've got a party to plan.'

Before long we had smooth balls of pastry in front of us.

'They need to rest in the fridge for at least half an hour,' I told him. 'So, we've got time for a coffee.'

'Do you want to try making some meringue swans?' asked Patrice.

'I'll go and get coffee,' said Noah, looking down at the table of swans with an expression of fear.

'Coward,' I said.

'Absolutely. Be back in a while.'

By the time he came back with coffee, I'd almost perfected a meringue swan, although for accuracy's sake, ugly duckling would be a better description. The wings were a bit short and stubby as was the neck, and the base was rounder and fatter than Patrice's swans.

'At least I'll be able to spot mine,' I joked.

Once we started assembling the mince pies, as usual Noah turned it into a competition, asking Patrice which she thought looked better, even though his holly berries were more like a pile of snowballs.

Patrice shook her head and refused to be drawn. Instead, she borrowed my pastry cutter and in half the time that either of us had managed, knocked up three mince pies and decorated them with perfectly placed holly leaves complete with three, in-proportion pastry berries.

She beamed at us, and Noah and I looked down at her mince pies, which looked a million times more elegant than ours. 'That's how it's done,' she said with a cocky smile, raising one of her dark brows in a perfect arch.

I glanced at Noah, but he was looking at me with a soft smile on his face. 'That's put us in our place.'

'It has, but we can't pass these off and pretend they're

ours. It's not the right thing. People expect homemade gifts to be a bit wonky. Otherwise, everyone would just buy M&S and pass them off as their own.'

'There is that. I do love the way you think.' Noah chuckled and gave me an approving look that warmed me all the way through. He caught my hand and pulled me towards him and kissed me on the mouth, completely unmindful of Patrice standing beside us. The spontaneous, unselfconscious gesture along with his words, eased my roughed-up ego, which was still smarting from losing my job. Inside I felt such a failure, but Noah managed to make me feel special and unique. I could get used to this feeling and that was far too dangerous.

Chapter Thirty-One

EVIE

I stretched and came to with a sleepy sigh, aware of the cold, empty space beside me. Funny how quickly I'd gotten used to Noah being there. I vaguely remembered the quiet snick of the lock behind him when he went out earlier to go training. I sighed again.

I swung my legs over the side of the bed, telling myself I needed to stop thinking like this. We were having fun. I didn't want it to be any more than that. I caught my lip between my teeth, ignoring how my feelings were starting to take root, like tiny weeds winding their tenacious way through the cracks in the pavement. I couldn't get used to this.

But when I heard the door open, my pulse gave a little kick and I couldn't help the broad smile that spread across my face at the sight of Noah, his hair damp with sweat, his chin dotted with peppercorn bristles and his T-shirt plastered to his body.

'Morning,' he said, looking pleased with himself.

'Morning,' I said huskily, just drinking him in.

He smiled at me, his eyes soft and warm, and I smiled back, a little dopey with love. I needed to get a grip. 'Good run?' I asked, suddenly bright, trying to be a lot less sappy.

'Yeah,' he gave me a slow appraisal, 'but no sexy ice skaters this morning.'

'Shame.'

'I'm going to get straight in the shower.' He paused, giving me a candid look. 'Coming?'

'Why not?' I hopped out of bed and sauntered towards the bathroom enjoying the sultry admiration in his eyes as he watched me.

Just by the door, he snatched me up and gave me a quick kiss before he began peeling off his clothes.

One of the joys of having a suite was the superior-sized shower with plenty of room for two, as we'd already discovered over the last couple of days.

'I love your hair,' murmured Noah a little while later, as he massaged shampoo into my scalp, his strong fingers delving into my curls.

'Mmm,' was all I could say, looking up at him from half-closed eyes, my hands wrapped around his waist to anchor myself as the water cascaded down over our slick bodies.

'We could go back to bed,' he whispered, rinsing the bubbles from my hair.

'We could, except we're supposed to be at the Rockefeller Center in half an hour.'

'I'm sure they won't mind if we're a bit late.'

I laughed. 'No. This is the big one. I get to skate in front of that golden statue like in all the movies.' The name escaped me all of a sudden.

'It's a real big deal for you, isn't it?'

'It is and it would be great if you could be my clumsy partner and make my *Serendipity* dreams come true.'

'You know I can't skate, right.'

'That's the whole point. We're recreating an iconic scene. Followers will love it.'

He grumbled a little as we vacated the shower and started to dress.

I waited until his back was turned and then pulled on my ridiculously expensive but also ridiculously cute Santa dress.

'Do you think—? Whoa! That's … a dress.' His enthusiastic gaze skimmed down my legs.

'Like it?' I did a little twirl so that the faux-fur-trimmed skirt flared out.

'I like it. Although I like what's in it better.'

'Nice answer. Smooth.'

He tugged at the cuffs of his sweatshirt. 'I like to think so.'

'There's a hat, too.' I pulled on the little white fur pillbox hat. It was totally over the top, but I loved every last inch of it. It was a homage to every New York Christmas movie ever, and today was my big moment. The one I'd dreamed off for a very long time. I hoped my mum would be looking down and watching.

'Come on,' I said and tugged Noah's hand. He already had a coat over his arm and his scarf, hat and gloves in his hand.

'I wonder where the tree comes from,' I mused as we went down in the lift. 'The one in Trafalgar Square in London is always sent by the Norwegians.'

'I know the answer to that one,' said Noah. 'The head gardener at the Rockefeller Center goes out and chooses one each year and afterwards the wood is donated to Habitat for Humanity which helps families build and improve homes all over the country and in others.'

'I love that it doesn't go to waste,' I said. 'That's brilliant.'

'You should see the crowds on the day the lights go on, it's a huge draw. The most iconic Christmas tree in the city. It was always the first thing my sister and I wanted to see when we came into the city.'

'Morning, Danny,' I called to the doorman, our feet crunching on the well-salted steps.

The snow had turned slushy at the edges of the road, spotted with grey, although the sun caught at the crystals of the heavy overnight frost, making the nearby branches of the trees glitter in the morning light.

'Morning, Evie.' He tilted his hat. 'I'm sure looking forward to your party.' His smile lit up his face. 'Everyone is. It's real good of you to think of us.'

I batted the comment away with my hand. 'It's nothing,' I said. Why wouldn't I invite all these lovely people who'd been so kind to me?

'You're a good girl, Evie,' he said.

'Not really.' As I shrugged, I caught Noah's quick smile. 'We're off to the Rockefeller Center.'

'Have a nice day,' he said and caught sight of Mrs Evans

clutching Monty in her arms. 'Taxi, Mrs E? Pumped-Up Pups?'

'Yes, please, darling. And then on to the AIRE Ancient Baths. I'm in need of a spa today.'

'Excellent.' He called over a cab and escorted the older woman to the car, opening the door for her.

'It's starting to feel like home,' I said with a spring in my step as Noah and I walked the now very familiar route down Fifth Avenue, the pavements completely clear of snow.

The Christmas tree was, as promised, iconic. It towered over us, at least seventy-feet high. The head gardener had chosen well; it was broad and bushy, epitomising the perfect Christmas-tree shape. On top the Swarovski crystal star glistened against the brilliant blue sky. I took a moment and stared up at it, dazzled by the glittering lights interwoven through the needle-clad branches reaching out, as if waiting to embrace those around it. A broad smile spread across my face. It was another pinch-me moment. I was really here. In New York. Just like Mum and I had dreamed about.

Except when we'd talked about it, it was in a future where Mum was better and I had gone on to lead my dream life.

The thought punched into my head like a train hitting the buffers. Mum might have died but I hadn't really moved on, not emotionally. Physically I kept moving all the time, so nothing would stick, so I didn't care too much about anything. Except I was starting to care about Noah. I cast a discreet glance his way and he smiled at me, those blue eyes meeting mine. My heart ballooned in my chest. Who was I kidding? I wasn't halfway in love with him; I was all the way and more.

Noah's phone rang and he waved his hand before it went to his pocket to get it out.

'Nope! There's no time for that. If we don't get down to the ice rink now, it'll get too busy to get any decent pictures.'

'Decent pictures of you?' teased Noah. 'I'm not sure I want evidence of my Bambi on Ice performance. The guys on the team will razz me.'

'I'll hold you up,' I promised and kissed him on the mouth, smiling up at him.

We walked down to the rink and hired a pair of skates for Noah. I laced on my own and put my hat on.

'You look like you could dance in those things,' said Noah, rising to his feet and clumping awkwardly to the barrier.

'Just practice,' I said with one of the quick shrugs that I was rapidly becoming much more aware of.

'A lot of practice.' He smiled and lifted my chin with one hand before tapping my lips. 'Don't sell yourself short. It takes dedication and commitment to build up any skill. I'm not the best player in the world, I just worked real hard at it.'

I smiled at him and squeezed his hand. He had a way of noticing and saying things about me that made me proud of myself. He had my back.

'Why don't you get on the ice first and do your twirly stuff in front of Prometheus and I'll get some footage? Then you can drag me round with you like I'm a shuffly old man,' suggested Noah.

'Okay,' I said. 'But you're not getting out of this.'

'Wouldn't dream of it.'

I gave him a quick wave and stepped out onto the ice. I pushed off, skating around the rink, revelling in the wonderful feeling. There was nothing quite like the easy smooth free glide across the glassy surface. Skating one slow circuit, I acclimatised, getting used to the frigid temperature as cold air swirled around my legs. The ice was fresh and clean, easy to skate on. In my happy place, I increased my speed, the wind streaking through my hair and my skirt whipping up. It didn't take long for me to warm up, the heat of my cheeks a stark contrast to the chilled air around me. Totally relaxed, I moved towards the centre, flipped backwards and skated in sinuous curves. A couple of people stopped to watch and so I prepared with a few turns and then completed a toe-loop jump, landing perfectly on one leg and gliding along in an arabesque.

When I glanced over at Noah, he was holding up his phone in hand, and with the other he gave me a thumbs-up.

I skated over to see him.

'Your turn now,' I said, holding out a hand.

'Be gentle with me,' he said, cautiously stepping onto the ice.

'I won't let anything happen to you, although do you want to give me your phone. You don't want to smash it on the ice.'

'Great, thank you, although I wasn't worried about my phone. I'm more worried about smashing my bones.'

'We'll take it nice and slowly. I won't leave you. Nothing's going to happen to you.'

'This probably isn't a good idea.'

I patted his arm. 'You'll be fine. Stop being a big wuss.'

'Who are you calling a wuss?' he growled and reached for me, almost falling over. I caught him quickly before he overbalanced and kissed him hard on the mouth.

'You're going to be fine.'

'If you keep kissing me, I'm sure I will be.'

I grinned at him. 'We're going to have a great time. Now let's skate.'

Chapter Thirty-Two

NOAH

E vie's skating was so easy and effortless, it was a shock when I finally got onto the ice. I'd forgotten just how fish-out-of-water the uncomfortable boots and the precarious, slippery and unforgiving surface made me feel.

After only two tentative pushes forward one skate took off without me and I did that cartoon running on the spot, trying to stay upright. Evie laughed but grabbed me around the middle and held me upright.

'This is the bit where I get to kiss you,' I said, holding her waist. Standing stationary, I felt quite stable.

She sighed and lifted her face. I tucked her hair back over her shoulder. The funny little hat she wore suited her. Her lips were cold, but she pulled me closer and I almost forgot where we were until some little punk skated past and yelled, 'Get a room, you geriatrics,' and my phone began to ring again.

'Do you want to get that?' asked Evie.

I shook my head. 'I think I should focus on staying upright.'

'You're doing just fine,' she said and took my hand.

I carefully pushed my feet forward one at a time and despite being very wobbly managed to keep my balance. Keeping to the edge, I made sure that I was in hand's length of the barrier as I gingerly crept forward. After almost a full circuit, my confidence increased although I'd hoped I might be better than this. It was a bit galling. There weren't many sports that I didn't take naturally to. Golf, tennis, squash, running and even dancing, I'd always had a natural aptitude at most physical pursuits.

Music started up and a loud waltz played. The memory of Grand Central Station slipped into my head, and Evie and I exchanged looks. She smiled one of those 'couple smiles', reminding me of Sophie and Todd. The music signalled more activity and lots of people began to speed up and weave around the rink in a more rhythmic way. Evie looked longingly at a girl who was sweeping round the rink confidently. Another skater, a man, crossed her path and the two of them, glided in and out of each other in a smooth dance. She was laughing, her head thrown back and he was skating backwards alongside her. Then the man swapped to another woman and another man took his place.

'You can go and join them,' I said.

She glanced at them and then back at me.

'Are you sure?'

'Yes. I'll stay close to the edge.'

'I'll be right back,' she said and swept off to join the fun in the middle.

I was doing fine, building up a bit of speed and I liked to think that I looked a lot less klutzy. Determined to improve – although I had a long way to go to catch Evie – I decided that I'd do a complete circuit without grabbing the rail once. The push-and-glide combo was coming more easily now, along with a sense of accomplishment. Out of the corner of my eye I watched Evie breeze by with a huge smile on her face. She looked so free and happy, and I got it. There was something about the motion, the lack of friction and the smooth glide that I was determined to conquer.

'You're doing well,' said Evie, coming to a graceful stop and turn beside me.

'Yeah.' I grinned at her. 'This is fun.'

'Told you,' she said, playful as ever. 'Come on.'

Together we circled the rink, and I stopped trying so hard, letting myself enjoy the rhythm and flow, feeling the air ruffling my hair.

'Do you miss playing football?' asked Evie. 'I get twitchy when I haven't been skating for a while.'

'Yes. I really miss it. I miss the routine, the train—' The words were ripped from me in the same way that my feet were ripped from under me. One minute I was upright the next I was on the floor and watching some guy tearing past, apologising over his shoulder. I slammed down hard, landing heavily on one knee and pitching forward hitting the ice with my forehead. I blacked out for a second and when I opened my eyes, I was cheek down on the cold surface and I could see Evie's skates in front of my face.

'Noah.'

I lay there for a second trying to figure things out. Pain radiated through my skull and pounded through my knee.

I blinked a couple of times. My head throbbed. A guy, the one who'd taken me out, crouched down beside me.

'Hey, man, I'm so sorry. You okay. Do you need a hand getting up?'

Between him and Evie, they hauled me up to my feet. The minute I was upright I felt sick and dizzy. I tried to focus but even that was difficult.

Evie's blurry face was filled with worry.

'Noah? Are you okay?' she asked.

'Mmm,' I said, still trying to clear my head.

'Let's get you off the ice,' she said, and together with the guy, they somehow shuffled me along the barrier to the nearest exit.

One of the rink employees came over. 'Hey, man, are you okay. You took quite a fall and hit your head. I'm a first aider. Anything else hurt? Can I take a look?'

I rubbed at my throbbing head and winced.

'Head and knee.'

'Looks like you banged your head pretty hard. Did you black out at all?'

I screwed up my face attempting to piece together what had happened. It was all a bit fuzzy. 'Yeah. I think I did. And I've banged up my knee.'

'You'd better go straight to the emergency room and get checked out. Sounds like you might have a concussion and you should check you've not fractured your knee.' The flood of anxiety that filled me made me wince. That could put me out for months.

'I'll call you an ambulance. Then you can get an X-ray. Can you walk to the sick bay?'

I hobbled behind him as he led the way, Evie holding my hand.

'Yeah. Thanks,' I said through gritted teeth, the pain exploding when I took a step.

'Shall I go and get your shoes and things from the locker?' asked Evie, her face screwed up with worry like an anxious mom. She was obviously desperate to do *something* useful.

I nodded again and blew out a breath.

'I'm really sorry, Noah. I feel like this is my fault.'

I shook my head. 'No. I'm a big boy. It's just one of those things,' I said, giving her a pathetic smile, because inwardly I was cursing myself. What a bloody stupid thing to happen and entirely preventable. What had I been thinking?

We reached the sick bay and sat on a long wooden bench.

When Evie returned, she perched beside me and took one of my hands. 'I'm so sorry.'

I squeezed her hand. That made two of us.

My phone rang again, and Evie pulled it out of her pocket. 'Do you want to take this?'

I glanced at the screen.

Crap! There were a dozen missed calls, some from Lara, some unknown numbers – and a couple from Marco, the team manager. He rarely called, he usually got his assistant to message me. My voicemail had blown up with seven notifications. What the hell was going on? Grateful for a distraction from the pain, I listened to the messages.

'Noah. Fuck's sake, pick up the sodding phone. Call me as soon as you get this message,' barked Lara. 'A story has broken in the press. "Rick Menzies. Habitual steroid user." You're off the hook. His bones have been weakened by the drugs. The FA have to reinstate you now. Marco wants you back on the team immediately. You need to get on the next plane.'

'Fuck!' I said. Quickly, I listened to the rest of the messages. A couple from journalists asking for my reaction and the main one from Marco telling me I needed to get back immediately.

'What's the matter?' asked Evie.

I sank my head into my hands. 'I don't fucking believe this.'

'What's happened?'

'My suspension's been quashed. Turns out Menzies is an addict. It's got me off the hook.'

'Oh,' said Evie. 'But that's good news, isn't it?'

I looked up at her and shook my head, which I immediately regretted when it throbbed. It was bad enough that my knee had swollen to twice its usual size, without worrying about swelling in my brain. I had a feeling the hospital might have to cut my jeans off to X-ray it and I was pretty sure I had concussion.

'Not exactly,' I said shortly, knowing that I shouldn't take my frustration out on her. It would be so much easier to blame her. If I hadn't come skating with her today, everything would be fine. Now … who knew?

'Do you think you've broken something?' she asked,

looking down at my knee, catching her lip between her teeth.

I shrugged. 'It's my own fault,' I said tightly. Knowing that didn't make it any better. Fuck. Fuck. Fuck. Why had I done this to myself? I've gone years without fucking ice-skating because I knew it was risky. Shit, it specifically said in my contract, no skiing. What would Marco say about ice skating?

'I'm sorry.'

'Stop saying you're sorry. This isn't your fault. It's my own. I knew it was risky and I should have had more sense. Shit.' I slammed my hand down on the wooden bench and swore again.

Evie closed her mouth, her eyes wide and anxious.

It was my fault for ignoring all the signs. I'd told myself umpteen times to keep my distance from her. Reminded myself several times that I should focus on my training and not allow her to distract me. And what had I done ... exactly that. What the fuck was wrong with me?

I sighed and went to unlace my skates and then had to lean back again as my head swam. I blinked.

'This was a mistake,' I said, turning to look at her.

Evie opened her mouth, and I glared at her.

'Wasn't going to say sorry,' she muttered. 'Do you want me to…' She nodded at the skate on my bad leg.

'No, it's fine,' I said, stretching over and ignoring the pain lancing up my leg.

'I don't mean the ice-skating was a mistake, although it was. I mean this,' I waved my hand from her to me and back again. 'Us. We're too different. You don't think about consequences. I'm trying to be more responsible and take fewer risks. You don't take responsibility for things. You came to New York and you're having a good time, but what will you do with it?'

'Do with it. What do you mean?'

'You never fight back or respond to what happened, or make a plan. You're a journalist, you could write about your experiences, write about New York. You just drift along having fun. Where's your purpose in life?'

Evie glowered at me, but I could tell I'd hurt her. Shit, I hadn't meant to let all that spill out. I just hated that she wasn't doing more with her life. She had so much energy and potential.

Her chin snapped up and seeing the fire in her eyes was an improvement on seeing the hurt. 'It's better than being so driven and determined that you take a man's legs out from under him with a risky tackle and break them both,' she spat.

It was like a sucker punch to the stomach. She was right, and the guilt would never go away.

'Yeah, I know, and I'll live with that every day of my life but I've learned from it. Not to take stupid risks – or rather I should have done. Today is a prime example. I took a stupid risk.' I make another attempt to take my skates off. 'I've learned my lesson this time.'

'Hmph,' said Evie with a disdainful sniff, coming to my rescue and kneeling at my feet, gently undoing my laces. 'Life is about risk. But there's a calculation to be made about what you stand to gain and what you stand to lose. I'm always aware of what I've got to lose.'

'Ha!' I snarled. 'That's rich coming from you, who never sticks to anything because there's a risk you might get attached.'

It was a low blow. I swallowed. 'Let's just face it, this was a big mistake.' Especially now that I might have fallen in love with her along the way.

'Yeah, you said.' Evie stared at me, her mouth set in a mutinous line.

'Surely, you agree. It was a mistake and it's not as if it was ever going to go anywhere.' Except I'd kind of been hoping it might.

'True,' she said, with one of her trademark shrugs. 'I knew that.'

Ouch. I thought of the trip I'd made just yesterday, when I'd thought about asking her to spend Christmas Day with me, maybe travelling home together and the gift I'd already put under her tree. Maybe she hadn't been that invested in the first place. We'd been having fun, maybe I read more into it. I thought… Well, it didn't matter what I thought now.

I needed to get on a plane home and put as much distance between me and Evie Green as I could.

Chapter Thirty-Three

EVIE

The first guest to arrive was Danny, clutching a few beers.

'This is for you, Evie. To go under the tree,' he said, handing over an endearingly badly wrapped parcel. 'I hope you'll like it.' His earnest expression almost finished me off.

'You didn't need to do that,' I said, swallowing hard as more pesky tears filled my eyes when he laid the parcel under the tree like one of the three wise men presenting gold. I didn't deserve presents. Or kindness. I was a terrible, useless person. The last thing I wanted was for anyone to be nice to me.

Noah might have said the accident wasn't my fault, but he wouldn't have been on the ice if it weren't for me. My guts twisted every time I thought of him hitting the ice head-first.

I glanced back at the door, hoping he might walk through it, even if it was just to tell me he was okay. What if he'd fractured his skull? Had a bleed on the brain? How would I know?

He hadn't answered my text asking if he was still at the hospital. He might not blame me, but I blamed myself and I wanted to make things right. I also wanted to know if he really meant that he'd made a mistake, because I wasn't sure it was a mistake. For the first time in my life, I wanted to see where things might go.

I caught my lip and realised Danny was staring at me. 'Thank you. I really wasn't expecting anything.'

There was a second knock at the door and my heart jumped. Noah? I hurried to open it. 'Help yourself to a drink,' I called to Danny.

Disappointment punched hard. Standing on the threshold of the door were Mrs Evans and Monty, along with Carol, Sofia and Angel.

'Happy holidays,' said Carol, who handed me another small package. Mrs Evans followed suit, hers beautifully wrapped in expensive paper and a big gold bow.

'Just a little something from me and Monty. You can put it under the tree.'

Angel also put a large gift bag in my hand. 'That's to go under, too.'

'You weren't supposed to bring me presents.' Tears leaked out again and I dashed them away again, hoping no one spotted them. I led them through to the lounge area and I was grateful when Danny took charge. 'Can I get you ladies a drink?' he asked.

I put my hands on my hips and summoned up an exasperated expression that had no substance. 'I'm supposed to be looking after you guys this evening,' I complained, although I was touched by the way Danny was still looking out for me.

'You are. You put on a party for us,' said Carol, patting my arm. I gave her a smile and hoped she couldn't tell how strained and false it was.

The room filled up with the various people who had looked after me during the last few weeks, but none of them were Noah. At each knock on the door, my heart gave a thud of hope and with every new arrival the weight of disappointment delivered another punch to the gut. Surely Noah would be here soon. I'd sent him a long, apologetic voice message and blown any sense of pride by begging him to come to the party. I'd heard nothing.

It wasn't long before everyone was chattering away drinking wine and helping themselves to the snacks that I'd arranged with the kitchen. There was a pile of cellophane-wrapped mince pies, which I'd mechanically spent the latter part of the afternoon preparing, grateful for something to do. They were ready to be given out as gifts as everyone was leaving, complete with a warning label that they were homemade and to be 'eaten at your own risk'.

'Where's Noah?' asked Angel.

I grimaced. 'I think he's at the emergency room. He wouldn't let me go with him.'

'Oh, no, he came back hours ago,' said Carol, with a blithe wave of her hand.

'What?' I said and automatically looked at the adjoining wall, wondering if he was on the other side hearing the noise.

'Was he okay?' I asked.

'I think so,' said Carol. 'He was just in the elevator doorway. I only saw him briefly, but he looked fine.'

'No crutches or a bandage around his head?' I asked.

'No,' she laughed.

My lips pursed. I was miffed. Why hadn't he come round? At least to let me know how he was? I needed to know that he wasn't badly injured. I crossed my fingers. He couldn't be. I'd fallen plenty of times on the ice, but I'd never broken anything, although plenty of people did. Once again, I looked at the dividing wall. Surely, he'd calmed down now and we could talk properly. I was sure he hadn't meant what he said at the rink, either; he'd been dazed and angry at the situation.

Glancing around, grateful that everyone was mixing so well and having a good time, I sneaked out of the room and knocked on Noah's door. There was no answer.

I sighed and knocked again, much harder this time. I knocked a third time.

'Noah. I know you're in there,' I yelled. 'Stop sulking and come and join the party.' I jiggled the handle.

I wanted the door to open and for Noah to appear. I wanted to hear him say, 'It wasn't your fault. It was an accident.'

I knocked again. 'Is your head okay?'

Still no response. I waited a little longer but there was no sound from the other side of the door.

Guilt pinched at my stomach. An accident that could have been avoided. That should have been avoided. I'd known the risks and ignored them, because I wanted to show off and realise my stupid dream, which now, in comparison to losing Noah, didn't mean a thing.

I wondered if I could ask Angel to use her master key to let me check on him. Make sure he was okay.

'Where've you been?' asked Patrice when I came back in.

'I was looking to see if Noah was coming to join the party,' I said with an isn't-this-all-jolly smile I was far from feeling.

'Noah?' said Danny. 'I put him in a cab to the airport about half an hour ago.'

The words sort of floated around in my head like errant feathers that were impossible to get hold of.

'What did you say?' I finally asked.

'He had to go home. Play soccer.'

'What about his leg? His head? Did he say anything?'

Danny looked bemused. 'He was limping a little. I asked him about it. Badly bruised, he said.'

'And he's gone?'

Danny nodded. 'Did he say if he was coming back?'

The doorman's eyebrows drew together like two caterpillars facing off against each other and he winced. 'Gave me one hell of a tip. You two had a falling out?' His face immediately signalled sympathy.

'No,' I said, aiming for breezy. Instead, my voice came out as a strangled croak. 'We were just friends. It was never anything. Just a publicity thing. You know. We both needed some good press.'

Danny frowned but before he could say anything, Mrs Evans interrupted. 'Evie, this is a simply lovely party. I just wanted to say thank you. Would you and Noah like to join me and Monty at lunch tomorrow?'

'That would be lovely,' I said, my ultra-brilliant smile hiding the way I collapsed in on myself inside, wondering when I should tell her Noah had gone.

He hadn't even said goodbye.

Chapter Thirty-Four

EVIE

The cork fired out of the bottle with a satisfying pop. Still wearing my pyjamas, I filled my glass and crossed to the window to look out at the city. I'd always envisioned the way I'd spend Christmas Day from the moment I knew I'd be here.

'Happy Christmas, Mum. I made it.' I lifted my glass and looked heavenwards hoping that she was looking down on me. I took a hasty sip to combat the painful twist of my heart. What would she think of me? Noah had made it clear what he thought of me. I sighed. Not thinking about him today.

Would Mum be pleased I'd done all the things we said we'd do? Or might she have wanted more for me?

It was no good. Noah leaving when I wanted him to stay had shown me that I'd been avoiding any kind of permanency. I sighed. It was long past time that I got some help. The idea had been haunting the back of my mind ever since the day I'd spoken to Debbie, the stylist at

Bloomingdale's. She'd talked a lot of sense. I realised that she'd been right, too. I hadn't given therapy enough time. A scant few sessions were hardly enough to unpack and process so much emotion. Grief did funny things to you. It had convinced me that the pain would never be cured and that it was easier to run away from things that reminded me of Mum, or to indulge in the pretend reality we'd created as we'd watched all those films together. What had I really achieved by coming here? Living out a fantasy that had been built on desperate hopes and dreams as Mum faded away. This wasn't real life.

Tears ran down my face. I'd made such a mess of things this year. Coming to New York had been an excuse to avoid Christmas, just like I'd done every year for the last five years.

Except this year, Noah had helped me create some traditions of my own and shown me what Christmas could be like. I looked over at the gorgeous tree in the room and all the special decorations he'd bought for me. I moved to stand in front of it, inhaling the scent of pine. My first real tree. I trailed my fingers over some of the ornaments, my touch releasing a snow globe of memories tumbling through my mind. Eating hot dogs on the street, mustard on Noah's very kissable lips, the trip to the Edge where Noah had been the one to support me. The little yellow taxi, reminding me of Noah humouring me when I insisted on walking instead of hailing a cab. He'd been unfailingly kind on all of our trips, even when I irritated the hell out of him.

I paused. I did irritate the hell out of Noah. And no wonder. He was riddled with guilt about injuring Rick

Menzies, and I'd insisted on posting pictures on Instagram of him having a good time at every opportunity. I never really gave him a chance to say no to any of our excursions. It was hardly surprising he'd bailed at the first opportunity. I didn't blame him. It wasn't as if he'd ever made any promises to me, and it certainly wasn't as if I'd expected any.

I was too commitment-shy to even give whatever it was between us a name. Relationship. Friendship. I'd refused to put a label on the simmering, obvious attraction between us because it made things so much simpler. If he left – it was as expected. People leave you. Nothing is forever. So, I'd made it easy for Noah to leave by never expecting anything from him or asking him for his view on what was going on between us.

I felt a leaden sensation, hard and heavy as a rock, in my chest. It made it difficult to breath properly, as if I could only draw in three-quarters of the air I needed.

Even though it was the last thing I should be doing, it appeared I needed a full-on wallow in misery, so opened up my Instagram account and looked at my current story – still available. Not quite twenty-four hours had elapsed since Noah and I had stood under the Christmas Tree at the Rockefeller Center. I studied the selfie. Noah, complete with cheesy grin pointing to the tree with a double thumbs-up. I'd captioned it in red lettering – Is this the most iconic tree in New York?

There were so many likes. Our second-highest engagement. Alicia would be delighted, although it would take some going to outdo the toyshop piano reel that had garnered over fifty thousand likes. It seemed you couldn't beat a spontaneous kiss.

I traced Noah's smiling face, those amazing blue eyes and put myself back in the moment, remembering the feel of his hands on my waist, pressing his body against mine to protect me from the crowd around us.

I shivered, suddenly cold, and wrapped my arms around myself, trying to combat the sudden pang of loneliness. It was a good few hours until lunchtime and I was not going to wallow a single second more. I refused to feel sorry for myself. It was Christmas Day. I was in New York. In a suite. With my own Christmas tree and presents.

I sat down on the carpet, putting my champagne glass beside me and pulled out the stack of mismatched presents, taking Danny's first. I'd planned to savour each one and take my time with them but the paper on his gift came apart as soon as I touched it, revealing a pack of Starbucks ground coffee, a glittery thermal mug and two packs of Oreos. I smiled, thinking of all the times I'd passed him with takeout cups of coffee. Danny, a sweetheart, who become a familiar face very quickly, greeting me every day.

The next present was wrapped with so much parcel tape that I had a hard time getting into it, which was rather appropriate as it was from Bernard and the maintenance team. They'd given me a little toolkit that included a tape measure, a screwdriver and a small hammer, along with a roll of duct tape with a sticky label attached, which read 'in case you take up serial-killing' which made me laugh.

Carol had bought me an insider's guide to New York for next time I came back, while Angel had given me a New

York keyring and some hair scrunchies made by her daughter. There were also a couple of boxes of chocolates, a Plaza bathrobe with my name embroidered on it from the whole front desk team, as well as a very fancy New York notepad and pen from Alicia. Everyone had been so thoughtful and kind.

I decided to keep Mrs Evans's gorgeously wrapped present to open at the table, glad that I'd also bought her and Monty gifts.

As I pulled her parcel out, I spotted, right at the very back, a blue Tiffany bag. Puzzled, I looked at the label.

To Evie

Merry Christmas. Don't open before Christmas Day.
Noah x

I drew my knees up to my chest and stared at the bag.

When had he put that there? He must have hidden it earlier in the week. For a moment I wondered if I ought to open it. Maybe he didn't want me to have it now.

I peeked inside the bag. Inside was a familiar blue box, tied with a white satin ribbon. I took the box out and set it on the carpet. I picked up my champagne and sipped while considering the box with all the caution of an explosives expert studying an unexploded bomb, not daring to touch it.

Would Noah still want me to have this? Where was he? What was he doing? Was he spending Christmas on his own?

Was it a test? He probably just didn't have time to retrieve the box before he left. With the stress of his injury and the rush to leave, he'd no doubt forgotten it was even there.

Should I return it to him? That would be the responsible, moral thing to do, wouldn't it? The sort of thing, he would do. I picked up the box and popped it back into the bag. I'd return it via his agent as soon as I got back to the UK. It would be wrong to keep it.

Then I pulled the box out again and gave it a little shake. There was an enticing metallic rattle. There was no harm in looking, not if I wasn't going to keep it. I eyed the perfectly tied white bow on the top of the box that I could never replicate. No. I wasn't going to give him the satisfaction of even thinking that I'd been tempted. It was better that I didn't know.

For a moment, it was tempting to text him and tell him that I'd found it and that I would be returning it. But that would be for my own satisfaction. Me, saying, 'Here, you were wrong about me. I can do the right thing.'

Before I could change my mind, I stood, picked up the bag and went and put it in my suitcase out of sight and hopefully out of mind.

I watched half of *It's a Wonderful Life* before I showered and put on the Christmas dress that Debbie had insisted I needed. The dark navy velvet hugged my figure, the dress skimming my legs just above the knee and making me feel glamorous and Christmassy. Like this was a special occasion. It was nice dressing up, and I was glad I'd listened to Debbie. She knew her stuff. I put the red bow in my hair for an added festive touch and did my makeup properly for a change.

Funny how clothes could make you feel so much better. Not only did dressing up give me a purpose but it also heightened the sense of anticipation. I was looking forward to lunch and all dressed up, doubly so. 'Sorry, Mum,' I whispered. She'd been right all along. I slipped my feet into heels and with one last look in the mirror, I headed down to the dining room to meet Mrs Evans and Monty.

Chapter Thirty-Five

EVIE

'Merry Christmas, Mrs Evans. Merry Christmas, Monty. Happy holidays, Martin.' The waiter pulled out a chair for me.

'Happy holidays, Evie, and thank you for a lovely party last night. That was real fun,' he said.

'Pleasure,' I said. 'You've all looked after me so well.'

'All part of the service.' He nodded. 'Now, can I get you ladies a mimosa?'

Mrs Evans sniffed. 'Mimosa my ass, Martin. Give me a straight champagne. It's the holidays.' She winked at me. 'And Evie will have the same.'

'Excellent choice, madam,' said Martin with a wry smile. 'And anything for Monty?'

'Champagne plays havoc with his digestion. A bowl of water will be fine, thank you.'

Martin retreated and Mrs Evans turned to me. 'Now, my dear, you must call me Reine. It is Christmas, after all, and I don't think we should be standing on ceremony anymore.'

'That's a lovely name,' I said.

'I know and rather fitting. It's the French word for Queen. Oh, look at those dear little girls, the Greenford Family.' She waved over at them.

'Happy holidays, Mrs Evans,' said Mrs Greenford coming over with the youngest of her girls who was dressed in the cutest little black velvet dress with a taffeta tartan skirt and a matching bow in her hair. 'Hello, Evie. Merry Christmas.'

'Merry Christmas,' I replied, as usual struck by how calm and serene she always appeared. At her side, Sasha bounced on the spot like a little jack-in-the-box.

'Happy holidays.' She held up a wrist decorated with an assortment of friendship braids. 'Santa came. He found us.' She nodded and then added confidingly, 'He always finds us.'

'Of course he does, darling,' said Mrs Evans. 'He's very clever like that.'

'I made these. There's one for you.' From her pocket she produced a little wrapped package and gave it to Reine. 'And one for you, Evie.'

'Can we open them now?' asked Reine.

'Yes. Sorry I haven't got one for Monty, but Mummy thought that it would be dangerous to have on his neck.'

Mrs Evans beamed at Mrs Greenford. 'How thoughtful,' she said, opening the little parcel. Inside was a friendship braid woven in hues of purple, orange and lime green.

I followed suit to find one of sky-blue and lime green. 'Gorgeous. Thank you so much Sasha,' I said, touched that I'd been included.

'Oh, isn't that lovely,' exclaimed Mrs Evans – it was taking me a little adjustment to think of her as Reine. She immediately held out an imperious wrist. 'I have to wear it right now.' With great delight the little girl tied it on to her wrist.

'I think Monty might be a bit jealous,' Mrs Evans declared. 'Thank you so much. I asked Santa to bring you a little something, too. It's probably on your table.'

'Really?' The little girl's eyes widened, and she looked hopefully towards the table.

'That's really kind of you, Reine. You really shouldn't.'

'I know,' said Reine and then after a brief pause she gave Mrs Greenford one of her classic mischievous grins. 'But I get so much pleasure out of it. They are sweethearts.'

'These are for you.' Mrs Greenford handed over a large box of Godiva chocolates.

'You're very naughty, too. Are you trying to sabotage my waistline?'

'Of course,' said Mrs Greenford, glancing over at her husband. 'Duty calls. Have a lovely day and we'll see you later in the lounge for the carols.'

Mrs Evans held up her wrist to admire the little braid. 'I'm not going to take this off until I go home. It will go with everything. It's perfect.'

Sasha bobbed a little curtsy and dashed away.

It seemed the right time to offer my gifts.

'Here you go. One for Monty and one for you.'

'Oh, how kind of you!' trilled Reine. 'I do love presents. My first husband was wonderful at buying gifts.' She lifted a diamond pendant hanging at her throat. 'He bought this for our thirtieth wedding anniversary.'

'Very nice,' I said. It was very beautiful, tasteful and discreet but very, very sparkly.

'How many husbands have you had?'

She laughed. 'Just the one. Sadly, he died ten years ago, and lovely as he was, he was troublesome. It's so much easier at my age living on my own. I can be deliciously selfish.'

Her eyes danced with their customary, naughty twinkle. Then she sobered. 'But it gets lonely. Life is a long road when you're on your own. It's so much more fun when it's shared.' She glanced around the room as if she didn't want to be overheard. 'I miss him terribly.' She clutched the diamond between her fingers, and I realised it was a familiar gesture. 'That's why I come here every year. I can't bear being on my own at this time of year. Everyone is busy with their families, and I hate being the ghastly old hanger-on – the spectre at the feast as it were.'

'You don't have any family?' I asked.

She shook her head. 'Wilf and I left it too late. Too busy with our work. I don't regret it. We had a ball. Children would have slowed us down.'

I nodded. I eyed Sasha on the other side of the room, laughing with her sister as she tugged off the wrapping paper.

'So, what happened with Noah?' Mrs E went straight for the jugular. 'If I'd known you were throwing him over, I'd have made a pitch.'

'Who said I threw him over?' I tried to sound cocky and failed miserably, I sounded more like a sulky teenager.

'Because he was smitten, girl. I can tell, especially as the man can't keep his eyes off you.'

'He left,' I said with a shrug, grateful that Noah wasn't around to identify it for what it was. 'We had a disagreement. The end.'

'You're giving up far too easily.'

'Not really,' I replied. 'It's not as if it were a proper thing. Circumstances brought us together for a short period. A Christmas-holiday affair. We had fun, and now after Christmas everything goes back to normal, doesn't it? All the decorations get put away. You eat all the leftovers and life carries on.'

'Aren't you the cheery one.'

'Christmas is just one day. Beneath the tinsel there's no real sparkle.'

'Wash your mouth out, Evie Green. Christmas is about building traditions and sharing the joy. It gets us through the long winter days. I don't have any family, but I can still enjoy the season. You can give a lot; you don't have to receive. In fact, giving is much more fun.' She smiled and looked over at the Greenford family. 'They're having a lovely time.'

Sasha waved and then jumped off her chair and came racing over, clutching a Barbie in one hand.

'Thank you. Thank you. Thank you. I love her. She's my favourite present. Mommy says you chose it for Santa.'

'I did.'

'And Daddy got a Ken doll!' Her eyes were round with awe.

'I think he probably needs it with all the ladies in the house,' said Mrs Evans, her wrinkles deepening as she chuckled.

'That's what he said,' said Sacha before she darted back to the table.

'Did you buy that?' I asked.

'Yes, I thought he'd see the funny side of it.'

We both glanced across the room and Mr Greenford raised the Ken doll and waved it with a big grin on his face.

'I think he does,' I said, loving that despite us all being in a big hotel where it might have been very impersonal, there was still a strong sense of community.

'Ladies, your champagne, and would you like to help yourselves at the buffet?'

'Lovely, thank you, Martin.'

My mouth watered as I considered the glistening roast turkey, glossy glazed hams, golden beef Wellingtons. What to have? Then there was an extensive seafood selection, with orange-veined lobster, plump pink prawns and dressed crab, along with a range of sauces. There were roast potatoes, mashed potatoes, potato dauphinoise, new potatoes and even chips, along with creamed kale, roast parsnips, baked carrots, red cabbage and big jugs of steaming gravy. And of course, there were stuffing balls, pigs in blankets (although they were in pastry blankets rather than bacon – still looked delicious) as well as cranberry sauce, mustard and even tomato ketchup.

It was hard not to go crazy, and around us several

people had piled their plates high with considerable engineering prowess. Managing some restraint, I opted for a seafood starter of prawns, a tiny bit of lobster and some salad before going back for roast potatoes, beef Wellington, parsnips and carrots covered in a ton of gravy.

Even Monty had his own plate of turkey, gravy and a couple of little sausages.

We drank a delicious red wine, which Mrs Evans ordered, and she told me all about the places she'd lived in the States.

'I love New York. I always come back, but there are some wonderful places to visit. Definitely Alaska. And some of the national parks. Yosemite's one of my favourites but it gets very busy in the summer. And you should visit Long Island. I have a place there. Come stay this summer.'

I smiled knowing that people said these things but didn't really mean them.

'This is a once-in-a-lifetime trip,' I said.

'Why? You wouldn't have to pay for accommodation in Amagansett. And you could come and go as you please. The beach there is wonderful.'

'I...' I genuinely didn't know what to say. 'I never thought past getting to New York and now I'm here...' I swallowed. 'I'm all out of ambition.'

'Well, that can change,' said Mrs Evans – I was never going to be able to call her Reine. She smiled, her kind eyes studying me.

I gulped down a glug of wine, feeling tears swimming in my eyes. 'I think I need to do a lot of changing.'

Chapter Thirty-Six

NOAH

The emergency room had been crazy. Thankfully, a quick X-ray showed that I'd have a whopper of a bruise on my kneecap but there'd been no internal damage. Since then, I'd been on to the team physio (Shelley – less than impressed with my choice of antics) at regular intervals, with a determined strategy to ensure I'd be fit in less than two days' time. I didn't mention the concussion or the fact that I probably shouldn't be flying.

Flying on Christmas Eve evening was even crazier. JFK was bedlam, filled with anxious, busy people, pushing and shoving in their desperation to get home for the holidays. Christmas spirit was in short supply especially with me. I'd snagged the last seat in first class at an exorbitant price because I just wanted to get home. Not even the cabin crew wearing jolly Santa hats could improve my mood. I elevated my leg all the way home but that didn't stop me brooding and cursing myself. I could have really screwed my career up. What if I'd done my ACL – that would have been six months off. As it was, I didn't know if I'd be able to play on Boxing Day.

I limped through arrivals at Heathrow on Christmas morning and was immediately faced by a wall of people, excited faces scanning each newcomer with great anticipation. The sight made me doubly aware that I'd be returning to an empty flat without so much as a Christmas tree.

I thought of the tree in Evie's hotel room. For the first time I allowed myself to think of her. She'd be fast asleep. Guilt twisted in my gut, even though I was still furious with myself. This was for the best. I shouldn't have allowed her to distract me from my original purpose. But ... she'd be alone. I remembered the gift I'd hidden under the tree. In a couple of hours, she'd find it. I wondered what she'd think. I hoped she'd like it and maybe forgive me for not saying goodbye.

But my brain thought otherwise and helpfully supplied me with a slew of memories: Evie's laughing face, her infectious grin, her mad, morning hair, her slender willowy form and the magic she made on the ice.

Then I spotted the first photographer – or rather he spotted me.

'Noah! Noah Sanderson!' The call went up like a wolf to its pack. Suddenly there were a crowd of them around me, snapping away and I remembered why I'd left. I hadn't missed any of this.

'Hey, Noah. What do you think of the news about Menzies' drug use? Did you have any idea?'

'When were you made aware he was on steroids?'

'Has he reached out to you?'

'Are you going to sue?'

The questions rained down on me as thick and fast as hailstones. It seemed as if Todd's friend had been right. Menzies had been using steroids.

I held my up hands. 'Merry Christmas, guys. No comment at this time.'

Exactly as promised, the private car was waiting to pick me up, and while the airport might have been busy, the M4 was quiet, and it didn't take long to drive back to Chelsea. I looked up at my apartment block, some windows lit up with trees and Christmas lights, others blank, no doubt because the occupants had decamped to spend the festive season elsewhere.

The apartment felt eerily quiet when I stepped through the door. I'd got used to Evie's noise and colour. Everything here, not just the sound, was muted. I glanced at the sand-coloured sofa, before moving my gaze to the amber-desert walls and the striped ikat rug in shades of pale brown – all chosen by a very expensive interior designer. Everything was beige. Even my bedroom was dull, containing the full spectrum of pale grey.

I huffed out a dissatisfied sigh and opened my suitcase, sorting through and unpacking. I wondered if I would be one of the only people in London to put the washing machine on today, such was the excitement in my life.

Christmas dinner turned out to be a pizza for one in front of the television watching *It's a Wonderful Life* for about the fifteenth time. Every ten minutes, I'd take a turn around the apartment in an attempt to keep my knee from stiffening up, before reapplying the ice and propping my leg up on a pile of cushions. At 3pm. I sent a picture of my slightly less swollen knee to the team physio. My head felt okay, apart from a dull headache and a slight lump on my forehead.

> FFS Noah. It's Christmas Day. No decision can be made until I see you tomorrow. I'll get to the ground early but I'm not promising anything.

Three o'clock here. Evie was probably awake. Had she opened her presents?

No text from her.

At five I made myself a protein shake and stood in the kitchen, drinking the unappetising sludge. Lunch time in New York. Evie would be in the Palm Court dining room. Would she be drinking the Californian Syrah we'd drunk that first night at dinner? Would she be enjoying her first proper Christmas in years?

And I had no right to ask any of those questions. I'd told her as much. I regretted it now. It had been anger and frustration talking. I'd been too quick to say the words, and she'd done one of those careless shrugs, but this time it suggested maybe she really wasn't that bothered. Perhaps if I kept telling myself that, it might finally get through, because otherwise I was going to be full of self-recrimination, wondering if I should have called her from the airport when I'd landed.

Jetlag caught up with me and I fell asleep on the couch falling into a dream world full of Evie. We were eating

Christmas dinner on a boat in the ocean, surrounded by pirate Santas on small bamboo rafts who were tossing stockings out to hungry sharks – and all the while Evie was promising that no harm would come to me if I jumped into the water. Apparently, the sharks would be much more interested in the contents of the stockings.

I woke with a smile on my face because that was so typical of Evie's logic, and then I realised I was cold and alone in the dying embers of Christmas Day. It was easily the worst Christmas I'd ever had.

'Hey, Sanderson,' called one of my teammates in the car park, getting out of his Porshe Cayenne. 'You're back.'

'I'm back.'

'Good to see you, mate.'

I followed him into the underbelly of the stadium for my meeting with the team physio, hoping that my attempts to hide my slight limp were working. All I needed were some strong painkillers and I'd be in business.

'Let's take a look, soldier,' said Shelley, the physio, who, despite being a bare five foot had more strength in her upper arms than a weightlifter. The bruise had come out in peacock glory, a colour palette of purples and dark grey.

'Ouch. That must have hurt.'

I shrugged, which immediately reminded me of Evie; I'd even picked up her habits. Another good reason to put her on the top shelf at the very back of my mind. Unfortunately, as with all things Evie, she didn't want to stay there, and I'd already thought about her a dozen times this morning.

'I presume you didn't tell Mario that you were ice skating.'

'What do you think?'

Shelley smirked at me. 'I think I've got me some blackmail material.' Her quick retort reminded me of Evie. Agh. That damn woman was lodged in my head.

'I know, bloody stupid. You don't need to tell me.'

Shelley rolled her eyes. 'Get over yourself, Sanderson. Shit happens. It's not a sackable offence.' She began poking and prodding my leg. Twisting and manipulating the knee.

'You been icing it.'

I nodded.

Her mouth twisted.

'I can run on it,' I said.

'No,' she replied, reminding me, despite her diminutive size, of a small tank. Immovable.

'All I need is a bit of pain relief.'

'It's badly bruised. You need an MRI scan to see if the bone is bruised.'

My shoulders sagged. 'Seriously?'

'I'll fix one up for this week. Sorry, Noah, I can't sign you off as fit to play yet.'

'So, why aren't you playing?' Lara's drawl came from behind me.

'Happy Boxing Day to you, too,' I said, as she took the seat next to me in the Chairman's box.

'I flew you back for the game. What happened?'

'I'm not match-fit.'

'You told me you were still training in New York.'

I sighed. 'I went ice skating. Banged my knee. Shelley wants me to have it scanned before I can play again.'

'No wonder you're looking so down in the mouth. But at least you're back in the game. And your rep has been revitalised. Actually, your approval ratings are through the roof.'

'Approval ratings?'

She laughed. 'You know what I mean. I had two sponsorship enquiries last week and an endorsement pitch. Free boxer shorts for life, if you want them. People really loved the chemistry with Evie. Good job there. I had no idea you were such a good actor.'

I closed my eyes. 'I wasn't acting.'

Her head whipped round to look at me so quickly, I'm surprised she didn't dislocate her neck. 'Noah, you dark horse. That's cool. When's she back from New York?'

'I don't know. It was a thing when I was there. It's not a thing now.'

'A thing. You old romantic.' Lara shook her head. 'What did you do to fuck it up?'

'Why do you think I fucked it up?'

She scrunched up her mouth and looked at me with utter disdain. 'Of course you did.'

'There was nothing to fuck up. We got on well, we had fun but long term we're not compatible.'

'Not compatible? What are you, a robot? What's wrong with her? Everyone in social-media land believes you're the perfect couple. They're going to be sad you didn't get your happy ending.'

'Boo-hoo,' I said.

'So, you're not seeing her again?'

'No.'

'That's a shame. I could have done a lot with that.'

'Sorry to be so disobliging.'

She snorted. 'You been reading Jane Austen or something. Seriously, Noah, I sometimes think you need to loosen up a little. When you were with Evie, it looked like the two of you were having a blast. I've never seen you look…' she clicked her fingers, summoning up the word, 'carefree. That's it. Carefree. It was a good look on you.'

It had felt good, too, I thought, picturing Evie with windblown hair on top of the Empire State Building, mischief in her eyes. That was before … I wouldn't forget that night in a hurry. The piano. Her makeshift piano keys. The feel of her body pressed against mine. The breath caught in my lungs, and I had an involuntary moment of panic. What if I never saw her again?

'Hey, Lara, how's my favourite rottweiler?'

The voice of one of the management team snapped me back to the now as he came to sit with us.

I took in a couple of shuddery breaths and let their conversation about transfers and deals wash over me. Evie was no good for me. I had to put her out of my mind. Focus on getting back on the pitch and forget New York.

Chapter Thirty-Seven

EVIE

'Here you go, dear,' said Reine passing me one of the pristine napkins. 'Wipe your tears.'

'Thank you.' I sniffed and used the pure white damask to dab at my face. 'Sorry, I didn't mean to let all that out.'

'As they say, better out than in, and a bit of drama makes a change from the usual boring lunch, doesn't it, Monty?'

The dog had come to sit on my lap and kept nudging my hand as if to say, 'See, it isn't so bad really.'

'Yeah, but it's Christmas Day,' I sniffled. 'I shouldn't be spoiling it.'

'You're not,' said Reine although she put her hand out and patted mine to take the edge off the comment.

'Thanks for listening. I feel better for getting it off my chest.'

'Good. So now what are you going to do about it? He clearly cares about you.'

'Cares about me? I think he hates me.'

'You're feeling sorry for yourself, dear, and playing the

victim doesn't suit you.' She poured us each another glass of wine, finishing the bottle and then waved over at Martin. 'We're going to need another one of these – and dessert.'

While I mopped myself up and drank a few fortifying sips of wine like a proper damsel in distress, Reine persuaded Martin to bring us a selection of sweet things from the buffet. Then she turned her attention back to me, steepling her fingers as she fixed me with a stern stare.

'Do you think he's right?' she asked. 'In his character assessment of you. Was it a true summation of what you're like? I have to say, I like Noah and he's a fair man. I think a good judge of character. Take a minute before you answer and consider it properly.'

It didn't take me long before I nodded miserably and whispered, 'Yes.'

'In that case there's nothing to be done.'

I gaped at her. 'What do you mean?'

'If you think you're all those things and agree with him. Then there's no argument is there?'

'Pardon?'

'Sorry to be blunt. But if you accept that's the way you are – you're the only one with any control over it. If you're not happy being seen that way – you have a problem.'

'What do you mean?'

'Do you want to be irresponsible? Do you want to live life without worrying about consequences and the future? If the answer is yes, then you don't have a problem, do you? Noah was right.'

'That's brutal,' I said, more than a little shocked by her candour.

'No point telling you he was angry and didn't mean it if you agree with him, is there? If you don't agree, then you have a right to feel pissed at him. Your choice.'

I stared at her, stunned by this revelation.

'Ah, Martin. What have you brought us?'

He put a large plate on the table filled with fat, chocolate profiteroles, pecan pie, delicate macarons and a festive cheesecake – along with a couple of ramekins of chocolate mousse and crème brulée.

'There you go ladies, enjoy.'

'Nothing like sugar to cure heartbreak,' said Reine.

'I-I'm not h-heartbroken…' I stammered.

She tilted her head and gave me a don't-give-me-that-crap look.

I sighed. Somehow along the way I'd fallen for Noah.

'The big question, my dear, is what you're going to do to get him back?'

I swallowed hard, facing the reality. 'I don't think that's going to happen. I'm not what he wants.'

'There's a big difference between what the head wants and what the heart needs.'

I shook my head. 'Noah won't come back, and to be honest, I don't blame him. I need to sort myself out before I can even start to think about the future. I haven't got a job, I need to make amends with my flatmates, and I need to … to get some counselling.'

Reine moved seats to come and sit next to me, taking my hand and clasping it between both of us. 'I think you've already taken the first step to healing yourself. Noah may not be in your future but there are lots of bright stars out there for you to reach for, and I have no doubt you'll catch them. And in the meantime, I have a suggestion for you.'

I couldn't help myself. On Boxing Day afternoon, after a morning of board games with the Greenfords, Reine, Monty and assorted other guests, I excused myself and took a glass of wine up to my room. All day I'd been keeping an eye on the time.

An hour before kick-off, 7pm UK time, I checked the Fulham team sheet online, scanning the names.

Noah wasn't playing. I stared at the screen on my laptop. Not playing? But he'd gone home. I'd assumed that what was why. The news hit me hard, a hand reaching into my chest and grabbing my heart with a rough squeeze.

All the hope that I'd been holding on to was extinguished like a blanket over fire. I let the tears roll down my face. He was gone. I looked down at the blank screen of my phone, still willing a text to appear, still clinging to the possibility that he was still travelling. Couldn't get a flight earlier and was still in the air. His phone had run out of charge. He hadn't got home yet. He'd had a brain haemorrhage and was in hospital – okay, unlikely, and way worse, but a measure of my desperation that he was physically unable to call.

The truth was – I wasn't going to hear from him. Not now. Not ever. Like he'd said, he was done with me. Because I was reckless, had no purpose and didn't stick at things – all the things he'd hurled at me like little knives had left a thousand cuts. And they hurt because now I knew they were all true. Reine had forced me to take a good, hard look at myself.

I sat back in my chair and stared out of the window, the lights twinkling in the New York sky, the tall, long shapes of skyscrapers silhouetted against midnight blue. I winced at the stark beauty. Time to say goodbye to New York. I realised the room was in near darkness apart from the glow of the Christmas tree. I crossed over to it and began to remove the ornaments that Noah had bought for me. I would keep them. For my tree next year.

I straightened and brushed my tears away. Reine was right. I had choices to make. And first up was accepting her very generous offer of going to spend New Year with her at her house on Long Island.

Thinking about it, I carefully wrapped each of the ornaments in toilet paper and packed them away in my case. A few long walks on the beach over the next week sounded a perfect plan and would help me get myself set up for the future. One thing for certain was that next year I would celebrate Christmas. No more running away from it.

Switching on the lights, I made myself a cup of tea and sat down at the table, straight-backed and filled with purpose. I opened up a new document on my laptop and began to type. My fingers flew over the keyboard as a flood of thoughts poured out. All the things I needed to do, an action plan, a timeline, ideas, plans.

After two hours I sat back and smiled to myself. Early days, but I knew what I needed to do. First on the list was to arrange a meeting with Sophie to pick her brains. The second thing was long overdue; I was going to find a counsellor. The third was working out how I was going to apologise properly to my flatmates for stealing from them. Yes, stealing, not borrowing. I'd justified taking the money to myself instead of admitting that I had stolen it for my own selfish reasons.

'Blimey, Evie Green,' I said out loud to the silent room. 'Look at you, all grown up.'

I smiled again. Despite the sadness that I'd made a mess of things, Noah and I had had a good time and I'd always have the memories, even if it hurt too much to let them in just now.

Chapter Thirty-Eight

EVIE

Both Esther and Jamie were at work when I walked into the empty flat at ten in the morning on the third of January, fresh from landing at Heathrow. I'd spent the last week alternating between card games with Mrs Evans, taking Monty for long walks on the endless beach at Amagansett and furiously typing away on my laptop. I'd made a lot of progress in those blissful days.

I was immediately hit by that stale, eau de bin-needs-emptying scent when I opened the front door. Funny how quickly you get used to your surroundings, and for a moment I longed for the distinct fragrance of my room at The Plaza or the scent of lavender at Mrs Evans's house.

Dumping my case in the hall, I followed the less than fresh aroma into our kitchen. Because our landlord maximised the rental income, there was no lounge, that was Jamie's bedroom. Our only communal area was the kitchen.

As always it needed a good clean. There were a few plates

waiting by the sink to be washed up, and an overflowing bag of rubbish beside the already overflowing bin, along with a fine collection of empty wine and beer bottles.

I considered the room with fresh eyes, I'd been away for a long time and coming back felt like stepping into a much smaller, darker world. The kitchen, like the rest of the flat, looked as tired as I felt, but also as if it had given up, or rather, we had given up. I straightened my spine. Change started here.

Despite the pall of jetlag hanging over me, I set to, ferrying the rubbish down to the ground floor and the big refuse bins outside the front door.

By ten past six, when Esther walked into the flat, I was absolutely knackered.

'You're back,' she squealed and threw her arms around me. 'Why didn't you tell us you were coming home. Did you have an amazing time?'

I nodded, surprised by the warmth of her welcome. We'd barely been speaking when I left.

'And what's that amazing smell?'

'I cooked dinner,' I said, still a little astounded. My plan had been to woo them with food and wine so that I could apologise properly.

'Oooh, yummy.'

Before she could say anything else, footsteps thudded up the stairs.

'Jamie! Evie's back.'

He burst into the hallway. 'Welcome home, matey. How was the trip?'

'Good,' I said, still bemused. 'I've … I've cooked dinner and I bought some wine. Would you like a glass?'

'Hell yeah,' said Jamie and shucked off his heavy winter coat. 'It's brass monkeys out there, although I guess it was colder in the States. Did you have snow?' he stopped dead as he walked past me and Esther and into the kitchen.

'Whoa! What happened in here?'

'Flipping heck,' said Esther as they both stared around the room.

I'd cleaned every last inch of it.

Jamie poked my arm.

'What?' I asked at the sharp prod.

'I'm just checking it's really you.'

'Very funny,' I said. 'Why don't you both sit down, and I'll pour the wine.'

'Good stuff, as well,' said Esther watching me take the bottle out of the fridge.

They both took their seats while I poured the wine and handed them each a glass.

'Have you got something to tell us?' asked Jamie suspiciously. 'Are you moving out?'

'No, but I have got something to say, that I should have said before. I'm really, really sorry that I stole the money.' I held my hand up to fend off their quick interruptions. 'No. What I did was wrong. And don't try and be nice about it, because it was wrong, and I should have apologised properly at the time instead of making excuses. You had every right to be furious with me and I'm really, really sorry that I let you both down.'

Jamie started to say something. 'No, let me finish.'

'I've had a lot of time to think and…' I screwed up my face. 'I need to change. Start looking forward and stop being so laid-back and laissez-faire about everything. I've been crap.'

'Enough,' roared Jamie. 'You were fucking stupid, and we were mad as hell at you. And yeah, you can pay the interest on my overdraft. But seriously, Evie, we were shits, too. Putting that reel up of you. That was mean.'

'Yes, Evie,' Esther burst out. 'I'm sorry. I was so angry with you. I didn't think about it properly. It was a seriously crappy thing to do to a friend.' Tears were running down her face.

'But I stole from you.'

Esther jumped up and put an arm around me as I started to cry. 'Borrowed. You were always going to pay it back… Stealing is when you have no intention of doing that.'

We were both crying and hugging now. Jamie stood up. 'Oh, for fuck's sake.' He pushed his chair back and put his arms around both of us. 'Group hug.'

'You're forgiven,' said Esther sniffing. 'If you forgive us.'

We settled a little and sat back down at the table, the emotional outburst making me a little woozy. I was starting to run on empty and feel light-headed. Jetlag is a funny thing.

'We talked about it,' said Esther. 'To be honest, it was such a typically Evie thing to do. You never think ahead and jump in … but that's part of your charm, too.'

'Though you can be irritating, as well,' chipped in Jamie.

'I know,' I said. 'But I'm going to try to do better.' I

glanced around the kitchen. 'Cleaning up this place made me realise that we pay a lot for this shithole. We deserve better. You might not want to carry on living with me, but I think it's time we moved on and looked for a new place. We've been here for a whole year, and we've done nothing to make it homely.'

'You know I've been thinking the same,' said Esther.

Jamie hunched in his seat as we both looked at him.

He waved one hand. 'I'm a guy, but it would be nice to have a sofa to stretch out on instead of having to watch TV in my room all the time, or you two taking up all the space on my bed when we're playing PS5.'

'And we've got a confession to make,' said Jamie, catching Esther's eye.

'Yeah, we have.' She winced. 'That video. Of you.'

'I deserved it.'

'No!' howled Esther. 'You didn't. You really didn't. It was really mean and … I was horrible. Thing is, it made us stupid money. I posted it on my TikTok shop, where I sell my crocheted animals.' She put her head in her hands. 'That video was seen over two million times.'

She told me the amount, and I almost fell off the chair.

Chapter Thirty-Nine

EVIE

Six weeks later…

'Who wants to come to the pub with me?' I asked brightly as if I'd only just thought of the idea.

'I'll come with you,' said Jamie, then added with a smirk. 'What time's kick-off?'

'Half three,' I said.

'See, she knows without even having to look it up,' said Jamie. 'Who are they playing?'

'Palace,' I said, and then blushed.

'Ha!' Esther pointed at me. 'Why don't you just call him?'

Jamie ran over to the blackboard on the kitchen wall and added another chalk line to the tally count. Apparently, it was the ninety-seventh time Esther had asked that very question in the last six weeks.

'Because…'

Both Jamie and Esther rolled their eyes.

They didn't understand. They were dozens of reasons. Namely, that I'd never heard from Noah after I'd dropped off the Tiffany box at his agent's office with a little note apologising and thanking him for making me reassess things.

I cringed now, thinking of the note and the hours I'd spent crafting it – it really was my last-ditch attempt to reach out to him.

10 January

Dear Noah,

I hope you've fully recovered from the injury to your knee and head, and that neither were too serious. Thank you for the gift. But I felt it wouldn't be right to keep it under the circumstances. But thank you for the thought.

I also wanted to thank you for opening my eyes and making me realise that I've been living in la-la-land for too long. You were right, I was hiding from real life and using my grief as a shield, as an excuse to avoid investing in the future. I'm having counselling. Early days, but hopefully it will help. I've also set up a TikTok channel to highlight fraud, inviting people to share their experiences to help stop others falling victim. So far, so good. Again, early days, but I've been invited to write a few freelance articles.

Good luck with everything, and thank you for the time we had in New York. I know it didn't end well, but boy we had some fun. I hope you'll remember the good bits.

With best wishes,

Evie Green

'You've really got to stop stalking him,' said Esther. 'Why don't you just text him?'

Jamie added another mark to the tally chart. 'Arrange to meet up.'

'I don't want to,' I said, knowing I sounded slightly sulky but there was no point. Noah had had plenty of time to contact me. I had to get used to the fact that he never would.

———

The pub was busy, full of Fulham and Palace supporters trading fairly low-key insults, but the game hadn't started yet.

'There's a space over there,' said Jamie. 'See if they'll let you join their table. They're more likely to say yes to you two hotties. I'll get the drinks in.'

We approached the table, where two men were sitting facing the big screen high up on the opposite wall.

'Mind if we sit here?' I asked, glancing at their black-and-white-striped football scarves. The older of the two, clearly father and son, responded with a cheeky grin. 'Palace or Fulham?'

'Fulham, of course,' I said.

'That's okay, then. If you were Palace fans you could sing.'

We sat down, half-turned towards the screen. The usual pre-match discussion was taking place with a panel of pundits all talking about each team's chances. My ears pricked up when I heard Noah's name – when didn't they?

I was primed for it, even when I hoped I might be over him.

'So, what do you attribute to Sanderson's change in form?' said one pundit to another. 'I mean five assists in four matches plus a couple of goals. He's on fire this season. What do you think's changed about his style?'

'He's always been a great forward. I mean he's a great striker but this year…' The other pundit shook his head.

Esther slyly turned to me. 'What do *you* think, Evie?'

'No idea,' I said.

'No special insight?'

The dad opposite us caught her eye. 'He's doing something right. I thought at first he'd lost his nerve after the "tackle that must not be mentioned" – but he's all over it. Being a lot more considered when he's taking chances, but also setting up some cracking goals. That one against Arsenal two weeks ago has to be goal of the season.' His son nodded enthusiastically. 'I mean, he could have easily taken the shot himself, even though it would have been risky. Instead, he passed it on the inside and Welton hammered it in.' The man laughed. 'He's positively selfless these days.'

'Probably because he had a mid-season holiday,' I pointed out. 'Came back refreshed.'

This weekly, masochistic Saturday ritual was based on the theory that if I kept seeing Noah on the screen I'd build up some kind of immunity, which would stop thoughts of him being triggered. It wasn't working. Memories intruded when I caught sight of someone with his colouring on the tube, or his name was mentioned on Radio 5 Live, or there was another picture of him celebrating a goal with his teammates.

Jamie returned with three pints of lager, just in time for kick-off. Once the game had started, the pub went quiet as the two teams settled and got rid of their initial nervy energy. Then things began to heat up as Fulham got possession of the ball, working their way down to the goal. The camera panned in on Noah running down the wing, his long legs pumping, followed by a close-up of his face, stern and determined. Every time I saw him I'd forgotten how gorgeous he was.

Esther nudged me and I realised I'd not been as subtle as I thought. I ignored her as the camera homed in on him. Was I the only person that noticed he'd had a haircut?

'Evie, either phone him or stop crushing on him. He's really not that…' The expression she pulled said it all.

But he is, whispered my sad little heart. Was she blind?

I focused on the screen, watching and concentrating on his lithe movements as he weaved through the defence. My pulse picked up. Surely, he was never going to try and score from—' The pub erupted as at the last minute he chipped the ball over to the other striker who had a clear shot. It sailed into the top-right corner of the net missing the post by a whisker.

Jamie punched the air. We were all on our feet. 'What a goal.'

'Belter.'

The replay was shown several times, with admiring punditry from the three ex-footballers in the TV studio. Biased as I was, it was without doubt a superb goal, which might not have happened if Noah had taken the shot himself.

A hot bubble of pride burned in my chest even though I had absolutely no right to feel it.

'He's got magic boots, that boy,' said the man at our table. 'Something's put a rocket up him, make no mistake.'

The rest of the team were hugging and jumping all over Noah and the scorer, and he disappeared from view beneath a flurry of white shirts.

With Fulham one–nil in the lead, it was a nail biting second half as we prayed they'd hang on to the lead, and then in the seventy-sixth minute, Noah scored again. One of those goals that came out of nowhere, he just seized a chance and made the shot and to our amazement it went in. He looked pretty surprised, too.

'Somehow, if he keeps this form up, I don't think he'll be playing for Fulham next season,' said the man to his son. 'Someone is going to snap him up. He could go to Europe again.'

The final whistle blew, and I watched as the players shook hands and trooped off the field, the camera favouring Noah the most. This was the last time, I told myself. I had to stop this. No more watching Fulham. Noah had no interest in me.

I was ready to leave, but Jamie had got another round in so we stayed while the post-match dissection began.

'Look,' Esther nudged me again with her ever-sharp elbows. 'They're interviewing Noah.'

There he was, slightly sweaty, his chestnut hair damp around his forehead, and those smoky-blue eyes sharp and alert. I couldn't take my eyes off his jawline. The jawline I'd kissed. Those lips. Urgh. I was a tragic mess.

'Great game, Noah. Another two outstanding goals. I mean everyone is commenting on your form. What do you attribute to this change of tactics?

Noah looked directly at the camera and a little shiver ran down my spine. Good job we weren't at home, I'd probably have kissed the television screen or something daft. My heart ached just looking at him.

'I realised that I wasn't in love with the game like I used to be. After that tackle, I was terrified of taking a risk. So, I started looking at the way I played and I realised that there's such a thing as a calculated risk and that's what I weigh up every time I'm on the pitch.'

The interviewer waved his microphone under Noah's mouth, as if trying to snake-charm more words out of his mouth.

'What brought on this change of approach? Was it the accident with Menzies?'

Noah shook his head. And then he smiled, right at the camera.

A desperate urge to run away seized my limbs and I jiggled my legs.

'I met someone who showed me that you need to have some fun in life otherwise none of this is worth having. You need to take risks to live and it's easy to play it safe, but it might not make you happy.'

I could have sworn he was looking right at me, and my heart did its best to jump out of my chest cavity or give me fatal palpitations, I couldn't make up my mind which.

Hope flared bright and sharp, almost taking my breath away. Was he talking about me? Did he mean I should take a risk? Or was he crediting me with changing his outlook.

'Sometimes you need to glimpse a different reality to realise that there are other ways,' he continued. 'We need to be open to alternatives and not just walk the same path. Someone once told me that life is about risk. But there's a calculation to be made about what you stand to gain and what you stand to lose.'

The interviewer frowned at that one as he tried to make sense of it, and I giggled to myself, amazed that Noah had remembered the phrase that I'd cobbled up out of anger and indignation.

'Right, and where do you see the team finishing at the end of the season. You're already mid-table and have won the last five games.'

'There are no guarantees in football.' Noah grinned. Despite this vague answer, the interviewer had more airtime to finish, so he asked a couple of the typically inane questions that no one was ever going to commit to answering.

Eventually, they cut back to the studio, where there was now an analysis of Noah's words.

'Do you think he's working with a sports psychologist?' asked one pundit.

'Certainly sounds like it,' said another.

The funny man on the team who could always be relied on to add a laugh cut in, 'Or he's met a woman.' They all collapsed with laughter at this before moving on to start a new topic.

Esther and Jamie both turned to look at me. I glanced at the man and his son who were standing up to leave. As soon as they'd gone, the two of them started whispering furiously.

'I bet he means you,' said Esther.

'Don't be daft,' I said, although my heart rate was still up there. I could feel my pulse thudding in my temple.

'It's entirely plausible,' said Jamie, tilting his head like a concerned doctor. 'His form improved dramatically after he shagged you.'

'Shhh,' I said looking fearfully around the pub.

'Jamie's right,' hissed Esther in a not-so-stage whisper.

'No,' I said emphatically.

'Yes,' said Esther.

'Then why hasn't he messaged me? He's the one that left me without a word. He never responded to my note.' I buried my head in my hands. 'Guys, please don't do this.'

That ever-optimistic sense of hope raised its happy little head, even though I was desperate to smack it down and I was back on the roller-coaster, wondering whether I'd imagined that connection between us. But then, I couldn't bear the rejection again. Once was enough. Noah wasn't coming back. How many times did I have to tell myself before it finally registered?

Chapter Forty

NOAH

I raced up all five floors from the gym to my apartment without giving my legs a rest. I'd cut short my training by ten minutes. But that gave me five minutes to make a cup of coffee before I tuned into my new guilty pleasure.

Grabbing my coffee cup, I settled into the armchair in the window and scrolled through my phone. A dozen texts from Lara, with more offers for interviews, podcasts, TV appearances and my least favourite type of offer – to escort an up-and-coming young actress to a black-tie shindig across the city. My currency had never been so high.

My lip curled as a couple of headlines popped into my news feed. How the tide had turned. All those papers that hadn't had a good word to say about me were now desperate for the inside story into my new-found success.

I checked my watch and then opened up TikTok.

'Welcome to *You've been Scammed*,' came the familiar voice. I caught the inside of my cheek with my teeth at the sight of Evie, looking earnest and confident. 'This week we're going to be looking at one of the latest scams doing the rounds. Tell your friends, your family, the guys next door. The more people who know what to look for, the less chance they'll be scammed.

'And remember, there is no shame in being scammed. Even the most financial savvy of us fall foul to these people. They're skilled at what they do and it's important we share knowledge to stay one step ahead of the game.

'As always, if you have a story you want to share, please DM me. Today, I'm talking to Tracy, who booked a flight to Thailand through a reputable travel company. Unfortunately, that's just the start of this story.

'Hi, Tracy. Would you like to tell us what happened to start with?'

I listened to Evie's warm voice encouraging the young woman to share her story. She had a deft way of handling her interviewees, never judging them, stopping to let them cry and empathising with them. I'd heard her say, 'You just feel so stupid, don't you?' at least once in every episode.

Tracy began her unhappy tale, where it transpired that the website was a counterfeit that looked virtually the same as the legit site and that once she'd passed on her bank details, the scammers phoned her and convinced her to give them remote access to her phone.

'They w-were so c-convincing,' sobbed Tracy.

'I know,' said Evie. 'Bastards.'

Tracy gave a sniffly giggle before relaying that once they got access to her phone, they then got access to her bank card and used it to spend thousands before she even knew what had happened.

'I can't believe I was so stupid.'

'Hey,' said Evie. 'These people use every psychological trick in the book. You have to remember, they're experts at what they do. Thankfully your bank picked up on the fraud.'

'Yes. They've been good and refunded all the money that was spent. Bloody galling that they bought a Gucci handbag. I've been wanting one for years.'

'Even bigger bastards,' said Evie, making Tracy laugh again.

I smiled because she really was great at this. Evie was building a steady following on TikTok. She put out three of these short pieces each week, but also had a linked website where she relayed more detailed information about the current scams, how to avoid them and what to do if you have been scammed.

The girl had done good. Really good and I was proud of her, even though I was sad that I'd never got the chance to tell her how much she'd changed my life. Every time I was interviewed, I tried to get the message across in case she ever got to hear or see me on TV. I wanted her to know that I was sorry about the things I'd said to her on that last day. Sorry that I'd left without saying goodbye. When I didn't hear from her, not even an acknowledgement of the gift I'd left for her, I gave into temptation and called her, only to find that I'd been blocked. It told me all I needed to know.

The video finished with Evie giving her trademark

wave. 'Stay safe, folks. And if something looks too good to be true, it probably is. Until next time.'

She was an absolute natural at this and I noticed she'd already been on breakfast TV again this month. That's where I'd first heard about her new channel.

I put my phone down to jump in the shower and head into the West End for a meeting with Lara. A potential sponsor wanted to meet me, and the deal was incumbent on this meeting. Did I really need any more men's grooming products?

'So, Noah, what do you do when you're not playing football?' purred Denise Moulden, Marketing Director of Golden Tresses, who were launching a new men's shampoo range.

'I like playing chess,' I said, and Lara shot me a startled glance. 'And I love potholing. And, don't tell anyone,' I lowered my voice and whispered, 'also trainspotting. There's nothing like seeing the "Evening Star", a locomotive nine two, two thirty. They only ever made ten of them before the nine two thirty-one came in.' I winked at her, I had to admire the way Denise managed to keep her composure.

'Fascinating,' she said, retracting her hand from my thigh.

'Yeah, I think so. I know it's not for most people, standing on a train platform for hours in the pouring rain but…' I shook my head, thinking of Evie and channelling her natural mischief. She'd love this conversation. 'It's great. You should come along some time.'

'Mmm,' said Denise. 'Unfortunately, I have a very busy schedule. Talking of which, I need to get back for a meeting. It was lovely to meet you and I'm thrilled that you're going to be the head of our campaign.' She laughed at her painful pun.

I nodded. Lara was looking a little alarmed, probably worrying that I'd just screwed up a lucrative deal, even though the ink was down on the pieces of paper in front of us. All I had to do was show up for a photo shoot and film an ad and tell everyone I used the product.

I felt a tiny bit guilty about the trainspotting, but then Denise had pushed for the in-person meeting. I bet she regretted that now.

We all shook hands, the managing director, the financial director and Denise, before they trooped out of Lara's boardroom.

'Noah Sanderson!' Lara burst into peals of laughter. 'Trainspotting? Where the hell did that come from?' She bent over double making very unladylike snorting noises. 'You bugger. I nearly spat my tea out.'

I grinned at her, feeling quite pleased with myself. 'Inspired, huh?'

'I'm not sure what's got into you recently.' She shook her head and then sniggered again. 'But I'm quite enjoying this new, improved version. I think your fans are, too. The quality of gifts is going up. I forgot to give you this.'

She ferreted in her desk drawer and took out a large brown envelope. I opened it up and pulled out a turquoise bag. It felt as if all my organs had ground to a halt as I stared down at it.

'Tiffany's? Nice gift, eh?'

I took the box out of the bag. My mouth drying with sudden awareness.

'When did this come?'

'Oh God, weeks ago. I'm sorry. I just forgot about it.'

'How many weeks ago?' I asked, my fingers stroking the perfect white ribbon on top of the box.

She sighed and opened up her desk diary, riffling through the pages. 'Early January.'

'Early January,' I echoed.

'Oh, and there was a card with it.' She produced a white envelope tucked between the pages of her diary.

My name was scrawled across the front and I recognised the handwriting straight away. Scrawly and loopy. Evie to a T. Her penmanship was like her: fast, impatient and always wanting to get to the end so she could do the next thing.

'Aren't you going to open it?' asked Lara.

I shook my head. 'Not just now.' I didn't want to share the contents with anyone. If Evie was returning the gift I'd left her, unopened, it was a fair indicator of what she had to say.

'Do you want to pop out for a drink to celebrate?'

'No, thanks, I need to go,' I said and turned and walked out of the office without even bothering to say goodbye.

As soon as I was outside, I strode quickly up to Soho

Square and to the little park there, searching out an empty bench. As soon as I sat down, I ripped open the envelope and read Evie's words.

> *… I hope you remember the good bits.*

I was never going to forget the good bits. But now I had a little bit of hope.

Chapter Forty-One

EVIE

'Thank you to Helen, my guest today, who shared her story of being spoofed by a scammer who convinced her that it was her bank calling. Thankfully, her bank had an extra layer of protection. Voice recognition. So, the message today is, where you can, make sure you have two-factor identification. And just because it looks like your bank's telephone number, remember scammers have the technology to make it appear that the call is coming from that number. It's called spoofing.'

I gave the screen a little wave from my cosy armchair tucked in the corner of our lounge.

'DM me to share your stories. Remember, you could save someone else from being scammed. And that's all from me today. Stay safe, folks. And if something looks too good to be true, it probably is. Until next time.'

I pressed stop and sat back, exhausted. It was 10:30am and I was a little punch drunk as I'd been working most of the night to prepare this episode. Helen had only been able to speak to me after eleven last night, and I'd been working nonstop for the last week since we'd moved into our new place, building up a body of material, so that I always had something ready to go.

'You're really good, you know that,' said Esther from her spot, where she sprawled on the sofa opposite me, her feet resting on Jamie's lap. The joy of having extra space had yet to wear off for all three of us. 'Want a cup of tea, Miss Workaholic?'

'I'd love one,' piped up Jamie.

'You don't deserve one,' said Esther.

'Who built all the bookshelves,' he protested.

'I'd love one, too,' I said interrupting their good-natured bickering. 'I'm not a workaholic, there's just so much to do. That poor woman, she was really upset. She honestly thought the call was legit. If it hadn't been for the voice thingy—'

'Love how techy you are,' said Jamie.

'You know what I mean. But she could have lost everything in her bank account and savings account.'

'I'm only teasing you,' replied Jamie.

'Honestly,' said Esther. 'What you come up with scares me. I would have done exactly what she did if my bank rang and said I'd paid Curry's four hundred quid. I didn't know people could do that spoofing thing. Makes you think.'

'That's the whole point of the channel,' I said.

'I know, but you've really brought home just how many scammers are out there.'

'Sadly, it's a full-time job for some people.'

'And you, too, now. What time do you have to get up tomorrow? I can't believe you're going to be on breakfast telly again.'

'Four, but it's okay, the TV studio is sending a car for me.'

Jamie yawned. 'That's not human.' He shuddered.

'I hope they've got good makeup,' said Esther, pushing his feet off her lap. 'No one, not even you, looks good at that time.'

'Thanks, Esther. That's very reassuring.'

She gave me a bright smile. 'But brilliant that they keep asking you back.'

'Yeah,' I said with more than a little pride. I'd come a long way since New York. 'They've offered me a regular slot. Every two weeks. And the money's amazing.'

'Good.'

'And…' I'd been dying to tell them this but I wanted official notification, which had arrived that morning, '*Money Weekly* has offered me my job back.'

'Really? What did you say. Go shove it up your arse?' said Jamie.

'No, but I said I'd write a regular fraud column for them on a freelance basis.' It felt like a triumph that rather than turn down the offer outright, I was able to turn it to my advantage. I was bossing life, and enjoying being in charge of it for a change, instead of rolling along.

Esther disappeared to the kitchen, again far nicer than our previous one. I began reading my DMs, always slightly upsetting as every week there were more people with awful scam stories. Some folks were a little naïve, but that didn't make them any less of a victim, others were shocked that they'd fallen for it, but everyone that contacted me had a sad story to relate and it made me even more determined to highlight the different ways scammers kept dreaming up ways to part people from their hard-earned cash.

Butterflies suddenly swarmed in my stomach, almost overcoming me. There in my DMs. A message from Noah. If I hadn't have blocked him, would he have been in touch earlier? I'd been trying to protect my heart from further battering, although it had never really worked.

> In the absence of the Empire State Building, meet me at the top of Horizon 22 on 14 February at twelve noon. I have something for you. Noah x

I stared at the message and my eyes blurred. And for some stupid, sappy reason I leaned forward and touched the words on the screen, pressing my lips together trying hard not to cry.

'Evie! What's the matter?' asked Esther, retuning with three mugs of tea.

I looked up and gulped, sniffing because the tears were coming through whether I wanted them to or not.

'Oh God, girl stuff. Do I need to leave?' asked Jamie.

'Noah!' I said, giving Esther a wobbly smile.

She raced to my side and virtually plonked herself in my lap.

'Oh, my God. Oh, my God. Oh, my God.' She squealed, and squeezed my arm. She read the DM and squealed again, almost piercing my ear drum.

'*Sleepless in Seattle* vibes. Oh, my God, he's a keeper.'

Jamie looked worried. 'What are you talking about?'

Tears were streaming down my face. What was with me? I wasn't a crier.

'Film stuff,' I said between sniffs.

'Oh, Evie, that's so romantic.'

'Kind of is,' I said, wiping tears.

'You've got to go,' implored Esther, rather unnecessarily because of course I was going to go.

'What are you talking about?' asked Jamie with frustration.

Esther rolled her eyes and then read out the email.

Jamie nodded and waited a beat before saying, 'You do know it's Valentine's Day today?'

There was a silence as Esther and I absorbed this information, and then screamed. Both of us jumped up and started running around like a pair of Keystone Cops.

'Whattimeisit? Whereisit? Howlongdoesittake-togetthere?' Barely coherent I tugged at my clothes. 'I'm a mess. I can't go like this.'

Jamie was on his phone. 'Liverpool Street. Nearest tube. It'll take you three quarters of an hour to get to the tube station. Probably another fifteen minutes to reach your destination.'

'Fuuuck,' said Esther.

I looked at my watch. I had fifteen minutes. I had pyjama bottoms and carrot-shaped slippers on my bottom half. Luckily, I was wearing video-worthy makeup and my hair was clean.

Esther, who's always good in a crisis, grabbed my shoulders and steered me into my bedroom.

'Shower first. I'll sort your outfit. Go, go, go. We've got this.'

'What if I'm late and he doesn't think I'm coming?'

'He's going to wait.'

'What if he doesn't?' Panic like a hungry wolf prowled in my stomach.

'Fuck's sake, Evie. Get in the shower. Let me do the worrying,' snapped Esther, clearly just as stressed as I was.

I was manhandled into an outfit that I didn't even have time to approve, Esther attacking me with perfume and a hairbrush to create a messy updo.

Ten minutes later, she and Jamie shoved me out of the door. 'Text as soon as you get there. Just let us know you made it.'

'Okay,' I said.

'You look gorgeous,' said Esther, elbowing Jamie in the ribs.

'Scrubbed up well,' he said and leaned forward and kissed me on the cheek. 'Go get him, tiger.'

Chapter Forty-Two

EVIE

Of course, the train stopped in a tunnel right outside Liverpool Street Station. I tapped my foot and kept looking at my watch. Ten to twelve.

'Come on. Come on. Come on,' I muttered.

The man next to me looked very tempted to change seats.

I closed my eyes and said a silent prayer to St Christopher. I was pretty sure he was the patron saint of travellers, although I suspect he was all about keeping people safe rather than getting them to their destination in a timely fashion. When he was around, people relied on mules and donkeys, which back in the day were probably a lot more reliable. It was a sure sign of anxiety when my mind started to charge off down these idiotic tangents.

We sat for what seemed like forever. Every time I looked at my watch another minute had passed. It was now four minutes to twelve. Finally. I almost cheered aloud. Like a geriatric dinosaur, the train lumbered into motion and slowly, oh, so slowly, rumbled into Liverpool Street station. Bah! It was exactly noon.

I was up and at the doors at the first chink of light from the platform. The second the doors parted, I flew out of them, frantically casting about for the yellow Way Out sign. I raced towards it, feeling damp patches gaining purchase under my arms. Bugger, I was going to arrive hot and sweaty.

I careered up the escalator, taking the left side for once, forcing my lungs to keep breathing with the unfamiliar exertion. I petered out before I reached the top and had to slink back into the lane on the right.

Breathless, I arrived at the top. And because I was too quick off the mark with my Oyster card after the previous person, I ran into the barrier full tilt. 'Oof,' I said, trying again.

Stepping out into the grey pallor of February in London, I consulted the map on my phone. Five-minute walk. Ha! I could walk quicker than Google. It was now six minutes past. I set off at an Olympic pace, run-walking, puffing in sync with each step.

At ten minutes past, I reached Horizon 22 and stared up at the skyscraper towering overhead and was immediately cast back to New York. My head tipped back and my neck craned to look up the vertiginous wall of glass.

I hurried into the building, following the signs to the lift to the fifty-fifth floor. There was a queue. A huge queue. Of course there was. This was my life. I looked at my watch. Twelve minutes past.

Noah would wait. Wouldn't he? I caught my lip between

my teeth; how long would he wait? I'd wait all day but ... he'd probably give it half an hour and assume I wasn't coming. I could have texted him at that point to tell him I was on my way but ... hey, this was all my romcom dreams coming true and I wasn't going to spoil the great romantic reunion by forewarning him. Besides, he could sit and stew for a minute or two. I was worth it.

At 12:17pm the lift doors opened and I managed to squeeze in with the last of the other visitors. Even before the lift began its lightening ascent, my stomach was already on a spin cycle.

Nerves jittered in every synapse as the doors opened.

I looked around at the large, bright space and like a homing pigeon immediately spotted Noah. He was there, sitting hunched on a bench looking down at his watch as if it held all the answers to the universe.

Something inside me settled and I took a moment to drink him in. It was like a lava flow stopping, the waters receding, the storm abating – everything felt calm again. My steps were steady as I walked over to the bench and stood next to him waiting for him to look up.

'Is this seat taken?' I asked.

His head jerked up and I saw the flash flood of emotions race across his face as he recognised me. He jumped up. 'Evie. You came.' A look of wonder filled his eyes.

I nodded, all the butterflies in my stomach exploding into life. 'I did.'

'Sorry it's not the Empire State Building.'

I almost shrugged, but stopped myself in time. 'It's more than adequate.'

He stared at me, as if he were inventorying my face, or maybe that was projection, because that's what I was doing with his.

He smiled. 'It's so good to see you.'

This was going to take forever.

'Noah,' I remonstrated. 'Are you going to kiss me or not?'

He laughed out loud. 'Evie Green, I've missed you.'

'Enough with the talking,' I complained. 'I—' I never did remember what I was about to say.

When his mouth covered mine, his hands cupping my face, it was just like Christmas should be, a beacon of light and hope in the dark midwinter. The sun came out inside me, and I wondered if I was glowing like a Dr Who regeneration.

My fingers touched his face, mapping his features so that I wouldn't forget them again.

His hands slipped down my neck to my shoulders where he pressed me against him. I could feel his tenderness as his mouth roved softly over my lips, searching to make sure that nothing had changed and that I was still me.

I softened against him, sighing into his mouth.

At last, he pulled away and rested his forehead against mine. 'I missed you. I'm sorry I left without saying goodbye. I'm sorry I was a complete idiot.'

'You were but … you're my idiot, so I forgive you.' I paused and smiled solemnly up at him. 'And it only hurt so much because you were right.'

'No. No, I wasn't. I've realised that sometimes taking risks and having fun with them can pay off.'

'Whereas I've found that taking responsibility for myself and facing up to the future also pays off.'

'*You've Been Scammed* is brilliant. I'm so proud of you.'

'Top goal scorer at Fulham. I'm proud of you.'

'I've been thinking that the sum of our differences might just equal a great team. What do you say?'

'Noah!' I punched him in the arm. 'I fancy the pants off you. We're compatible and you're hot.'

'Thanks. You're not so bad yourself.'

'I know. So enough of the mushy stuff. Are you going to take me out for a drink and then take me home?'

'Sounds like a plan,' said Noah, putting an arm around me and kissing my face. 'Can you wait long enough to get your hands on my body to take in the view, or are you in a hurry?'

I tilted my head and gave him a considering look before sighing. 'I'll manage.' I dropped my hand and squeezed his delectable butt and grinned at him. 'Just to keep me going.'

He kissed me again. 'Don't ever change, Evie Green. I love you just the way you are.'

The L word was as unexpected and shocking as a battery jump start to my heart but then the thought settled, and I tried it out for size. It fitted perfectly.

I grinned at him. 'Funnily enough, I love you just the way you are, too.'

'By the way. I still have your Christmas present.' He pulled the Tiffany box from his pocket. 'You never opened it.'

'I didn't feel I should.'

'I bought it when I realised I loved you … before I chickened out.'

I tugged on the white ribbon to open the box. Nestled inside was the gold key pendant.

'Oh, my God. This is … too much. This was…' My eyes are so wide I think they might pop out of my eye sockets. 'I can't…'

'It's all right, we can go halves for lunch,' he said, reminding me of our conversation when I'd looked up how much professional football players earn.

'Okay, it's a deal,' I said.

He put his arm around my shoulders and the two of us sauntered over to the huge glass windows to share the view together. There was a lot to see but it looked as if we had all the time in the world.

Epilogue

'I'm hungry,' said Barney, shifting from foot to foot in the queue.

'You're always hungry,' said Jeannie, with a grandmotherly smile. She came to stand next to him and put her arm around him. 'Just think, when we get in there, you can choose whatever you like.' Noah's mother was still a little starstruck and kept looking round at the Christmas decorations – and I actually saw her pinching herself at one point last night over dinner in the Palm Court restaurant.

Jeannie was possibly one of the nicest women on the planet. Today she was sporting the Tiffany starfish earrings to match the necklace Noah had bought her last year.

'I expect a blue box, every year now,' she declared this morning … after she'd finished crying.

Noah had arranged for the whole family to stay at The Plaza on Christmas Eve. His sister, Rachel and her husband, John, their two kids, Barney and Oscar, as well as his mum and his dad, Ronnie. We'd arrived at his parents' house, in

JULIE CAPLIN

Bridgeport, Connecticut, three days ago. Luckily for us, Noah's team wasn't scheduled to play on Boxing Day, although we would be catching a flight home this evening as he was playing on the 27th.

I touched the little Christmas-tree earrings dangling from my ears that had been in my stocking this morning, along with a pair of felt Elf slippers with bells on – Jeannie had seen the infamous reel – and the cutest gloves with tiny ice skaters embroidered on each one, along with chocolates and smellies. To be honest, I cried, too, because I really hadn't expected to be enveloped by her warmth and made an instant part of the family.

I looked at them all now, Noah's dad engaged in an earnest conversation with Oscar. Rachel, another new designer handbag resplendent on her arm – orange this time. She kept stroking it when she didn't think anyone was looking as she stood with her mom, their arms linked. Their love for one another was palpable and they made spending time together for the holidays look easy.

I squeezed Noah's hand, and he looked down at me.

'You okay?'

I nodded. How could I not be? These people, who completely embraced Christmas, had also completely embraced me.

This was what Christmas looked like. My mum would have been happy for me. I'd learned that I needed to learn to live and know Mum wouldn't have wanted me to stagnate and never move on from the point at which she died. Yeah, she would definitely be happy for me.

'You do realise that if we ever split up, I'm still coming for Christmas with your mom, dad and sister.'

Noah sighed. 'Yeah. I got that memo. Mom loves you.'

'I know,' I said smugly.

He tugged on one of my curls. 'Good job I do, too. I'm not planning on letting you go anytime soon.'

'Just as well. I'm not planning on leaving. You're far too rich…' I stood on tiptoes and whispered in his ear, 'and too good in the sack.'

'Evie! Honey. How lovely to see you,' Raoul, wearing a very swish Santa hat, grabbed me by the shoulders and kissed both my cheeks. 'Welcome back.'

'Hey, Raoul. How are you doing?'

'Missing my favourite elf. Where you been?' He looked at Noah. 'I guess I've got you to blame.'

'Sorry. This is a flying visit.'

'No worries. You ready to come in?' Raoul looked down at Noah's nephews who were beside themselves at the prospect of a buffet and being able to help themselves to whatever they wanted.

Along with the rest of the people waiting to join in the famous buffet Christmas lunch at The Plaza, we entered the iconic restaurant. I looked around and there at a huge table was Mrs Evans, with Monty on her lap, waving his paw at us.

Noah and I went straight over to her.

'Evie, my darling. Noah. Happy Christmas. Now, how have you been since I last saw you?'

We'd spent a blissful week in the summer at her house during the off-season.

'All good,' I said. 'And thank you for the Christmas decoration.' I beamed at her. 'You should see the size of the tree Noah bought this year. Ridiculous.' Despite rolling my eyes, Noah knew I absolutely loved it. We'd had so much fun, and definitely of the X-rated variety, putting the tree up and celebrating afterwards, creating our very own Christmas tree-decorating tradition.

'My pleasure, and thank you for the box of mince pies. Your friend Sophie is now taking orders, they're so popular. I ordered a dozen boxes for the staff here. They were so pleased to hear you were coming back.'

'I know. I had coffee with Angel and Carol yesterday.' Coming back to The Plaza had felt like coming home, and to top it off, this morning I'd enjoyed some of the Sanderson family traditions. My favourite was the Secret Santa, where we all had to buy each other a book. Rachel had bought me a copy of *Eloise*, which was just perfect. I'd bought Oscar a copy of one my favourite books, *Jesus's Christmas Party*, the nativity story told from the point of an exasperated innkeeper. Smiling to myself I recalled just how much of a kick I'd got out of reading it to him as he perched on my knee and roared with laughter as I brought the grumpy innkeeper to life. That memory would live in my head for a long time, as well as all the others: everyone gathered around the tree in their dressing gowns, Oscar and Barney's wide-eyed delight at seeing all the presents under the tree in mine and Noah's suite, and the smile Jeannie gave her son when she opened her earrings. The look Noah gave me when I gave him sky-diving tickets. What I had yet to tell him was that they were for the indoor variety. I'd get round to that later.

As I was helping myself to a slice of beef Wellington and handing one to Noah, a lady sidled up to me. 'Excuse me, you're Evie Green, aren't you?'

'Yes,' I said warily.

'I just have to say a massive thank you.' She paused and looked earnestly at me. 'Because of *You've Been Scammed*, I found out that I was being conned. My daughter's been watching you on your TikTok thingy and warned me just in time. Honestly, if she hadn't told me, I wouldn't have believed her because the call came from my bank's telephone number. How do they do that?'

'They're very clever I'm afraid. But I'm so pleased they didn't catch you out.'

'So am I. You're doing a real service. If it weren't for you, I might have lost a lot of money.' Her face revealed the full extent of her horror. 'Sometimes I wake up in the middle of the night and think "what if my daughter hadn't been there?" I tell everyone to watch your channel.'

'Oh, thank you. I'm so glad that you found out in time.'

'You keep up the good work.'

'I will.' She walked away and I felt a glow of happiness.

'I'm so proud of you, Evie Green,' Noah said.

'I'm quite proud of me, too. Do you know what? That might just have been one of the best Christmas presents ever.'

Noah laughed. 'So, I won't bother with Tiffany again next year, then?'

I eyed the diamond bracelet on my wrist that sparkled in the light.

'Now, steady on,' I teased. 'I said "one of".' I leaned forward and kissed him. 'Although you make quite a tasty package. I'd be happy with just you.'

'Evie Green, I swear you're getting positively mushy,' said Noah.

'Shh, don't tell anyone,' I said with a laugh and whispered in his ear. 'But if you're being competitive about it, I'd say you're the best present ever.'

Acknowledgements

Trying to immerse myself in snow and ice proved tricky during a very hot summer, with the added complications of broken ribs, a chest infection and a stomach complaint. So I'm extremely grateful to my writing crew, Bella, Sarah, Rachel, Phillipa, who kept me going throughout and put up with my whinging. Special thanks go to my dear friend Donna Ashcroft, without whom this book might not have made it into print. We message virtually every day, supporting each other through the highs and lows of writing. As any writer will tell you, it can be a lonely job. Everyone needs a cheerleader like Donna, and I'm so grateful to have her in my life.

There are lots of people involved in publishing a book; it really is a collaborative process. I'd like to thank all the lovely people at One More Chapter who work behind the scenes, particularly Sofia Salazar-Studer, the sales team and many more. Also, thanks to the fabulous Rights Team, led by the lovely Zoe Shine and including Aisling and Ashton, who do so much to share my work across the world.

I always thank my editor Charlotte and my beloved agent Broo – because they are both extraordinary women and demonstrate their brilliance time and time again. I'm so glad they are on my team. Ladies, you're both awesome and I love you to bits.

YOUR NUMBER ONE STOP

ONE MORE CHAPTER

FOR PAGETURNING BOOKS

The author and One More Chapter would like to thank everyone who contributed to the publication of this story...

Analytics
Imogen Wolstencroft

Audio
Fionnuala Barrett
Ciara Briggs

Contracts
Laura Amos
Inigo Vyvyan

Design
Lucy Bennett
Fiona Greenway
Liane Payne
Dean Russell

Digital Sales
Laura Daley
Lydia Grainge
Hannah Lismore

eCommerce
Laura Carpenter
Madeline ODonovan
Charlotte Stevens
Christina Storey
Jo Surman
Rachel Ward

Editorial
Rosie Best
Kara Daniel
Paris Ferguson
Charlotte Ledger
Jennie Rothwell
Sofia Salazar Studer
Caroline Scott-Bowden
Emily Thomas
Helen Williams

Harper360
Emily Gerbner
Ariana Juarez
Jean Marie Kelly
emma sullivan
Sophia Wilhelm

International Sales
Peter Borcsok
Ruth Burrow
Bethan Moore
Colleen Simpson

Inventory
Sarah Callaghan
Kirsty Norman

Marketing & Publicity
Chloe Cummings
Grace Edwards
Katie Sadler

Operations
Melissa Okusanya
Hannah Stamp

Production
Denis Manson
Simon Moore
Francesca Tuzzeo

Rights
Ashton Mucha
Alisah Saghir
Zoe Shine
Aisling Smyth
Lucy Vanderbilt

Trade Marketing
Ben Hurd
Eleanor Slater

**The HarperCollins
Distribution Team**

**The HarperCollins
Finance & Royalties
Team**

**The HarperCollins
Legal Team**

**The HarperCollins
Technology Team**

UK Sales
Isabel Coburn
Jay Cochrane
Sabina Lewis
Holly Martin
Harriet Williams
Leah Woods

**And every other
essential link in the
chain from delivery
drivers to booksellers
to librarians and
beyond!**

Read More Romantic Escapes

BY JULIE CAPLIN

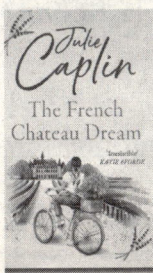